one of us is a jerk (spoiler: it's him)

One of Us Is a Jerk (Spoiler: It's Him)

ISBN: 979-8-9932140-0-9

Many thanks to:

    Cynthia A. (layout inspiration and title)

    Cynthia A., Christine L., and Amanda S. (editors)

    Joshua L., Matt B., Jennifer G., and Carson L. (early readers)

one of us is a jerk (spoiler: it's him)

paige ellsworth lyman

For Joshua

chapter
one

Outside the car window, palm trees flash by, and there's sand by the side of the road. Mom's window is rolled down a crack. The breeze coming in smells salty, like the ocean. But all that does nothing to change the fact that I'm on a vacation I'm not looking forward to.

"Is it the introductions, Jim?" Mom speaks out of the blue, as if she can read my thoughts, though we've been sitting in silence for a while. Maybe the silence is what she can read. "Is that what you're dreading?"

I pause before answering, sounding more sullen than I intend. "Part of it."

Mom turns around in her seat. "Matt doesn't think it will be that bad."

I look at her in disbelief. "Of course he doesn't! He doesn't have to be here until tomorrow." My next statement comes out even poutier. "Another thing you could have solved by letting us switch days. He could have flown *and* gone through the awkward introductions he doesn't dread as much as I do."

Mom frowns. She's been through this many times—with both me and Matt—and isn't excited to go through it again. "We don't switch days, Jim. It's a rule." She faces forward. "And Matt will have ten times as many introductions as you at the reunion tomorrow. You should be grateful you got the days that you did."

I slump back, making the leather seat creak. It's never fun to realize that your parents are right about something.

"Come on, Jim." Dad glances at me through the rearview mirror. "It won't be that bad. At least you get a few days off from schoolwork."

I don't reply. Last time it was bad.

"Think about the fun stuff we'll do." Dad repositions his right hand, which is balancing his phone (and driving directions) against the steering wheel. "The beach, out to eat...Rick said we might go to a state park on Sunday."

I lean against the car door and let my head fall against the glass. Rick is one of the main problems. Taking us to a state park won't make up for the way he's going to treat me.

"The sun and water should feel nice after being stuck on a plane." Dad is having a hard time leaving the car in silence. He signals and turns the car down a sandier road. "Aren't you excited for the beach?"

"Sure," I mutter. "Just *not* excited about everyone forgetting everything about me, if they remember that I exist at all."

That isn't the only thing that will make this trip lame. I have a whole list of things that are making me miserable at the moment:

1. I probably won't be called by my own name for the next few days.
2. People are going to get my likes, dislikes, and memories mixed up with Matt's all weekend long.
3. I forgot to pack a toothbrush, so I'll have to share with Matt, who will chomp all the bristles flat.
4. I'm tired and feel dirty from being in airports and on a plane all morning.
5. The rental car smells weird.

"Jim." Mom's tone tells me I'm pushing it. "Please stop pouting. You have to give everyone a chance. Maybe this time it will be different."

"Why should it be different?" I lean closer to Mom and Dad. "They just don't get it. If you tried to explain it to them last time and they got confused, why should this time be different?"

"Well, their kids are older now." Mom rolls down her window a bit more, letting in a stream of warm air. "They'll have a better chance of understanding you and Matt. At least your cousin Maddy."

"Michelle, too." Dad avoids my eyes, and I feel guilty since it's his cousin's family I'm complaining about.

"And Rick?"

Mom and Dad glance at each other. Maybe they know a lost cause when they see one.

I lean back in the seat, wondering again why we have to stay with family at all. This whole trip would be better (not perfect, but better) if Mom, Dad, Matt, and I could just stay in a hotel. But Dad's cousin Michelle and her family are going to the same huge family reunion we are, and they invited us to stay with them for the whole trip. And last time we stayed at Michelle and Rick's house—four years ago—I didn't enjoy it.

Then again, maybe Mom's right. Last time we saw them, Maddy was ten, Jill was four, and Dan was two. You couldn't fault them for not understanding how Matt and I are different people.

We pull into a sandy parking lot. "Why don't you give them a chance?" Mom picks up the swim bag she pulled out of her suitcase at the airport. "At least Maddy."

Dad looks for a parking spot. "You two might have fun together this trip."

"Especially if you explain you and Matt to her."

I groan. I hate explaining me and Matt. "Can't you do it?"

Mom smiles at me. "It would be more natural coming from you."

"OK." I sit up straighter. "But that doesn't change the fact that people will confuse us. Even if they all understand how me and Matt work, they don't know us well enough to treat us like individuals or tell us apart." I remember something. "Did Matt agree to wear a hat on his days like I asked him to?"

Mom puts on a pair of sunglasses, and Dad avoids my eyes as he replies. "He said—these are his words, not mine—that if you're the one who's bothered by it, you should be the one to wear the hat."

"But it's his hat!"

Dad doesn't respond as he parks the car.

I frown and lean back against the seat. Mom and Dad are unbuckling and climbing out of the car. Realizing there's no way out of this, I unbuckle my seatbelt.

Slipping on my sandals, I adjust my swim trunks. They felt weird to wear walking out of an airport, but we're in Florida. I couldn't have been that out of place. I open the door and step out.

It's sunny, warm, and windy outside the car. I can see the blue gulf between gaps in a row of beach grasses and shrubs. Dad's right—I do like the beach, and the sun and wind should feel good. But it's hard to muster up the excitement.

Voices call and people walk toward us. Dad calls out in greeting and heads their way. I have one last moment to face my mom.

"Mom," I plead. "It bothers you, too. I know it."

She frowns and takes off her sunglasses. I know she can't deny it. She likes me and Matt to be treated as individuals as much as I do, and she works hard to make it happen.

"OK." She leans close to me. Everyone's getting nearer, and we're running out of time. "Yes. I know. It's hard. I recognize that. But it's important to your dad. So...?" She smooths out my T-shirt at my shoulder. "Do it for him?"

Mom's eyes move beyond me, and she beams at the extended family members approaching. Before I know it, we're surrounded.

We say hi to Dad's cousin Michelle, her husband, Rick, Grandma Mickelsen, and a couple other adult first cousins once removed. I know them less well than Michelle's family. Rick calls me Jett and, worse, asks which "personality" I am today, "the Matt one or the Jim one?" I send my mom a *See? I told you* look that she ignores.

My second cousins are down at the beach. I slip away from the adults to put my shoes and shirt on a beach chair under the canopy they've set up and make a beeline for the shore before Mom or Dad can stop me.

This close to the water, even the air tastes salty. I'm standing alone ankle-deep in the water, looking out at the gulf, when someone splashes in the shallows behind me. I turn and see my cousin Maddy, looking a lot more grown up than when she was ten. Behind her, I can see Mom in her sunglasses looking at me. She nods, and I guess she sent Maddy over. My younger cousins are out playing in the waves.

I resume staring into the gulf as Maddy comes to stand by me.

"Hi, Jett." She sounds nice enough.

"It's Jim." I do not sound nice.

Maddy's confused. "Oh...I thought my mom said I could call you Jett."

Yeah, and I could call you dumb, but you don't see me doing that.

Out loud, I say, "I prefer Jim." I can feel my mom watching me and reluctantly go on. "Matt and I can go by Jett, but around people who know me and know who I am, I'd rather go by my own name."

"Oh. Sure. Sorry." Maddy moves back to where the waves occasionally wash over her feet. "Jim."

I come to stand by her. "That's OK."

"So..." Maddy shifts her weight from side to side and starts to bury her feet in the sand. "I haven't seen you in like four years. You're sixteen now?"

I nod.

"And taller. With longer hair."

I half-smile. "You too. For both." Then I tell myself to act less like a jerk. "Are you still into singing? Last time I saw you, you had started taking lessons, right?"

Maddy brightens, lifting her head. "Yeah. My teacher said I have a good chance of making JV choir when I start high school next month."

"Cool."

But before I can start feeling any better, Maddy has to make me feel worse. "You and Matt are musical, too, right? Do you still play the drums?"

"*Matt* plays the drums. Not me."

"Oh. Right." Maddy is confused. "But...if it's the same body..." she says, her voice higher and uncertain, "...does it matter?"

And here we go. "Yep." I look at the foamy bubbles on top of the wet sand. "Yes, it matters. Just because we take turns in the same body doesn't mean we like the same things."

"So, you don't like the drums like Matt does, so you choose not to play?"

"No. I can't play."

"But...if the knowledge is in your brain..." Maddy scrunches up her nose. "Can't you access it?"

"Nope."

"Huh." Maddy looks in the same direction I do—out to sea. "Weird."

Yep. There it is. Weird. Less than five minutes and I've been called weird.

"Well..." Maddy turns toward me. "Then...does Matt still play the drums?"

I sigh. I'm being a jerk again, I know it. But I can't help it. "I guess you'll just have to ask him tomorrow."

Saturday, June 5
Matt

"Matt."

Someone's saying my name.

"Matt!"

I'm distracted, looking into the park as a guy plays fetch with a brown dog that reminds me of Termite. I turn around. "Yeah?"

"Buffet line is starting." Dad pulls me up from my seat. "Go get a plate."

"OK." I grab a paper plate and fall in line behind Dad. Mom must be somewhere with Dad's cousin Michelle. I don't know where my second cousins are.

Someone plops a scoop of potato salad on the plate I'm holding. At least the food looks good. Was it catered? I wouldn't know. All the people at this mega reunion are as unrecognizable to me as any caterer would be.

The potato salad is joined by a hamburger, a scoop of fruit salad, potato chips, and a slice of watermelon. My plate is so loaded, I'm surprised it doesn't collapse. I move away from my dad so I can stop and dress my hamburger, grab a water bottle from an ice chest, check behind my shoulder to make sure Dad's talking to someone, and head for the trees.

"Matt!"

I stop, grimace, and turn around. It's Mom. "Where are you going?" She's with Michelle and Maddy, the oldest of my second cousins.

"Uh...nowhere." My answer is pointless. Mom's face tells me she knows I'm trying to sneak away.

"Well, why don't you take Maddy with you." Mom's stern look is replaced by a kinder one.

I perk up. She isn't going to make me sit at the table with all the great-aunts and second cousins I don't know?

Maddy walks up to me. She has her own plate, which holds no hamburger but twice as much watermelon.

"You're not going to go sit with everyone?" I nod toward the white canopy set up under the trees. "All your extended family and cousins and stuff?"

She snorts. "They're your family, too. And I don't know most of them any better than you do. If you get to sneak away, so do I."

I laugh.

We take our plates to an old wooden picnic table under a tree, brushing aside pine needles from the bench before we sit down.

"The food's not bad." Maddy starts on her potato salad.

"Yeah." I swallow a bite of hamburger. "Still, I'm bitter Jim got to miss this mega reunion *and* go to the beach."

"So, you really weren't there at the beach?" Maddy sweeps aside her dirty-blonde hair from her face. "Like, Jim was there, and your body was there, but you don't remember it at all?"

I'm surprised. Jim mentioned in his video message that he had attempted an in-depth explanation of our condition with her. I would have thought they would have covered that.

"No." I put down my hamburger. "No, I don't remember it. When Jim's in our body, I'm out of it. Like I'm in a coma. Dormant."

"And that's what he is now?"

"Yep."

"Huh." Maddy takes a juicy bite of watermelon.

I tap my white plastic fork against the edge of my paper plate. "Didn't Jim explain that yesterday?"

"Well, yeah..." Maddy wipes up watermelon juice with the back of her hand. "I was wondering if you'd say the same thing."

I raise my eyebrows and go back to my food, glad that she said that to me and not Jim. That sort of thing annoys him. I wonder what else she might have said yesterday to get on his nerves.

Friday, June 4
Jim

"Hey, look at this one." Maddy pulls a white, almost complete, shell out of the sand.

"Not bad." I show her the most recent shell I've found. It's flat and iridescent.

"Ooh, Jill will like that one." Maddy holds out the plastic bucket, and I drop it inside with a fragile *clink*. Her younger brother and sister are building a sandcastle, and Maddy and I volunteered to find seashells to decorate it with. Well, Maddy volunteered, and Mom made me come along, hoping, I'm sure, that it would give me a chance to get Maddy to fully understand what it's like living with *duocordis unuscorporosis*. I don't even have to try to keep my cousin on topic.

"What I don't get..." Maddy bends down for another shell, "...is how your two personalities are so aware of each other."

"Our two what?"

"Personalities?" Maddy straightens and slips into that high, uncertain tone. "Yours and Matt's?"

I grunt as I kick through a mound of wet sand. This is one of the misconceptions that annoys me the most. "We're not two *personalities*." I look at her to make sure she's listening. "We're two different *people*. What you're talking about is dissociative identity disorder. That's something different."

"Oh."

I stop walking. "Look. I know your parents aren't as religious as my mom, so maybe they've never explained it to you this way, but you know what a soul is, right?"

"Yes, Jim." Maddy's annoyed. "I'm not dumb."

"OK, then." I look away from her to a kite someone's flying in the distance. "Matt and I are two separate souls."

Maddy resumes strolling. "But...how do you know? What's the difference between that and multiple personalities, really?" She says it innocently, like she's trying to understand. At least I tell myself that to boost my patience as I start walking again.

"Well, science knows, for one."

"Science has proved the existence of a soul?" Her voice is flat with disbelief.

I roll my eyes. "Call it a consciousness, then. You can read an article about it if you want. My mom could send it to you."

"OK, OK." Maddy sidesteps to avoid a dog racing down the beach.

"And..." I sidestep to avoid the dog's owner. "Can't you tell? When he's here and when I'm here, can't you tell that we're different?"

Maddy's hair blows in the wind, and she tucks a strand behind her ear as she looks up at me. Her eyes are the same shade of brown as Dad's. As mine, too. "Well, I haven't seen you in a few years. Give me a chance to hang around Matt and I'll see."

"OK." I nod. "Tomorrow, you do that."

"It can't be sooner?"

I take a slow breath, trying to focus on the confusion evident on her face to keep myself from getting offended. "No, we only switch places when we go to sleep."

"Oh. Right. I forgot." She pauses. "Um...how come?"

I look over Maddy's shoulder, out to the ocean. "There's a device in our brain that controls it. We got it when we were two and diagnosed."

"Got it." Maddy walks to the left so the waves wash over her bare feet. "So tomorrow, I'll pay extra close attention and see if I *can* tell the difference between you and Matt."

I smile. That feels like progress.

Saturday, June 5
Matt

"Yesterday, Jim told me to do something." Maddy dusts the crumbs off her fingers from her sugar cookie. We had made a quick trip to the buffet line for dessert and then retreated back to our private table. "He told me I should see if I could tell the difference between you and him."

"And?" I take a bite of a chocolate chip cookie. "What do you think?"

Maddy looks unsure. I smile, thinking that Jim is a little unfair to put our fourteen-year-old cousin through a test like this when she hasn't seen us in almost four years. But he loves it when people can tell us apart. If he had warned me, I could have played it up, trying to act super extroverted or impulsive or something. Of course, Jim wouldn't want that. He'd want it to be natural.

"It's OK," I say to Maddy. "I know we look exactly alike, and—"

"Well, duh. Of course you look exactly alike—" She cocks her head as if something occurs to her. "But I guess you don't have to, do you? Why don't you style your hair differently or something?"

I shift on the rough wood bench. "I like my hair like this." I know I sound stubborn. "I'm not going to change it just because Jim likes it, too."

Maddy studies me.

"Anyway," I go on, "people who know us well—like our parents or our best friend—they can tell we're different, even though we have the same body. Promise."

Maddy nods. But she still looks disbelieving.

"Here." I put down my cookie and pull my wallet out of my back pocket. "Want to see my driver's license? It's just got my name on there, 'Matthew Mickelsen.'" I hand it to her. "Jim has his own. Even according to the government, we've got our own identities. Even social security numbers."

In the silence, we can hear a murmur of voices from the white canopy as Maddy studies my license. "But if you were driving and got pulled over and handed over Jim's license, what would keep the cop from being fooled?"

"Nothing," I admit. I pretend to get thoughtful. "Hey, that's not a bad idea. I should *always* drive around with Jim's license on me, just in case I do get pulled over. Great idea, Maddy! I'll tell him you thought of it."

Maddy's jaw drops, and I laugh. "I'm kidding. You think I'd be able to get away with that? My parents would find out eventually. Then I'd have to kiss my license goodbye."

Maddy studies me with narrowed eyes as she hands me my license back.

"Not to mention Jim would be pretty mad." I put my wallet back in my pocket.

"What would he do?" Maddy starts idly twisting her paper napkin.

"If I got a ticket in his name?" I exhale. "Oh, I don't know, probably hide the car keys from me or something." I stop to consider. "Probably worse. Probably some mean prank. Mean enough that I'd do something back, and then he'd retaliate, and I would, too, and then..."

Maddy rolls her eyes.

I smile. "Yeah, a prank war seems to be the natural course of events that follows any disagreement between me and Jim."

"A prank war?" Maddy now picks up two pine needles to twist. "Isn't that a little immature?"

"Well, it's not like we can talk it over and shake hands on it." I let that sink in, watching the shifting spots of sunlight that shine through the wind in the trees, until she rolls her eyes.

"Yeah, duh, the shaking hands part I know," she says. "But what do you mean you can't talk it over?"

"Well, we can't talk it over in real time. Which makes a big difference."

"In real time?"

"Yeah. Like we're doing now." I gesture to the space between us. "You say something, I hear, and I respond right away. Jim and I don't get that."

Maddy nods thoughtfully. "But...you're in the same body. Can't you just...I don't know, wake him up and talk with him inside your head for a second?"

I smile wryly. "No."

"Not even at night?"

"Not an option. Jim and I can't talk to each other, not even if we were both awake in our body at the same time."

"Really?" Maddy's surprised.

"Well, we can't read each other's minds or anything."

"Wait." Maddy snaps the brittle brown pine needles she's been fidgeting with. "Your two minds occupy the same brain, and you can't talk to each other mentally?"

I shrug.

"That seems kind of unfair."

"Yeah." I take a drink from my water bottle to wash down my cookie. "Go figure."

Friday, June 4
Jim

"So, you don't even have a desire to learn how to play the drums?" Maddy and I are now finishing Dan and Jill's sandcastle. The six-year-old and eight-year-old lost interest and ran back into the waves with their dad. Maddy and I did all that work gathering the shells, and it seems like a waste not to use them.

I squeeze a fistful of half-wet sand. "No. Just because Matt likes it doesn't mean I do." I pause and add—lest she think Matt's the only one with musical talent—"I play the guitar." Then I can't help but say, "And soccer. Matt doesn't play those."

"Oh." Maddy places a seashell above an archway. "And he doesn't want to learn how to play either of those?"

I shrug. "I guess not." I look down at the sand. We're under the shade of the canopy, and looking outside at the bright sunlight makes me squint.

"He plays the drums, and you play guitar and soccer...don't you guys do anything together?"

I look at Maddy, unamused. "Um, no. We can't do *anything* together." I'll be really disappointed if that hasn't sunk in.

Maddy rolls her eyes. "That's not what I mean. I mean, if you guys worked together to learn the same skill or talent or something, wouldn't it make it easier on you both?"

I shrug and push up a wall of sand.

"There's not anything you both do?"

"Um..." I exhale. "We both play the piano. Or played. We don't take lessons anymore. We both took swim lessons."

She's watching me expectantly.

"Oh. I got it. We learn the same viral dances."

Maddy smiles.

I smile too. "But here's the thing. Most of the time, it's not like, 'Hey, Matt, let's learn to do this thing together!' It's more like, 'Hey, Matt, I can do this better than you!'"

Maddy laughs. "You guys are competitive."

"It comes naturally." I sift through a mound of dry sand with my fingers. "But it's not that weird that we like to do different things or use our body in different ways. We don't always like the same foods."

She's surprised. "Really?"

"Yeah."

"Even though you have the same taste buds?"

"Yeah, go figure." In the distance the waves roar, and I can hear kids laughing. "We agree that corn dogs are gross, though."

"And you both like learning dances."

"And swimming," I remind her.

Maddy smiles. "So, you have some things in common, some things not. You kind of sound like normal twin brothers."

Maddy's looking down at the sandcastle and not watching me, but I smile at her anyway. Does she know that's one of my favorite things to hear?

"Anything else you and Matt have in common?" Maddy continues to decorate a wall of sand with white shells.

"Besides a body?"

She smiles.

I'm leaning on my left arm, but I sit up straight and dust off my hands. "We have the same best friend. We both like going to the gym. We have a favorite show. And yeah, we both like listening to the same music and playing the same music, though we play different instruments." I pause. "We both like where we live."

"Any other ways you're different?"

"Well, yeah, but if I list them all, we'll be here all day."

Maddy smiles.

"Jim! Maddy!"

We both look up and squint at the sun. Dad's joined Rick and the younger kids in the waves and beckons us over.

Maddy and I glance at each other, stand up, dust ourselves off, and head into the gulf. The water is warm, but it does feel refreshing as it washes off all the sand.

Out in the waves, I'm going over in my head what I'll say to Matt when I leave a message for him tonight. I decide I'll optimistically tell him that our extended family is beginning to understand us better. But as Rick calls me Jett and waves me over, I grimace. At least one family member is.

Saturday, June 5
Matt

Maddy and I finish our lunch and dessert, and her mom and my dad glance over at us. It's probably time to quit avoiding everyone and head back so they can introduce us to all their aunts, uncles, cousins, and anyone else we've never met before.

"OK." I sigh as I stand up, collecting my trash. "Time to face the inevitable."

Maddy stands up, too. "Thanks for explaining you and Jim."

We step off the concrete square around the picnic table and into the grass as we start to walk back together.

"Sure. Thanks for listening. He told me he talked to you about us yesterday, but that you might have some more questions."

Maddy looks confused. "I thought you said you and Jim can't talk to each other."

I smile. "Not in our head." I balance my trash-filled plate in one hand and pull my phone out of my pocket. "There *are* these amazing message-leaving devices called phones..."

Maddy hits me lightly on the arm, then her eyes get wide. "Oh! That's who Jim was talking to last night!"

I raise one eyebrow at her as I pocket my phone, and we continue on.

"I didn't mean to overhear," she apologizes. "I was walking by the bathroom, and I heard Jim talking inside. At first, I thought he was talking to himself, and I was like, 'That's weird,' but now I realize he was leaving something for you, wasn't he?"

I smile to myself as we walk out from under the shade of the trees into the sun. Staying at our cousins' house and sleeping on an air mattress in the living room means the bathroom is the most likely place where Jim and I can have some privacy as we send and watch each other's video messages. I did the same thing.

"Is that something you do often?" Maddy asks.

"Every day."

"Yeah?"

"Sure." The murmur of voices by the canopy is getting louder. "It's the only way we get to talk to each other. We'll send video messages and other stuff, too—we text each other every day, and usually have a couple message threads about school for different topics."

Maddy nods. We're nearly at the white canopy.

"We can say something to him now if you want," I say.

"What do you mean?"

We reach a trash can and drop our plates and napkins inside. On my phone, I open Vimer, stand next to Maddy, point the phone at our faces, and tap record.

"Hey, Jim! Just here at the mega family reunion with Maddy."

Maddy goes along like a natural. She smiles and waves. "Hi, Jim!"

"It's been lame, but the food was good. Maddy ate, like, five cookies."

She smacks my shoulder.

I laugh. "Anyway, you're lucky you were spared the torture. Now we're off to be introduced to a ton of extended family members we've never met before." Maddy and I make exaggeratedly fearful faces, then I tap to end the message.

"Just like that? That's what you do every day?"

"Every day." I put my phone away. Some kids are running for the trash can with hands full of garbage, so I step out of the way. "Usually, we leave a few short videos throughout the day, and then one longer recap at night."

Maddy and I face each other. She smiles. "Like a digital pen pal."

I force a laugh. Yeah, a pen pal I'm separated from by time, not space. A pen pal I have never and will never meet. A pen pal I share a ridiculous amount in common with. A pen pal who happens to be my brother.

Maybe Maddy sees through my fake laugh because her smile fades. "I guess that's actually kind of hard, huh?"

"Oh, yeah?" I act casual. "Why's that?"

"Well, I had thought that you might—well, the way you would feel about Jim—" Maddy gestures with her hands as she struggles for words. "I mean, since your condition is so, um..."

"Crappy?"

Maddy looks down. "Um, yeah. But hearing the way you talk to each other, it seems like you're actually..."

"Friends?"

She smiles apologetically.

I look down at the weedy grass we're standing on as I consider how to answer the "How is it that you and Jim are friends?" question this time. Our mom made us that way? Life would be even more miserable if we hated each other? It makes sense because we have a lot in common? He's actually an OK guy?

I end up shrugging and using the same answer I gave her earlier. "Yeah. Go figure."

Maddy smiles, but before she can say anything, we're interrupted by a call.

"Madison!" Her mom waves at us from where she's sitting at a long folding table.

"Matt!" Dad waves, too. "Come over here. I have some people I want you to meet!"

I take a breath. Maddy and I look at each other.

"My introductions are worse," I point out. "It took me and Jim two days to fully explain ourselves to you. I've got to do that like twenty more times with people I've never met before."

"Matt!" Dad calls again. I turn toward him and sigh.

Maddy pats my shoulder. "Poor Matt."

***

The introductions *are* awkward. I try to change the subject away from me and Jim as often as I can. The easiest way is to ask lots of questions about whoever I'm talking to. Maddy and I spent quite a bit of time at our secluded picnic table, so the giant Mickelsen family reunion ends soon. I get into the rental car with Mom and Dad so we can drive back to Rick and Michelle's house.

"Whew." I lean against the headrest in the back seat as I buckle in.

Mom turns around and smiles at me. "You survived."

I pretend to be so weak I can only manage a halfhearted smile and a thumbs-up.

"Thanks a ton, Matt." Dad pulls the car out of its parking space, and we wait with the cars lined up to get out of the parking lot. The afternoon sun has heated up the car, and he turns the AC on high. "It means a lot to me to be here."

"Sure, Dad. But Jim owes me one. He would have hated that."

Mom smiles. "He would have been fine. Like he was yesterday."

"He told me Rick was annoying." I get more comfortable in the back seat and watch the trees pass by as we pull onto the main road. "Even if Maddy was nicer."

"Seems like you've both gotten along well with Maddy." Dad's trying not to sound too pleased with himself.

"Yeah." I try to sound disinterested. "I guess she's cool." I don't miss Mom and Dad trying to hide smiles as they look at each other.

Matt—Mon, Jun 7, 7:52 AM

so hey look at that
we survived the trip to rick and michelle's

Jim—Tue, Jun 8, 7:02 AM

yeah
it would have been worse without maddy
she was pretty cool right? at least there was someone
there who tried to understand us and tell us apart

Matt—Wed, Jun 9, 7:04 AM

what do you mean? everyone could tell us
apart. they all told me so on my days

that i was the cooler more awesome more fun one 😎

also better looking
they just didn't want to hurt your feelings

Jim—Thu, Jun 10, 7:03 AM

hardy har har
i still think it would have helped if you had worn the hat

Matt—Fri, Jun 11, 7:11 AM

i'll only wear one of these

get me an authentic one of those next christmas
instead of a baseball cap and i'll wear it all you want

Jim—Sat, Jun 12, 7:02 AM

watch out i'll take you up on that

Matt—Sun, Jun 13, 10:02 AM

oh but only if I have the mustache to match

Jim—Mon, Jun 14, 7:05 AM

😎 like we could grow one anyway

chapter
two

Monday, June 7
Matt

I wake up on Monday morning in Jim's bed like usual. Jim, Mom, and Dad flew back from our trip the day before. We're home in Austin, Texas.

Following my normal morning routine, I climb out of Jim's bed, make the bed, walk to the Mastermind game on the table in the corner, study the board, make my daily move, walk into my room, grab my phone, and flop down on my back on my bed, sinking my head into the pillows.

First, I watch the Vimer messages Jim sent yesterday. There's a short one from the morning and one from later in the day with Maddy and the younger cousins waving goodbye to me in front of their house. That makes me smile. Then there's a recap of the day, during which Jim looks tired and glad to be home.

"So, I'm glad we're back," Jim sums up at the end of the message. "Even though it wasn't as bad as I thought it was going to be." He smirks. "Oh, by the way, Mom says you're going to the dentist this week."

My jaw drops.

"Take it up with her if you want, but the appointment is made. Have fun with that. Oh." Jim's smirk fades. "But I also heard from Leo, and he's getting home on Friday. So you'll get to see him first. Lucky."

I grumble. Seeing Leo first doesn't make up for the fact that I'll have to go to the dentist twice in a row.

The message ends with Jim lying back on his pillow, getting comfortable and ready for bed. "Anyway, welcome home, Matt. See ya."

I send a response, telling him I'm glad for my sake that the trip he had been dreading so much hadn't killed him, and complaining in general about how many unpleasant things have been landing on my days lately.

Then I check all my other messages and accounts. You'd be surprised how much builds up after only one day of being out of it. There are photos to like and posts to comment on, and a friend request from Maddy that I accept.

After I scroll and update to my heart's content, I head downstairs for breakfast.

"Mom!" I call before I reach the bottom step. "I have to go to the dentist this week?!"

She's in workout clothes standing at the counter in the kitchen. "Yes, and there's no use complaining about it."

"But it's Jim's turn!"

Mom shrugs. "I'm sorry, Matt. I tried to schedule it for a blue day, but it was the only opening they had before your dentist goes out of town for two weeks."

I grumble under my breath as I walk into the kitchen and lean against the counter. Like living each day, Jim and I take turns at the dentist. One checkup, it's his turn to go. Six months later, it's mine. I guess having to go to the dentist once a year instead of every six months is one of the few perks of sharing a body with a brother. If you can call it a perk. Especially when I have to go twice in a row.

Mom smiles and gives me a hug. "Good to see you, too, Matt."

I can't complain anymore before I'm bombarded by a wiggling, knee-high, short-haired, brown dog.

"Termite!" I smile and get down and grab his face. It's hard to stay frustrated while being showered by that much love. "Hey, boy! Hey, did you miss me?"

He wiggles and whines until I sit down and let him flop in my lap. After a few belly rubs and ear scratches I stand up laughing.

"Somebody missed you." Mom smiles down at Termite, still wiggling on the tile floor. "Jim didn't get a reception this warm."

"Of course he didn't." I go get a bowl and spoon. "Termite loves me more. Who wouldn't?"

Mom is unamused. She turns back to the counter where she butters a piece of toast. "Well, you're up late today…"

I shrug.

"If you cut your workout down a bit, you should be home to start history on time."

"Right." I flop into a seat at the kitchen table. I forgot it was a school day.

I know it's June, but Jim and I are homeschooled. With our weird, irregular schedule—with each of us awake every other day—there isn't a way we can work out public school. So ever since kindergarten, Mom's homeschooled us. Partly because we get half as much time as any other teenager, and partly because we have the flexibility, our school year doesn't match a typical public school calendar. We go year-round, but with lots of breaks throughout the year. Still, we look forward to the summer because Leo's out of school. At least, I remind myself, I'd get to see him first.

Tuesday, June 8
Jim

I smirk as I watch Matt's response about the dentist. He complains about having to go to the mega reunion, too. But I know that's for show. He hadn't minded the reunion that much.

After I make Matt's bed and get dressed, I go down to the kitchen. Mom's up. She's an early riser and wakes up and exercises before I come down. She's still in workout clothes, sitting at the bar with her laptop in front of her.

"Good morning, Jim." She stands up and gives me a hug.

"Hi, Mom." I hug her back. "How's your website?" Mom runs a combo recipe/literature site with her two sisters.

"Good." Mom sits down at the computer again. "Aunt Theresa made the cake from *The Cat in the Hat*." She shows me her screen. The cake is pink and whimsical. One of the photos shows a toy ship sunk into the icing. "I thought Aunt Lizzie did a fun job with the photos."

Mom likes working on the website with her sisters. They make a good team. Aunt Theresa is the chef, Aunt Lizzie takes the pictures, and Mom writes the book reviews.

"Fun." I watch Mom scroll through the pictures. "But I'm always sad we don't get to eat Aunt Theresa's creations."

She sighs. "Me, too." Mom's two sisters live close to each other in Virginia.

After a second of looking distracted, Mom sits up straight. "But right now I'm actually reading over the paper Matt finished yesterday."

I had started to get a bowl down from the cupboard, but I set it on the table and walk over to her, looking over her shoulder at the computer screen. "The one on *The Book Thief*? He finally finished?"

"Yes." Mom types something in a comment box.

I snort. "Took him long enough."

"In all fairness, he didn't like it as much as you did. I don't think historical is his thing."

Termite comes over, and I pat him on the head before washing my hands and going back to my cereal bowl, grabbing milk and a cereal box on the way. Mom wants me and Matt to be on the same schedule as far as school goes because sometimes she has us do projects and assignments together. I finished *The Book Thief* and my paper on it before we left for vacation. I've been waiting for Matt to finish so we can move on to something else.

I sit down at the table. "Who wrote a better paper? Me or him?"

Mom looks up at me. "You know, I think the best paper either of you has written was that one on *Lord of the Flies* you wrote together."

I roll my eyes and pour cereal into my bowl.

"Well." Mom stands up and joins me at the table, where I'm starting on my breakfast. "You're reading *Fahrenheit 451* next. Matt picked yesterday."

"Alright." I continue to eat while Mom clears an empty plate and cup from the bar.

"You're going to the gym this morning?" Mom asks from the sink. She and Dad are always encouraging me and Matt to take care of our body.

"Yep." I scoop up the last spoonful and bring my bowl to her. "What'd Matt do yesterday? He forgot to tell me."

"I think he lifted weights."

"Got it." I'll run on the treadmill.

***

I get home from the gym, shower, and head downstairs to the homeschool room, where the laptop Matt and I share is plugged in. I sit at the table, log out of his account, log into mine, and start reading my newest history chapter.

Mom has a room set up in our house that we call the homeschool room. When we were little, the room was decked out with colorful posters, charts, our artwork, craft supplies, and stuff like that. Now that Matt and I aren't eight, we insist that it stay less kiddy feeling. There's a small table with two chairs, a comfy armchair in the corner, a bookcase with some textbooks and novels, and a desk with office supplies.

The rest of the day is normal: history, math, lunch with Mom, doing the dishes (my and Matt's daily job). I take a minute to look at the Mastermind board on the table in the corner of my room, studying Matt's move from the day before and responding to it. Then English with Mom, chemistry online, and I'm done with school for the day.

Soccer season hasn't started yet, I don't have private lessons, it's too hot outside to do anything but swim, and Leo's out of town. So I use the afternoon to practice guitar and finish some schoolwork.

After dinner, Dad and I sit down in front of the TV in the basement. We've been working our way through an old show—me, Matt, and Dad—called *24*. It's about a counterterrorist agent and all sorts of dangerous threats, deaths, twists, and conspiracies. And a lot of action. Which makes it fun, even if it's old. We're halfway through season two. Dad's cool about watching the episodes twice. I think there's enough going on in each episode that he doesn't mind. But it's cool because it gives us all something we *almost* feel like we're doing together. And watching an episode with Dad tonight puts me one episode ahead of Matt. It's always fun to hang spoilers over his head, threatening to ruin things for him.

In the end, another normal day at home. I don't have much to tell Matt that evening (other than pretending to reveal spoilers). I'm looking forward to Leo getting home.

Friday, June 11
Matt

On Friday, as soon as I finish my last chemistry assessment, I shut the laptop and head out the front door.

"Bye, Mom! I'm going to Leo's!"

Mom's goodbye comes from somewhere in the kitchen, and I'm off.

I cut across our lawn and the neighbors', dodging the edging, mulch, and plants, and walk up to the front door two houses down. I knock twice before putting a hand on the gold doorknob and opening it.

"Ms. Roberts? Leo? It's Matt!"

"Hey, Matt!" calls a voice from the kitchen. "Come in."

I walk in to see Leo and his mom, home from vacation at last. They left before we did and have been gone for weeks.

Leo's mom is working on shifting things around in a big pile of stuff that takes up the entire kitchen table. Leo stands at the counter eating a Pop-Tart.

"Matt." Leo comes up and gives me a bro hug. "How's it going?"

"Good, bruh. How was Cancún?"

"It was wonderful," Leo's mom says. "So beautiful. And you can see Leo got plenty of sun."

I laugh. Leo *is* tan—if you can call it that. More like a shade of pink. It makes his usually fair skin almost as dark as his dirty-blond hair, which is in its typical style of stiff, messy waves.

"How's your summer been?" Leo says around a mouthful of toaster pastry.

"Oh, same old, same old. We took that trip to see my cousins and had a mega family reunion, but otherwise, it's been schoolwork. It's been boring here without you."

"Well, I'm back now." Leo finishes up his snack with a glass of milk. "Want to watch a movie?"

"Yeah!" I pull out my phone to text my mom that I'll be at Leo's the rest of the evening.

"After you unpack, Leo." Ms. Roberts puts a laundry basket of dirty clothes in his arms. "Take that to the laundry room, then empty your suitcase and start your clothes."

Leo rolls his eyes at me as he walks out of the room. I follow.

"You and Jim are so lucky your mom does your laundry for you," Leo says over his shoulder as we walk down the hall. My mom says Jim and I have half as many hours as we should. Laundry doesn't have to be one of the things on our plate.

"Yep," I say. "That's what me and Jim are. Lucky."

Leo pauses at the doorway and winces at me. "My bad."

I laugh. "Don't worry about it."

In his room, Leo starts emptying his suitcase (which turns into gathering clothes that have ended up all over the room). I pick up a gray T-shirt off his desk chair and toss it into the basket, then reach into the giant plastic jar of candy on Leo's desk and pull out a taffy.

Finished gathering clothes, Leo grabs a taffy of his own and leads the way out with the laundry basket under one arm.

"So, what 'movie' are we going to watch?" he says as he chews.

I grin. Movie is a code word. It really means video game.

***

See, Dad won't let me and Jim play video games. He's actually really strict about it. Which is totally lame.

"I read a statistic," Dad said once as I was giving him some pushback. We were in his car, driving to a concert downtown. "The average teenager who plays video games spends at least six hours playing per week. That's five percent of their awake time playing video games." Dad glanced away from the road to look at me. "But for you and Jim, who have half the time as normal teenagers, that's *ten* percent of your time. Ten percent!"

I opened my mouth to protest. Dad's math didn't seem quite right on that one.

"The point is," Dad cut me off before I could speak, "you and Jim have half as much time as anyone else. That's just the way it is. With so many things to do in life, you can't afford to waste any of your time on video games."

So, no video games for us. Mom and Dad won't even let me and Jim download games on our phones.

The only time I get to play is at Leo's house. Dad doesn't know about it, and Jim hasn't told on me yet.

***

As Leo and I flop down onto the cushy couches in his game room, I make a suggestion. "*Neutron 2?*"

Leo smiles and pulls the game up.

Later that night, Leo and I are still in the game room. Leo's mom celebrates their return from vacation by getting pizza. That, combined with a bowl of candy Leo finds in the pantry and some soda, makes for a great dinner. Leo and I lie on the couches, stuffing ourselves.

"Jim's gonna hate me tomorrow..." I take a big bite of my third slice of triple-meat pizza.

Leo tosses a candy wrapper into an empty pizza box and laughs. "Too much junk food and too little sleep?"

"Yeah..." I look at the newest text on my phone. "Man, my mom's on my case. I gotta get going soon."

Jim and I have a strict bedtime. A consistent schedule, our parents are always telling us, is critical to managing our condition. Yeah, well, we're sixteen years old. Nobody's perfect. So our body won't get as much sleep tonight. So Jim will be tired in the morning. Oh well, right? We each do it to the other sometimes.

Leo puts on a motherly voice. "Is it past your bedtime, Matt?"

"Shut up." I move to the floor, where I set my piece of pizza on the empty box and grab a piece of candy. I pull over an orange throw pillow and stretch out on my stomach on the rug. It's quiet as I chew.

"It's good to be back." Leo rolls over onto his back, and the old leather couch creaks. "Mexico was fun and all, but you know how my extended family is. Want to know the craziest part about the trip?"

When I don't answer, Leo looks at me. "Matt?"

I don't reply.

"Did you zone out?"

"No." My mouth is busy chewing. "It's this caramel. How old is this candy from your pantry, anyway?"

"Um, last Halloween?" Leo closes his eyes and stretches his arms above his head.

I prop myself up on my elbows and roll my eyes. "I think I almost pulled out a tooth. They're clean, too. I went to the dentist today."

"Well, maybe the Tooth Fairy would pay extra for it, then."

I stop for a second and try to process what Leo said. I'm tired. Maybe I missed something. But after a few seconds of trying to make sense of it, I give up. "What?"

"You know, the Tooth Fairy?"

I'm quiet.

"What parents say to their kids about losing teeth?"

I crane my neck to stare at Leo from my spot on the floor. "What the heck are you talking about?"

"You've never heard of this? Really?" Leo sits up. "Like, when you and Jim were little, and you lost a tooth, didn't your mom have you put it under your pillow and then the 'Tooth Fairy' would come in the middle of the night and take it away and swap it out for money?"

Now I'm really lost. I sit up, too. "*What*?"

"It's not real," Leo goes on. "It's just what parents say, but, you know... the little fairy who pays kids for teeth?"

I'm done with the too-sticky caramel, so I spit it out and put it back in its wrapper. "A little flying lady who sneaks into kids' rooms and takes their teeth in the middle of the night?"

"OK, I admit it sounds creepy when you say it like that, but—"

"That's weird. Why does she steal the teeth?"

"She doesn't steal them. She gives you money for them—"

"What does she even do with them?"

"Um...I don't know..." Leo rubs his face. "I feel like when I was little my mom read me this book once where the Tooth Fairy built a castle out of all the teeth, but—"

"A castle? Out of little kids' teeth? Gross!"

Leo laughs and lies back down on the couch. "Well, what did you do when you lost a tooth?"

"We gave it to our mom and dad, and they paid us for it." I take a bite (my for real last bite, I tell myself) of pizza.

"Just straight-up paid you for it?"

I chew. "Well, yeah. That's less weird than believing a little fairy flies into your room at night." I get up and sit down on the other couch, sinking into the saggy leather like always.

Leo puts a throw pillow under his head. "Who'd they pay? You or Jim?"

"Whoever was awake when the tooth came out. But they gave us two dollars. So, if it was Jim, he kept one of the dollars and put the other under his pillow for me to find the next morning. Then when I woke up in the morning with a new gap in my teeth, I'd know to look under my pillow and find a dollar." I pause, remembering, and smile. "It was kind of fun."

"Yeah, well, believe it or not, so was the Tooth Fairy."

I shake my head. "Nope. Not as fun. Couldn't be. Definitely weirder."

Saturday, June 12
Jim

Waking up this morning, I feel tired. Like, extra tired. Tired and gross. I groan as I stand up and walk to my room. Matt. What had he done last night?

I grab my phone and flop down onto my stomach on my bed. Matt's latest message in Vimer *had* come in late last night. He's outside. It's dark and the light and shadows from the streetlamps roll across his face as he walks.

"Sorry, Jim, I was out late tonight. Also, I ate a lot of pizza. And candy. And soda. My bad. But good news—Leo's home!" Based on the background in the video, I can tell Matt's walking through our front door. His voice lowers as he says, "Oh, and for a good laugh, ask Leo about the Tooth Fairy tomorrow. You'll get a kick out of it."

I get up and get dressed, still feeling tired and gross, but excited. Leo's home.

***

That afternoon after my schoolwork, Leo and I know we have to do something fun. He's been gone for weeks. So, it's a little kiddy because we haven't been since before we could drive, but Leo and I head to the local arcade and bowling alley.

It's dark and cool inside, and it smells like stale popcorn like it always does, but it's fun. Nostalgic. Leo and I go to the games we used to play, all our favorites from a couple summers ago. We're finishing a dinosaur shooting game when Leo asks a question.

"Let me get this straight." Leo puts his gun back in the holder. "This doesn't count as a video game?"

"Not to my dad." My gun makes a power-down sound as I put it away too. "Because he views it as a one-time thing? Not something Matt and I would be tempted to do on a regular basis?" We walk away from the game. "What did you and Matt do yesterday, by the way? Besides eat too much junk food?"

"Oh, you know, we watched a movie."

Of course.

Leo pulls a token out of his pocket and fingers it. "You know, if you tried it, I bet you'd pick it up quick. The muscle memory in your fingers and all? I bet you'd master the controls faster than Matt did."

I dodge a little kid running by with a handful of tickets. "You think I'd have muscle memory? How often do you and Matt play, anyway?"

Leo looks up as he thinks. "Not all that often. Yeah, now that I think about it, Matt is pretty terrible at video games."

I smile. I don't care what Matt does with video games. I'm not going to tell on him. But it does make me feel good to know that at least he isn't much better than me.

Pop music playing over the speakers clashes with the bells and whistles of all the games we pass as we walk through the arcade. Far across the room, a tumbling sound indicates that someone knocked a group of bowling pins over.

"We should make some plans for the rest of the summer." Leo walks up to an old-school arcade game with a button and a joystick. "School's gonna start before I know it." He puts a token in the game and starts to play. I lean against the game and watch.

Summers are always nice because Leo is around so much. Matt and I, even when we have school, have a flexible schedule and can see him during the day. Mom is good about letting us do that.

"Yeah." I watch a little plane move across the screen, beeping as it shoots out little bits of white light. "Summer plans would be great." I remember something as Leo jabs the joystick button repeatedly. "Oh, and

I'm supposed to ask you about the...what was it? Teeth Fairy? What's that all about?"

Leo laughs.

Jim—Mon, Jun 14, 7:03 AM

so how was the dentist?
man i hope it wasn't too uncomfortable
having your teeth scraped
sitting in that chair with your mouth wide open and the light
shining in your eyes
getting that gross fluoride painted on

Matt—Tue, Jun 15, 7:44 AM

yeah yeah rub it in

well you'll be happy to know our teeth are healthy

all thanks to my good flossing

Jim—Wed, Jun 16, 7:07 AM

think you mean my good flossing
but glad to know we have good teeth

Matt—Thu, Jun 17, 7:10 AM

yeah great teeth!

it stinks we only have one smile between the
two of us but at least it's a good one

Jim—Fri, Jun 18, 7:09 AM

chapter
three

Matt

This morning there's a boastful message from Jim about finishing one of his *Fahrenheit 451* essays. There's one about the team chemistry project Mom assigned us. But the one that makes my still-sleepy eyes open wide is Jim's last Vimer of the day.

"Alright, I'm going to bed. Oh, by the way, Mom asked me to cut our hair today. She said it's getting too long, and I agree. So I'll go on Thursday and get it cut."

I sit straight up in bed and send a message back.

"NO! DO NOT CUT OUR HAIR! It looks great! I'm starting to feel like a legit drummer. Do *not* cut it! Didn't we agree on the longer look? That way we can style it differently and people can tell us apart more. You can wear that dorky part like we talked about."

We hadn't talked about a dorky part. Well, I mentioned it once, and Jim never responded. Still.

First thing I say to Mom when I walk downstairs is about the haircut.

"Mom! Jim and I don't need a haircut!"

"Good morning to you too, Matt." Mom has just gotten back from the gym and is rubbing the back of her neck with a towel.

"Mom." I walk up to her. "It's not too long!"

Mom eyes the hair hanging over my forehead. (I should have combed it before talking to her. Oops.) "It's a little too long," she decides. "I'm going to have Jim get it cut tomorrow."

"Argh." I walk to the pantry to get a box of cereal. "It's not fair. Normal teenage boys don't have to deal with sharing a haircut with a brother."

"But plenty of 'normal' teenage boys have to deal with a mother making sure they look presentable. It's my word that's law. Jim happens to agree with me."

I continue to grumble as I pull out a box of Cap'n Crunch. Dad doesn't like buying sugary cereal like that. If he had his way, Jim and I would eat oatmeal every day. We find a way to sneak it around him sometimes. But speaking of my dad...

"Dad, will you tell Mom that Jim and I don't need a haircut?"

He's heading across the kitchen, on his way out the back door for work. He eyes me then the look Mom is giving him.

"Matt, listen to your mother." He gives my smiling mom a kiss. "Love you both!" Dad walks out the door.

I plop down at the kitchen table and pour a heaping bowl of Cap'n Crunch. It's so full that some dry pieces overflow onto the table. I'm finishing off the box on purpose so there won't be enough for Jim the next morning.

"Can you make sure he doesn't cut it too short?" I plead with my mom as she sits down at the table with me.

"How short were you thinking?"

I hold up a hand to my hair. "Like half an inch. See?"

Mom eyes my hair like she's appraising its value. "At least a whole inch. But it doesn't have to be any more than that."

I slump down, content to take Mom's compromise.

Thursday, June 24
Jim

After I wake up in Matt's bed and get my phone, I stand and watch Matt's messages while I pick out my clothes. The first one from yesterday is an adamant message that I not cut our hair.

I smirk. I figured he'd take it like that. The next Vimer is of him standing in the kitchen with Mom in the background.

"OK, Jim, I talked to Mom. You can take off an inch. No more than that!"

I walk downstairs, dressed for the gym. Mom is at the table pouring herself a bowl of cereal.

"Hey, Mom."

"Good morning, Jim."

I look in the pantry for breakfast. "Hey, Matt ate all the Cap'n Crunch!"

"Matt ate *the last of* the Cap'n Crunch," she corrects.

I turn around and scowl. "On purpose."

She smiles and holds out the box of sugar-free oat cereal she's eating. I sigh and take it.

"If you want, you can get your hair cut in the middle of the day." Mom pours milk in her cereal. "Since you don't have anything going on this afternoon. You can study a little later than normal and free up your evening."

I smile. "Sounds great."

Friday, June 25
Matt

When I wake up, something about my forehead feels different. I put a hand to my head right away. Jim definitely cut our hair. I hurry to the bathroom to look in the mirror—and then yell.

"MOM!"

She walks into the bathroom sighing.

"We said an inch!" I stare at my now way shorter hair. It doesn't even cover my forehead!

Mom leans against the doorframe. "Jim was the one to talk to the stylist. He told her how short to go. It was up to him."

"It's not fair! It's not just his hair! It's mine, too!" I look into the mirror and moan. "It's so short...I look like a loser."

"No, of course you don't." Mom puts a hand to my hair. "I think you look very handsome."

I shoot her a look. In return, she kisses me on the cheek and walks out of the bathroom. I look in the mirror and moan again.

After I get sick of looking at my shorter hair, I stomp to my room, grab my phone, and check to see what Jim has to say for himself.

The last Vimer of the day shows Jim in his room with our new haircut. His cheery attitude only makes me madder.

"Hey, Matt! Like the look? OK, so the stylist went a little short. She talked me into it. But I think we look fine. And think of it as all about convenience. It's summer; it's hot outside. Won't this shorter hair feel nice? And it's so much easier to take care of when it's this—"

Disgusted, I toss my phone to the foot of my orange bedspread, not caring to watch the rest of the message. I don't send anything back.

***

I have to do schoolwork like normal that day, and I take some time to bang on my drums, which feels good. I'm still angry, though.

That night, after I say goodnight to my parents and leave a Vimer for Jim, I stand in our bathroom, looking at my reflection in the mirror. I hold a black Sharpie in my hand. And I smile.

Saturday, June 26
Jim

On Saturday morning, I'm expecting Matt to be angry about the haircut, and in his Vimer he definitely doesn't act happy, but he doesn't bring it up. After I get dressed, I head into the bathroom.

Then I look in the mirror and yell.

"MOM!"

My voice is distressed enough that I hear quick footsteps up the stairs. Mom appears in the doorway.

"Look what Matt did!" I turn to her. Her face falls as she comes forward and tries to rub off the bold, black letters that spell LOSER across my forehead.

"What? What is it?" Dad appears in the doorway in running clothes. Mom and I both turn to face him. Mom's face is disappointed and mine is livid.

Dad catches a laugh in his throat. I can't believe it. Mom shoots him a look and I turn away, back to gaping at myself in the mirror.

"Sorry." Dad puts on a straight face. "Will it wash off?"

Mom rubs at my forehead with a wet rag and soap. "I'm sorry, Jim. It looks like permanent marker."

I exclaim in frustration. "I have a soccer lesson this morning!"

"I think Matt knew that." That earns Dad a glare from me. "Here, I'll go look it up online." Dad walks away. "Maybe there's an easy way to wash it off."

I moan as I rub my forehead some more and lean close to the mirror. That's when I notice the note taped to the bottom.

Betcha wish your hair still covered your forehead huh? WHOOPS!

I grit my teeth, rip it off, and crumple it up.

Mom had walked off down the hall. She comes back with Matt's Avengers baseball cap I gave him last Christmas. "Here." She holds it out. "Wear Matt's cap. It will cover it up."

"To soccer?" I can't believe this.

Dad walks back holding his tablet. "OK, there are about fifteen different things we could try."

Mom checks her watch. "And you have about fifteen minutes before you need to leave."

I still hold Matt's note in my hand, and it crinkles as I slowly crumple it into a tighter ball.

Dad scrolls through his tablet screen. "Do we have any rubbing alcohol? If we soak and wipe it with that it should help it fade." He looks at me apologetically. "It probably won't come all the way off, though."

I growl.

"Dave, I keep the rubbing alcohol above the washing machine." Mom takes the rag and rubs my forehead again. My skin's starting to feel raw. "Grab it and we'll see what we can do."

Matt. That jerk. Leave it up to him to do something like this.

In a minute, Dad comes back. "It wasn't there, Jane."

"What about the nail polish remover?" Mom turns to him. "In our bathroom."

Dad comes back a minute later empty-handed. Mom and Dad look at each other, and I watch them. We all have the same thought at the same time.

"Do you think Matt hid them?" Dad asks in disbelief.

"Matt!" I hit my fist on the bathroom counter so hard, I wince.

***

Forty-five minutes later I'm walking into Capital Soccer Club, the private league I'm a part of. Since I don't go to public school, private teams are the only way I can play soccer. Capital Soccer offers everything I need: high school–age teams, two seasons (spring and fall), other teams to compete against, and private or small-group lessons. The season hasn't started yet, and I have no team. Instead, I'm doing small-group lessons over the summer.

I walk across the artificial grass of the indoor field and up to the two other guys who are taking lessons with me, Kahlil and Steve. They notice my cap right away.

"Nice hat, Jim," Kahlil jokes.

"Wrong sport, ace." (Steve is the less nice of the two.)

I keep my head low and try not to respond. In a few minutes, Coach Jordan, our instructor, walks up with a soccer ball under one arm.

"Alright, y'all—" He stops. I look up in apprehension to find him looking at me. "Jim, ditch the hat, man."

I want to hide. I should have skipped practice. But it's not like I get to go every Saturday. I reluctantly take off the baseball cap, feeling it slide across my head and down over my lowered face.

Kahlil and Steve burst into laughter.

"What happened to you?" Steve laughs.

"Matt," I grumble. "Matt happened."

My coach and the other guys know about Matt, know about our condition. How else could I explain that I'm only able to play every other day? But all my coaches have been understanding. They let me play when I can and excuse me when I can't.

Kahlil and Steve keep laughing. The sound of it echoes around the metal walls of the big indoor field, and I look around the room nervously, watching some kids standing around some orange cones stare at us.

"Must be tough sharing a body with a brother," Kahlil says.

"Yeah," I mutter. "A real jerk of a brother, too."

Coach Jordan looks at me, and I swear he's trying not to smile. "Well, you wear the hat if you want to, man."

***

Later that day, after practice and after schoolwork, I'm up in my room, supposedly doing math homework but instead idly spinning the little black and silver globe by my desk, thinking of possible ways to get back at Matt.

"Jim!" Mom's voice from downstairs interrupts my thoughts. "Leo's here."

I give the globe one last spin before getting up and dragging myself to the front door, my footsteps heavy on the carpeted stairs. As soon as Leo can see my feet on the steps, before he can even see my face, he starts talking.

"So, now that we're all back, I was thinking, you, me, and Matt, we've gotta—" He stops as I step into the entryway and he sees my face. Then he bursts out laughing.

"Ha, ha," I grumble. "Yeah, laugh it up."

"Sorry, I'm sorry." Leo breathes in deep as he sincerely tries to stop laughing. "OK, let me guess. You got your hair cut, Matt hated it, and he retaliated?"

As annoyed as I am that Leo finds it humorous, I'm pretty impressed by his accuracy.

"Alright," I mutter, twisting the one wooden banister spindle that's been loose for years. "I've been coming up with some ideas. I was thinking that if I changed Matt's ringtone to something super embarrassing and had you call it at an awkward time—"

"Oh, no." Leo puts up his hands and takes a step back. "I stay out of these, remember? I was going to say we should make a movie, for old times' sake. But I'll start thinking of some ideas on my own. Let me know when you guys like each other again. I'll catch you later." And he walks out.

I sigh as the front door closes with a thud. Well, I know one thing. No way Matt is getting away with this.

Sunday, June 27
Matt

A loud and intense guttural sound is blasting in my ears. *Blasting.*

I suck in a huge gasp of air and jerk up, ripping off the headphones I'm wearing. Even with them off, I can hear the music coming from them. "*This ain't a song for the broken-hearted...*" The rock song "It's My Life" by Bon Jovi.

I grope on Jim's nightstand for his phone, but it's missing. Clumsily, I fall out of bed and start searching through the pitch-black room. Finally, I find his phone *in his closet.* I fumble around with the screen to turn off the alarm, which is labeled "YOU KNOW YOU DESERVE THIS."

I breathe in deep in the finally quiet room, crawl out of the closet, and lean against the wall with my eyes closed.

Jim and I take a sleep medication every night that helps us sleep soundly to avoid switching places with each other unexpectedly during the night. It takes a lot to wake me up before morning, but Bon Jovi had done it, blasting at full volume through the over-ear Bluetooth headphones Jim and I had saved up for.

I rub my face and look at the time.

4:45 AM.

"Jim..." I mutter as I realize what he's done.

He set the super-early alarm for me on purpose. It's worse because it's Sunday, the one day of the week Mom lets us sleep in. And I can't go back to bed, because if I do, when our body wakes up in a few hours, Jim will be the one awake inside it. Not me. And Sundays aren't just great because we can sleep in. Sunday is the only day we don't have school. (To even out the school week, Saturday is a school day. That way Jim and I each get three school days a week.) Sunday, my free day, the one that I only get every other week? No way I'm letting Jim take that from me.

I give a long, low moan and drag a hand over my face. If I want this Sunday, it's now or never.

But I still have a problem. My body's super tired because of the medication. I usually don't wake up until around seven. What to do to keep myself awake?

The drums are out. I'd wake up Mom and Dad. Instead, I trip down through the dark house, bumping into walls and doorframes.

A jingling of metal dog tags as I reach the kitchen tells me that I've woken Termite.

"Jim is a *jerk*, Termite." My voice is slurred, and my body feels sluggish. I reach out in the dark until I clumsily pat his head. "Next time you see him, bite him for me."

Termite just licks my hand before his nails click back over to his doggy bed. I sigh and stumble down to the basement to watch an old Marvel movie.

I say basement, but it's more like the first story, because our house is built on a hill. From the street, the middle story (with the kitchen and living room) is the main story. But walking out the back of the kitchen leads you to a second-story patio, with stairs that lead down to a lower porch, the yard, and sliding glass doors that open to the basement.

I leave the lights off as I start my movie, but because of the sliding glass doors, the room eventually gets lighter as the sun rises. When the room is light enough, and I'm not feeling so groggy, I leave one short, straight-faced Vimer for Jim.

"This. Means. War."

***

When I stumble upstairs from the basement, wrapped in a flannel throw blanket, Dad's making a hot breakfast like he usually does on Sunday mornings, and Mom's sitting on the couch with an open book.

"Matt?" Mom looks up. "You were in the basement? How long have you been up?"

"Since four forty-five." I scowl and flop down at the table. "It was Jim. He set an alarm for me so I couldn't sleep in!"

Mom frowns. Dad turns around and sees my tired face and messy hair (less messy than it should be because it's way too short). He slides a plate of pancakes and bacon in front of me.

"That is not acceptable." Mom closes her book and stands up. "We will definitely be talking to Jim about that."

"Do you need a nap today, Matt?" Dad sits down at the table with me.

"And give my Sunday up to Jim? No way!"

"We could make Jim go back to sleep," Mom offers.

I think. As tempting as that sounds, you can't *make* someone sleep. Jim would get away with it. I know he would. No, I won't let him win. I'm keeping my Sunday.

"No, I'll stay up," I say wearily. I let the throw blanket fall off my shoulders and pull the plate of food closer. "I want my Sunday."

"Well, we're leaving for church in a few hours." Mom rubs my back as she turns away from the table. "Maybe a shower would wake you up."

I nod as I dig into my breakfast. Mom heads upstairs, and Dad goes to work on the dishes.

"Wait!" Mom's shout is loud enough to make me jump. She stops and turns around.

I freeze with my fork in my mouth. I have a bad feeling about this.

"The Sharpie, Matt!" Mom's eyes are murderous. "We have to talk about the Sharpie! You wrote LOSER for Jim and he had to go around with it all day!"

I swallow a mouthful of syrup and pancakes and wash it down with a gulp of milk, all while staring at her wide-eyed.

Mom takes a calming breath. "First of all, bring out the rubbing alcohol from wherever you hid it and wash that word off your head."

I touch my forehead. Guess the word is still there.

"And for your punishment…" Mom takes a few not-quite-as-calm-as-before breaths.

"Jim did get his revenge," Dad says quietly to Mom. "Maybe we leave it be for now."

Mom huffs and turns around. "I'll think about it! Now get ready for church!" And she disappears up the stairs, leaving the novel she had been reading lying on the couch.

"She's a lot less sympathetic now," I mumble to Dad. "What happened to the nice 'go try a shower, Matt'?"

"You did do something pretty mean." Dad turns to the sink to finish the dishes. I swear I see him hide a smile, but then he continues. "You know,

Matt, you and Jim are going to have to work things like this out on your own one day."

I just grunt.

Monday, June 28
Jim

When I walk into my room on Monday morning, I almost don't recognize it. Everything in my room—books from my bookshelves, clothes from my closet and dresser, pens and notebooks from my desk, the older keepsakes I keep in the trunk at the foot of my bed, my old guitar that hangs on the wall, framed photos, the bendy lamp on my desk, my old trophies, even my blue and gray bedspread—is dumped in a pile on the floor. Only the Mastermind game in the corner is untouched.

"Mom!"

She and Dad come in together.

"Look what Matt did!" I stand inside the doorway and point to the floor.

For a second they stare. "Wow," Dad says.

Mom sighs. "OK, Jim, before we talk about your room, we have to talk about Sunday morning. You set an alarm for Matt!?"

I'm worked up about my room. "What about what Matt did?"

"Jim, don't ignore your mother." Dad looks at me. I grunt and kick at the carpet. This is so unfair.

"Jim." Mom waits until I look her in the eyes. "No more alarms."

"OK, fine," I mutter. "Now what about...?"

"We'll talk to Matt about this." Dad pushes my door open wider and nods to the messy pile of clothes, books, and keepsakes on my floor. Even my desk organizer has been taken off the wall.

Mom nods, too. "Tomorrow before he does anything fun, he'll have to put it all back—"

"No!" I hold up my hands. "I don't want him putting it all back. He'll do it wrong."

Mom's clearly frustrated. "Maybe you should work it out with him, then."

I glower. "Hey, I'd love to." (I really would. Slugging him would feel so good right now.) Out loud I say, "If he were actually *here*."

Mom groans, then turns to walk out. "Then I'll think of some other punishment!"

Dad gives me a look that says *See what you did to your mother?* I look back at him in disbelief.

I pick up my phone to see if Matt has anything to say. There's one Vimer from him, and it's short. He's looking at the camera with a straight face.

"This. Means. War."

I snort. Fine by me.

After a normal day of schoolwork (during which I notice my forehead no longer says LOSER, and I try to tiptoe around Mom, not wanting to be punished for the Sunday morning alarm) and before I go to bed, I sneak a combination lock down to the basement and leave a message for Matt.

Tuesday, June 29
Matt

When I wake up this morning, I look around Jim's room and smirk. He's made some progress, but it's still a mess. And no early morning alarm. I bet Jim got in a ton of trouble for that. I'd say the war is going in my favor.

"Matt." Mom appears in the doorway, frowning.

"Yeah, Mom?" I stand up.

"Matt, what you did with Jim's room was *not funny.*"

I sit down on the bed again.

Mom sighs as she adjusts her ponytail. "He doesn't want you touching his stuff, so I don't want you to put it back, but you're taking over his dish duties for the next two weeks."

I'm confused. "How am I going to do that?" I won't be awake on his days to do the dishes.

"You'll have two days' worth of dirty dishes to do instead of one." Mom gives me a look that dares me to argue. I don't.

"Now out and to your own room." Mom points toward the door. "I want you to the gym, back, and showered by nine."

Not feeling as happy as I did a few minutes ago, I head to my room. I'm not expecting any messages from Jim, so I'm surprised to open my phone and see one.

"Hey, Matt." Jim's sitting on his bed and his voice is calm—nice, even. "Look, sorry about the alarm on Sunday morning. Let's call a truce, alright?" My eyes narrow. Something feels off. Jim goes on. "I thought maybe we could jam together. I recorded myself playing a few Distorted Tides songs today on the guitar. Go downstairs and play along on your drums. I'll be excited to see what you send back."

Something is definitely fishy. I drop the phone on my bedspread and hurry downstairs. As soon as I'm in the basement, I see that someone has messed with my drum kit.

My hi-hat cymbal has been dragged around to the right side of my kit. When I try to move it back, I hear a metal clinking sound, and my ride cymbal stand starts to get dragged with it. I bend down for a closer look and see that Jim's chained the two cymbal stands, along with my bass drum, together with a combination lock.

"MOM!"

In a few minutes, Dad comes down the stairs, dressed for work. "Your mother wants to know why you and Jim by default shout her name instead of mine."

"Dad, look what Jim did to my drums!" I show him the lock. Dad bends over and frowns as he pulls at the metal chain.

"Well?" I say impatiently. "He can't treat my stuff like this! And I can't play like this! He knows that!"

"Yeah..." Dad clicks the numbers of the combination lock a few times before straightening up. "And these things aren't cheap..."

"Exactly!" I stand up. "So can I tell Mom now?"

"Hold it, Matt." Dad grabs my arm before I can go up to the kitchen. "You're one to talk with the mess you made in Jim's room."

"But what about my drums!?"

Dad turns around and looks at my kit. "We'll talk to Jim tomorrow about it. For now...don't you have school to worry about, anyway? Then after school you'll have to find something else to do."

"But Bradley is coming over today!"

Bradley's my drum tutor.

Dad's eyebrows go up. "Oh..."

"Well?"

Dad sighs. "There's no way we can guess Jim's combination. And I don't have anything to cut through a lock like that."

I grit my teeth and clench my fists. Jim. I *hate* Jim.

"Sorry, Matt. We'll have to reschedule your drum lesson." Dad sees me glancing angrily at Jim's guitar hanging on the wall next to the sliding door. "And do not touch his guitar! Do you understand? Matt?"

I sigh and look at him.

"No more touching Jim's stuff, understood?"

"Fine," I mutter.

"Excuse me?"

I speak louder. "Yes, sir."

It looks like I need to get more creative than that.

Wednesday, June 30
Jim

When I wake up, I'm feeling gross. My stomach feels awful—sick and knotted. Things feel...*off*, down there.

I groan, pulling Matt's two-toned orange and gray bedspread over my head with one arm and holding my stomach with my other. Maybe Matt and I are getting sick.

After an unpleasant trip to the bathroom, I head to my room (which is still a mess) and lie down on my bed. Matt hasn't said anything to me since he declared war, but out of habit I open Vimer. Maybe he started feeling sick yesterday and can explain why my insides feel like I've eaten a live octopus.

There's one Vimer from Matt.

"Hey, Jim, how's it going?" He's sitting on the floor in his room, in front of his bookcase. His tone is casual. "So, it's time for bed, and I'm about to take our sleep medication." He pops a pill in his mouth, takes a drink of water, tips his head back, and swallows. Then he looks at a bottle in his hand, which looks like an over-the-counter medication and not the orange canister we keep in the bathroom. I start to realize something is up.

"Oh, my bad..." Matt says in the video. "I must have gotten mixed up... what is this I took?" Matt reads the bottle. "A laxative? Whoops...hmm, takes effect in six to twelve hours...common side effects may include stomach slash abdominal pain, cramping, nausea, diarrhea, and weakness." Matt looks at the camera and winces. "Yikes." Then he leans closer and smiles wickedly. "Have a nice day, Jim."

"MOM!"

She and Dad both come in this time.

"One morning." Mom shakes her head as they walk in. "Just one morning, can we *not* start a day like this?"

"Look what Matt did." My voice is strained because my stomach starts to knot again. I hand over the phone and curl up on my side while Mom and Dad watch the message.

"Is that...?" Mom asks.

"Uh-oh..." Dad says.

The message ends and they both look down at me, lying on top of Matt's crumpled bedspread, holding my stomach.

"Yep. He really did."

"OK, I agree it's gone too far this time." Dad turns to me. "Jim, by the way, you need to go to the basement and unchain your brother's drum set."

Mom gives a frustrated sigh. "I forgot you caused Matt to miss his drum lesson yesterday." She shakes her head. "This has gone on long enough. Jim, come down to the basement, please."

***

After another unpleasant trip to the bathroom, I'm dressed and (once I unlock Matt's drums and hand over the combination lock and chain to Dad) sitting on the basement couch next to Mom. Dad's left for work.

The basement TV is hooked up with a nice camera that makes it easy for me and Matt to record good, high-quality videos for each other. We use it for Christmas and birthdays, and to play music for each other and then pretend like we can jam together. There's not any music today, though.

I hold my stomach as I slouch on the beige leather couch next to Mom, my knees bent and my feet on the ottoman. She turns on the TV and hits record on the remote that controls the camera.

"OK, Matt." Mom looks at the camera. "This has gone on long enough. No more war. No more pranks. Jim." Mom turns to me. "Apologize to your brother for the haircut and for everything that's happened since."

"Fine." I lower my eyebrows and glare at the small black camera on top of the TV. "Sorry. Jerk."

"No name-calling."

I roll my eyes and sigh. "OK, fine. Sorry, alright? Truce."

Mom nods.

I take my feet off the ottoman and sit up straight. "But the laxative was downright low and I—"

Mom switches off the TV before I can finish.

Thursday, July 1
Matt

This morning, I don't get to wake up slowly. Mom is waiting for me.

"Matthew Mickelsen."

I want to hide my head under my pillow. I know I'm about to get it for the laxative.

"What were you thinking, taking a laxative for Jim?"

I roll over and open my eyes. I try to put on a placating smile.

"Pretty funny, right, Mom?"

She pulls out a spray bottle and sprays me in the face.

"Aah! Mom!" I sit up. "What the—"

"It's water, Matt, relax."

When I rub my eyes and chance to open them, she sprays me in the face again.

"Mom! Come on!" Water drips off my face and onto the front of my pajamas.

"Jim has a video for you to watch downstairs. Come with me, please." Mom leads the way out of Jim's room, and I don't dare disobey. I follow, still wiping water off my face, meet Dad in the kitchen, and walk down to the basement with my parents.

After we all sit on the couch, Mom plays the video. It's of her and Jim sitting on the couch and Jim giving an obviously forced apology.

As soon as the video is done, Mom leans forward, pushes record on the remote, and looks at me expectantly.

I sigh. "Alright, Jim. I'm sorry for the laxative...and the mess in your room...and writing LOSER on your forehead in permanent marker..." I can't help smiling. "You've got to admit, I've got style, right?" A look from both Mom and Dad causes me to straighten my face. "OK, so, sorry. Truce." I look at Mom, and she switches off the TV and the camera.

I lean my head back against the couch. Luckily, I don't feel sick. I had hoped the effects of the laxative would wear off by the time I was awake again. I'm glad I was right.

But not feeling sick doesn't help the guilt I'm starting to feel as Mom and Dad both stare at me.

"What?"

"You see that it went too far, don't you?" Mom puts the remote down. "When you and Jim are willing to mistreat your body to retaliate in your little wars..."

"That's not how we want to see you treating each other," Dad finishes, his arm around my mom's shoulders.

"Yeah." I sigh. "I know."

Friday, July 2
Jim

Friday there are no unpleasant surprises to wake up to. Mom meets me soon after I get up and takes me downstairs to watch Matt's apology from the day before.

"So no more war?" Mom asks, looking at me sternly. "You agree that it's over?"

"Whatever," I sigh as I sink back into the couch cushions. I won't admit it out loud, but I think Matt might have come out on top in that one.

Still on the basement couch, I lie down on my side, my head resting on one of the blue throw pillows, and pull out my phone to watch Matt's Vimers.

"OK, so, war's over and all that," he says in his latest one. "And I have an idea. Next time we need a haircut, can *I* be the one to get it cut? Then if it's not short enough, you can go and get it cut again."

I send a response. "Alright. Deal—if I get to eat the last bowl of the next box of Cap'n Crunch."

Mom groans. I look up to see her standing at the bottom of the stairs leading up to the kitchen, one hand on the railing. "Would that have been so hard to work out a week ago?"

I just shrug.

She grumbles as she walks upstairs.

Jim—Fri, Jul 2, 9:47 AM

i like your haircut idea but next time we
could always try something like this

Matt—Sat, Jul 3, 7:08 AM

yeah mom would love that

Jim—Sun, Jul 4, 10:13 AM

or maybe the asymmetrical look isn't the best
what about you choose the middle and i choose the sides?

Matt—Mon, Jul 5, 7:57 AM

Jim—Tue, Jul 6, 7:14 AM

Matt—Wed, Jul 7, 7:30 AM

mom would love that even more

chapter
four

When I walk down for breakfast in the morning, Mom isn't in the kitchen. My eyes wander over to her laptop, which is left open on the bar.

I walk over to the computer. How funny would it be if I find Jim's paper on *Fahrenheit 451,* check if Mom has started grading it yet, and then rewrite all her comments to him? If I keep the comments light, it will make them both laugh. Smiling at the thought of Mom's and Jim's faces when they read it, I sit down on the stool in front of the laptop and swipe my fingers across the touchpad. I get lucky. It's unlocked.

The screen shows Mom's email and a full inbox, and I'm about to minimize the window to look for Jim's paper when a message catches my eye.

It's from Dr. Anand, the specialist who treats me and Jim for our condition, and the subject is "Information on the procedure."

I glance behind my shoulder. There's a basket of unfolded laundry on the white fabric couch and a gray throw blanket draped over the ottoman, but no sign of Mom. I turn back to the computer and surrender to the funny little pull from the email that says *open me.*

The text from Dr. Anand is short: "Here's the paper on the procedure I mentioned to you. If you have any questions, please reach out." I click the paper attached to the email and start to read.

It's scientific; there are a lot of big words. I start skimming. Certain phrases start to pop out at me...*siblings with duocordis unuscorporosis... location of consciousness...possibility of separation....* I get more engrossed as I read. ...*progressive surgical procedure...as of yet untried...tumor which destroys a consciousness but leaves the body intact...*

It feels like my stomach is standing over a trapdoor that someone just opened. My eyes go wide, and I can't stop reading.

...the transference of one consciousness to the donor body...only discovered permanent cure to duocordis unuscorporosis...

"Matt?"

I jump about a foot in the air and turn around. Mom is standing at the base of the stairs in gym clothes. Her forehead wrinkles in an expression that's half disappointment, half concern. "What are you doing?"

I stand up from the barstool and point at the screen. "Why didn't you tell us about this?"

Mom walks over and looks at the computer. She closes her eyes and sighs. "Matt, don't get mad—"

"How long ago did you find out?" I check the date on the email. "You found out back in March!"

Mom puts her hands on the laptop.

"Wait!" I grab the edge of the screen before she can fold it shut. "Is that what it sounds like? Is that a procedure that could fix us?"

"Matt." Mom pulls the computer away from me and closes it with a snap. "Please stay out of my emails. If the procedure were a possibility, I would have told you and Jim about it." She holds the laptop under one arm and walks back toward the stairs.

"What do you mean *if* it were a possibility?" I jump up and follow her. "It says right there that it is!"

Mom transitions to holding the laptop against her chest with both hands, as if trying to keep its secrets from me. She doesn't look at me. "You're talking about things you don't understand. It's not what you think it is."

"I still want to know about it!"

Mom shakes her head. She's already up the first few steps. "No. Please forget about it." She disappears with the laptop before I can stop her.

I have to read the rest of that paper. I *have* to. I can't get it out of my thoughts all day. And it isn't available online, not anywhere I can find. I have to act quickly.

After Dad gets home, and while Mom is making dinner, I find him in their bedroom. He's on their unmade bed (Jim and I have always been way better at making our beds than our parents), watching something on his tablet.

I knock on the doorframe and Dad looks up.

"Hey, Dad, want to help me play a prank on Jim?"

He lowers his tablet and looks at me warily. "Maybe..."

I walk over to the bed. "Don't worry. It's harmless. He finished a paper, and I thought I could make a copy of Mom's graded one and change all her comments to funny things." I sit down next to Dad's feet. "Make him and Mom laugh."

Dad bends his knees and scoots back, rumpling up the blue bedspread and white sheets some more, until he's sitting up against the blue-and-white-striped pillows. He smiles. "You'll probably get an extra assignment from your mother for that."

"Sometimes a good prank is worth the effort."

He chuckles and closes his tablet. "Alright. What do you need from me?"

"Just log into Mom's laptop for me so I can copy it to my shared folder?" I glance at Mom's laptop sitting on the long dresser across from the bed.

Dad's still in a blue golf polo from work, with a barbell and a solid silver V embroidered over the chest. "Real quick?"

"It'll only take a second."

Dad nods and motions toward the laptop. I don't let him see the victory fist I make as I grab Mom's computer and bring it to the bed.

Dad sits up straighter as I hand him the laptop. He flips it open and types Mom's password. Then he rotates the computer around, keeping it on his lap, so I can use the trackpad and see the screen.

I lean forward, sliding my finger across the trackpad, looking for her email. I feel jumpier than normal. "Will you keep watch?" My eyes never leave the screen.

The laptop shifts as Dad laughs. "So serious."

"Yes, I take my pranks very seriously."

"Alright. I'm watching the door." Dad sounds more amused than anything.

I find Mom's inbox, but I don't see the email. The keys click as I run a search for it.

Dad sits still, the computer on his lap. "Good thing I'm keeping watch. It would ruin everything if Jim walked in on us."

I force a laugh. I finally find the email, copy the paper attached to it, and send it to myself in a new message. I exhale and lean back.

"Done?"

"Done." I smile. "Thanks, Dad."

Saturday, July 10
Jim

I scoot my chair up to the white table in the homeschool room. The laptop Matt and I share is in front of me. I open it with one hand as my other hand runs a towel over my still-wet hair. I've been anxious to get back from the gym and shower and open the laptop, but not because I'm excited about history.

Matt's Vimer from yesterday was so strange, I've been curious about it all morning. His voice was serious.

"Jim. There's something on our computer I want you to read. When you open it to my account, it should be pulled up. Just make sure Mom's not around when do you because she doesn't know I have it."

What would Matt have that Mom shouldn't know about? It doesn't seem like a surprise or a prank because Matt's face had been so somber. Now I can finally find out.

In Matt's account, there's some sort of scientific paper pulled up. It's titled "The Implications of the Burke-Dalton Surgical Procedure for *Duocordis Unuscorporosis.*"

Huh? I scoot my chair in closer and start to read. As I do, my eyebrows gradually lower in concentration, and the hand that's running a towel over my hair slows to a crawl. Then it drops the towel altogether.

Tuesday, July 13
Matt

I'm watching a chemistry video at the table in the homeschool room when my phone vibrates with a new call. I see who the call is from and jump up. Then I creep down the entryway and glance into the kitchen and living room to make sure Mom isn't around. The coast is clear, and I walk outside to the back patio before I answer. "Hello?"

"Matt," Dr. Anand's voice says kindly in greeting. "It's been a while. How have you and Jim been?"

"Fine." I pace across the patio. It's sun-warmed and hot. "Did you get my message? You know the paper I mentioned? The one about the Burke-Dalton procedure? I need to ask you about it." I move quickly down the steps to keep the wood from burning my bare feet.

I can feel Dr. Anand's reluctance in the silence that follows. "Did your mother share that paper with you? I was under the impression she wasn't going to share it with—"

"Yeah," I lie. "Now, I want to make sure I understand it. It sounds like you could take my consciousness and upload it into a new body?" I reach the bottom of the stairs and step under the shade of the patio.

"That's...maybe not exactly how I would put it, but yes."

"A donor body, right?" The concrete and shade are cooler than the sunshine, but that's not why my arms are covered in goosebumps.

"Right." Dr. Anand's voice is reluctant. "It's all recently discovered, but there's a certain type of brain tumor that renders a consciousness lifeless but keeps the rest of the brain and body intact."

"Yeah?" I pace on the concrete now as I wait for Dr. Anand to explain. He does so reluctantly.

"*Duocordis unuscorporosis* is the only condition we know of that could allow the consciousness transfer. With your condition, because there are two consciousnesses in your and Jim's brain, you're both only...semi-attached to it, in a way. We think we would be able to remove the part of your brain with either your or Jim's consciousness, transfer it to a donor body, and preserve your life." Dr. Anand pauses. "Does your mother know you're speaking to me?"

"But there's a risk, right?" I'm so engrossed that I almost walk into the basement's sliding glass door. "Because it's never been done before?"

The pause before Dr. Anand answers is just long enough to indicate discomfort. "Correct. It's estimated that there is a forty percent chance of failure—"

"That's to me, right? To the one who would be transferred? Is there a risk to Jim, too?" Through the sliding doors, I can see Termite coming down the basement stairs. He must have heard me.

Dr. Anand sighs. "Matt, I don't know if I should be talking with you about this. Do your parents know that you know? I—"

"Is there a risk to Jim?" I repeat forcefully. Termite bursts out of his doggy door to my right.

Another pause. "Yes. Not as big of a risk, but yes, there's a chance that the consciousness of the sibling remaining in the original body would—"

"What's the chance?"

"Twenty percent." Dr. Anand doesn't pause this time. "A twenty percent chance of failure."

"O—OK." I take an unsteady step to the side as Termite reaches me and jumps up my side. "Thank you, Dr. Anand. Bye."

"Matt, wait—"

"Yeah?" I'm too distracted to give Termite the attention he's clearly asking for as he runs circles around me.

"How did you decide you would be the one to be transferred?"

I don't know how to answer his question. But Termite is whining, thinking I'm outside to play, and I figure it's a good enough excuse for me to end the call. "Sorry, Dr. Anand, I have to go. Thanks for everything."

Termite barks and wags his tail, but I hardly notice. Instead, I clutch my phone and stare into space as I walk slowly back inside.

Wednesday, July 14
Jim

Like the message from Matt I got on Thursday, in his message to me this morning, he's serious. Somber. Intent.

"You read the paper, right, Jim? The one about the procedure to fix us?"

I'm on my back on my bed, watching Matt's Vimer. I roll to my side and listen as he goes on.

"I want to do it. I want to be transferred. I want to get my own body." Matt sits on his bed, all the lights off in his room but the reading light illuminating half his face. "But you've got to be on board with it first. I talked with Dr. Anand, and there is a risk—to both of us. Forty percent risk of failure to me and a twenty percent chance of failure to you. And yeah, failure means—" Matt stops. "Well, what you think it'd mean."

"So, listen, Jim." Matt looks down at his lap. "You can guess how much I want this. And I know I can be bad sometimes about...well, talking you into doing things you don't want to do." The video jiggles as Matt readjusts, propping his arm up on a knee. He still avoids the camera with his eyes. "But I don't want to talk you into this. This is big. And risky, for both of us. So..." He takes a breath. "I'm not going to say anything else about it. Just let me know what you decide."

Thinking about the possibility of the Burke-Dalton procedure is kind of mind-bending.

I think about what it could mean. Matt and I in our own bodies. He could grow his hair out. I could cut mine short. He could stay out late and eat all the junk food he wanted, and I wouldn't wake up feeling tired and gross the next day.

And time? What would *twice* as much time feel like? I wouldn't be the guy on the soccer team who's only there for half the practices and games. There's a new season coming up in August, but I'm going to miss tryouts because they'll be on Matt's day. What would my life be like without any more "Matt days" at all?

And then meeting Matt. In real life. What would it be like to hang out together? To play music together? Would I have complained so much about the family reunion if he had been there with me the whole time, someone to joke, laugh, and talk with? Wouldn't it be great to watch *24* with Dad and Matt together? How cool would it be to drive around or watch movies or even play video games, me, Leo, *and* Matt?

Sunday, July 18
Jim

The hallway leading to Mom and Dad's room is dark. The carpet feels worn underneath my feet as I approach the door and knock.

"Mom? Dad?"

I hear Mom's voice. "Hi, Jim. Come on in."

I push open the door and step inside.

"What's up, bud?" Dad's sitting next to Mom on their bed. He flips the cover shut on the tablet he's been reading, and she slides a bookmark into her book and closes it in her lap.

I have great parents.

I climb onto their bed and sit at the foot. "Don't be mad." I look at each of them in turn. Dad is wearing an old marathon T-shirt and looks back at me with an open face. Mom's dark hair, often in a ponytail and never quite straight, is down around her shoulders. Her expression looks a little more ominous than Dad's.

I take a breath. "Matt and I have been talking about the Burke-Dalton procedure for the past few days."

Dad's eyebrows shoot up, and Mom's mouth drops. "How did—"

"Matt told me. He showed me the paper from Dr. Anand."

"But—" Mom sits up straighter. Her voice is agitated. "How did he *get* the paper?"

I shrug. "I don't know. He didn't tell me." I decide to go on. "Matt and I both want to do it, and—"

"Jim." Mom makes eye contact with me and speaks like she's breaking bad news but wants to do it in the gentlest way possible. "I'm sorry you misunderstood, but the Burke-Dalton procedure doesn't work like that. It can't be performed—"

"It can be," I correct. "It just hasn't been yet. But Matt and I have been talking to Dr. Anand and—"

Mom's expression becomes even more ominous.

I flinch. "This could change our life, Mom. We want to do it. The thing is, Matt says he wants to be the one to be transferred, but I feel bad about it, like that's maybe not fair."

"Neither one of you will be transferred!" The striped bedspread shifts as Mom's legs underneath it move to a cross-legged position so she can sit up even straighter. "This isn't a life-changing decision—it could be a life-*ending* decision! It's not happening!" She turns to Dad and puts a hand on his arm. "You remember how risky it is, right, Dave? *Forty percent* for one and *twenty percent* for the other. Forty percent!"

Dad sits up straight too. He puts an arm around my mom and leans in close to her. "It's OK, Jane." Dad turns to me. "We'll talk about this more. But not now."

Monday, July 19
Matt

"I told Mom and Dad we've been talking about the Burke-Dalton procedure," Jim says in his Vimer from last night. "Mom didn't take it well. She might bring it up with you today if you don't. Good luck convincing them. I'm sure you'll do a better job than me. But that's not saying much."

By the time I go downstairs, Dad's gone and Mom's sitting at the bar on her laptop, an open novel on one side of her and a plate with a crust of toast on the other. She's still in her pajamas.

"Hey, Mom," I say cautiously as I walk into the kitchen.

Mom shuts her computer and stands up. She doesn't look at me. "I found out you stole that paper from my email."

Her accusatory tone makes me defensive. "I just forwarded it to myself. I think I have a right to read it."

Mom picks up her plate. "And I didn't know you had been talking to Dr. Anand."

"He's our doctor, isn't he?" I open the cabinet to pull out a bowl. "Don't we have a right to contact him?"

Mom puts her plate in the sink and turns around to face me for the first time. Her eyes look different, and it takes me a second to realize it's because she isn't wearing eye makeup. (Mom *always* wears that eyelash makeup and is constantly touching it up. She keeps extra tubes of it everywhere: her room, the kitchen, her purse, her car.) She sighs. "Not about this. This isn't a discussion we should be having. The Burke-Dalton procedure, however appealing it sounds to you, is not something that—"

"But it could change our life!" I guess we're getting right into it.

Mom shakes her head as she starts wiping down the counters. "It's too risky, Matt. Way too risky. If there were a *ten* percent chance you or Jim wouldn't make it, that would be too high. A forty percent chance is unthinkable—"

"But think about what it could do, Mom!" I forget about my cereal bowl and walk around the bar so I can face her.

"No. Absolutely not. We're not discussing this." Mom turns her back to me again.

I walk around the bar, back to her side. "But this is my ticket to a whole life! Not a half-life anymore!"

Mom finishes wringing out the rag she's been using. She drapes it over the sink and forces herself to take a deep breath. "I know, Matt, I can see you're excited. But you and Jim are young. This is an exciting breakthrough in the medical field. But give it another five or ten years. They might test it on another pair of siblings, the science will improve, the risk will go down—"

"Five or ten *years*?" I gape. "Mom, this is my *life* we're talking about. I want to live it *now*."

"You are living your life!" Mom spins to the side and faces me. She gestures with her hands. "You have a great one! Dad and I have done everything we can to let you and Jim live as normally as possible—"

"Normal!?" I laugh in disbelief. "What about us is normal?"

Mom shakes her head like she's done discussing it. She turns back to the sink and starts doing the dishes (which means her distress is really distracting her, because that's supposed to be my job).

I walk around to her other side and keep talking over the sound of the running faucet and dishes, glasses, and silverware clanging. "Mom, there's so much we can't have. We can't go to public school. We get *half as long* to live! And what about relationships? Isn't that a normal part of life? Not for me and Jim. Girlfriends, marriage, kids—not for us. Don't you want grandchildren, Mom?"

Mom shuts off the water so fast and hard, the faucet clangs. "Stop it, Matthew!"

I'm stunned to silence.

Mom closes her eyes, takes a breath, and continues in a quieter voice. "Do you think your condition is only hard for you and Jim? For me and your dad, the first two years of your life were full of constant confusion and worry. After you were diagnosed and got the implant, we were so happy, but it was still *hard*." Mom picks up a dish towel and dries off her hands as she goes on. "Your condition has affected everything. Where we live, me homeschooling you, even the fact that Dad and I never had any other—" She stops like she's said more than she wanted.

I swallow.

Mom starts to get emotional. "And do you think it doesn't tear me up inside when we can't all be together as a family? Do you think I don't miss you and Jim *every single day* you're not here? And yes, knowing you won't ever be able to have your own families—" Mom purses her lips and finally puts down the dishcloth, which she's been distractedly still rubbing over her hands even though they're dry. "No, Matt, this isn't just hard on you."

I stand at her side, staring at her wide-eyed.

Mom's next words are still quiet, but more gentle. "Believe me, I would love for you and Jim to be normal." She puts a hand on my cheek. "But I would so much rather have you both here with me the way you are than lose either one of you."

Wednesday, July 21
Matt

I flop down on my back on my bed.

It's after lunch, around the time that Mom usually sits down with me for English, but she isn't home from the grocery store.

This morning, I woke up to a handwritten note from Mom telling me she loves me and she's sorry for getting upset the day before. Then I gave her a hug and told her I was sorry too. But it's still been a subdued kind of day.

Now I just lie on my bed. No music, no phone. Just lying.

Next to my bed is a big bulletin board, which I admit is crowded. There are notes, drawings, playbills from Leo's high school plays, old projects, photographs, and other random stuff. One piece of paper catches my eye, and I sit up to pull it down.

It's an art project, mine and Jim's, from years ago. We were six or seven. The paper is covered with handprints in blue and orange paint—mine in orange, Jim's in blue. But does it matter? It's the same hand.

Mom did a lot of stuff with our handprints when Jim and I were little. I didn't realize it then, but looking back it's easy to see how hard she worked so Jim and I could establish a relationship with each other. It's like she knew what her challenge would be, having two sons who shared so much with each other yet could never meet. So, aside from videos and messages to and from each other, we would do games and scavenger hunts. I would hide some small treasure or candy on my day and leave clues for Jim to find it on his day. Then Jim would hide something for me. We did crafts together, too. One of us would start a painting or drawing and the other one would finish it the next day. Like the paper I'm holding.

Someone knocks on the door, and I look up. Mom is standing in the doorway.

"Mind if I come in?"

I shake my head and scoot over so she can join me on the bed. The mattress shifts as she sits next to me, folding her legs underneath her.

She looks at the paper in my hands and smiles. "Do you remember asking me when Jim could come over and play?"

I smile and look up at Mom. "No. When did I do that?"

"You were maybe five. And you would ask me every day, 'Mom, can Jim come over and play today?'" Mom's smile fades. "Sweetest and saddest thing ever."

I look back at the handprints, running my fingers over the paint that's thick enough to make bumps on the paper.

Mom touches the paper, too. "It made me feel happy because I did everything I could to help you and Jim be friends. But I hated having to tell you, over and over, that Jim couldn't come play."

I let the paper fall to my lap and lean my head back until it hits the wall. "I used to wish so bad that I could talk to him. In real life. I used to imagine what it would be like." I turn my head toward Mom. "I still do."

Mom fingers the cuff of her sweater in her hands and nods.

"Mom..." I'm as gentle with my words as if they were bird eggs. Or, maybe more accurately after the argument yesterday, ticking time bombs.

"Since I found out about this procedure...thinking about the future and continuing to live with our condition...it's almost torture. Knowing that there's another option out there." I lift my head off the wall. "Knowing that I could be normal."

Mom takes a slow breath. "Matt...you don't remember what it was like before you got the implant. Before you and Jim were diagnosed. But I do. You couldn't talk. You couldn't crawl. You couldn't even sit. All of the normal milestones babies are supposed to hit."

I look down at the floor, trying to find something to focus on, and end up staring intently at the pajamas I dropped on the beige carpet that morning. I never like hearing about life before the implant.

"But *now*..." Mom leans closer to me. "Look at you now, Matt. You're smart. You're creative and funny. You're strong and healthy. You have friends. You have talents." She puts her arm around me. "Like being the best drummer I know." It's one of those cheesy mom compliments, but she's smiling when she says it, so I do my best to smile back.

Mom's arm around my shoulder, which already feels awkward because I'm taller than her, squeezes tighter. "Compared to before, you *are* normal. You and Jim already got one amazing life-changing miracle from science. Let's just be grateful for that."

looks like my magnificent power of persuasion wasn't enough to convince mom and dad

i was so excited about it but I don't think the burke dalton procedure is going to happen 😧

yeah I know 😔
i was getting so used to thinking about it
going through all the amazing changes
if we had our own bodies

seriously

but i wouldn't bring it up with mom if i were you

not unless you want her to get super sad

and whatever you do don't mention grandchildren

ok

noted

chapter
five

Monday, July 26
Jim

Monday morning marks the first day of a summer school break for me and Matt. Leo's just as excited as we are because he's there in the morning when I wake up.

"Jim!" He bangs the bedroom door open. "Finally! I've been waiting for you guys! Ready to make a movie this week?"

I yawn and rub my still-closed eyes. Leo doesn't seem to care I'm still waking up as he walks into Matt's room and opens the blinds.

"Your haircut war took forever." The desk chair creaks as Leo plops down in it. "And then summer school? Bruh, I don't care how short your school days are. Having them in the summer is still a crime."

"We get more breaks spread out through the year," I say around another yawn as I sit up.

"And what's up with Matt lately?" Leo goes on. "He hasn't seemed like himself."

I open my eyes fully. "Oh." I straighten up. "Yeah..."

I know why Matt's been down. The sting of our parents saying no to the Burke-Dalton procedure hasn't worn off. But I don't know what to tell Leo about it. Matt and I agreed we didn't want him to know. No use getting his hopes up like ours had been.

"So what's up with him?" Leo presses.

"I don't know."

"You don't know?" Leo spins in the desk chair.

I force a smile. "What do you want from me, Leo? I've never met the guy." The oft-used joke works, and Leo laughs it off.

"We're making a movie this week?" I'm ready to change the subject.

"For old times' sake." Leo stands and rubs his hands together theatrically. "I have been working on the best idea we've ever had, so when you two slackers are finally ready, we can start."

***

Leo moved onto our street when Matt and I were eleven years old. It only took him a couple of times talking to each of us before he got our condition. That summer, the three of us got into making movies. Matt and I had gotten our own phones the year before, so we had an easy way to take videos. Our first movie was silly, a reenactment of a spy film. But soon they became more elaborate. That summer, and the summers following, we continued to make movies. Some were parodies of other films. Some were original scripts written by the three of us. Leo was the best actor and played two or three roles. Matt got good at video editing. I found that I loved planning costumes and sets. We made a good team.

Leo moving in was a lucky thing for me and Matt. At first, we were jealous of each other. We each wanted to be Leo's best friend. I wanted to spend as much time with Leo as Matt did, paranoid that Leo would end up liking Matt better and I'd be ignored. But that's not what happened, and the videos we made with Leo gave me and Matt something to do together, another way for us to interact.

The videos helped Leo out, too. Aside from being fun, they launched his junior high and high school drama career.

***

"You're sure we're not too old to goof around with homemade movies?" I ask Leo as I walk back into Matt's room, pulling on a shirt after I've taken a few minutes to get caught up on my phone.

He stands up from the desk chair. "*Goof around?*" he repeats. "Please, Jim. Is that what we do? Who was cast as one of the leads in *Our Town* this year?"

I sigh and humor him. "You—"

"And who's been getting better and better at video editing software?"

"Matt, I guess—"

"And who's designed two—no joke—award-winning Halloween costumes?"

I finally smile. "Me?"

Leo pats me on the back. "You bet you have."

I lead the way out of the room and down the stairs. "Alright, alright. What's it about?"

Leo smiles. "Time travel."

Friday, July 30
Jim

On Friday when I wake up and walk into my bedroom to grab my phone, I stop short. Leo is sleeping in my bed.

I smile wryly, not surprised. Leo often sleeps over after hanging out with me or Matt, crashing in whichever of our beds is vacant.

I grab my phone and let him sleep, heading back to Matt's room. Instead of the bed, I flop into Matt's extra chair in the corner. It's like a fold-out camping chair, bright green and super padded, with a headrest tall enough to lean back into comfortably.

Matt's last Vimers of the day include Leo and show them goofing off down in the basement. They're choreographing a fight scene for the movie we're making. (It actually doesn't look half bad.) Then they fill me in on Leo's plan to sleep over, and Leo grabs Matt's phone and tells me about a concert at a restaurant he wants to go to later tonight, while Matt acts jealous in the background.

I breathe a deep self-satisfied sigh and balance the camp chair on its back two legs, enough so I can reach back and twist the blinds open with one hand. It's good to see Matt having a good time with Leo. From what I've heard from Leo's comments and Matt's Vimers, things started out strained between them this week. It's taken Matt a while to come out of the slump he's been in since Mom and Dad told us no. This might be the first time I've seen him laugh since then. But it looks like he's finally feeling more like himself.

Saturday, July 31
Matt

Leo rolls down the passenger window of the truck, letting in a blast of warm air. As I turn out of our neighborhood onto the main road, picking up speed, the air starts blowing faster.

"Would you roll that up?" I ask Leo above the sound of the wind rushing by. "The AC will kick in eventually."

"Bruh, your truck is so *old*." Leo rolls up the window.

"Well, hey, at least I have a car." I twist the AC dial. It *better* kick in eventually.

Leo scrolls through his phone. "Can you even call this a car? Doesn't it turn into an antique if it was made over a decade ago?"

"Hey, don't hate on the Silverado." The truck Jim and I share may be old, so old the exterior paint walks a fine line between "faded red" and "pink," but we both love it.

Leo smiles as he continues to read his phone screen.

"And are you sure we have to drive across town to film this scene?" I ask. "We're driving past like three other parks."

"For sure." Leo nods. "Trust me. It'll be the perfect setting for a time travel movie."

"Alright," I sigh. "You're the director."

"How's the video editing going?" Leo's eyes leave his phone, and he runs his fingers over a rip in the leather seat. "Did you do those first scenes with Jim yet?"

"Yeah." I drum my hands on the steering wheel along to the music. "And now that me and Jim are done with school for a few weeks, I should have plenty of time to get it done."

"Even the fancy stuff? The cloning?"

I smile. For this video, I'm going to attempt some fancy video editing and do things like clone us so it'll look like we have more actors than we do.

"Don't you worry." I normally don't like sunglasses, but Jim keeps a pair in the truck. I pick them up and put them on for effect as much as to block out the afternoon sun. "It's gonna look amazing."

Thursday, August 5
Jim

For the next week, Leo, Matt, and I work on our movie every day. We film at locations all over town: Leo's high school, a park, our neighborhood, the grocery store.

Late Thursday night, Dad takes me and Leo to his gym. We have a scene we want to film at a pool at night, and the indoor pool at the gym will be perfect. Since Dad is the owner, we can go after hours when no one is there. (I have to get permission from Mom to stay out late—which is *totally lame*, by the way. But since Matt's cool with it, she said OK.)

After we park and Dad unlocks the building, we walk inside. The gym looks different in the dark—empty, silent, with only the silhouettes of the weight machines visible. Kind of eerie.

Dad goes to his office while Leo and I head to the pool.

"OK." Leo puts my phone on a tripod and points it at the deep end. He turns around. "Ready?"

I step up to the pool. The surface reflects the few dim lights we have on. "Why do I have to be the one to do this again?"

Leo smiles. "Because your character is the one the jock pushes into the pool!"

"Matt could have done it," I point out.

"Yeah, but Matt's not here, is he?"

I sigh.

Leo taps record. He walks over to me, we say our lines, and he shoves me into the water. I fall in, fully clothed.

The water is cold. When I surface with a gasp, Leo's laughing, until he calls "Cut!" Then (trying to hide more laughter) he goes over to stop the video.

"You wrote that scene just so you could push me in the pool, didn't you?" I swim over to the edge and heave myself out, sopping wet.

Leo isn't listening. His eyes are on the camera, watching the scene we filmed. When he laughs again, I know it's a good take. I walk over to a towel and attempt to dry myself off and warm up my arms enough to get rid of my goosebumps.

The door to the pool opens.

"Hey, guys, are you—" Dad stops when he sees me. "Jim, you're soaked!"

I look at Dad, the towel wrapped around my shoulders, and shrug.

Leo takes my phone off the tripod. "You didn't think we were going to film a scene at a pool and not get in it, did you, Mr. Mickelsen?"

Dad rolls his eyes. "I guess I should have seen that one coming."

He and Leo talk while I change, and then we head home. It's a good thing, too. Though I hate to admit it, I'm really starting to yawn.

Friday, August 6
Matt

"Good morning, Matt." Dad hasn't left for work yet when I come downstairs. He's standing by the counter, reading something on his phone with a smoothie in one hand.

"Are you tired?" Mom sits at the table with her own smoothie glass. Her face is concerned. "Jim was up so late last night."

I roll my eyes. "I'm fine, Mom. We're sixteen. Going to bed past midnight every now and then isn't going to kill us."

Dad smiles down at his smoothie, but Mom still looks worried.

"Besides..." I pull down a bowl and some cereal. "It'll be worth it to see that shot of Jim getting pushed into the pool. Did it turn out good?"

"They seemed to think so." Dad takes a last sip of his smoothie and puts his glass in the sink.

He says goodbye to us, kisses my mom, and heads out for work. The gym chain he owns has three locations around the city, and he's heading to the furthest one. If it were one of the days he was going to our local branch, I might have ridden with him because after breakfast that's where I'm going.

***

One nice thing about Dad's job is that we all get gym memberships for free. Mom and Dad always stress how important exercise is for me and Jim. We have to take extra good care of our body, they say. Somehow, the fact that Jim and I share a body makes it especially important in their eyes. I'm not sure why.

So anyway, we work out at Dad's gym. And the best part about Dad's job is that Jim and I get our own memberships. Had it been some other gym, we would have had to share a membership (why pay for two when one would do?), which would have meant one of us would have to pretend to be the other or we'd have to go as Jett.

But at Dad's gym, Jim and I each get our own membership under our own names with our own accounts. This means that everyone there can call us by our own names. People know us because we're their boss's kids. They're nice to us. Most of them think Dad has two normal identical twin boys (who for some reason never do anything together). Only a few of Dad's closer employees know about our condition. It's not that Dad tries to hide it...it's just simpler that way. Jim and I are all for it. And as long as we don't get some horribly apparent facial injury, we can keep pretending to be normal twin brothers. I like that.

***

Jayden at the gym's front desk greets me as I walk in. "Hey, Mickelsen, which one are you?"

"I'm Matt." I scan my membership code from my phone. "Hey, Jayden."

"Working a whole year here, and I still can't tell y'all apart." He shakes his head as he types something into a computer.

"It's OK." I smile. "Not many people can." I walk away to my favorite weight machine still smiling. It's nice to be seen as a normal person sometimes.

But when I walk up to my machine, I frown at the thin laminated sign taped to it. "Out of order?"

I turn away. What to do now?

Out of the corner of my eye, I see the yoga room to the left. I know they have yoga classes, but I've never been to one before because each class is 98 to 99 percent middle-aged women (and 1 to 2 percent women older than that). But I stop and watch as a guy walks into the room. He's a little older than me, either in college or maybe recently graduated. He's wearing gym shorts and carrying a yoga mat. His hair is thick, blond, and long. He looks... cool.

I walk over to the door and glance at a schedule hanging on the wall next to it. A class is about to start. I look over my shoulder at the other weight equipment, then back into the yoga room.

You know, what the heck. Why not? If he can do it, so can I. I walk into the room, leaving behind the loud music, clangs of weights, and whirr of treadmills.

And you know what? I enjoy it, despite being the only teenage guy in the room. I stay for the whole class. There are some poses where, in my head, I'm like, "You want me to do *what*?" But the instructor is nice, and I'm able to follow along, even with zero yoga experience.

At the end of the class, the other guy in the room gives me an accepting nod, and the instructor catches me as we're walking out the door at the same time.

"I don't usually see people as young as you in class." She looks older close up than she did from across the dimly lit room.

"Yeah." I shrug. "I'm homeschooled so I have a flexible schedule." Plus, my dad owns the gym.

"How did you like yoga?" She slings her purple yoga mat on a strap over her shoulder.

"I liked it," I say honestly. "I might be back."

She looks thrilled that she's converted another male to her class. "Every Thursday and Friday at eight AM!"

I laugh to myself as I walk into the parking lot. I tried a yoga class. I can't wait to tell Jim.

Saturday, August 7
Jim

When I wake up this morning, as soon as I get out of Matt's bed, I'm sore. Like, really sore. What did Matt do yesterday?

His last Vimer of the day reveals the answer.

"OK, Jim." Matt smiles brightly. "I tried a new class at the gym today. Yoga. Don't laugh!"

I'm already laughing.

"No, really, you should give it a try. I liked it. I'm going to try it again. And oh," Matt adds as an afterthought, "I did do a lot of stretching. I'm not sure, but you might wake up a little sore tomorrow."

I snort. A *little*? I'm tempted to do yoga again so Matt will have to live with the pain. Or can I do something else to make him sore? Go shovel some dirt or load some heavy boxes? Take a long run? Dad's always training for a marathon or race and would be happy to go with me.

I decide I'm too stiff to get dressed and instead zombie-walk down to the kitchen.

"Guess what Matt did yesterday?" I laugh as I take down a bowl and some cereal. "He took a yoga class!"

Mom's sitting at the kitchen table, scrolling through her phone next to a bowl of bran flakes. She looks up and smiles. "Yes, he said he liked it."

My smile drops as I lower myself into a chair. "Well, easy for him to say. My body is *sore*, all thanks to him. He's lucky I don't have a game today or I'd be mad."

Mom winces as she watches me. "Sorry about that. If Matt does keep doing it, your body should get used to it, and the soreness will go away." Mom pauses. "Maybe it would help if you did more yoga today."

I snort. Yeah, right. Maybe a class specifically for teenagers, preferably teenage guys...then I'd give yoga a shot. Not in front of a bunch of middle-aged women I don't know.

Jim—Mon, Aug 9, 4:02 PM

oh i saw a flyer in the gym today for a new class
you'd like. water aerobics on thursdays at 3 pm

Matt—Tue, Aug 10, 7:21 AM

very funny. you're the one who's gonna be thanking
me for all the benefits our body's gonna get. increased
balance and strength, not to mention the mental benefits
like concentration and focus which only i'm gonna get
because i'm the one doing yoga. you're missing out

Jim—Wed, Aug 11, 10:43 AM

yeah...i'll take your word for it
i'll stick with weights and soccer thanks

Matt—Thu, Aug 12, 7:12 AM

https://www.fitforlife.com/10-reasons-men-should-do-yoga/

Jim—Fri, Aug 13, 7:56 AM

#mattsnewfriends

Matt—Sat, Aug 14, 7:25 AM

#mattandjimsnewbodythankstomatt

Jim—Sun, Aug 15, 7:13 AM

ha yeah you wish

chapter
six

Saturday, August 14
Matt

Leo, Jim, and I just barely finish our movie in time for school to start. Monday's the first day for all of us. And I gotta say, it turns out pretty good. We decide to celebrate with a "film festival," watching some of our past movies and ending with this newest one. Leo is willing to do it twice. We plan to do it after the first few days of school (Jim on Thursday, me on Friday) as a kind of farewell to summer. And we invite our parents to come watch the premiere of our latest movie.

***

On Saturday afternoon I'm in my room, scrolling through our past videos and making a list of the ones I think would be fun to watch. I'm also scrolling through my phone, looking at Distorted Tides' social media feed. They're my favorite band of all time, though they're older and not well-known. Jim and I agree they're the best, and we've turned Leo into a fan too. I jump in excitement when I see a post announcing that they're touring—they haven't done that in years! They're from the UK, so I'm not sure if there's a chance, but I read over the cities listed and...

I sit straight up in bed so quickly my headphones fall into my lap with a clatter. They're coming here! To Austin! Live! How amazing is that? I'm thinking about how fun it will be to tell Jim when I read three words next to the concert date that make my face fall: ONE NIGHT ONLY.

I shove my computer aside, trip on Termite as I jump out of bed, and run out of the room. March 19. Saturday, March 19. Please let that be my day, *please* let it be my day...

We have a calendar in the kitchen, a calendar where Mom marks out, in blue and in orange marker, my and Jim's days for the next year. The days that are set in stone and that we're not allowed to switch. I know the blue and orange color-coding seems silly. It was a system Mom worked out early on to stay on top of our condition. She even dressed us in blue and orange when we were little.

The calendar comes in handy when we plan things in advance, like, for example, going to a concert.

I run up to the calendar, flip through the months, find March, let my eyes follow the columns over to Saturday and down to 19...

"Dang it!" I yell.

It's marked with a strip of blue marker.

It's Jim's day.

Tuesday, August 17
Jim

This is the first message Matt left for me yesterday:

"Jim, guess who's a little hyper today?" Matt's voice is overly cheery as Termite squirms next to him on the kitchen floor. "Guess who missed his walk?" Matt turns to Termite and talks in that sappy voice he always uses with our dog. "Poor Termite, poor boy! You let us down, Jim!"

Termite thumps his tail on the kitchen floor, then jumps up to lick Matt's face.

In the video, Matt laughs and stands up. "But seriously." His smile drops and he brings the camera closer to his face, looking menacing. "Don't. Let it happen. Again."

I sigh.

Termite is supposed to belong to both me and Matt. He was our shared Christmas present five years ago. (Each Christmas, in addition to clothes, Matt and I get two presents from our parents: something for us to share and something for us individually.) When we were eleven, Matt begged and begged for a dog. He tried to talk me into begging for one, too. I guess Matt is the more persuasive one, because when Christmas came, guess what we got.

We celebrate Christmas separately, of course, on our own days. Whoever has Christmas Day will open presents with our parents first, then the day after Christmas, the other of us will do the same thing. Our parents rewrap whatever present they get for us to share so we can both open it.

Termite was our shared gift that year. Matt had his Christmas morning the day before, and on my Christmas day, Mom and Dad prefaced their gift.

"Now Jim," Mom said. "This sharing gift is something that Matt really wanted, and maybe you not so much, but we think it's something you can enjoy, too..."

"It's a puppy, isn't it?" My voice was flat and unsurprised.

Mom gave an apologetic smile and pulled out a twitching, yapping box.

I'll admit Termite was a cute puppy, all wiggly and excited, a nice red-brown color with white paws and dark fur around his eyes, nose, and ears. At the beginning, taking care of him was fun, even if he did chew on everything. As Termite's gotten older, he's come to be a well-trained dog and a part of the family.

It sounds funny, but one of my favorite things about Termite is the way he loves Matt more than me. I like the thought that Matt and I are individual enough that even our dog can tell us apart. I don't know if Termite has some sixth sense that lets him know which one of us, Matt or me, is awake in our body at any given time. Maybe it's just that Termite can sense the differences, however small, in the way Matt and I talk to him, treat him, touch him. Either way, he gets more excited around Matt.

When I go down to breakfast after getting dressed that morning, Mom also reminds me about Termite's walk.

"OK, OK, Mom. Matt reminded me, too. I'll take him after practice."

My fall soccer season started two weeks ago, and it feels awesome to be on a field with a team again...even if I'm not thrilled about the actual team I'm on. Capital Soccer Club players in my league get to try out at the beginning of each season, but I missed tryouts because they had landed on Matt's day. (Lame.) So when I get assigned to the lowest team in the league, I just say "thanks" and live with it. Next season, I tell myself, hopefully I'll be able to make tryouts.

***

After practice in the afternoon, I take Termite on a walk like I promised. I walk into the kitchen afterward to find Mom standing in front of the calendar, the one that marks my and Matt's assigned days.

I unclip Termite's leash and turn him loose in the house. His nails click on the tile as he runs off. Mom's holding up some of the calendar pages, frowning.

"What is it, Mom?" I fill up a glass of water and gulp some down.

"I'm just double-checking the dates next spring..." Mom mutters, flipping the page from one month to the next. Her tone doesn't sound particularly pleased.

"How come?" I say, out of breath as I finish off my glass.

"Let's just say I have a sneaking suspicion someone got into my colored markers." Mom's tone is stern enough to make me wince. "*Yes*," she finally announces. "At the beginning of next March, Matt has two days in a row. At the end of the month, you do. All of the days in March have been flipped." Mom turns her head to look at me like an 1800s schoolteacher about to scold a child. "You wouldn't happen to know anything about this, would you?"

"No!" I take a step back. "It wasn't me, I swear! If someone did it, it was Matt, and I'll find out why."

It takes some detective work. I check his phone first and look at his messages, but I don't see anything suspicious or out of the ordinary. I log into his account on our laptop and check all the open tabs online. Nothing fishy there, either, until I look at his browsing history. I read through the list of pages until two next to each other make me pause. One is the website of our favorite band, Distorted Tides, and a page labeled "Concert Tour." The next entry is the website of a concert venue...in Austin.

I open Distorted Tides' website, and it's confirmed. They have a concert in Austin! I check the date and hurry out of the homeschool room.

"March nineteenth." I nearly run into Mom, who's walking back into the kitchen from the office, a new freshly printed March calendar in her hands. "Whose day is March nineteenth?"

"In the modified version?" Mom reaches the bar and puts the new March calendar next to the old one. "Matt's."

I exclaim in frustration. "I can't believe it!"

Mom looks up. "What?"

"It's Distorted Tides!" I pace away from the bar, then back again. "They have a concert on the nineteenth. Matt saw it was my day, and he switched the calendar around!"

Mom frowns. "It hurts to see him think he can get away with something like that."

"It hurts that he'd try to steal something like that from me!" I keep pacing. "We're switching it back, right?"

"Of course." Mom's marking the new March page already, highlighting the days in blue and orange. I dig in a drawer for a pen, walk over, and write DISTORTED TIDES CONCERT—JIM GETS TO GO in big letters on March 19. Then I pull out my phone and open Vimer.

"I can't believe you, Matt!" I yell at the phone. "You tried to steal the Distorted Tides concert from me?" I flip the camera around to show him what I wrote. "But guess what—*I'm* going. Nice try. Jerk."

When I put the phone away, Mom's frowning at me.

"What?" I sit down at the bar and start ripping up the counterfeit March calendar Matt made.

Mom reaches over and holds my hands still. "Matt should be punished for this. And Dad and I will take care of that. But...maybe you could take it easier on him."

"What!" I can't believe she's saying that.

Mom sighs. "Look, I'm not saying what he did was right, but try to look at it from his point of view."

I roll my eyes and lean heavily on one arm, which slides across the slick granite countertop and makes me slouch even more. I *hate* when people tell me to look at things from Matt's point of view.

"He does love Distorted Tides." Mom finishes marking the new page of the calendar and hangs it up with the other months. "If you found out that Matt got to go to one of their concerts and you didn't, how would you feel?"

I grunt.

"Just..." Mom comes back over to me and gathers the paper shreds I ripped. She sweeps them into one hand and sighs. "I don't like it when you two are mad at each other."

"Then tell Matt to stop acting like a dirty rotten thief."

Mom looks down at me, but instead of looking mad or like she's going to reprimand me, she looks sad.

I grunt again, but after the rest of the day—after I shower and when I'm in my room getting ready for bed—I feel calmer and send Matt a Vimer with a different tone.

Wednesday, August 18
Matt

Jim's first message to me this morning is one of him with Termite on a walk, proving to me that he took him. He's in a good mood.

In Jim's second Vimer, he's ticked. "I can't believe you, Matt!" He's standing in the kitchen. "You tried to steal the Distorted Tides concert from me?" He shows me something written on the calendar (DISTORTED TIDES CONCERT—JIM GETS TO GO). "But guess what—*I'm* going. Nice try. Jerk."

My mouth drops open as I sink back into my bed. Caught! And now Jim gets to go. I moan and lie down on my side. It isn't fair.

Jim has one more Vimer for me. It starts playing automatically.

He's on his bed at the end of the day, illuminated by his reading light. "You were a jerk to try to take that concert away from me. And you're *so* going to get in trouble for that."

I groan. So he told Mom and Dad, too.

"But..." Jim's smirk drops. "I get why you did it. I know I wouldn't have stooped to your level and done the same thing if I were you, but..." He sighs. "Well, I know you're bummed you don't get to go."

Thursday, August 19
Jim

On Thursday, I spend some time getting the basement ready for the film festival Leo, Matt, and I have planned. I pull up the old videos I want to watch, plus the ones Leo wants, plus our latest film, which only Matt has seen all the way through. Then I pop some microwave popcorn, and by the time Leo comes over that night we're set.

Leo brings his mom, and Mom and Dad walk down the stairs as we're about to start.

"Wasn't one of you going to watch with Matt tomorrow?" I glance up at my parents as I balance my laptop on the TV stand and connect it to the back of the TV.

That's a common strategy our family uses. Dad will do something with me, and then the next day Mom will do the same thing with Matt (or vice versa). It prevents our parents from having to sit through lots of things twice.

Mom frowns. "Matt's film festival tomorrow night is cancelled."

"What?" Leo, who is already getting comfortable on the couch, looks up in surprise.

Mom sits down next to my dad. "I'm sorry, Leo. It's a punishment."

Leo stands and walks over to me. "What'd Matt do?" he says in an undertone.

I reply in a murmur over our parents' chatter. "He tried to switch the days around next March, behind my parents' backs." I pick up the remote and get ready to turn on the TV. "Distorted Tides are playing live in Austin—"

Leo's face lights up.

"But only on my day. Matt, of course, really wants to go, but he tried to do it by secretly changing the calendar."

The TV's on, but Leo hasn't sat down yet. He's staring at the rug, frowning. I watch his face, guessing that we're both thinking the same thing. *I wish we could do these things—film festivals, concerts, hanging out—with all three of us.*

Matt—Wed, Aug 18, 8:30 PM

jim! let me go! please! 🙏 pretty pretty please!
i'll give you anything! i'll let you choose the length
of our hair for the rest of our life! please!

Jim—Thu, Aug 19, 7:15 AM

look even if i wanted to give the concert up to you
and i DON'T
It's against the rules
we can't swap days for anything
mom and dad won't let us
you know that

10:04 PM

you're already missing your film
festival with leo just for trying

(the film was awesome btw)

Matt—Fri, Aug 20, 10:18 AM

mom and dad don't have to know! so come on!
PLEASE! I HAVE TO GO TO THIS CONCERT!!!

Jim—Sat, Aug 21, 7:09 AM

I HAVE TO GO TO THIS CONCERT TOO
i like distorted tides just as much as you do matt

Matt—Sun, Aug 22, 7:16 AM

ok how about this. let's leave it to chance. pick
one of us randomly to go see it. that way it's fair

Jim—Mon, Aug 23, 7:46 AM

what are we going to do play rock paper scissors?
but come on
you know i dont wish for anything more than that we could
both go to this concert together
but we just can't matt

Matt—Tue, Aug 24, 7:24 AM

Jim—Wed, Aug 25, 7:14 AM

i'll take lots of videos for you!

Matt—Thu, Aug 26, Oct 20, 9:20 AM

i hate you

chapter
seven

I goofed up, and I hate myself for it.

Why did I go with the calendar-switching plan? My plan B for seeing Distorted Tides live for the first time ever was to travel to another city on their concert lineup—L.A., or Las Vegas, or even somewhere on the East Coast if I had to. But that would have been expensive, and it would have eaten into Jim's days, and I knew my odds of talking Mom and Dad into it would be low. So I went with the sneaky route. And now I'm paying for it.

After I get caught trying to mess with the calendar, I try to humbly suggest getting me to another city to see my favorite band of all time. Guess what Mom and Dad say? That would be a big fat "no." And then I do something even more stupid and bring up the Burke-Dalton procedure again. Can't my parents see that events just like this one are the reason the procedure could be so life-changing? Apparently not. They shut down that conversation fast.

So...life gets easier if I try to pretend to myself that Distorted Tides *aren't* coming to Austin next year. That's better than obsessing over it, being tormented by the fact that my favorite band will be so close, but I won't be able to see them. Instead, I try to forget and move on with life.

Leo starts school in August, and so do Jim and I. We started our sophomore year curriculum this summer, so we don't have any new classes. Just plowing ahead through the same US history, chemistry, geometry, and English.

Jim started his fall soccer season too, which doesn't change much for me. He goes to the gym less as he hits more practices, scrimmages, and games. It means I pick up more weight training at the gym. I'm not giving up my weekly yoga class, though. I've really come to like it.

With Leo back in school, I can't head over and eat lunch with him in the middle of the day. I eat with Mom at home instead. After my math, she has me help her make a pasta salad.

"So..." Mom measures some pasta to boil. "I found something interesting this morning while you were reading."

"What's that?" I chop a bell pepper into strips.

"It's a camp." Mom dumps the pasta into a pot of water and pulls out some tomatoes and a knife. "For teens. I guess you'd call it a summer camp, but it's in September. And since it's in the middle of the public school year, it attracts kids who are homeschooled, or completing their education in more creative ways."

"Really?" I pause from my chopping to eat a bell pepper strip.

"It's called Camp Waller."

"And it's next month?"

Mom looks down at the tomatoes she's now dicing. "Yes."

"And Jim and I can go?" I wipe my hands on my pants and reach for the phone in my pocket.

"Well, I didn't say that." Mom puts her tomato dices in a bowl. "We need to talk about it and see if we could work around your condition, but if we talk to the camp, I don't see why we couldn't work something out. And it could be a good opportunity for you and Jim to—"

"Can we tell Jim now?" I have Vimer open. I point the camera at my face.

Mom looks up, realizing for the first time I have my phone out. "Matt, wait. I didn't say you're doing it—"

I ignore her and tap record.

"Jim, Mom found a camp for homeschooled high-school kids, and she says we can go!"

Mom sighs, picks up a cloth to wipe her hands on, and steps over so she can look into the camera. "Jim, I said you can *maybe* go. We'll need to work some things out, but—"

"And I think we should go as Jett!"

"What?" Mom looks at me. "What do you mean, go as Jett?"

I smile into the camera, talking to Jim, ignoring Mom. "I'll try to talk Mom and Dad into it tonight, but there'll probably be more convincing for you to do tomorrow. Good luck!"

I end the message and grin at my mom. She lays the dishcloth she was holding on the counter and gives me an unamused look.

***

Jett is an identity we created, a way for Jim and I to pretend to be normal. When we're around someone for a short amount of time, sometimes it's simpler not to have to explain our condition, to pretend to be what we look like to everyone else: one person. Jett makes it fair because neither of us has to pretend to be the other. We can be Jett, this third identity who's like both of us combined.

Jett plays the drums like me, and he plays the guitar like Jim. He has some sweet dance moves, and he's good at soccer. Jett is a way for both of us to be ourselves, sort of, without anyone having to know about our condition.

At church, we're Jett. We go to a big non-denominational Christian church but don't get too involved. It's easy for us to go to Sunday services and the occasional activity and blend into the background.

As soon as I hear about Camp Waller, I know we should go as Jett. What's the alternative? Explaining our condition to everyone at camp? Going over all the weirdness of it every time we meet someone new? No, no way. Camp Waller will be a bunch of people we won't have to see again. While it lasts, during that week, Jim and I can pretend to be totally normal. No one will have to know.

Unfortunately, my parents don't see it the same way. That evening, I go with Mom and Dad to the grocery store, and we discuss it.

"No." Mom's arms are folded, her beat-up wallet-phone-case-combo hanging from one wrist. "I do not like this going-as-Jett idea."

"Why not?" I push the grocery cart through the produce section. "We're Jett plenty of times. You let us go to church as Jett."

Dad adds a bag of apples to the cart. "Church is different."

"Come on." I lean across the grocery cart. "You guys want us to be Jett at church because you don't want everyone thinking our family is weird. Me and Jim want the same thing."

Mom looks away from the head of broccoli she's holding to frown at me. "That's not why you're Jett at church. And you don't know what Jim wants. Not yet."

"Anyway." Dad turns into the deli section, and we follow. "Whether you both want to go as Jett or not, there're reasons it won't work."

I lean my weight onto the cart and push it along with one foot. "Like what?"

"Well, first of all…" Dad pulls out his phone. "We checked the guidelines." He shows me the Camp Waller website. "Camp Waller's whole thing is that they're a technology-free camp, all about 'unplugging—'"

"Which is a great idea." Mom adds lunch meat to the cart.

Dad glances at her. "Right. But the point is, how would you and Jim possibly coordinate with each other enough to pretend to be the same person if you don't have your video messages?"

"If we go as ourselves, we'll still want Vimer," I point out.

"But that's just it, Matt." Mom pulls me up from where I've been essentially lying across the cart. "If we tell the camp directors about your condition, I'm sure we can work something out. I wouldn't be surprised if they make an exception and let you and Jim use your phones each night to talk to each other."

Dad takes over pushing the cart, sliding it away from me. "But if they think you're Jett, no such exception."

"So what?" I follow as Mom and Dad walk up the cereal aisle. "We'll write it down. We'll use a journal. We can still communicate that way. It'll be fine."

Dad shakes his head. "I don't see it working." He sees me trying to sneak a box of Cap'n Crunch into the cart and takes it away.

"And..." Mom surprises me by taking me by the shoulders. "You and Jim don't have to be ashamed. You have a rare condition, it's true. But you should be—"

"I'm not ashamed!" I back away from her and spread my hands out. "I just want the chance to be normal for once!"

Mom sighs, and she and Dad look at each other. Eighties music plays over the speakers, and other grocery carts in the aisle squeak as they're pushed.

Dad looks at me. "We'll talk about it."

I take that as progress. Now I need to convince Jim.

Matt—Wed, Sep 1, 7:34 AM

come on lets go as jett! it'll be fun!

Jim—Thu, Sep 2, 7:12 AM

i don't know

i don't like jett a ton

Matt—Fri, Sep 3, 7:07 AM

don't you want to be normal?

Jim—Sat, Sep 4, 7:02 AM

don't you want to be yourself? i don't
want to spend a week being you

Matt—Sun, Sep 5, 10:04 AM

you wouldn't be me! you'd be jett! jett's both of us

you can tell everyone you play soccer and the guitar

jett is just super cool because he's ALSO a drummer and
a good dancer and of course our super good looks

jett is awesome!

Jim—Mon, Sep 6, 7:16 AM

i don't know

(also side point i'm just as good of a dancer as you are)

Matt—Tue, Sep 7, 7:28 AM

(this is me refusing to acknowledge your side point)

you really want to be known to everyone
in the whole camp for our condition?

because you know that's going to happen right?

it'll be all that people want to talk to us about

or they won't get that we're two different
people and think we're split personalities

i know how much you hate that

Jim—Wed, Sep 8, 7:43 PM

well if you really think we can pull it off...

Matt—Thu, Sep 9, 7:28 AM

Matt

chapter
eight

Monday, September 13
Matt

Mom looks around the parking lot. "You're sure you're set?" We're surrounded by other cars with parents saying goodbye to teenagers.

"Fine, Mom." I give her a hug. "We'll be great."

"Make sure you take your sleep medication on time each night." She pulls away. "No matter how late you want to stay up."

"OK, OK, we will." I'm eager for them to leave. "We'll be fine, I promise." I look around the parking lot, taking in all the other teenagers, teenagers who I can be completely normal around...

Dad sets my duffel bag on the gravelly asphalt next to me. "Matt—"

"It's Jett, Dad," I say in a low voice.

Mom and Dad glance at each other. They're still not happy Jim and I are going as Jett.

"Maybe it's not too late to change your mind." Mom glances around the parking lot as if she's searching for someone. "We could talk to the head of the camp and—"

"Mom, it's fine!" I try to keep my voice forceful but low. "We already decided, alright?"

"OK, OK." Dad steps back. "Jett," he adds with a pointed look. I roll my eyes as he gives me a hug.

Mom hugs me again. "You're sure you're—"

"I'm sure, Mom!" I laugh as I pull away. "I'm sure, we're sure, I'm fine, we're great, it'll be awesome." I give her a big smile and a thumbs-up.

Mom looks at me, makes a determined face, nods, and gets in the car, followed by Dad.

"We love you!" She waves from the window as Dad reverses the car and heads for the camp exit.

"See you in a week, bud!" Dad waves, too. Their tires kick up dust as the car pulls away. "Have fun!"

I smile. "Oh, we will," I say quietly to myself. Then I call out, "Bye, Mom! Bye, Dad!" I wave until they pull out of the parking lot.

I pick up my duffel, turn around, and take a deep breath. Wow. Alone at a week-long camp. We've never done anything like this before. I walk into the main building to check in.

***

Inside, I join a line of other kids with luggage. In the foyer of a low-ceilinged building with long windows, I surrender my phone for the week and get our name tag (Jett Mickelsen), a week-long schedule, a camp map, and a dorm assignment.

As I walk outside and start up a hill toward the building marked on my map as my sleeping lodge, I fall in line with three boys walking the same direction.

"Yeah, they changed a lot since last year." One of them points to the left. "That building over there? That's all new."

"You've been to Camp Waller before?" I adjust my grip on my duffel and lean forward into my steps up the hill.

"Yeah." He has short blond hair and speaks with a slight Southern drawl. "This is my third year. What about you?"

"It's my first time."

"Mine, too." A black boy walking next to him with a duffel bag slung over his shoulder waves.

"This is Chase." The blond boy points to a dark-haired kid with glasses walking next to him. Chase salutes. The blond boy goes on. "He and I met last year. I'm Joel."

"I'm Christopher," the other first-timer says.

"Hi." I smile. "I'm Jett."

***

Chase, Christopher, Joel, and I are all headed to the same place: the Arvel Taylor lodge, which has two big rooms lined with metal bunk beds. The whole lodge is filled with boys.

Chase and Christopher claim two bottom bunks, and Joel and I claim the two on top of theirs. The whole walk up the hill to the lodge, Joel told us all about Camp Waller and what we can look forward to. Some of the highlights, according to him, are the ropes course (I consult my schedule and find that it's on Thursday, Jim's day) and the dance (on Friday! YES!).

After we slide our duffel bags under the bottom bunks, we have free time before lunch, so Joel leads us down to a river where the four of us kayak. At lunch, we sit together. Joel, Chase, and Christopher are becoming my good friends. That's perfect. In my and Jim's case, it'll be much easier for Jett to have a few close friends than trying to get to know dozens of kids.

After lunch is tie-dyeing T-shirts, then the whole camp gathers together for the first time outside. I've never been part of a group of teens so big. There are probably two hundred of us. The camp leaders talk to us for a while, and then they have a party set up for us down by the river for the rest of the afternoon until dinner. There are all sorts of games going on, like soccer, Frisbee, kickball, sand volleyball, and games with nets and balls I've never seen before. There are ice chests with water and cans of soda and popsicles and tables of snacks. It's awesome.

My three new friends and I end up with a bunch of other kids playing with a giant beach ball on a sand volleyball court. I'm having a blast. I feel like a normal teenager. It feels like maybe what public school feels like. Or summer camp.

Once, the beach ball comes sailing over the net, and I make a dive, swatting it up into the air before it touches the sand.

"Nice save."

I push myself out of the sand and stand up. A pretty girl is smiling at me. She has on a blue shirt, which she must have planned to match the shade of her blue eyes. She has long blonde hair. And a nice smile.

I smile, feeling like a dork with sand all over my shirt. "Thanks." I turn back to the game.

***

At dinner, my roommates and I sit down with our trays of lasagna and salad and laugh about the volleyball game and the time the ball hit Chase in the face. (He isn't really athletic, but he's funny about it.)

"Mind if we sit here?"

I look up to see the blonde girl from the volleyball court. She smiles and slides into the plastic chair next to me, setting her cafeteria tray down on the table.

"Sure. I'm M—Jett."

"Hi, umm Jett." She giggles.

Smooth, Matt. Real smooth.

The girl has three friends with her (none of them are as pretty as she is). They all sit down with us. The blonde girl says her name is Andie. Her friends are Emily, Ivy, and Zoe. Turns out that Emily and Joel know each other from last year, too.

I smile and wave as I meet them, loving it all—loving the attention, loving meeting new people, loving meeting girls.

***

After dinner, we go on a walking tour of the camp, which is fun because the weather is good, the camp is pretty and has a ton to do, and there's a nice sunset, but it makes me feel bad for Jim because there's no way I'm going to be able to communicate all the information from the tour to him. It's one of the times I wish we could share knowledge. Oh well. He'll have to manage with the camp map and help from the other teens.

After the tour, we all sit in a kind of outdoor amphitheater formed by a rocky hill, with benches made from stone. Adults talk to us about Camp Waller, its history and unplugged philosophy (which apparently doesn't extend to microphones or the outdoor lighting that switches on as the sun goes down).

I put my hands in my hoodie pocket, grateful I have it to protect against the light night chill. Andie's found a seat next to me, and she keeps leaning over to talk. It's small talk, where are you from, how old are you, what type of school are you doing, what do you like to do, etc. I answer all her questions, and she answers them back unprompted. She's easy to talk to, even if it's because she's the one asking all the questions. Once, Joel on the other side of me shoves my shoulder. I turn around and, even in the fading light, can see his knowing look. I grin back and shrug.

As one speaker wraps up a talk about the history of the camp, I lean over to Andie and say something about pretending we'll have to study for a test later. She laughs. I smile. Jett is funny. Jett is getting attention from a girl. Jett is awesome.

***

Later in our dorms, before bedtime, Joel and the other guys sit and talk, but I pull out the journal Jim and I brought, climb up the squeaky ladder to my top bunk, and start to write.

"Jett?" Joel calls. "What're you doing?"

"Writing in my journal." I don't lift my head. "I never go to bed without writing in my journal first."

A few of the guys laugh, but I can't take the time to care.

I'm glad I write fast. A counselor comes in and enforces lights out. I close the journal and slide it under my pillow. Then I make sure the little battery-operated alarm clock is set and next to my head. As I lie down and close my eyes, I smile. This has been one of the best days I've ever had. I'm already a huge Camp Waller fan. The only thing bringing down my high spirits is resentment that I have to give Jim a turn.

Tuesday, September 14
Jim

A soft beeping wakes me up. I open my eyes.

I'm in an unfamiliar place. I've known it was coming, but I never like waking up in an unfamiliar place.

I turn off the alarm clock that's sitting next to my head and sit up. I'm on the top bunk in a room that's filled with bunk beds and sleeping guys. There are windows on the wall behind me that let in soft light. No one else is awake. It's early morning.

I reach under the pillow and find, like Matt and I planned, the journal. The creaking of the leather binding feels too loud in the silent room as I open it. The last written-on page is filled with Matt's handwriting.

Hey Jim! Camp Waller ROCKS! It's awesome here. Summary on today: check in this afternoon, then free time. We went kayaking. Lunch, then making tie-dye shirts (I made ours blue and orange... kidding! It's dark and light blue and there's a chance it will turn out OK.) Then there was this party down by the river with tons of sports and games and snacks. I played beach ball sand volleyball with a bunch of kids. Made an awesome save. Then dinner and we went on a tour of the whole camp, which looks really cool. But there's no way I can write down everything we saw. Sorry. You'll have to rely on the map.

After walking around the camp we sat and heard some people talk about Camp Waller's mission and history. I can't fill you in on all the details either because I wasn't paying attention to half of it. I'm sure it's not important.

I shake my head. Typical Matt. I hope all his updates for the week won't be similar.

Here's all the names to remember:

- Mike: our counselor. Has curly dark hair. He's a little strict, but cool
- Joel: top bunk to left of ours. Short blond hair. He's nice, was here at Camp Waller last year. Knows a lot about the camp
- Chase: bunk below Joel. Dark hair and glasses. Not very athletic, but funny. Chase met Joel last year at camp
- Christopher: black kid on bunk below you. A newbie like us. He's also pretty funny

Those were the only guys I hung out with. I tried to keep it simple for you. Now for the girls:

- Andie: small, long blonde hair, blue eyes, really pretty. She talked with me at dinner and during the meeting at night. Also I impressed her during the volleyball game

- Emily, Zoe, Ivy: Andie's friends. I can't remember who is who. I'm sure Jett won't be seen as too inconsiderate if he has to ask for their names again

Not gonna lie, I'm super bummed I have to miss even one day of Camp Waller. So enjoy it for me. Don't forget to leave me a report. Have fun!

There's a gap, and then something Matt seems to have added as an afterthought.

Oh, I think Andie likes me/Jett/us. She was flirting with me all evening. She's cute. I would just go with it.

I glance over to the side. Joel in the bunk next to me (if Matt's notes are correct) has his head hanging off his pillow, his mouth open, and his eyes closed. He's fast asleep. I grab the pen and write a quick response.

Are you serious? We can't flirt with a girl. What if she finds out?

Then I reread Matt's notes, trying to commit it all to memory. When a counselor (Mike, I presume) calls from the doorway that it's time to get up, I shut the journal and stuff it under my pillow. Time to meet everyone.

Chase, Christopher, and Joel are easy to recognize. I find our schedule, map, and name tag. I hang the name tag lanyard around my neck and make sure to grab the schedule and map. Those will come in handy. Then I follow everyone to breakfast, fitting in as casual as can be.

The camp is beautiful. It's hilly and green and most of the buildings are made of white stone. There are birds chirping and wildflowers growing by the side of the path.

On the walk down the hill to the cafeteria, I remind myself that, if Matt and I are both going to be Jett, I have to act more like him. With that thought on my mind, I walk into the cafeteria.

The room is crowded and noisy with kids, and I stick close to my three new friends. Just after we walk through the glass doors, a group of four girls walks up to us.

I recognize Andie right away. First, she's cute, like Matt said. She has long, wavy blonde hair. She's short and small and has noticeable blue eyes. But what makes Andie the easiest to recognize is the way she looks at me— like she's really, really into me.

"Jett!" She's beaming as she comes over and gives me a side hug.

"Hey, Andie." The hug surprises me, but I'm on top of it enough to hug her back.

She falls in line behind me as we pull plastic trays from a stack and slide them along a metal runner. Andie talks about yesterday, and I smile and nod as cafeteria workers add plates of pancakes and fruit to my tray. At the table, she sits by me, and our friends gather around.

"Did you see the schedule for today?" A dark-haired girl scoots her chair in next to Andie. "In the morning, it says we choose a workshop. What does that mean?"

"Oh!" Joel sits up straight, excited enough to pause with his fork in the air. "It's super cool. Every morning, we get to choose a workshop to go to." He puts down his fork and pulls out his schedule, which he points to as he explains. "They have a bunch of them—music, art, engineering, theater. Even cooking. You can go to a different one each day or the same one every day. But it's best to go to the same one every day because you work on a project that you build on all week. We should all pick one and go together!"

Everyone starts discussing the workshops. I half listen as I chew my pancakes and study my camp map and schedule. All the workshops sound cool to me.

It turns out most kids in our little group play instruments because they settle on the music workshop.

"That's cool with you, right, Jett?" Joel slides his schedule in his pocket. "You can show us your drum skills."

I look up from the map I've been studying.

"Or the guitar, right?" Christopher elbows me. "Didn't you say you play both?"

"Yeah." I'm glad that Matt mentioned Jett plays the guitar, too. "And I gotta say today feels like a guitar day."

***

After breakfast, Joel leads all of us—me and the two other guys and Andie and her three friends—to the music workshop. We walk up the path to the stone building and open a wooden door to reveal a large, white-tiled room cluttered with musical instruments.

"Hey, look, an open drum set!" Joel walks with me toward the drum kit. I change directions and head for an acoustic guitar hanging on the wall.

"I'd rather play guitar." I pull it down, pretending to focus intently on the strap and strings, and cross my fingers that someone else will sit at the drums. Luckily another kid does. Whew.

Instruments are claimed and tested, filling the room with noise and pandemonium that drowns out the voice of an adult urging us to be careful and only pick up instruments we know how to play. The many string instruments can still be heard above the loud brass, piano keys, deep bass notes, wind instruments, and drumbeats. I can barely hear the notes of my own guitar.

Joel finds a saxophone. Chase finds a violin. Andie plays the piano. (She heads for it and waves me over to stand by her. I hesitantly oblige.) One of Andie's friends with light brown hair finds another violin. I can't remember if it's Emily, Zoe, or...the third one.

We're all quieted by a shrill whistle. At the front of the room is a man in a green Camp Waller polo and jeans. He has dark hair long enough to tie back in a ponytail and wears thin-rimmed glasses.

"Thank you for choosing the music workshop!" His accent is something East Coast. "I'll be your director, and this week we'll be learning the Camp Waller theme song."

He and some helpers start handing out sheet music. Music stands are passed around. Kids who don't have an instrument are given tambourines or shakers and sing. Then we're led by the director as we follow the sheet music and start playing the Camp Waller song called "All We Need." It's upbeat, catchy, easy, and comes with a lot of hand-clapping and "hey-heys" and "whoa-ohs." The director is very flexible, adapting parts based on everyone's skill level.

We spend the rest of the morning practicing. At first, it's cacophony, but after a few times through we start to get better. Our last time through the song, I have the chorus memorized enough to look around the room as I play along. Everyone's singing or clapping or making music, getting into the song, full of energy and smiles. I can't help smiling myself.

At the end of the song, the director congratulates us.

"Well done, all! Now, if you'd like to check out another workshop this week, feel free." He starts collecting sheet music from kids up front. "But I hope a significant portion of you stay because we'll be practicing this song all week and then performing at the camp variety show on Friday."

I look up from the sheet music folder I'm closing. Friday? Uh-oh. That's Matt's day. I realize how dumb I've been, coming to the music class, with me and Matt playing different instruments. I should have opted out. Maybe Matt can opt out tomorrow, but judging by the excited look on all our friends' faces, he might have to do that alone. I'll have to let him deal with it.

The music workshop takes all morning. At lunch, Andie sits by me again. Matt was right. She's definitely flirting with me. I try to do what Matt said: go along with it, let it happen, enjoy the attention. But I never feel totally at ease talking to her because part of me still feels like it's a bad idea.

After lunch is free time. The cafeteria is highly air conditioned, and the afternoon air feels warm and comforting as we walk outside.

"There's a lot to do down by the river." Joel leads the way down a gravel path toward the water. "We could kayak, or even swim..."

As we walk onto a flat, grassy area next to the river, we pass a plastic tub full of balls and Frisbees. Underneath, I can barely see a soccer ball.

What would Matt do? What would *Jett* do? He would be proactive. He would start something. I tell myself I can do that.

"Hey, who wants to play soccer?" I dig the blue and orange ball (a color scheme that feels like a good sign somehow) out of the tub and squeeze it between my hands, testing the firmness. It's scuffed and just a tad flat, but it'll work.

"Yeah, sounds great!" Joel comes up behind me. He's nice, like Matt said, and an agreeable guy. That's coming in handy.

The rest of our group agrees, and we walk out to the big, grassy field to play. Some kids are already there tossing a Frisbee around, and they accept our invitation to join our game.

Kids drop hats and jackets on the ground to make makeshift goals. Joel sticks his arm down the middle of the group to sloppily divide us into two teams. The day is warm, but it's partly cloudy and a little breezy. I can't help grinning as we start to play.

Not to brag, but I stand out at the soccer game. Most of these kids don't play on a team. It's easy. It's fun. It makes me feel confident, like Jett would feel. I end the game smiling.

The rest of the day is packed and awesome: an entertaining science presentation, getting dirty doing yard work on the camp's grounds, dinner, and at night a bonfire and s'mores.

Everything is amazing. I'm liking Camp Waller just as much as Matt does.

***

That night, after we're all herded into our dorms, Chase, Christopher, and Joel start a card game. I ignore them and climb up to my bunk, grateful for the bright fluorescent lights that are still on.

"Journal writing again, Jett?"

"Yep." I pull the lid off my pen. "I'm an avid journal-writer. You should try it sometime."

Wednesday, September 15
Matt

When a soft beeping wakes me up, I'm at first confused by stiff sheets and a scratchy bedspread.

Then I open my eyes and sit up. Camp Waller! Yay! I'm back at Camp Waller! I glance around, making sure everyone is asleep, and pull out the journal. What awesome stuff have I missed out on? Time to read Jim's report. First is a message from him on a line by itself:

Are you serious? We can't flirt with a girl. What if she finds out?

Then the actual update starts:

Hey Matt! You're right, Camp Waller is great! I loved it. Super fun day. We had a bonfire and s'mores tonight, and we helped out the camp by digging flower beds, where we got super dirty. It was a blast. We played soccer after lunch, and not gonna lie, I'm pretty sure I impressed everyone. Jett's coolness level increased.

I hope Jim hadn't impressed everyone so much that I'll be asked to play soccer today. That won't go over well.

All morning there was a music workshop. The way it works is you can pick between like five different workshops to go to in the mornings. All our friends want to go to the music workshop every day. The bad thing is...I played the guitar. So tomorrow, you'll have to either find a way to hand off the guitar to someone else, fake it, or go to a different workshop on your own (all the workshops did sound cool though). If you stick with the music class, we're learning the Camp Waller theme song, and it's easy and catchy, and there were a lot of kids there, so hopefully you can get by faking if you want. Oh, but one other complication... We're performing the song in front of the whole camp on Friday. So if you fake it all week, you'll have to fake it there. Sorry, I didn't know beforehand or I would have skipped it.

I sigh. Great. Thanks a lot, Jim. Can I pull off faking the guitar? Will it be better to go to a new workshop all on my own? And will I ever get a chance to play the drums?

I sit up straighter and lean against the wall, careful not to make the bed squeak as I keep reading.

Here's everyone else's instruments in case you need to know:

- Joel – Saxophones
- Chase – violin
- Andie – piano
- Ivy – violin

- Christopher and Emily and Zoe - sang
- Took me a while to sort out Andie's friends, but this should help:
- Emily - Asian. Excited, fun
- Ivy - light brown hair. Quieter
- Zoe - I think she's Hispanic. Seems nice and easygoing

That actually is helpful. Thanks, Jim.

Also, talked to Andie a lot. She hung around me all day. You're right, she IS a flirt. I tried to go along with it like you said. But I don't know if it's a good idea. First, what if she figures out we're two people? And even if she doesn't, isn't it kind of inconsiderate of us?

I address Jim's comment about Andie right away.

It's fine, she's just into our super good looks more than either of our personalities anyway. It's nothing serious, but since she's into Jett, I say go with it. We're getting attention from a girl. Kinda cool right? It's only this week and we'll never see her again, why shouldn't we enjoy it?

By then, other guys are starting to wake up. Our counselor comes in and makes sure we're all getting ready. I snap the journal shut before stuffing it under my pillow. Time to start the day. I can't wait.

All through breakfast, I try to decide what I'll do when the workshops start.

I don't like the idea of going to another workshop alone, so after we deposit our cafeteria trays on some metal racks, I follow along as the others lead the way to the music workshop, all of them humming the song they started learning the day before.

Walking into the room, I wonder if it's what walking into a high school band class feels like. There are musical instruments and stands everywhere, and colorful signs painted on butcher paper lining the walls.

Before I can take in the whole room, Andie holds out a guitar to me with a smile. The noise level in the room rapidly increases as instruments are picked up and tested.

I slide the fabric guitar strap over my shoulders, preparing myself to fake it for the whole practice, wondering if I can get away with it, when I hear two of Andie's friends talking nearby.

"Yeah, we learned the same song last year." One friend tucks her dark, straight hair behind her ear. That one's Emily, right? "I played the guitar."

"You play the guitar?" My voice is too loud and eager, and she and her friend are startled. But I don't care. "Here, do you want a turn?" I slip out of the strap and hold out the instrument to her.

Emily speaks loudly over the noise in the room. "Oh, no, you keep it."

"No, really." I push the guitar at her, but she takes a step back. I take a bigger step toward her. "Here."

Emily stammers a bit, but I don't drop the instrument or step away, and she finally takes it from me.

"Thank you." She smiles and puts the strap around her shoulders.

I try to smile and nod nicely and not reveal that I'm as relieved as I had been when Dad signed me up to run a marathon with him but Mom got me out of it.

Chase is nearby. "What are you going to play, Jett?"

Music stands and chairs scraping across the tile add to the noise level in the room and I almost have to shout to reply. "I can sing. It's OK!"

"Yeah, join the singers!" Christopher puts an arm around my shoulder and a tambourine in my hand. I still feel like exhaling in relief, but I beat it a few times and act excited.

Andie touches my shoulder, smiling her bright white smile. "That was sweet of you." She isn't that hard to impress. I again chalk it up to my and Jim's good looks.

(OK, a quick note on how Jim and I look. Yeah, we were born sharing a body. That sucked. But we do commiserate with each other by agreeing that at least the universe made it a good-looking one. Our brown hair is thick. Because of our gym membership and Jim's soccer, we're fit. We have good teeth and a good smile. We even have good skin—well, for your average teenage guy. I've told Jim that what happened with our body was this: God made such a perfect human form, he knew it was too great of a blessing for any one person to hold alone. So he sent down two of us to share it.)

So, with me not having to play the guitar, it turns out the music workshop is a lot of fun, and I'm glad I'm there. It's neat to come together with so many other kids and instruments to make something that sounds good (or will eventually, I assume). And because the kids who are singing also have a stomping and clapping/tambourine bit, I'm still involved in percussion.

The rest of the day comes, action-packed and fun. Lunch, then an "act of kindness" activity where we get the chance to make cards and write letters to family and friends. I make some for my parents, then feel awkward as Andie gives me a purple envelope and I don't have anything to give her in return. Then there's a nature walk, and rappelling, and dinner, and outdoor team-building games on the lawn. Later that night we go stargazing.

At night after I leave an update for Jim, I'm again bummed out that I have to miss the next day.

Thursday, September 16
Jim

Thursday morning, I wake up excited and ready for the day. Matt's notes are helpful and only make me a little jealous. He got to go rappelling? And stargazing? Lucky. I'm happy for his sake that he was able to get out of playing the guitar. If I don't end up playing the rest of the week, I won't mind.

The day is fun, like Tuesday. At the music workshop, Emily keeps the guitar, and I stick with singing. And our song starts sounding good.

The highlight of the day is a ropes course. There's a rock wall, several zip lines, and a bunch of other fun climbing challenges.

Andie wants to climb some things at the same time as me (which is annoying; there's a lot of squealing involved). But when it's time to climb the rock wall, she makes a big enough deal of acting scared that I end up climbing up the wall next to Andie's friend Zoe.

"Can't keep up, Jett?"

I squint up into the sun to see Zoe already several feet ahead of me.

"Wow, you're fast!"

She stops, flat against the wall, and turns around to look down and grin at me.

Well, I know what I have to do then. I quickly reach for the next rough weather-worn climbing hold and pull myself up.

In the end, Zoe wins, but only barely. And she's huffing and puffing as she pulls herself onto the flat wooden platform at the top. (Well, I'm huffing and puffing too, so we laugh about it.) As a guide hooks our harnesses up to two zip lines and we catch our breath, we talk about past rock-climbing experiences. I find out she's from Austin, too, though the opposite side.

As I step off the platform and slide down the metal wire, listening to the buzz of the pulley and the wind rushing by me, I can't help feeling frustrated at Matt. How many more girls like Zoe are there at camp? Down-to-earth girls who would be more fun to hang around than self-centered Andie, who practically never leaves my side?

By the end of the day, I really am getting tired of her. I try to tell myself to do what Matt said. Go along with it, try to enjoy getting attention from a girl. It's one week, and we'll never have to see her again. Despite all that, there's no way that I didn't treat her at least a little more coldly than Matt does. But I can't help it. I'm not Matt.

And, even more annoying, Andie doesn't seem to notice.

Friday, September 17
Matt

Jim's update this morning is shorter than his last one.

Hey Matt. Right now I'm sitting alone on the ground in the trees. We all brought notebooks and we're supposed to write deep self-reflective thoughts inspired by the beauty of nature or something. Ha, yeah right. Not in the journal I share with you anyway.

Well the day's been super fun. At music class, I let Emily play the guitar and it was fine. I'm glad that worked out. I think you guys will sound pretty good tomorrow.

We got our tie-dye shirts. I was impressed. Ours turned out really well. I even got compliments, which I should pass on to you since you're the one who made it. So nice job, bruh.

The best part of the day was the ropes course. We got to climb all sorts of things hooked up to harnesses, and then jump off and go down zip lines, plus a bunch of fun team building exercises. I'll try not to go on about it too much. Don't want to make you too jealous.

I exhale through my nose, frustrated. Sure. To not feel too jealous, I tell myself that tonight I have the dance.

OK, back in the dorms now. We played a new card game Joel taught us. That's why I don't have as long to write. I hope you don't have to play the game again, because you'll have to relearn it. Sorry.

Great.

Hope you enjoy your last day!

That's it? I hope that's all I need.

Friday, like the other days, turns out to be an absolute blast. We spend the music workshop practicing the Camp Waller song, getting it down just right. At the end there's some downtime, and I seize the opportunity to mess around at the drum kit for a few minutes, impressing all of Jett's friends.

As we walk out of the music room, we see that it's lightly raining. There are already puddles on the road, and it smells like rain on concrete.

Joel holds his jacket over his head as we sprint up the road to the cafeteria. "Hey, if the rain clears up, we should go play soccer again after lunch!"

Oh *please,* rain, don't go away...

During lunch the guys want to teach the girls the card game they played last night. That's embarrassing because it's obvious that I apparently forgot how to play. Luckily Joel has to teach the girls, anyway.

As we walk out of the cafeteria, I wince at the sun that's now peeking out from behind the clouds. Great.

Sure enough, Joel brings it up. "So should we play soccer again?"

Everyone else gets excited and follows as he leads the way.

"Are you sure?" I jog a few steps to catch up with him. "We could go practice our song one more time." Or I could play around at the drum kit some more. I could have done that all day.

"They close the music room after the workshops are over." Joel points ahead to a grassy area by the river. "Look, the field is open. I call team captain, and I call Jett!"

Andie's at my side, and she puts a hand on my arm. "I call being on Jett's team!"

"Picking teams doesn't work like that, Andie!" Emily giggles. I try to laugh along, but inside I'm filled with dread. This isn't going to go well.

***

It doesn't go well. My saving grace is the muscle memory Jim's drilled into our body. At least part of me knows what it's doing. But *I* don't, and I'm sure it shows. The most embarrassing part is when I'm trying to get the ball past a defender and trip, ending up in the grass.

"Come on, feet," I mutter to myself as rainwater soaks through the knees of my pants. "You do this for him. Do it for me!"

Joel comes jogging over. "What happened, Jett?" He reaches down a hand and pulls me up. "On Tuesday, you were way better than this."

"I told you, it doesn't feel like a soccer day." I pick wet grass off my hands. "Sorry."

As the rest of the kids scatter to the other end of the field and I watch them, I can't help imagining what it would be like if Jim and I were normal, if we were in our own bodies. If we got the Burke-Dalton procedure. He'd still be better at soccer than me. But I wouldn't have to pretend to be him. And then, just as quickly as the thought comes, a dozen other thoughts follow. *If we got the procedure...* I wouldn't have had to miss the ropes course yesterday because I would get to be at every day of camp. So would he. We'd be here together. Together! What would that even be like?

Sometimes I feel like half a person. And here, at Camp Waller, with a big secret and pretending to be someone I'm not, a lonely half person.

I swallow hard and try to force the feeling down as I jog up the wet field. Nothing would make me more un-Jett-like than brooding about that.

***

The variety show comes later, and that ends up being a lot more fun than soccer. All of us from the music workshop perform our song. The whole camp joins in on the chorus by the end.

And then, after we have the chance to go back to our dorms and change, the highlight of the day comes. The dance. It's outside on a big pavement slab. The earlier rain has cooled the weather down, and the sky is clear now. With the music playing and the strand lights, lanterns, and a slight breeze, the whole feel is...I don't know if I should say magical, but something like that. I love it.

Joel, Christopher, Chase, and I dance by Andie, Emily, Ivy, and Zoe all night. Any embarrassment I've caused for Jett on the field is made up for on the dance floor.

The DJ scatters in a few slow numbers, and every time, Andie's right there, expecting me to dance with her without even having to ask. So I do. I notice that we aren't the only ones pairing off. Joel and Emily dance with each other more than once, too.

Despite Andie practically hanging on my arm, for one slow number a guy from another dorm asks her to dance, and she reluctantly follows him. I exhale, glad for the space, and look around.

Joel and Emily are dancing again. Off to the side, Zoe and Ivy stand talking.

I only get to go to a dance like every other year. I'm not sitting out even one song. So I walk up to Zoe and asked her to dance.

"So...you and Andie, huh?" Zoe looks at me knowingly as we start to move to the music.

I shrug and try to smile. "Yeah, we just...hit it off, I guess."

"Evidently."

For a second we dance quietly. I look at a silver hummingbird necklace around Zoe's neck until I can think of something to say. "So, um, is this your first year here at Camp Waller?"

"Yeah." Zoe's sweater is fuzzy under my right hand. "I told you that yesterday."

Oops. I try something else. "Are you from close by?"

"Yes." Zoe squints at me. "Austin, actually. Like you. Did you forget our whole conversation yesterday?"

"Oh!" I give an awkward laugh. "Oh, man, I'm sorry. There's been a lot of new people to meet this week, you know?" Inside, I grumble at Jim's lack of details on whatever conversation that was.

"Are you a forgetful guy, Jett?" Zoe leans forward and gives me a teasing look.

"No!" I try to laugh it off. "No—"

"Because you forgot how to play cards, too."

"Hey, that was a complicated game."

"Did you also forget how to play soccer?" Zoe's cheeks pull in like she's trying not to smile.

"It wasn't a soccer day." I start wishing I had never asked her to dance. Why couldn't she go on about herself like Andie did? Maybe pairing off with a self-centered girl all week has been a good thing after all, as far as not blowing my and Jim's cover.

"But it *was* a drum day," Zoe says. "You were really good, by the way."

I smile. "Yeah, I love the drums."

"Yeah, we could tell. But you didn't touch them until today." She's making me nervous the way she's talking. But what Zoe's just said isn't anything compared to what she says next. "You're a weird guy, Jett. It's almost like you're two people."

My stomach drops to the floor. Really? Are Jim and I that obvious? Are we failing at being Jett? But no, I tell myself. Andie's clueless. And Joel and the other guys? Maybe they've noticed Jett has some off days. But no one's said anything close to the eerily true thing Zoe just said.

I shuffle to the music with my mouth half-open like an idiot for a full three seconds until I pull myself together enough to respond.

"Good one, Zoe." I straighten my shoulders, lift my head, and use an exaggeratedly confident voice. "No, I'm really just twice as talented as your average guy."

She laughs, but I can't quite tell if it's the laugh that says *Haha, you're so funny* or *Yep, you're as weird as I thought.*

***

As I go to bed that night, I have a lot to fill Jim in on. I skip out on more card games to give him an extra good report.

OK, biggest news of tonight: after the dance Andie held my hand. She caught me by surprise and did it all on her own. I let it happen because I didn't want to be rude and I didn't know what else to do. So, as a heads up, keep your hands in your pockets tomorrow if you don't want it to happen again. (And I'm guessing you don't.) Andie's really forward, huh? She hung around me all night long. I danced with her most slow songs. She expected it.

Despite that, the dance was way fun! Oh, and we played soccer today. AND the card game you guys learned last night. Those both went poorly. Soccer more so. Super embarrassing. Lucky for you, there's no more dance or YOU would be embarrassed trying to live up to my dope moves.

The variety show was fun. We did end up sounding good. And it was cool to perform in front of so many people. I feel bad you missed it. I wish this weren't a technology-free camp or I would have recorded it for you.

So anyway back to Andie. She might try to hold your hand tomorrow. Good luck with that. And...sorry I started that whole thing. Looking back it was probably a bad idea. I should have listened to you. Well, one more day and we'll never see her again. Remember, you can tell people to follow us and stuff but don't give out either of our numbers. Especially to Andie.

Enjoy the last day of camp. Can't wait to get home and swap more details with you about each day!

By the end of the entry, I'm really missing our phones and Vimer. My hand is starting to cramp.

Saturday, September 18
Jim

The quiet beeping of our alarm clock isn't what wakes me up this morning. It's our counselor, Mike.

"Come on, come on, it's leaving day! Get up and get packed!"

I sit up. Guys are rubbing their eyes, climbing out of bunks, heading to the bathroom, throwing clothes in duffel bags. I grab our journal from under my pillow and start to open it, but I don't have time. Mike is walking down the rows of beds and calling guys down.

"Jett, down from your bunk, time to pack up!"

I climb two steps down the ladder and jump the rest of the way. Maybe I can pack up and read Matt's latest entry afterward.

By the time I get everything packed away, Mike is there again, calling for all of us to zip up our duffel bags so they can be taken to the parking lot. I have to stuff the journal inside. It'll probably be OK. I bet Matt's entry is just more, "Yay, camp was awesome!"

Breakfast is rowdy, with more talking and laughing than usual, plus some cheers and songs the counselors taught us over the week. Andie sits by me, giving me an extra-big smile.

We're walking out into the sunshine when it happens. I'm walking along, talking to Joel, when someone grabs my hand. I look down and almost trip over my own feet. Andie is holding my hand.

I feel my face getting warm. I'm holding hands with a girl. It feels unnatural. How am I supposed to swing my arms when I'm holding her hand? Am I holding my arm too stiffly? When can I let go?

Based on how casual Andie looks, gesturing with her free hand while she talks to Emily, this isn't the first time this has happened. If I wasn't so focused on feeling nervous and uncomfortable, I'd be angrier at Matt. One thing I do know is that I *really* regret not reading his latest entry.

***

The rest of the day isn't as action-packed as the other days at camp, but it's fun: a nature walk, a service project, time to hang out with each other. And me trying to keep my hands busy or in my pockets around Andie as much as possible, when I'm not avoiding her altogether.

And then, too soon, it's time to leave. We're taken to the gravelly parking lot where our duffel bags are waiting for us. Our counselors give us back our phones, and kids go crazy. Soon all I can hear are excited voices, the beeps of message alerts, the sounds of ringtones, and the artificial clicking of phone cameras.

There's one update I want to read more than anything on a phone. The second I have my duffel and the opportunity, I slip our journal out and hold it in my hands. But I feel awkward opening it up and reading it then. Plus, I'm distracted by requests for pictures, which I smile for, and for my number, which I turn down every time. "This isn't my phone," I lie to everyone. "It's my parents'. They gave it to me just in case. I don't have my own phone. Yeah, my parents are funny like that. Look me up instead."

Everyone gives me their number anyway, but Matt's right. We'll never have to see these people again. They come from all over the state. True, Zoe's from Austin, but from the opposite side. Next to her, Joel outside San Antonio is the closest. Andie, thank goodness, lives all the way down in Corpus Christi.

***

When my parents pull into the parking lot to pick me up, my cheeks are aching from smiling for selfies. Mom and Dad get out of the car, give me big hugs, and put my duffel in the trunk. I keep the journal in my hands, wanting to read it the second I have the chance.

Right before I climb in the car, Andie comes running up.

"Bye, Jett!" She hugs me. "Call me, OK?" And then, taking me by surprise, she stands tall and kisses me on the cheek.

My eyes get wide, and I climb into the car without saying anything. My cheeks feel hot, and my body feels stiff as I buckle my seatbelt.

Dad pulls the car out, and I look up to see Mom gaping at me. I shrink down in the seat.

"Jim?" She pulls off her sunglasses. "You are Jim, right?"

I nod.

"What was that all about? Who was that girl?"

Dad also stares at me through the rearview mirror with eyebrows raised.

"Just a friend?"

Mom doesn't buy that for a second.

"Who...had a crush on us all week?"

I know Mom's serious when she turns down the volume on the movie scores she and Dad have been listening to. "So you discouraged her from the start and kept your distance?"

"Um...maybe encouraged? Just a little?"

"What!?" Mom's shocked.

"It was Matt's idea!" I quickly say. "He started it!"

"You and Matt can't have girlfriends—let alone the *same* girlfriend!"

I don't respond. Instead, I open the journal on my lap, flip to the right page, and start reading.

"Jim!" Mom's voice is frustrated. "Did you hear what I said?"

"She...wasn't a girlfriend," I mumble, distracted as I keep reading.

"What are you doing?" Mom leans between the seats, blocking the AC I can feel blowing from the front.

"Reading Matt's last entry. I didn't have time this morning—"

"We knew Jett would be a bad idea," Dad says from the driver's seat.

"It—it was fine." I close the journal. "It was only this morning. They made us pack up early. But Matt tried to warn me about the girl. She was just super forward—"

"And that makes it OK?" Mom's voice is getting louder. "If I'd have known you and Matt would use your little...charade as Jett to start a relationship with a girl—"

I roll my eyes. "It wasn't a relationship! That's ridiculous, Mom. And seriously, I don't like her *at all*. Her name's Andie, and she's self-centered and shallow. And I know Matt and I tried to act like the same person, but the truth is we're not, and even though she hung around us all week she didn't even notice—"

"I knew this was a bad idea." Mom turns forward and puts on her sunglasses again.

"It was fine, Mom!" I stretch my seatbelt as I lean forward. "Seriously! And are you going to ask how our week was? Because, despite Andie, it was AMAZING—"

She interrupts me again. "You and Matt know better. Now, I know that your condition is hard. And I know that it's not fair. But there are certain facts about you and Matt that can't be changed, and certain rules that can't be broken. As appealing as it is, starting a relationship with a girl—"

"Ugh!" I lean back against the seat. "Mom!"

Mom turns around and stares at me. Even with her sunglasses on, the look is stern enough to get me to close my mouth.

"We're disappointed," Mom ends. "And I don't want either of you to contact this Andie girl again—"

"Hey, no arguments there. Seriously, Mom, haven't you been listening? *Neither of us likes her.*"

"It sounds like you don't." Dad chooses to join the conversation. "What if Matt doesn't feel the same way?"

I look out the window and huff a breath through my nose. "Then he has terrible taste in girls."

***

For a while, the only sound in the car is the thrum of the tires on the freeway (and me humming the Camp Waller theme song under my breath). I'm afraid of getting lectured and Mom's mad. After about thirty minutes, Dad turns on the music again, and I take that as a sign that I can talk.

I do want to tell Mom and Dad about camp. They start to loosen up and, after we drive through for burgers and fries, and by the time we pull into the driveway at home, I have them both smiling and asking questions as I tell them about the highlights. (Maybe they'll forget about the whole Andie thing.)

Unfortunately, later that night Mom comes to see me in my bedroom. "Jim."

Her tone doesn't sound good. I wince as I turn around from my desk chair to see her standing in the doorway. "Yeah?"

She sits on the edge of my bed. "Can we talk about the girl, please?"

"You mean can you lecture me about the girl?" I've been reading my phone, but I swivel my chair around to face her and fiddle with the case.

She smiles. "I want to make sure that what you said is true—that you don't like this girl, and you're not interested in starting a relationship with her."

I cringe at the embarrassing *start a relationship* phrase. "Completely true, Mom. And did I tell you where she lives? Corpus Christi."

Knowing that Andie lives on the bottom border of the state does seem to make Mom feel better.

"I promise, Mom," I say. "And I know the rules. I won't break them. Matt won't, either. He doesn't think this Andie thing counts as a girlfriend. He never wants to see her again, either."

Mom flattens my gray bedspread with one hand. "Are you sure?"

"Pretty sure."

"You haven't talked to him all week."

I smile. "Still, I know him pretty well, right?"

Mom smiles, too. "Well, despite the girl incident, which I hope you and Matt never repeat, I am glad you had fun."

"A ton of fun!"

Mom really does look happy as she stands up and moves to the doorway. "Good. I'm glad."

Sunday, September 19
Matt

It's nice to be in Jim's comfortable bed instead of the squeaky bunk with its stiff sheets, but I do miss camp. The week was all too short. (Of course it was. Three days instead of six? Like everything for me, half as long as it should be.)

I hurry to my own room and flop on my bed to open up Vimer. Jim's latest update is the first thing I watch.

"Hey, Matt." Jim is at home, sitting in his room still dressed from the day. "We're home! And first of all, heads up, you're in for a huge lecture about Andie."

I groan. Jim ratted me out?

He goes on to tell me how Andie held his hand, kissed his cheek, and thoroughly embarrassed him in front of Mom and Dad. He tells the story so well, I laugh out loud. Miraculously, he doesn't seem too mad at me. Instead, after more info about the lecture, he fills me in on the most entertaining parts of all his other days at camp. The video is long, but I don't mind. It's good to see his face and hear his voice. I realize, surprised, that I've missed him the past three days.

In addition to Jim's long message, I have so many other posts to catch up on that I'm downstairs to breakfast late. I'm wary, but not surprised, to see Mom and Dad sitting at our round kitchen table in front of mostly empty breakfast plates, watching me come downstairs.

Termite bombards me first, so I have to kneel and pet him and give him some attention while trying to ignore the stern looks my parents are giving me. Finally, I clear my throat and stand up.

"Mom!" I make my voice excited and hold out my arms to her as I take my seat. "Dad! I haven't seen you guys all week! So good to see you, too!" (Dad cracks a smile, but not Mom.)

"Of course we're happy to see you, Matt." If Mom really is happy, her stiff posture and tone of voice haven't gotten the memo. "And we want to hear all about camp. But first—"

"A big lecture about Andie. I know." There's a bowl of strawberries in the middle of the table, and I pull it over and pop one in my mouth.

Mom and Dad glance at each other with a look that says *Dang, Jim already gave him the lecture, and it probably came out more funny than firm.* They're right.

"Look." I sit up straight in my seat and swallow my mouthful. "Everything Jim said is true. I agree with him. I don't like Andie at all. She was just..." I shrug. "Super forward. I thought I'd go along with it. I didn't want to be rude."

Mom and Dad don't move, just stare at me, ignoring their plates of mostly eaten waffles and Termite wagging his tail next to me.

"And..." I slide my bare feet across the smooth tile underneath my chair. "I promise I won't contact her again. And I'll tell Jim I'm sorry if the whole thing made him uncomfortable."

"I think having a girl kiss him on the cheek made him feel pretty uncomfortable." Dad starts to chuckle, so I do, too. Then Mom sends Dad a look and he straightens his face.

"Well..." Mom fingers her glass of orange juice as she studies me. "As long as you learned your lesson and promise to follow the rules."

"I will. No girls. I promise."

Dad leans back from the table and refills his own glass with juice from a pitcher on the table. "Jim told us you didn't think Andie counted as breaking the rules."

"Yeah." I scratch Termite's ears when he puts his head in my lap. "I didn't. I mean, it was only a week."

"Well." Mom's knife and fork clatter as she stacks them on her plate. "Just so you know, what you did with Andie *does* count as breaking the rules."

I sigh. "OK. Noted."

"And you won't do it again?"

"I won't."

Luckily, Mom and Dad let the subject of Andie drop, and I'm able to fill them in on all the other awesome stuff that happened at Camp Waller.

They're a good audience, and it's cool to see how happy they are that Jim and I had a good time.

Jim—Sat, Sep 18, 7:19 PM

ok camp waller was fun
but andie was a big mistake

Matt—Sun, Sep 19, 10:13 AM

yeah i agree with you on that one
she didn't end up being as fun as
i thought she would be

Jim—Mon, Sep 20, 7:02 AM

yeah
and being jett wasn't as fun as i thought it would be either
like andie was way into us but she couldn't
even tell we weren't the same person

i mean we have a DOG that can tell us apart
being around andie every day for a week and she
couldn't tell? yeah i know we tried to hide it but i didn't
like that there wasn't anyone who could tell us apart

Matt—Tue, Sep 21, 7:14 AM

well there was zoe. wasn't it worth it though?
to have a normal teenage experience?

Jim—Wed, Sep 22, 7:08 AM

wait what about zoe?

Matt—Thu, Sep 23, 7:10 AM

i didn't tell you? it was at the dance. we were
talking and she told me that jett was a weird
guy. that jett almost seemed like two people

Jim—Fri, Sep 24, 7:12 AM

what!? you didn't tell me that!

Matt—Sat, Sep 25, 7:05 AM

sorry guess i forgot it in the giant info dump i gave
you friday night. which was way more than you gave
me on thursday. and which you didn't even read

Jim—Sun, Sep 26, 7:12 AM

we're not going over that again
but i can't believe you left that out
it would have made me feel at least a little better

Matt—Mon, Sep 27, 7:12 AM

yeah well it made me feel worse

chapter
nine

Saturday, October 9
Matt

After Camp Waller, it's back to life as normal. When friends from camp message Jett online, Jim or I say a quick hello and then ignore them.

School starts for us. We go back to our subjects, back to reading, back to math, back to working together on the partner assignments Mom gives us. We record drum and guitar videos back and forth. Leo gets busier with school and theater, but we hang out with him as much as we can.

Jim and I do the daily jobs our parents assign us (dishes and taking out the trash). Jim's in the middle of his soccer season, and he's excited to play in the games he can. I have my drum lessons twice a week (once with a tutor at my house and once at a music studio in town). We go with our parents out to eat sometimes, we have meals at home, and we enjoy the cooler weather. We go hiking, biking, and kayaking at parks nearby. We watch *24* with Dad and movies with both our parents. We listen to and play music from our favorite bands, like Distorted Tides and Chaos of Quincy. We hang out with Leo on the weekends. Except for soccer, Jim and I do a lot of the same stuff. Just, like always, never together.

Friday, October 15
Matt

As the end of October draws closer, Jim is more sullen in his Vimer messages. I know why. It's my year for Halloween.

Most holidays, like Easter or Christmas or our birthday, Jim and I can both celebrate. When we were little, Mom and Dad explained that they could ask Santa Claus and the Easter Bunny to make an exception for our special family and make two visits. And for our birthday, Mom and Dad split it over two days. We both get to blow out candles and have a party or go out somewhere fun with Mom and Dad.

Halloween, though, that's different. There's only one trick-or-treating night. Only one Halloween costume party and dance at our church. Only one of us who gets to go.

So, like so many things in life, Jim and I take turns. This year, I get Halloween. He got the Fourth of July. Next year, the opposite. It's fair that we take turns with Halloween because we both love it.

When we were little, it was all about trick-or-treating. But now it's about our church's Halloween party. Which, for me, is all about the dance. For Jim, it's about the costumes. He's placed in the costume contest two times (a zombie and Professor Dumbledore). He loves making costumes. He'll spend weeks or months on one.

So we both love Halloween, if for different reasons. And this year, my year for Halloween, Jim is noticeably bitter. Not much I can do about that, though.

Monday, October 18
Jim

Monday night Dad asks me to help him with yard work. There aren't many leaves to rake, but there are bushes that need trimming and weeds to pull.

Dad is clipping extra branches off a bush. "So. Jim."

"Yep." I stand with a trash bag in my hands, held out and ready for bush scraps.

"I know it's not your year for Halloween..."

I give an exaggeratedly loud sigh and lower the trash bag to the ground. He thinks I needed another reminder?

Dad pauses between clips so I can hear him over the metal hedge trimmers snapping shut. "But maybe we could still do something fun."

"Yeah. I guess." My voice is low, and I stare into space. I admit I'm moody. Not only am I going to miss the Halloween party this year, but I'm also going to miss a soccer game while Matt goes to the party. Way unfair.

Dad straightens up and wipes flecks of leaves off his face with his sleeve. "You know, there's a new haunted house I heard about. Maybe we could check it out."

I look at Dad dubiously. "Really?" The last time we went to a haunted house—based on Dad's face when we walked out—I had figured he was more likely to buy me and Matt a new truck than take either of us to one again.

Dad takes a breath and smiles at me. "Tell you what. Next April there's a 10K here in Austin—"

I lean my head back and groan aloud.

"And it's on your day! You train with me for the race, and I'll take you to a haunted house." Dad sets the trimmers down and starts picking up branches and leaves off the ground. He comes up with a handful, pulls my arms up again, and dumps them in the bag.

I squint. "Isn't that like blackmail?" The black plastic starts to stretch in my hands, and I readjust my grip.

Dad looks wounded. "Blackmail? Please, Jim. Get your means of coercion right. This is a bribe."

I roll my eyes, and he smiles.

Dad drops another bunch of leaves in the bag, then motions for me to bend down and help him. "Jim. If all I had wanted was a trash can, I could have brought one over. Come on."

The smell of cut leaves is heavy as I bend down to pick up a handful. I try another angle. "You know, Dad, I totally would, but training this body for a race would have to be something Matt would need to get on board with, too. And I just don't know if I could talk him into it."

Dad shakes his head as he picks up the trimmers and goes back to snipping stray branches. "You two always say that about each other. What's it going to take to get one of you to run a race with me?"

I smile as I straighten up. Dad's always training for some race or marathon. And Matt and I are always coming up with excuses not to run with him.

"Two sons." Dad trims so forcefully a few leaves fly out toward my face. "And neither likes to run."

I dodge the leaves, then bend down to pick up more scraps of bush to throw away. "You're right. I just don't like to run."

"And I don't like haunted houses." Dad pauses to drop his arms and catch his breath. "That's why this was going to be such a great deal."

I just laugh.

look will you lay off the guilt tripping about me getting halloween? i know you're bitter but it's my turn this year

there's nothing unfair about it

Jim—Mon, Oct 18, 7:13 AM

well you could lay off rubbing it in my face
if you send me another clip of you practicing dance moves i'm gonna hide the basement camera

Matt—Tue, Oct 19, 7:25 AM

if you love making costumes so much why not make me one?

i'll just end up throwing something together anyway. why dont you use your creative juices and make me something awesome to wear

Jim—Wed, Oct 20, 7:03 AM

no thanks
pass

Matt—Thu, Oct 21, 7:10 AM

but you love making costumes

Jim—Fri, Oct 22, 7:12 AM

it's not the same when i don't get to wear it

Matt—Sat, Oct 23, 7:04 AM

your body gets to wear it

Jim—Sun, Oct 24, 10:11 AM

still not the same

Matt—Mon, Oct 25, 7:24 AM

chapter
ten

Monday, November 29
Jim

Halloween comes and goes, and Matt, to his credit, tries not to rub the party in my face too much.

In early November, Matt and I get the flu, which is crappy. Especially because Matt somehow swings it so that almost the entire time our body is sleeping, I'm dormant. That means *he's* dormant when our body is awake, making me the one who has to deal with the chills, fevers, and aches. We're allowed to nap when we're sick, so we'll switch places up to five or six times a day then, but it's no fair how he manages to do that.

Later in the month, Dad runs a marathon in the Texas Hill Country. It's on the same day as my last soccer game of the season, so Dad and I give each other a hard time about who Mom will go see (she chooses Dad).

Before I know it, it's Thanksgiving. That's never a big deal at our house, unless we're traveling to see family. This year we stay home and it's low-key. I guess it's hard to celebrate a holiday about gathering family together when our whole family can never actually gather together. Mom, Dad, Matt, and I end up eating a lot of food, sleeping in, relaxing, and streaming some new movies.

Tuesday, December 14
Matt

Leo's school play, *You Can't Take It with You*, happens in December. Mom and I go to a Friday performance, and Jim and Dad see it on Saturday. Leo does great and the play is really funny, but mostly I'm excited his rehearsals are over, and now he'll have more free time.

Jim and I are about to start a break from school, which is great, but I'm bummed about something else. My drum tutor is going out of town, and then we're going out of town, and so I'll go for a month without playing with him.

Bradley's a college student. He's been a drummer for a few different bands since he was in high school. One day a week, I go to a music studio for drum lessons. And one day a week, Mom and Dad pay Bradley to come over and teach me. He has been since he was in high school.

When I was younger, Bradley stood and watched me play, giving me pointers and guidance. But my lessons with him have changed over the years. Now they feel more like jam sessions than lessons because he plays along on the guitar.

He says he's not that good on the guitar, but I think he's fine. And what I love is playing the drums with someone else playing guitar. It feels more like a real band. And that's what I would love more than anything else in the world.

***

At the end of our last session before the holiday break, I hit a final beat on a cymbal to wrap up a song.

"Great!" Bradley ducks out of the strap of Jim's electric guitar (which he probably plays more than Jim does). "You're doing really well, Matt."

I stay sitting at the drums and catch my breath. "Are you and your band playing any time soon?"

Bradley hangs the guitar on the wall, then turns around wincing. "Tomorrow night." He watches my dejected face. "But we've got another gig in January. I'll check the dates."

"Yeah! Let me know!" I watch him wrap up the guitar cord and lay it next to the speakers. "I'm so jealous you get to play in a band."

"What about the group that plays at your church?" Bradley straightens up and swings his brown messenger bag strap over his shoulder. "Weren't you going to talk to the drummer there? Ask him if he ever needed a sub?"

"You think I should?" I tap my drumstick idly on my floor tom, listening to the low thumps it makes.

"Yeah!" Bradley holds out his fist. "You'd rock it, Matt."

I smile as I bump his fist. "Yeah, that'd be lit! It wouldn't be the same as a rock band, but..." My smile falls and I look down. "Well, I'll take what I can get. What band is going to want half a drummer?" I look at the two drumsticks I hold in my right hand and run my other hand through my hair without looking up. "Let me know if you hear of any, alright?"

"Will do, Matt." Bradley's face, when I look up at him, is full of pity.

It's not fair. Jim's able to play soccer with our condition. His team is big enough to make do without him on the practices and games he has to miss.

But a band? If I wanted to be a drummer in a band, what could they do? Only have gigs and practices every other day? Yeah, right. Could I find a band with a drummer who was OK letting me sub for him on *my* schedule rather than his? Yeah, right again.

I would even be stoked to be part of the group that plays in church every Sunday, even though I don't love Christian gospel music. Any chance to play with other people on a stage…it would be so dope. Unfortunately, the whole only-alive-every-other-Sunday thing throws a wrench in that plan.

I first got into the drums five years ago. Now I wish that Jim had, too. Then we could be in a band together. Share it. We're good at that.

Friday, December 17
Jim

I noisily slurp the last of my slush out of its Styrofoam cup, then zip my jacket up to my chin. "Man, I'm cold."

Leo sits at the red picnic table next to me. Bright menu signs and fluorescent lights illuminate the notebook he's reading. "Weird. I mean, it's not like you're sipping a frozen drink outside at night in the middle of December."

I smile. It *was* my idea to come to Sonic. Leo has been studying for finals, but I told him he needed a break. And yeah, it's chilly, but not cold enough to keep me from enjoying my cherry limeade in the brisk night air. I love Austin.

Leo shuts the notebook, pushes it away, and rubs his eyes. Then he takes a long drink of his own slush.

"Ready for finals?" I set my cup aside and pull out my phone.

"Meh." Leo yawns as he stretches his arms above his head. "Ready to be done."

I smile, not envying him. I'm homeschooled, and I have to share a body with a brother. But all my huge school tests aren't crammed together in a big cluster twice a year.

In one of the drive-in spaces in front of us, a car engine revs up. I squint at the headlights that shine in my face. "What do you think I should get Matt for Christmas?" The car pulls away, and I open my eyes and go back to scrolling through my phone. "I found a Distorted Tides shirt." I hold the screen up for Leo to see. "Think he'd like it?"

Leo glances over from his own phone. "As long as he's not still bitter about having to miss their concert."

I make a face. Good point. Back to scrolling.

"How about this?" Leo shows me his phone screen. "Speaking of winter weather. Heaters for the seat of your car."

I smile wryly as I look at the product on Leo's phone. "Yeah, but he'd know I'd use it just as much as him."

"So?"

I swipe my screen again. "I guess the gift doesn't seem as sincere that way."

"Who said I was going for a sincere gift?" Leo flips his body around so he can lean back against the table and stretch out his legs in front of him. "I was suggesting it mostly for me."

Saturday, December 25
Jim

Christmas is no Halloween, but it's still one of my favorite holidays, whether I get it first or second.

We do presents in the basement in front of the big TV. We record the whole thing, so Matt and I can watch each other's Christmas morning.

I sit cross-legged on the gray rug in front of the TV, in the same spot I have every Christmas since I was a kid. My feet are snug in some striped socks I just opened from Mom and Dad.

Dad half-lies, half-sits on the couch. Mom leans out from under his arm to reach forward and hand me a gift. "This is from Matt."

The wrapped gift is heavy as I take it, but it isn't big. I pull off the paper to reveal...

"Wow." My voice is flat. "Body wash." I hold up the bottle to the camera. "A little self-serving, don't you think, Matt?" Leave it to him to do something like this.

Dad sits up. "Matt wanted me to point out that it's an expensive body wash. It's from a London company." He wads a ball of wrapping paper and tosses it in the general direction of the corner of the room.

I look at the bottle and make a face.

Dad laughs and reaches to the side of the couch. "OK." He tosses me a lighter wrapped present. "Here's Matt's real gift."

It's a soccer jersey. I smile at the camera. "Good one, Matt. And thanks for the jersey, it's great! Merry Christmas!"

Sunday, December 26
Matt

On my Christmas morning, I open presents before watching Jim's Christmas from the day before. Jim got me a Sonic gift card. To share, Mom and Dad got me and Jim a fitness tracker band, which, I admit, is a disappointment, until they reveal their individual gifts for us: new phones.

After all the gifts are opened, and the morning recorded for Jim, Mom turns on the video of Jim's Christmas from the day before. I'm looking forward to seeing him open my gag gift (which hadn't been cheap because I knew Jim would see through the joke otherwise). But watching his straight face, followed by his smile, is worth it.

***

Almost as good as Christmas morning is church later on because I finally do what I told Bradley I would. I talk to the drummer.

Each week at church, in addition to a message from the pastor and worship and prayer, some musicians play on the stage while everyone sings. A drummer, a bass player, someone on keyboards, a couple of acoustic guitar players, a couple of singers. The gospel music they play isn't fast or my favorite type of music, but at least it has a beat.

The drummer in the band is dark-skinned, tall, and thin. Each Sunday, I watch him from my seat in the auditorium, wondering what it would be like to be him. It's not like service is a concert, but he's playing on a stage, under lights, in front of an audience.

Until this Sunday, I've never talked to him. But after church, I find him and introduce myself as Jett. He says his name is Elijah and—best part—if he ever needs a sub he'll come and find me.

I cross my fingers it will be my Sunday and not Jim's.

Mon, Dec 27, 7:46 AM

so I'm looking at our new fitness tracker
and you got a pretty low activity score yesterday
better step it up matt
you know you've got to do your part
to keep this body healthy

Matt—Tue, Dec 28, 8:31 AM

oh shut up

worst present ever

like we need something else to gripe at each other about

at least the new phones were a good gift

Jim—Wed, Dec 29, 8:02 AM

yeah the new phones are great!
also that body wash is actually really good stuff

Matt—Thu, Dec 30, 7:46 AM

you think i'd get you anything less than the best?

i'm totally using it every time I shower tho

chapter
eleven

Tuesday, February 1
Jim

In January we get back from our trip to Virginia to visit Mom's family, and the rest of the month passes quickly, but not without some tension.

Soccer tryouts for my next season fall on one of Matt's Saturdays, which is a bummer because I have to miss them again. And then Matt actually gets asked to sub for the drummer in church, but it's on one of my Sundays, which drives him crazy. He pleads with Mom and Dad to let us switch the days around, but they of course say no. Then he's mad at them for being too strict, I'm mad at Matt for making a big deal out of it when I missed tryouts without begging for an exception, he's mad at me for not backing him up about switching days, and Mom and Dad are frustrated with both of us for complaining. Then amid all that the Burke-Dalton procedure gets brought up again. When Mom and Dad come down hard, it affects Matt so much I don't hear from him for a day.

Despite all that, school and life go on.

Thursday, February 10
Matt

"Mom." I walk into the kitchen and hang up my keys. "I want to get a job."

"What?" Mom is sitting at the table on her laptop. She has a novel open next to her and a photo pulled up of a soup Aunt Theresa made.

"A job. These things teenagers have. They get paid money for working. I'm surprised you haven't heard of them before, Mom."

"Very funny."

I go to the sink and wash my hands with dish soap (because the hand soap Mom keeps by the sink smells like roses).

"How was the gym?" she asks. "Was it yoga today?"

I ignore Mom not-so-tactfully trying to change the subject. "A job, Mom. Most teenagers have them. Can't I get one, too?" I open the fridge. The door is covered in silver magnets and various papers and flyers, one of which flutters to the floor. A business card for a lawn care service. I hang it back up and pull out an apple.

Mom stands up from the table. "I don't know, Matt. I don't know if it's a good idea." She pauses. "No, forget whether it's a good idea or not—I don't know if we'd be able to make it work at all."

I turn around from where I'm getting peanut butter out of the pantry. "Why not?"

"Matt, you're only awake every other day. Most employers aren't OK with their employees skipping every other day of work."

"It'll be a part-time job." The silverware drawer clatters as I bump it closed with my hip.

Mom rubs her eyes. "And not only that—your days change. You'd be a Monday-Wednesday-Friday employee one week and a Tuesday-Thursday-Saturday employee the next."

"So, we'll have to find the right employer." I sit down at the table with the apple, the peanut butter jar, and a knife. I dig the knife in, spread peanut butter on a section of the apple, and take a bite.

Mom sits down at the table again, looking down at her computer, shaking her head. "I don't know. I don't know if we could work it out with you and Jim."

I swallow my bite. "Well, what if Jett gets a job? Jim and I could share it."

"Jett doesn't have a social security card."

I sigh and sit back, then sit up straight again as I think of a different angle. "Well, us getting jobs has to happen someday. Unless you and Dad plan on supporting us the rest of our life?"

Mom sits up straighter, too. "We've got time to work that out. For now, you don't need a job. I don't know if you'd have time for a job."

I lick peanut butter off my fingers. "Can we at least talk about it with Dad?"

Mom looks at me. "And Jim. Even if he's not sharing the job with you, you should talk to him."

"Why? It's not his business what I do on my days."

"Well..." Mom brushes her hand across the white fabric tablecloth that covers our round kitchen table, trying to flatten out wrinkles. "Sometimes it is, like it or not. Also, Jim has good judgment. It's normal to ask close family members opinions on new life choices." Mom gets a sneaky smile on her face. "And Jim is *very* close family."

I snort. Mom doesn't usually joke about our condition. I take another bite of apple.

Sunday, February 13
Jim

Walking out of church that afternoon, Dad starts a conversation. "So, what's the deal with Matt and the job?"

I shrug. "He wants a job. We've been talking about it for the past two days. He thinks we should get one and share it."

"What do you think?" Mom walks next to me across the asphalt parking lot.

I shrug again. "I don't really want to. I feel busy enough." Soccer just started, and my new coach, Coach Turner, is really working us hard.

Mom nods in approval and pulls her sweater tighter around her. It's colder outside than it had been in the building.

"That's what I told Matt this morning." I reach the car and open the door to the back seat.

"You told him no?" Dad opens his door.

"Yeah."

I climb into Dad's car and slide into the leather seat, which is warm from being parked in the sun, despite the cooler weather. "But he says he's still going to get one."

"If we give him permission." Mom and Dad are both in the car now, and they glance at each other. I can tell they both have things they want to say. They aren't going to say them with me there, though.

It doesn't surprise me that Matt wants to get a job, and it's pretty obvious to me why. Coming off the drama in January about switching days and getting told no about the procedure again, he's searching for something he can get excited about. Searching for a way that, even though we have to live the way we do, he can be as normal as possible.

Monday, February 14
Matt

Tonight, I do something Jim and I like to do sometimes: eavesdrop on our parents. In my pajamas I crouch in the dark dining room, after I fake taking our sleep medication so Mom and Dad will think I'm in bed. I listen to them talk in the kitchen after they get back from their Valentine's Day dinner.

"I don't know about this whole job thing, Dave," Mom says.

"We have encouraged them to be as individual as they can," Dad points out over the sound of the sink running.

"I know. But he already has half as much time as everyone else."

I move to my knees, careful not to make any noise on the hardwood floor, and lean against the wall by the doorway.

"Jane, I think Matt needs this." Dad's voice gets quieter, and I have to strain to pick it up. "You know how he's..." He keeps talking, but he's moving across the room, and his voice is too low to make out.

Mom's voice sounds like it's close to the fridge, and I think I hear the freezer door shut. "Maybe you're right."

"I think we just have to set up clear rules." Dad crosses the room again, and I see the strip of light falling from the kitchen momentarily darken with his shadow. He goes on. "It's got to be something Matt can do on his own days, with no temptation to day-swap." Chairs scrape across the floor. Mom and Dad are sitting down at the table. "And it can't take up too much time. It can't disrupt his school, or his music lessons, or his exercise."

"And he has to tell his boss everything about his condition," Mom adds.

A spoon scrapes against a bowl as Dad speaks. "It'll be a tough search."

"Maybe he won't find anything," Mom says (sounding a little too hopeful).

I smile. Boy, am I going to prove her wrong.

jim help! i can't find a job! 😔

it's got to be super flexible with hardly any hours. dad said he'd look into getting me a job at the gym but it would mess up our whole cover story and get complicated. any other ideas?

wait you mean you haven't found something yet? i'm shocked

come on help me brainstorm! everything i can think of requires me to work the same days each week

ok i got it. two words. gig economy like giving rides with uber or picking up groceries or takeout

or i bet you can find stuff online like tutoring or proofreading

uber: too young

groceries and takeout: not that desperate yet

online stuff: NOT sitting at home on my computer would be a plus

but maybe the gig economy idea could work. what about i rent out your room as an airbnb when you're not here?

ha you're hilarious on airbnb you can sell experiences too like those sunset kayak tours downtown something you're an expert in like...

hmm...

dog yoga!

Matt—Tue, Feb 22, 7:32 AM

ok you've ceased to be helpful
forget i asked

Jim—Wed, Feb 23, 7:25 AM

chapter
twelve

On Saturday, I wake up feeling weary. And it isn't because of any workouts Jim has done.

Two weeks and my job search is still coming up empty. I just can't find anything I feel like I can apply to. The condition makes it all so complicated. I find some ways online to make money, like the gig economy stuff that Jim mentioned. But I don't want that. I want a *real* job, with a boss and a paycheck.

Maybe I'm being too picky, because I can't find anything. But the more I think about having a job, the more obsessed I become. I'm convinced there's no way I can ever be happy without a job—it doesn't even have to be minimum wage. But I'm feeling more and more hopeless.

Which is why Jim's first Vimer comes as a happy surprise.

"Hey, Matt!" He's sitting in our truck, which is parked on a street somewhere. "I have a job idea for you! And no, this one isn't sarcastic."

I smile bitterly. I'm watching in the bathroom while I brush my teeth, in a hurry because Mom and Dad declared this a deep-cleaning day, and the sooner we're done, the sooner we're going to my favorite taco truck for lunch.

Jim flips the camera around so it's pointing out the front windshield. "See that?" his voice says off-camera. He zooms in on someone in an orange shirt walking a dog down the street. I don't get what the big deal is.

Jim flips the camera back around. "I saw someone else in the same shirt walking a dog earlier, and I got curious and looked it up. So, here's what it is. There's this company called Pals, right? And it's like Uber for pets." Jim's in a T-shirt sweaty from soccer practice. "They have an app, and people who work for them use it to claim pet jobs people have. From what I can tell, it could be anything—feeding, walking, food delivery, checking in on pets, playing with them."

I stand up straighter. I've been brushing my teeth long enough that the mint toothpaste is way past feeling gritty. I stand with the toothbrush slack in my mouth, too interested to look away.

"So," Jim finishes. "You should look into it! From what I can tell, you set your own hours and work when you can. And you like dogs. Maybe it's just what you're looking for."

I spit out my toothpaste, wipe my mouth on the back of my hand, and send a response right away. "Jim, you're a genius! I love it! I'm going to go look it up right now. Thank you!"

***

Jim's right. It's the perfect gig.

I start reading about the company online. Pals is just like Jim described. They employ people (who they fittingly call Pals) to basically act as pet concierges.

Before I can read about much else, Mom makes me start cleaning. It's not until later, when we're sitting outside the taco truck eating lunch, that I get the chance to check out their site some more.

"What're you reading, Matt?" Dad takes a bite of his fish taco.

"Just this study about dads with low spice tolerance being more likely to sing off-key." Two of Dad's traits that Jim and I mock him most for. "You sure you don't want a bite?" I hold out my jalapeño taco that's too hot for him to handle.

He rolls his eyes. I smile, then go back to my phone. If I bring up Pals to my parents, I'm pretty sure they'll try to talk me out of it or shoot it down. I scroll down my phone and keep reading. According to the Pals website, once you get hired and trained, you get access to their app, where you can claim nearby pet tasks.

Mom says something teasing to Dad (even she can stand spicier Mexican food), and I let them talk and keep reading. Pals employees do a lot of dog walking, but other stuff, too. Their website describes tasks having to do with rabbits, cats, reptiles, even birds. A lot of Pals customers are pet owners who leave town for several days. This seems to be an easy way for them to know their pets are taken care of while they're gone.

When I put up my phone to keep Mom and Dad from asking any more questions, I'm excited. There are lots of neighborhoods in Austin where I know it will work great, especially closer to downtown. As I eat, I picture myself outside in the fresh air, walking dogs all day and getting paid for it. It's perfect.

As soon as we get home, I go through the Pals online application process. It's intense. I have to supply three references and answer questions about me and my qualities and skills. When I get to the section asking about previous animal experience, I'm grateful I can list years of successful dog ownership thanks to Termite. There's even a place I can submit pictures of him. I've also volunteered at the animal shelter where we got Termite several times in the past. Maybe, I tell myself, I have a chance.

Matt—Wed, Mar 2, 7:35 AM

guess what?? I GOT THE JOB! its perfect you're a genius

thanks again for the idea

Jim—Thu, Mar 3, 7:01 AM

cool! im glad you got it

Matt—Fri, Mar 4, 7:17 AM

also I told pals about you (mom made me) and i bet they'd hire you if you want in on the action

or if you ever want to try the job out as me on one of your days you're welcome to

Jim—Sat, Mar 5, 7:31 AM

ha that's nice of you
i'm good for now
but keep me updated on how the pay is...

Sun, Mar 6, 10:11 AM

chapter
thirteen

Friday, March 4
Matt

I do the online training for Pals as soon as I find out I get the job. It isn't too hard. The way the company is structured, I get training in tiers. Being dog-trained is first. I can also get cat-trained, rabbit-trained, rodent-trained, reptile/amphibian-trained, bird-trained, and even bug-trained (that sounds cool and repulsive at the same time).

I start with just dog. The online training material includes some videos and things to read through and doesn't tell me much more than what I already know. (What can I say, I'm a stellar dog owner.)

On Friday, I sign up for an in-person dog training Pals is giving. I'm required to do both the online and in-person training before taking my first assignments, so I'm eager to get it done.

All the people that I meet at the training, my fellow Pals and the trainers, are friendly. I pay attention, am extra nice to all the dogs there, and pass the test at the end. When they present me with my uniform, I'm stoked. I can't wait to get out and start walking some dogs.

Wednesday, March 9
Jim

Matt really likes his new job. He has to go through a lot of training, but I think he likes that. He likes that the job feels official. And I haven't seen anyone prouder to wear an orange T-shirt.

On his first few days, he sends me videos of him walking various dogs. He's always excited, happy. Matt goes downtown to work for Pals a couple times a week, his shifts always arranged to make room for his schoolwork, drum practice, and exercise.

I'm happy for him. One day, I'll follow in his footsteps and get a job. A different job, my own job (if I can find something as perfect as Matt has). One day.

In his videos lately, Matt has been so excited with his new job that I'm surprised to see him with a long face this morning.

"Hey, Jim." His voice is heavy. "I looked at the calendar and realized what's happening in a couple weeks." He looks at the camera. "The Distorted Tides concert."

I make a face as I pull a gray shirt off a hanger in my closet.

"*But...*" Matt holds up a finger. "I have an idea."

I look at the phone suspiciously.

"Hear me out," he says. He's in his bedroom at night. "We both want to go, right? Well, what if we both do? You go to the first part of the concert. Halfway through, come out to the truck in the parking lot and take a short nap. Then I'll get to go in and watch the last part of the concert. When I go to bed that night, I'll set an alarm for the middle of the night so we can switch again, so when our body wakes up in the morning, it'll be me, and I'll have a normal Matt day. Mom and Dad never have to know. And, in return, I'll pay for gas for the truck for the next three months. What do you think? A good idea, right?"

I sigh and let my arm holding the phone drop to my side.

Thursday, March 10
Matt

First thing in the morning, I check Vimer, making sure Mom is nowhere near before finding out what Jim has to say about my concert idea.

Jim sent his message later in the day, in the afternoon, as if he took a while to think about what he was going to say to me. "Hey, Matt." He's sitting downstairs in the basement. "Look, I know you want to go to the concert. And I do feel bad for you. And your idea is smart. But..." Jim rubs his face. "I'm worried we won't be able to pull it off. What if I can't nap in the parking lot? I'll be in the middle of a concert. What if I can't fall asleep?" Jim shrugs. "I just don't think it will work. Sorry, bro."

I drop the phone on the bedspread and lean my head back on the headboard with a sigh.

come on jim please. it'll work
let me have the second half of the concert
mom and dad never have to know

i don't know

please! if i don't go to this concert i'm never
going to recover! i've been obsessed jim. i've
been listening to distorted tides nonstop

i know you've been listening to their music nonstop
you wore headphones to bed last night and I woke up with
sore ears
but still matt
i dont know

you remember they're my favorite band of all
time right? you remember the reason i wanted
to play the drums is their drummer justin right?
remember when you cut our hair and i was super
mad? its because it was almost as long as his

i'm not a normal sixteen year old wanting to go
to a concert, i'm a fellow musician! i play their
music all the time! can you imagine how amazing
it would be for me to see them in real life?

i know i know i know

five months. i'll gas up the truck for five months
or name your price

otherwise i might resort to something desperate like
using my savings to make a secret road trip and you'll
find yourself waking up unexpectedly in a strange hotel
room in some other city on their concert lineup

i just HAVE TO HAVE TO see them jim!

please please please please please
please pretty pretty please!!!

chapter
fourteen

Wednesday, March 16
Matt

I love working for Pals. I like earning money, getting out of the house, and spending time downtown. Add on top of that the fact that I get to meet a bunch of dogs and enjoy time outdoors walking in parks, and it's great. If it weren't for the Distorted Tides concert coming up, life would be perfect.

The concert is this coming weekend. I'm feeling pretty hopeless as Jim stands up to every bribe I offer. Maybe I have to accept the fact that I'm not going to go (or maybe I need to get serious about this secret road trip plan, though I have my doubts about whether I could really pull it off).

On Wednesday, I'm so discouraged I don't check Vimer right away. I don't even get out of Jim's bed. I just lie there, my arm flopped over my face. When I don't come down for breakfast, Mom and Dad come and find me.

"Hi, Matt." Dad knocks on the door. "That's you, right? Not Jim? Don't you want some breakfast?"

I grunt.

"I made a smoothie. I can pour you some before I leave."

I feel the weight of someone sitting on the bed. "Oh, come on, Matt." Mom surprises me with her fed-up tone. "Don't be this dramatic. I know you want to go to the concert. But there will be other concerts. You'll have to—"

I interrupt her by groaning loudly and flopping over on my side, facing the wall. I wonder what kind of look my parents are exchanging above me.

"Bye, bud." Dad tousles my hair. "See you after work."

I grunt again, staring at the grain in the wood on the wall by the bed. An accent wall. So formal-looking and nice and...boring. I prefer my room, with its colorful collage of concert posters. *I* love concerts. I should be the one to go. Not Jim. It's not fair.

Mom and Dad say goodbye to each other in the hall. I stay on the bed. I notice the room smells a little musty because the AC is running for the first time in months.

"OK, Matt." Mom comes back to Jim's room. She pulls me by the shoulders, so I sit up. "You're not six anymore. You don't need to throw a tantrum."

"This is a tantrum?" My voice is flat.

"It's a sixteen-year-old tantrum. And it's time to end it. Now come downstairs and eat breakfast. Then it's gym time."

***

It isn't until the afternoon that I watch Jim's messages from the day before. Leo is over after school, hanging out in my room. I'm sure he's not having the greatest time because I'm moody, and he's trying not to bring up the fact that he can't wait for the concert on Saturday. Leo's a good friend.

I'm sitting on the floor with my back leaning against my bookcase, throwing a big bouncy ball out the door into the hallway, where it bounces against the opposite wall and comes back to me. Over and over and over...

"So..." Leo's scrolling through his phone. "No luck talking to Jim, then?"

I sigh, let the ball roll across the floor, and pick up my phone. "I don't think he's going to change his mind. I didn't even check what he sent me yesterday." I tap his most recent Vimer and watch it play.

"OK, Matt." Jim sounds worn-out. The camera is close to his face. He sighs and hangs his head down, then looks up. "Make it six months' gas, and let's do it. Let's swap halfway through. You can go."

I stare in shock for a second, then jump up and whoop so loud I startle Leo.

"Wait, he's in? He says you're gonna switch?"

"Yes!" I pump one fist in the air. "I'm going to the concert!"

Thursday, March 17
Jim

In his message to me this morning, Matt is as excited as I've ever seen him.

"Jim!" His eyes are big, and he has one hand through his hair. "Jim! Are you serious?!" He laughs. "Yes, six months, you got it! Thank you! Thank you, thank you, thank you! I owe you one big! This is gonna be so great, bruh." Matt turns the camera around to show Leo sitting on Matt's bed. "Leo, isn't Jim the best brother in the world?"

"He's the best," Leo agrees.

It's impossible to watch the message without smiling. Matt did a good job of guilt-tripping me into giving him half the concert—or practically threatening me with his comment about running away to another city to see it. (But no way he'd do that. He'd be in so much trouble. Or...at least I think he wouldn't.) Well, call it a guilt trip or a threat, but at least he's grateful about it.

***

I don't bring up the concert to either of my parents that day, but Dad brings it up after dinner.

"So, the concert's on Saturday, right?" He hands me another plate to wash. I stand at the sink, doing the dishes, feeling the warm water and soap run over my hands.

"Yeah." I'm trying to decide if I should bring up Matt or not. Which would sound more natural? Mom decides for me.

"Matt was pretty pouty yesterday about missing it." She wipes down the counter next to me. "But by the end of the day, he seemed to perk up. I think he's come to terms with you going. You'll have to take lots of videos for him."

"Will do, Mom."

I know the real reason Matt has perked up, of course. But we can't let our parents know. They will *not* be happy if they find out what we're planning to do.

Saturday, March 19
Jim

On Saturday, after my soccer game, I rush home to shower and change. Leo meets me at my house, and we head out.

Forty-five minutes later, we pull into the parking lot of Vargas Hall, a smaller concert venue I've only been to once before. We find a spot that's as far away from the streetlights as possible (so I'll be able to fall asleep easier) and head inside.

The concert is amazing. Leo and I have great spots, right at the front. I've never seen Distorted Tides live before, and being there next to them while they perform the songs that I've listened to and played so many times is awesome.

The time flies by. The opening bands are OK, but when Distorted Tides takes the stage, it's like someone pushes fast-forward.

As they're finishing one of their fastest songs, Leo cheers and pumps a fist in the air while I end the video I've been recording. Bodies nearby bump into me as I try to keep my phone steady enough to check the time.

"I gotta go!" I shout in Leo's ear. "We're halfway through!"

Leo pats me on the back. "Alright, bruh, see you later!"

"Keep taking videos!" I start weaving my way through the crowd as Distorted Tides starts their next song. It's not one of my favorites, which makes me feel better. I can feel the vibration from the bass as I shoulder my way through all the fans and noise.

It isn't long before I make it to the parking lot and the truck. I unlock the door and climb in. Then I leave a Vimer for Matt.

"OK, Matt, here I go! I'm setting an alarm for fifteen minutes. Leo's close, off to the righthand side from the stage. Call him if you can't find him. And enjoy the concert! It ROCKS!"

I grab the pillow I brought, put in my earbuds with white noise, drape my jacket over my face, and lie down on my side.

But it isn't that comfortable. My knees are bent and hang over the edge of the seat. The steering wheel feels like it's in my way. We probably should have borrowed Mom's SUV so I could have more space to sleep, but we couldn't have done that without arousing suspicion.

Still, I try to fall asleep.

I can't stop thinking about the concert. You know when you drive a long time at night, then you close your eyes, and you can still see the highway lines passing? I keep seeing the lights of the concert behind my closed eyes.

I focus on the white noise playing through my earbuds. But, though I try to ignore it, I can still pick up the music from the band inside, especially the bass line.

As I keep lying there, eyes closed, trying to sleep, I can't help wondering how much time has passed. I know I shouldn't, but I shove my jacket off my face and check my phone. Almost ten minutes.

I sigh and lie down again, trying as hard as I can. I have to fall asleep. I *have* to. Matt will hate me forever if I make him miss the concert. But, try as I might, I can't do it. Five minutes later my alarm goes off, and I have to decide how much longer I'm going to spend trying.

Feeling low, I make my way back through the crowd and find Leo.

He turns and sees me.

"Hey! Matt! Took you guys long enough! But dude, this concert rocks!"

I'm tempted to lie, but he's bound to find out eventually.

"It's me, Leo! Jim!" I feel like mumbling instead of shouting, but I have to for Leo to hear me. "I couldn't fall asleep, even though I tried as hard as I could."

Leo's eyebrows shoot up, then he looks at me with a smile that, even by the flashing stage lights in the darkened room, I can tell is disheartened. "Guess I know what I'm going to be doing tomorrow."

"What?"

"Cheering Matt up."

Sunday, March 20
Matt

When I wake up, I'm dejected immediately. I'm in Jim's bedroom. I'm dressed in our pajamas. A quick look at Jim's phone confirms it—it's Sunday. The concert was last night. I missed it.

"Dang it!" I slam my head back into the pillow. I can't believe Jim did that! Did he do it on purpose? Was he enjoying the concert so much he couldn't leave?

I cover my face with my hand and resist saying a swear word. When I walk to the door, I see a handwritten note from Jim taped next to the doorknob.

I tried I swear

I rip the note off, wad it up, and throw it in the trash. As I move, I swear I detect a sweat-and-smoke-machine concert smell coming from my body. This makes me even madder.

In my room, I pick up my phone and slam myself on my bed on my stomach. I skip to Jim's most recent Vimer message, where he's in his bedroom, sitting on his bed in our pajamas.

"Hey, Matt..." His voice is downcast. "Listen, I'm sorry. I swear I tried to fall asleep. I did. But it was really hard. I never should have agreed to swap with you. But I did take a ton of videos, and when I couldn't fall asleep, I went back in and—"

I close the app and throw the phone onto the carpet. Liar. I roll over onto my back, seething. Of course he's going to say he tried to fall asleep. How much time did he spend trying? Five minutes? Suddenly I can't stay silent. I fall onto the floor, retrieve my phone, and send Jim a Vimer. I'm angry, and it shows.

"Well, hope you enjoyed the concert, jerk. It's bad enough that you stayed the whole time. But now you've got to lie about it on top of that? Drop the act, Jim. I know you stayed on purpose. Thanks for nothing."

There's a knock on my door. Mom opens it.

"Matt, honey?" If she finds it odd that I'm sitting on the floor, she doesn't mention it. "Jim said he took a lot of videos at the concert last night." Cautious pause. "He said it was a good one." Her voice is gentle. She knows I'm in a bad mood, but she doesn't know the half of it.

I grunt.

"Well, why don't you come down for breakfast? We've got church in a few hours."

It takes a few minutes, but I drag myself up and walk downstairs to the kitchen, still in our pajamas. Mom's there alone. I sit at the table, my eyebrows lowered, staring into space. I'm determined to be mad at Jim all day.

"It's spring break this week." Mom starts setting the table. Her voice is still cautious. "For Leo and for you. That'll be fun, right?"

I don't say anything.

"Did you watch any of the videos from last night?" Mom finishes setting the table with a pitcher of orange juice and a plate of waffles. Dad made a hot breakfast like he usually does on Sunday mornings.

Mom sees my face, and her voice becomes sympathetic. "I'm sorry you didn't get to go, sweetie. I know you really wanted to."

I know I shouldn't admit to Mom what Jim and I were planning to do. It's something we'd get in trouble for, something our parents were never meant to know about. But I can't help it. I have to expose his treachery to someone.

"Jim was supposed to give me a turn," I mumble angrily.

"What?"

"Jim told me he'd go to sleep at the concert last night, halfway through, so I could see the second half of it." I scowl at the tile. "But he didn't. He stayed the whole time."

Mom is silent, so I look up to see her face. She's frowning. "Well, I can imagine it would be difficult to fall asleep at a concert—"

"Mom!" I gape. "You're taking his side?"

"I'm not taking anyone's side, Matt! And you know that day-switching with naps like that is against the rules."

I look away, staring down at the table, eyebrows lowered. Then I sigh and put my head down on the tablecloth. "It's not fair." My voice is muffled from between my folded arms.

"What's not fair?" Dad walks into the room.

I stay silent, but Mom explains in a low voice. "Matt wanted to go to the concert last night. He and Jim had agreed to switch partway, but it didn't work."

"That makes it sound like it wasn't his fault," I say through gritted teeth.

"You're not supposed to day-swap like that anyway." Dad ignores my comment.

"I know," I mumble, head still down.

"We have that rule in place for a reason." Dad's voice comes nearer as he sits at the table with me. "If we let you boys start to get casual with the schedule, it's a slippery slope into—"

I sit up. "I get it, Dad!"

Mom and Dad are silenced. They exchange a look. I sigh and go on without shouting.

"It's just not fair." I know I'm being whiny, but I don't care. "That concert was a once-in-a-lifetime thing. And Jim got lucky that he was the one who got to go. If it were one time, OK, maybe it wouldn't be such a big deal. But this is going to be my whole life. Missing out on half of it."

"It wasn't a once-in-a-lifetime thing." Dad's voice is gentle now. "There will be plenty of other concerts and other opportunities to see Distorted Tides. I mean, they call Austin the live music capital of—"

"That's not the point!" I exhale sharply. Then I lower my voice. "Maybe...it would be different if I knew this *wasn't* going to be forever, if I knew that things were going to change one day, that me and Jim might get the procedure, that—"

"*No.*" Mom doesn't have to say anything else. It's clear I'm not to bring that up again.

So, I sigh and look down. "It's just not fair."

Mom and Dad are quiet. In the silence, I can hear the dryer running in the laundry room nearby.

"I'm sorry, honey." Mom rubs my back. "I know it's not."

I stand up from the table and start walking upstairs.

"Matt? Don't you want breakfast?"

Dad speaks. "I made waffles. Your favorite."

"I'll eat later." I don't turn around.

"They'll be cold."

"Who cares?" I mutter. I feel guilty again. But I keep walking.

***

Church is strained. I don't say much to Mom and Dad, and they let me be. Watching Elijah play the drums is painful. I don't sing along to any of the songs.

When we get home, I go straight up to my room and shut the door. There's a whine and a scratch outside, and I open the door to let Termite in. I sit on the floor and play a halfhearted game of tug-o-war with him.

After a while, there's a knock at the bedroom door, and Leo opens it and walks inside. "Hey, bruh."

I scowl up at him from the floor.

"Look, I had nothing to do with it." Leo puts up his hands.

Termite lets go of the rope I'm holding and walks over to sniff Leo, who ignores him and keeps talking to me.

"I know you're bummed and everything. But..." Leo looks like he doesn't know what to say.

I look up at Leo silently, then hold out a hand. Termite comes back to me, letting me scratch behind his ears, but then he turns and leaves the room. I stare at the carpet.

Leo sits down on the floor in front of me.

"Well...Jim wanted me to show you something."

I look up to see Leo holding out his phone. I grunt and turn away.

"Matt, come on." Leo shoves the phone at me. "Just watch it."

I take the phone but don't tap play. "I thought you stay out of these."

"Out of what?"

"Arguments." My eyebrows are low, and my voice is lower. "Between me and Jim. I thought you didn't pick sides."

"I'm not picking a side. I..."

I continue to glare, and Leo grunts and takes his phone back. "Fine. Forget it."

"Fine."

It's silent for several moments.

"You know," Leo says like he can't keep it in. "He really didn't mean it. He felt really bad when—"

"Leo!"

"Argh." He stands up. "Man, you guys are hard sometimes."

I grunt.

Leo heads out of the room but comes back in a second. "And here." He throws something at my chest. A blue Distorted Tides shirt falls into my lap. "That's for you."

I pick up the shirt and look at it. It's a nice shirt that I'd be excited to own if I weren't so mad.

"Is this from you?"

"Nope. Someone else." Leo stands in the doorway looking at me pointedly.

"Big deal," I mutter. "He's just going to wear it, too."

"Well, you're welcome anyway." Leo turns to go. "Let me know when you like Jim again!" he calls on his way down the stairs.

I throw the shirt onto the floor of my closet.

★★★

Later that day, I watch the footage of the concert. I'm still mad at Jim. Part of me doesn't want to watch it. But part of me does.

There's a knock at my door, and I look up to see both my parents in the doorway. I take off my headphones.

"Hi, Matt." Mom walks into the room with Dad. "So, your dad and I were thinking...maybe we can take a trip."

I'm surprised. "A trip?"

"Yeah." Dad's hands are in the pockets of his athletic pants. "To Houston."

I raise an eyebrow. "To see Dr. Anand?"

"No..." Dad leans against the doorframe. "See, Distorted Tides isn't playing there...but Chaos of Quincy is." He smiles.

"What?" I sit up straight, pushing my laptop aside. "Seriously?"

Mom smiles too. "We thought you could use something fun and special."

I'm tempted to bounce up and down on my bed. "When are we going?"

Dad gives me a funny smile and steps out into the hall. When he comes back, he's holding a suitcase. "As soon as you fill this."

I whoop, jump up from the bed, and hug Mom and Dad. Mom laughs.

"It's not a normal concert," Dad warns. "The big Houston rodeo is going on, and there's a performer each night after the show. Also, we've got the worst seats in the entire stadium."

"That's fine. I don't care." I grab the suitcase, toss it open on my bed, and pull open the top drawer of my dresser. "When are they playing?"

"Tuesday night." Dad picks up the laptop on my bed. "We'll drive down now, get a hotel and a late dinner, and see some sights with Jim tomorrow.

Then I'll go with you to the rodeo and concert on Tuesday night. We'll drive
back with Jim on Wednesday."

I break into a smile again. "Sounds awesome." I'm so excited, I don't
even mind packing for the brother I'm still mad at when Mom asks me to
(though picturing him freaking out when he wakes up tomorrow in the hotel
gives me a spiteful sense of satisfaction).

Monday, March 21
Jim

As soon as I'm the slightest bit awake, I jerk up. I'm not in Matt's bed, or
mine.

I look around. I'm in a hotel room, in a hotel bed. The curtains are
drawn, but sunlight shows around the edges. I turn my head from side to
side, confused, shocked, and—though I don't like to admit it to myself—
scared.

Dad walks into the room from the bathroom. At the sight of him, the
pressure in my chest immediately releases, and I breathe a sigh of relief as
the fear, at least, leaves me.

"Morning, Jim." Dad's buttoning up a non-work shirt as if nothing were
out of the ordinary.

"Where are we?" I run a hand through my hair.

"Houston. We took a spur-of-the-moment trip." Dad hands me a paper
restaurant menu. "We went here for dinner with Matt last night. Want to try
it for lunch? We thought you'd like their fajitas."

I look at the menu without taking any of it in, then around the hotel
room. Mom walks in from the bathroom.

I look back at the glossy paper menu, wondering what happened
yesterday. I wish I could ignore Mom and Dad and pull out my phone to
watch whatever Vimer Matt left me. But Mom and Dad are both watching
me.

I look up. "Did...Matt tell you about the concert?" I watch Mom and
Dad's faces and wince. "Was he mad?"

"He told us." Mom sits down on the bed. "And yes, he took it a little hard."

Dad speaks up in a stern voice. "I hope you learned your lesson about
switching days."

I look down at the bedspread. "Yeah." I run my hand over the maroon-and-green diamond pattern. "I know. I know I shouldn't have told Matt I'd swap, but he was so bummed about not getting to go."

"Well…" Dad stands in front of me. "I hope this doesn't bum *you* out too much, but I am taking Matt to see Chaos of Quincy tomorrow night."

I look up. I admit I'm tempted to get jealous. But then I think of Matt and how he must have been feeling for weeks now. I smile bitterly. "So basically, Matt did such a good job of throwing himself a pity party yesterday that you guys brought him down to Houston for a concert, and I happen to get to tag along, too?"

Dad sits down on the bed next to Mom. "Hey, you guys are a two-for-one."

"This trip is for *both* of you," Mom insists. "For all of us." She watches my face and speaks more gently. "I know you hate unexpected trips. I'm sorry. We made an exception."

She doesn't have to add why they made the exception—because I'm partly to blame.

"So," Dad stands up, "what do you want to do today, Jim?"

I really am tempted to get jealous of, or mad at, Matt. First, I really do hate waking up somewhere unexpected like this, especially somewhere so crazy as a hotel room. And seriously? He weaseled a whole trip out of my parents?

But at the same time, I know how hurt he is about the concert. And I can put myself in his shoes (ha). His favorite band of all time, the drummer he looks up to most, performing in our own city, yet he didn't get to go. He had been torn up about it for weeks. And then to be looking forward to it, thinking he'd be able to go, and to wake up at home in bed instead of in the concert parking lot—yeah, that had to have sucked. So, in the end, I'm not mad at Matt.

He's mad at me, though. His one Vimer from yesterday makes that clear. He calls me a jerk. And he doesn't say anything about the shirt or the concert he gets to go to.

Tuesday, March 22
Matt

　　The day of the Chaos of Quincy concert in Houston, I watch Jim's videos in the morning. He has a few of him and Mom and Dad around town, like one from a nature center. They went to the rodeo, too, but Jim didn't take any videos there because, "No spoilers," he says.

In the videos, Mom, Dad, and Jim are all happy, carefree, like nothing bad happened. But then there's one Vimer from Jim at the end of the day. It looks like he's standing in the hallway of the hotel.

"What the heck, Matt?" Jim's tone is mad, but his face is amused. "How on earth did you weasel a trip *and* a concert out of Mom and Dad? After you admitted to them that we were trying to break the rules? Must have been some pity party." His face grows more serious. "And look, I swear, I did try to fall asleep. And I bought you a shirt. That counts for something, right?"

I grunt.

Mom's standing nearby and hears the message. She walks over and sits on the bed. "He showed us a picture of the shirt he got you. That was nice of him."

I look up, annoyed. "Mom." I prefer to watch my videos from Jim each morning alone, as does he. Here in a hotel room with our parents, it's harder for us to have private conversations.

Mom starts to put on a pair of earrings. "You're going to send him something, right?"

"Sure." I lift my phone in front of my face. "Hey, jerk. I still think you're a liar."

Mom looks at me sternly.

I sigh. "That wasn't real, Mom, alright?" I show her the phone to prove I haven't sent a video. Mom nods and continues to watch me.

"Can I talk to Jim alone?"

"OK." She stands. "I'll go find Dad, and we'll head down to breakfast. Come when you're ready."

Dad already walked out to take a work call, and Mom heads out after him, shutting the hotel room door with a quiet click.

After she leaves, I send Jim a real message.

"OK, first of all, I didn't ask for this trip. Mom and Dad offered. I didn't manipulate anything. Guess I must be their favorite." I almost end it, then reluctantly add one more thing. "And...fine, thanks for the shirt."

Jim—Wed, Mar 23, 5:32 PM

thanks for the chaos of quincy shirt
and i'm glad you had fun at the concert

Matt—Thu, Mar 24, 7:29 AM

thanks
it almost made up for the fact that i
didn't get to see distorted tides

Jim—Fri, Mar 25, 7:45 AM

only almost huh?

9:39 PM

i overheard mom and dad talking about us tonight
they're wondering if they're spoiling us
you in particular
really what they did for us/you in going to
houston and the rodeo, that was a big deal

Matt—Sat, Mar 26, 7:23 AM

yeah i know
what did they say?

Jim—Sun, Mar 27, 10:08 AM

mom's worried they're spoiling us the way only children
get spoiled. she says it's like they're raising two only
children, which i can see. dad said living with our condition
is so rough he doesn't think a little spoiling will hurt us

Matt—Mon, Mar 28, 7:03 AM

what do you think?

Jim—Tue, Mar 29, 7:20 AM

i think you were pretty lucky to get to see chaos of quincy

Matt—Wed, Mar 30, 7:10 AM

well you were pretty lucky to get to see distorted tides

Jim—Thu, Mar 31, 7:02 AM

yeah well we can't have everything

Matt—Fri, Apr 1, 1:12 PM

no

we can't

chapter
fifteen

Friday, April 1
Matt

Friday morning when I go into my room to check my phone, I hold it up to my face, but nothing happens. The face ID feature isn't working. I enter my password. That doesn't work, either. After my third try, I look at my nightstand where my phone charges and notice a note. It's from Jim and it has a ridiculously long math equation on it. Except, instead of numbers, the equation has things like "date of Termite's last checkup," "number of unique words in my favorite Distorted Tides song," "circumference in centimeters of the kitchen table," and "number of pennies hidden throughout the basement."

I moan. How could I forget it was April Fool's?

Downstairs, Mom walks in on me measuring the kitchen table. I took the tablecloth off to make it easier.

"Matt? What are you doing?" She sees me marking the edge of the table in pencil. "Don't write on the table!"

"Then do you have a longer measuring tape?" I hold up the bendy twelve-inch ruler I've been using. "I need to know the circumference of the kitchen table." I look down at the ruler. "In centimeters."

Mom's confused. "Why?"

I hold up the equation. "Jim locked my phone."

Mom comes over and takes the paper. Then she smiles. "Happy April."

"Yeah, yeah, happy April." I take the paper back. "Except this is going to take forever. Any idea how many pennies Jim hid in the basement?"

Mom laughs and shakes her head. "No. But you're going to be late for the gym if you don't leave soon. This might have to wait until later."

I look at her, unamused. "Do you really think I can survive for that long without my phone?"

She redoes her ponytail and smiles. "You'll have to figure out a way."

"Well, I've got all day to figure out how to get him back." I go back to painstakingly measuring the table.

"Matt." She waits until I look up at her. She has a stern face. "Nothing mean."

I act offended. "What? A mean prank? Me? Come on, Mom."

***

I have to work on unlocking my phone in between schoolwork and the gym, and I barely get it unlocked in time to go to work. (If I hadn't, the prank would have gotten a whole lot less funny.)

Working for Pals is still great. I open the app before I leave the house, look for a good task to claim, and drive to the right neighborhood to complete it. It's usually walking a dog, either for half an hour or a whole hour. After my first task, I check the app and find another close by and keep going for about four hours until I go home.

Mostly, my tasks are walking dogs, sometimes just feeding them or checking in on them. I haven't done training for any other animals yet, but I want to soon. It'll broaden my options for tasks. There are a lot that I'm not eligible for, either for lack of training or because I'm what they call a solo Pal. Some tasks (like houses with two or more dogs) request a two-Pal team.

***

On Friday, I'm on a walk in Zilker Park with a brown poodle mix named Roger. Someone turns onto the path in front of me—someone in an orange shirt with the Pals logo on it, leading a chocolate Lab with a leash.

"Nice shirt!" I call out.

The other Pal stops and turns around. It's a girl with dark wavy hair pulled back in a ponytail. That's when I realize I recognize her.

"Zoe?"

"Oh! Jett!" She's easy to recognize from Camp Waller. She looks at me wearing my orange Pals shirt and smiles. "You work for Pals, too?"

Zoe has stopped walking, so Roger and I catch up with her.

"Yep." I pull up on Roger's leash and pat the dog's fuzzy head to keep him close to me. "It's pretty great, huh?"

"How long ago did you start?"

Before I can answer, I have to tug Roger away from Zoe's Lab. As Pals, we aren't supposed to let our dogs interact with other dogs on our walks. Zoe must realize the same thing because she tugs her dog's leash, too, and we back away from each other, realizing awkwardly that now isn't a good time to talk.

"Well, have a good walk," I say, leading Roger back the way we had come.

"You too, Jett!" And that's it.

Saturday, April 2
Jim

Saturday morning, I wake up apprehensively. I don't forget what day it is. But everything seems normal. I'm not wearing an old Halloween costume or tennis shoes that have been tied together. There isn't anything in Matt's bed that doesn't belong there. Nothing's written on my skin. I don't feel sick.

Still cautious, I go to my room, where I notice right away that my phone is gone. In its place is a note—a note that turns out to be the first clue in an hour-long scavenger hunt that goes all over the house, over to Leo's, to the truck, and finally back to my closet, where the phone is hidden (of course). Even without going to the gym, I'm late starting history.

"Congratulations," Matt says in his Vimer when I'm finally able to sit at my desk and watch it. "You found it. I think that took me even longer to set up than your stupid equation did. Thanks a lot, by the way." He acts annoyed but I can tell he thinks it was fun. Then he tells me some funny stories about trying to solve my math equation and setting up his scavenger hunt. I smile. Sometimes our pranks are mean. But sometimes they're not.

Matt stretches out on his bed as his update goes on. "Oh, guess who I ran into at work today. Remember Zoe from Camp Waller? Yeah, she lives on the other side of Austin, and she works for Pals, too." From the way Matt's moving, I can tell he's kicking off his shoes. "We couldn't really talk because we were walking dogs, but we said hi to each other."

I send a message back.

"That's cool, Matt—*as long as* she doesn't get us back in touch with Andie. If she does, I'm telling Andie the truth about our condition. And I'll give her your number and tell her you were madly in love with her the whole time. And then you'll be on your own."

Tuesday, April 5
Matt

After seeing Zoe on Friday, I'm not really expecting to see her again. But on Tuesday, I'm walking out of an apartment building empty-handed, after taking a dog back to its home, and guess who's about to head into it.

"Zoe?"

"Jett!"

I think we surprise each other. She has a big black dog on a leash. I smile as I pat it on the head. "This is Zorro, right? I was going to walk him, but the task got claimed. I just got back from walking a terrier instead."

Zoe smiles as she pats Zorro's side. "Guess you were too slow, Jett." It's sunny out, and she squints up at me. "How have you been since Camp Waller?"

"Oh, fine." I have my phone open, ready to find a new task to accomplish. "How long have you been working for Pals?"

"This is my second week. How about you?"

"I started a few weeks ago." I look up from my phone. "I needed a job with flexible hours, and this fit the bill."

"How's it going so far?" Zoe's starting to get dragged away by Zorro, whose tongue is hanging out of his mouth as he pants noisily.

"Good." I watch her, amused, as Zorro pulls her into the building.

"Talk to you later, then!" she calls breathlessly.

I smile and turn back to my phone. Time to find another task. I'm standing in a courtyard outside the apartment building. It's covered on one side but open to the sky above me. Nearby there's a park bench made of thick metal slats. I take a seat and browse Pals' map and listings.

"Looking for your next task?"

I look up to see Zoe walking toward me. Her own phone is in her hands.

"Yeah." I smile. "And I'm not going to let you steal it this time."

"Oh, really?" Zoe sits next to me. "We'll see about that."

For a few seconds, we look at our phones silently. I'm more serious now that it's turned into a competition. As we browse, I can hear the footsteps of people walking across the gray slab tiles of the courtyard.

"There's a beagle three blocks away..." Zoe mutters.

Then we both see it at the same time. A task pops up for a dog named Snowball in the apartment building we're sitting right next to.

"Got it!" Zoe calls.

"No way." I tap the task to claim it. But Zoe and I are both disappointed. In a few seconds the task comes up as claimed by another Pal.

"Bummer." I tap back to the map screen.

"Does that happen often?" Zoe frowns at her phone. It has a sleek case, a blue one with geometric designs trimmed in silver.

"Not very," I say. "I think it's because we're newer Pals, without as many reviews. Snowball's owner must have chosen a more experienced one."

That leads to me and Zoe comparing our Pals profiles. I have more reviews, but we're both rated five stars. I notice her full name is Zoe Estrada, and a second too late, remember that she doesn't know me by my real name.

"Matt Mickelsen?" Zoe reads off my phone. Her eyebrows crinkle. "I thought your name was Jett."

Oops. "Actually, Matt is my real name. At Camp Waller, I decided to try out a new nickname..." I'm thinking fast. "Like, do you ever feel like, with a fresh batch of people you don't know, you can sort of...reinvent yourself? Start over? Be someone new?"

"Um...maybe?" Zoe tilts her head.

"Well, at Camp Waller...I thought I'd be Jett. Someone new. Someone a little fake. Because we—I—didn't know anybody and thought, why not?" It's hard not to slip into first person plural as I speak. I glance at Zoe. Is any of this making sense?

"OK..." The way she's studying me is making me nervous, so I try to change the subject.

"Who's that?" I point to Zoe's phone, at her profile picture that shows her holding a small ball of white fur.

She smiles. "My dog. Mariposa." I don't know what the name means, but I can tell it's Spanish, and Zoe's pronunciation makes it sound like she's fluent. Also, luckily the subject change works because she nods to my profile picture. "Who's that?"

"Termite." I smile. "He's my dog."

"Your dog is named after a bug?" Zoe says with a flat voice.

"So?" I challenge. "What's yours named after?"

"A butterfly," she says coolly. I watch her expectantly until she opens her eyes wide in realization. "Which is still a bug! But a much cuter one."

I lean back. "Hey, I'd like to challenge that Termite has a lot more in common with actual termites than your dog does with actual butterflies."

She laughs and I smile.

"Well..." Zoe stands up and slips her phone into a cargo pocket on the black joggers she's wearing. "Maybe if I can't find anything, I'll head back to my car and see if there's anything closer to home..."

"Hang on," I say. "There *is* one task in this building. But it's..." I pause and Zoe watches me. "It's a team task," I explain. "Not a solo job."

For a second I sit, and she stands quietly. I think we're both thinking it, but we're both hesitant to say something.

For my part, I don't know Zoe that well. The main things I remember about her from Camp Waller are that she wasn't afraid to rappel, and she almost figured out my and Jim's secret. Not a lot to go on.

But this team Pals task is right here...

"We could team up," I finally suggest. "Just for this one walk."

Zoe seems hesitant, but we end up going for it. We figure out how to accept each other in our profiles as a "Pals partner" so we can accept team tasks. Then we volunteer for the task (walking two German shepherds) and get accepted.

Somewhat awkwardly, with neither of us saying much, we head into the building and take the stairs to get to the right apartment. Zoe follows the app instructions to enter the door code, and we let ourselves in.

Any awkward silences end there. The two German shepherds are animated and excited to see us, and for the next hour, Zoe and I are kept busy, walking and trying to control the huge dogs. We laugh a lot.

At the end, walking out of the building and catching our breath, still laughing, brushing dog fur off our clothes, Zoe speaks.

"That was a good idea, Jett."

"You can call me Matt." That comes out of nowhere. I hadn't really planned on saying it.

"Oh, right, sorry." She smiles. "I forgot." Zoe pauses to think. "You really went by a whole new made-up name at camp? Just because?"

I laugh. "Yeah, I know it's pretty crazy." Ha. She doesn't know the half of it.

"So..." Zoe still looks thoughtful. We're standing in the shade of the building, where the spring weather is just chilly enough for Zoe to wrap her hands around her arms. "This maybe explains why you were kind of weird at Camp Waller?"

"Right." And, not wanting to touch on her comment about Jett seeming like two people, I add, "...And it explains Andie, too."

"Aah." Zoe nods. I think I might blush. "So you weren't that into her?"

"Well, she was into me." I shove my hands into my jean pockets. "I thought, in the spirit of being Jett, I'd just let it happen."

Zoe shakes her head at me. "Heartbreaker."

I wince. "You and Andie are friends, right? Have you talked to her since camp? Are you going to tell her you've been hanging out with Jett?"

"I don't know," she challenges. "Have I? Or is this Matt now?"

I feel like grinning more broadly than I have all day. "This is Matt now."

Saturday, April 9
Matt

I walk along the path of Zilker Park until I see the orange shirt and dark wavy ponytail.

"Hey, Zoe."

She's sitting on a park bench looking at her phone, and she lifts her head. "Hey, Jett—oh, sorry. Matt." She smiles apologetically.

I smile back. "You're OK teaming up again?"

She stands. "It went well last time, right?"

"I thought so."

"Cool. Me, too."

So, for my shift that day, Zoe and I work together. We claim the team tasks, which usually involve two or more dogs to walk, often big ones. They keep us busy and laughing. Zoe likes dogs, too, and we have fun talking to them and giving them attention.

After our second dog walk, and on our way to the third, after Zoe says again that teaming up was a good idea, I speak. The task is far enough away that we drive there, so I'm taking us in my truck.

"So..." I tap my hands on the steering wheel. There's something I need to establish. "I should let you know I've got a funny schedule...this week I could work with you Tuesday and Thursday and Saturday, but next week I'll have to do Monday, Wednesday, or Friday. The week after that, Tuesday, Thursday, Saturday again." I glance at her. "Is that OK? Could you make that work?"

She looks at me curiously. "I guess so."

"We'll text each other to coordinate shifts? Other than the specific days, I'm flexible on time." I know Zoe is flexible, too. She's homeschooled like me.

"OK." Zoe sounds unsure as she faces forward and looks out the window. The trees we're driving by cast shadows on her face.

"And if you ever have to work without me, of course feel free," I say quickly. "Who knows, going back to walking one dog at a time might be a nice break."

"But it'll be less fun."

For some reason that comment makes me feel really happy inside.

We make easy conversation as we drive. The AC has kicked in just enough to feel refreshing, but we're on smaller streets driving slow enough that I open the windows a crack and let in the fresh air from outside. My music is playing (it's always playing when I drive), but I keep it quiet enough we can talk.

Zoe notices the music and me tapping along to it. "So have you been playing the guitar and drums a lot since Camp Waller?"

"Drums yes, guitar not so much," I say, feeling a little guilty. I'm ruining Jim's chance to be Jett around Zoe again (which I guess I've already done by telling Zoe to call me Matt). Hopefully, Jim will never get the chance, and it won't be an issue. "Do you play anything?"

"No." Zoe sticks her fingers out the crack in the window, feeling the breeze. "I do like to sing, though."

"What types of music do you listen to?"

"Um, let's see..." Zoe looks out the window. "Really, almost anything. I like musicals, stuff like Chaos of Quincy—"

"No way!" I interrupt. "I got to see them a couple weeks ago!"

Zoe's jaw drops, and she turns in her seat. "Are you serious?"

"Yeah! They were playing at the Houston rodeo—"

"No way!" Zoe says this time. "I went to the rodeo, too! I was so bummed we didn't get to go the night Chaos of Quincy played. What did you think of the actual rodeo?"

I stop at a red light. "I admit I would have liked it better if I wasn't waiting for it to end so I could see the concert. But my brother said—" Crap. I've gotten so comfortable talking, that slips out. "...He..." I try to recover. "He liked it more than me."

"I didn't know you had a brother." Zoe pulls up one knee against her chest. "He wasn't at Camp Waller, right?"

"No, he's younger than me," I lie.

Jim doesn't come up again until we're on our next dog walk (three full-size schnauzers) and talking about sports. Zoe is telling me about her favorite places to rock climb nearby. Then she asks me how soccer is going.

"Well, Jim's the one who—" I pause. Dang! I've done it again.

"Jim?"

"Yeah. Jim." I look down and watch Zoe's footsteps on the pavement. Her tennis shoes are gray with bright blue, hot pink, and bright green accents. "My younger brother. He's the one who's into soccer. I play along sometimes, but he plays in a league."

Then I try to change the subject.

Zoe and I talk easily our whole shift. And walk dogs, petting them and talking to them and laughing. We watch our five-star Pals profile ratings come in and high-five each other after.

Wednesday, April 13
Matt

I'm doing the dishes so I can have them done before Bradley comes over. I'm excited to tell him that I talked to the drummer again at church on Sunday. Elijah said there's a chance he'll need a sub later this summer.

Mom walks into the kitchen.

"So, Matt." She opens a drawer to put away clean dish towels. "Jim mentioned you started working with a girl."

"Yeah." I rinse off a plate and put it in the dishwasher. "Her name's Zoe. She works for Pals, too, and we saw each other and recognized each other from Camp Waller, and we realized we can do more tasks if we team up."

"Does she still think you're Jett?" Mom closes the drawer with a soft thud. "Plain, normal, boring Jett?"

I grab a pan and run the dish brush over it. "OK, first of all, Jett is *not* plain or boring. Normal, yes, but also awesome and—"

"Matt." She leans against the counter next to me and folds her arms.

"OK." I sigh and flip the pan over. The soap suds slide off under the running water. "Yeah, she thinks I'm Jett. Except I told her she could call me Matt."

"Matt!" Mom is surprised and angry.

"What?!"

"That's not fair of you."

"Why not?"

"You're hijacking Jett! He's supposed to belong to you *and* Jim."

I sigh. Why does this all have to be so complicated?

"Well, Jim and I talked." Mom starts helping me load the dishwasher. "And, like any friend you or Jim spend a good deal of time around, we think she should know the truth about you."

I shut off the water and my shoulders droop. "Do I have to?" My voice comes out more whiny than I plan.

"Yes. You do."

Monday, April 25
Matt

Both Mom and Jim ask me more than once if I've told Zoe about our condition. I'm loving being a normal teenager around her, but inside I know they're right. I have to tell her sometime.

During our next shift together, after we walk dogs for about three hours, I ask her if she wants to go to the park to sit for a bit. She agrees. When we get there, I lead the way to a stone wall overlooking the creek. We sit, our feet dangling over the edge, watching the reflection of the trees above us in the water below us.

I like that moment. I like being there with her. I hate to ruin it, but I have to.

"Hey, um, Zoe? I have to tell you something."

Zoe turns to me. "You have a girlfriend, don't you?"

"No!" I'm shocked. "No, not at all!"

My reaction is genuine enough for her to relax. She crosses her feet at the ankle and swings her legs. "OK." She smiles shyly. "Sorry."

"No..." The stone wall is gritty under my fingers. "No, that's not it. It's worse than that."

"Oh my gosh," she whispers. "Matt...do you have cancer?"

"Zoe!"

"OK, OK, sorry, I'll stop guessing!"

I shake my head. Time to get on with it—she'll never guess this secret in a thousand years. "OK...so...here it is. Remember my brother I told you about? Jim?"

"Yeah."

"Well, he's not my younger brother. He's more like...my twin brother. In a way."

This catches her interest. "In a way?"

"Well, yeah..." This seems worse than any explanation of our condition I've had to give before. I take a deep breath and forge ahead. "We have this condition... It's called *duocordis unuscorporosis*. It means...well, we share a body. One body we take turns in. Every other day." I look up. Zoe is staring at me. I can't read her expression.

"So..." I pause at the sound of a jogger's footsteps on the path and wait until he passes. "I...well, it explains some things. Like how I'm not available on certain days. Those are Jim's days. When it's his turn, I'm dormant. I don't see, or hear, or know what Jim does. Then when our body goes to sleep, we switch places and it's my turn for a day."

Zoe looks down at the creek below. Her feet have stopped swinging. She's quiet for several seconds, and I'm afraid to say anything. I let her think.

"This explains Jett, doesn't it?" she finally says. "At Camp Waller...that was both of you, wasn't it?"

I'm relieved that she's catching on. "Right. It was my idea, but we wanted to go to Camp Waller, and we get sick of explaining our condition to people. We wanted to try to be normal for once. So we pretended to be Jett all week."

She nods slowly, looking down and talking almost to herself. "That's why I said it seemed like you were two people. Because you were." She looks up and speaks louder. "Who did I say that to? You or Jim?"

"That was me. At the dance." I try to read her expression but feel like I fail. Her dark eyes stare past me into the park.

"So..." Zoe looks at her hands, which she folds in her lap. "Since Pals, since you've told me to call you Matt...that's been you the whole time?"

"Yeah." I nod. "Aside from Camp Waller, you've never met Jim."

"OK."

For a few minutes, Zoe and I avoid each other's eyes. I watch a little bird peck at the ground nearby.

"You believe me?" I ask after a silence.

"Yeah..." But she sounds unsure.

"I know it sounds crazy. But it's true."

Zoe sits still, looking down into the creek again.

I lean forward so I can look into her face. "Does this mean I'm a freak and you never want to hang out with me again?" I'm relieved to see her smile as she turns my way.

"Don't be silly, Matt."

And, despite the conversation, that last comment leaves me feeling happy enough as we get up and walk back to our cars.

Thursday, April 28
Jim

"So, hey, I was wondering if you could do something for me." That's how Matt's message to me this morning starts. I look at the phone suspiciously. With Matt, you never know what words can follow a sentence like that.

"You know Zoe? And you know how I told her about you? I was wondering...would you call her?"

I'm surprised.

Matt shrugs. "It's not that she doesn't believe me, but... Well, I thought the condition might seem more real to her if you talked to her about it, too."

***

So that evening, though I feel weird about it, I call her.

"Hello?" Zoe's voice sounds uncertain as she answers.

"Hey, Zoe? It's, uh, Jim. Matt's brother." I'm standing alone at the edge of Capital Soccer's outdoor field. Practice is over, and the afternoon sun is getting lower, casting long shadows over the field.

"Oh!" She's surprised.

"He asked if I would call you." I put one hand on the strap of my gym bag and take a few slow steps in the grass. "Since our condition is kind of bizarre, he wanted to make sure you believe him." I try to sound joking, but I'm not sure if that carries through. She's quiet. "Do I sound just like Matt?" I guess.

She laughs nervously. "Yeah."

"Yeah, I get that a lot." I remember I haven't taken off my cleats, so I sit down in the grass and shove my shoulder up to my ear to hold the phone in place. "So...anything I can say to you to convince you that Matt's telling the truth?"

She laughs, not nervously this time. "I believe Matt. I could tell back at Camp Waller that Jett seemed like two people."

"Yeah, that's what he said." I undo the laces on one shoe. "Kudos to you on your observational skills."

She laughs again.

"So..." I take off one shoe and try to think of what to say next. "Do you have any questions?"

"Um, I don't know..." Zoe pauses. "Wait. Yes. Which one of you did I beat at rock climbing?"

I smile as I pull off the second shoe. "That was me. But I'm pretty sure Matt wouldn't have done any better. Probably worse."

"And who played the guitar?"

"Me." I un-Velcro my shin guards and toss them with my shoes into my gym bag.

"But the one who gave the guitar to Emily was Matt?"

"Right." I pull on my sneakers and the phone almost falls away from my face.

"And it wasn't because he was being courteous?"

I laugh. "No, it was because he didn't know how to play it." Balancing the phone is getting hard, so I hold it with one hand and lean back in the grass, my legs sprawled out.

Zoe pauses. "Which one of you liked Andie?"

I feel my face get warm. "Neither of us. She was super into Jett, and I will definitely say that Matt started it, but since we were trying to act like a 'normal' teenager, we didn't discourage her. By the end of the week, we were sick of her."

"Hmm." Zoe pauses. "That's almost mean of you guys."

"Oh." That kind of hurts. The grass tickles my hand, but I don't move.

"But...I guess it turned out OK," Zoe says. "Andie was fine."

"Oh. Well, that's good."

There's an awkward silence.

"Well..." I stand up. "Matt wanted to make sure you believe him."

"I do."

I pick my gym bag back up and sling it over one shoulder. "He'll also be hoping you won't think he's weird now and ditch him."

She laughed. "I won't."

"Good. He'll be glad about that."

There's another awkward pause. I shift my weight from one leg to the other, looking out into the empty field.

"Well, Jim, thanks for calling."

"Yeah. Yeah, no problem."

"Bye."

"Bye."

Tuesday, May 3
Matt

"OK," Zoe says. We're eating burgers and French fries on a little round table outside a restaurant downtown. "So, what about learning stuff? If you learn something, does Jim know it, too? Does he get to access your knowledge?"

"You know..." I balance my stuffed burger in my hands. "As cool as that would be, no. We've each got to learn everything for ourselves. Though it would save time if we could share knowledge." I shrug and take a bite. "Oh well."

This is the first time Zoe and I have gotten food after working. But she suggested it, and I was all for it. The weather is perfect, too: sunny, clear, and warm enough not to need a jacket. And now that Zoe knows about Jim, she's curious.

"What about dreams?" Zoe's sitting on the edge of her metal seat, a fry ready to dip in one hand, looking fascinated. "Do you guys have the same dreams?"

"Haven't so far. Jim keeps hoping we will, but I don't think it's going to happen."

"And when he's awake, on his days, you don't remember anything?"

"Nothing." I take a drink of the soda I ordered. "I don't know what he does, or what he sees, or what he feels, or what he hears. I'm not aware of anything at all. Like I'm in a coma. When I wake up each morning, the last thing I remember is going to bed on my last awake day."

I admit I had been nervous to tell her about the condition. But the way she's looking at me now makes me feel...interesting. Special. I'm surprised by how much I like it.

"So, when do you actually switch places?" Zoe asks. "Sometime in the middle of the night?"

"The instant our body falls asleep."

"Wait..." Zoe is about to take a bite, but she stops. "Didn't you tell me you have your own rooms? If you switch places at night..." She tilts her head to one side. "Whose bed do you sleep in?"

"Well, I guess you'd say both." I swirl a fry in ketchup. "I go to sleep in my own bed, in my room. When Jim wakes up in the morning, he's *in* my bed. Then he'll go to sleep in his bed, and I'll wake up there."

Zoe nods slowly. "And sharing a bed is out because...?"

"Because we want our own rooms."

"And sharing a room is out because...?"

I smile and lean forward in my seat. "Because we're different, Zoe. We like having our own space and our own stuff."

"So, your rooms are different."

"Yeah."

"In what ways?" She takes a bite and watches me, prepared to listen.

"Well, if you asked him, he'd say his is cleaner and mine is messier." I suddenly have a desire to pick up my napkins and paper trash on the table, as if to prove I'm not messy. "If you ask me, I'd say his is more boring and mine is more artistic." I return her smile and go on. "But let's see...I like putting posters on my wall." Tons and tons of posters. "Jim doesn't put anything on his wall unless it's framed."

"That's neat of your parents then, huh? That they let you and Jim have your own?"

"Oh, yeah." I raise my voice over the sound of a motorized scooter zooming past us on the sidewalk. "Our parents are the best. Pretty much anything normal brothers would have their own of, Jim and I can get our own of."

"That's really cool, Matt."

"Even toothbrushes."

She gives me a funny look over her hamburger. "OK, that one's a little weird. Does it matter if you have the same mouth?"

"Well, Jim says I chomp down on my toothbrush and squish the bristles flat..." I get quiet, self-conscious. That's a lot of information to share with a girl. I clear my throat and shift. "Um, apparently he doesn't like that."

Zoe gives me a sly look.

We go on for a while, me answering more of Zoe's questions: how were you diagnosed, how does the implant in your brain work, what do you do about holidays, what would happen if one of you got sentenced to jail time someday, etc.

When we're gathering our trash to throw away, she turns to me with a small smile. "Well, you probably hate looking for a bright side to your condition—what's it called again?"

"Duo-COR-dis you-nus-cor-por-OH-sis," I enunciate. "Yeah. Kind of a mouthful."

"Right." Zoe drops her wad of wrappers into a trash can and slides her hands in the back pockets of her jeans. "Well, you probably hate looking for a bright side, but it could be worse. You and Jim could have narcolepsy."

I laugh out loud at that. It hasn't ever occurred to me to be grateful that Jim and I don't have a disorder that causes us to fall asleep at unexpected times during the day. "Good point," I say. "That would complicate things significantly."

Mostly, I'm elated that she's taking the condition in stride enough to joke about it.

hey jim do you ever think how lucky we
are that we don't have narcolepsy?

well i don't usually use the word lucky when i'm talking
about us
but ha thats actually occurred to me
that would be a nightmare

no kidding

and thanks for talking to zoe on the phone

no problem
you like working with her?

yeah i do

she seems nice
i'm glad

chapter
sixteen

"Mud, Mud, no! Down!" Zoe stands up from the park bench and backs away before the giant Labrador can climb into her lap.

I laugh and pull the leash. "Come on, Mud. Here, boy." The dog backs up and settles for a pat on the head from Zoe instead.

She shakes her head at me and puts down the fluffy white dog she's been holding.

I take a turn patting the black dog's head. "Mud just wants some attention like Poco."

"Mud just thinks he's the *size* of Poco." Zoe acts frustrated at the muddy paw prints on her pants, but then she laughs with me as we continue down the path. She holds the little white dog's leash, and I hold the Lab's.

"At least these two aren't as hard as those three dachshunds the other day," I say.

Zoe raises her eyebrows and gestures with her free hand. "And they were so little! But they were all over the place!"

Working with Zoe is one of my favorite parts of the week. We meet each other downtown, claim Pals team tasks on the app, and work for several hours. Most often, we walk three or more dogs at a time.

We're saying goodbye to Mud and Poco when I pull out my phone to look for the next assignment.

"Anything good?" Zoe closes and locks the door to the town home, and we head off down the street.

I swipe a finger across the screen. "There's a python two blocks over who needs his frozen mice thawed and fed to him. Too bad we're not certified for reptiles yet."

Zoe pretends to gag, and I laugh.

"Oh," I say, my eyes on the screen, "remember those two German shepherds? They need a walk. Could you go another hour?"

Zoe and I head to the German shepherds' apartment. Sometimes to get from task to task, we drive. Sometimes we rent the electric scooters you find all over downtown. Today, it's close enough we choose to walk, chatting along the way.

"What are you doing this weekend?" she asks.

"Me and Leo are going to see *The Last Edge* on Friday." I raise my eyebrows at her as we stop at a crosswalk. "You're sure you're not going to go see it?"

Zoe makes a face while we listen to the beeps that sound until the light changes. "Two and a half hours of car chases and fight scenes? No, thanks."

I laugh.

The next hour is fun, like always. The two German shepherds are energetic and keep us active and laughing.

At the end of their walk, we rent electric scooters and ride back to where we parked our cars.

As we're leaving our scooters, Zoe, hands in her back jean pockets, reaches a foot over and kicks my shoe. "Hey, come with me. I have something for you."

I follow her to her car. It's a silver sedan. She opens the passenger door and reaches in. When she stands up and turns around, she's holding a box wrapped in green, blue, and black shiny wrapping paper. "Ta-da!"

I smile. "Aw, Zoe."

"I didn't forget it's your birthday this weekend! You can call this a present for you and Jim both because you'll share it, but..." She holds out her arms straight, offering me the present. "Open it!"

I take the gift and open it to reveal...

"Is this an organizer for my truck? Thanks!" When I've driven us to tasks farther away, Zoe has noticed that my and Jim's truck has a flip-out center console, nothing fancy. But Zoe's gift has...

"Cup holders, a phone organizer, and the best part—a French fry holder!" She crinkles up the used wrapping paper.

I laugh. "No way, Zoe. Thank you."

"And," she says, "it's easily removable in case you want to fold up the console for your bench seat. Just in case anyone wants to sit in the middle."

Immediately I think of one thing. In case *she* wants to sit in the middle...

"Thanks, Zoe. It's great." I lean over and give her a hug. It's the first time I hug her. It's the first time I smell her perfume. But it feels natural.

Thursday, May 26
Jim

On Thursday, Matt and I turn seventeen years old. Like Christmas, we celebrate our birthday separately. Leo is great like he always is and, even though he's getting ready for finals, goes with us two days in a row to *The Last Edge*, a new spy movie we all want to see. Matt makes Leo swear not to reveal any spoilers when he goes with him to the theater on Friday.

Mom and Dad are always nice about our birthday. We have cake and candles and all that, both of us, two days in a row.

I get to celebrate first this year. Standing in the kitchen next to the bar, Mom slides a cake over to me. It's a small cake, 11x13 cut in half, covered in solid chocolate icing. (Mom used to be fancier with icing and sprinkles, until we got old enough to tease her about her lack of cake-decorating skills.) There are seventeen candles crowded on top.

I smile. "Thanks, Mom."

"OK, wait." Dad takes out his tablet and holds it in front of his chest, between him and Mom, the screen facing out. He taps play on a video.

The video shows Matt's face. Matt looks away from the camera, up over his shoulder, like he's looking out of the screen and up at Dad. "Ready, Dad?" He looks up out of the frame in Mom's direction. "Mom?"

Mom and Dad beam at me like they're in on the biggest birthday surprise of the decade.

In the video, Matt starts to count. "OK, one, two, three…" As he starts singing happy birthday in the video, Mom and Dad join in, still all smiles.

After the song ends, the video goes on. "OK, wait, let me help blow out the candles!" Matt leans forward and blows, like he's blowing out candles on a cake. I laugh and lean forward, too, blowing all the candles out.

In the video, Matt cheers. "We're seventeen, Jim! Happy birthday!"

The video ends, and Mom comes forward and gives me a side hug. "That was fun, huh? It was all his idea."

I hug Mom back. Times like this, when Matt and I figure out a way to make it almost sort of feel like we're actually together, are always nice.

Jim—Thu, May 26, 4:28 PM

hey where'd the nice organizer in the truck come from?

Matt—Fri, May 27, 7:12 AM

it's a birthday gift from zoe

nice right?

Jim—Sat, May 28, 7:30 AM

tell her thanks
and HAPPY BIRTHDAY!!!

Matt—Sun, May 29, 9:54 AM

HAPPY BIRTHDAY!!!

9:36 PM

thanks for the yoga mat 🧘

you had me going for a minute with
the fakeout pink flower one

Jim—Mon, May 30, 7:04 AM

i was tempted to leave you with it and not return it
hope you get better use out of the black one
(but really tho i hope you use it because i
admit yoga's treating our body well)

Matt—Tue, May 31, 7:00 AM

TOLD YOU SO

chapter
seventeen

Sunday, June 12
Matt

Once Leo's school year ends, I start to get excited about the summer. I get to hang out with him more, the pools are open, Jim and I have been on a two-month break from schoolwork since the beginning of May, and I get more time to work with Zoe.

The only thing that keeps the summer from being perfectly chill is an argument Jim and I have. Zoe has a birthday party, but it's on Jim's day. I can tell she wants me to go, but after the Distorted Tides concert, I don't think there's any way I can get Jim to switch days with me. So I ask him to go and pretend to be me instead. Which for some reason makes him mad. For a couple of days, we exchange angry messages and insults, until Sunday morning Mom finds me and tells me I'm not being fair and need to apologize.

Please. Like I'm gonna.

Still, it isn't fun, the way our arguments stretch on for days, even weeks.

I think it would be different if we were normal brothers, if we could see and hear one another in real life, in real time. Then he'd say something mean, I'd punch him in the stomach, and we'd be done. Instead, here I am, trying to think of creative places I can write the word TATTLETALE for him to see.

Monday, June 27
Jim

Matt and I always have a game going on, a two-person turn-based game like checkers or Battleship. We keep it on a small table in my bedroom. I keep trying to get Matt to agree to learn chess because it would be perfect, but he says it'll take too much of our precious time.

Right now, the game is Mastermind, one of our favorites. Each day one of us takes a turn. One round of the game can take weeks. A whole game can take months.

The game is kind of sacred. We never cheat. And back during the haircut war, even when Matt dumped everything else in my room onto the floor, he left the game alone.

***

On Monday, I win a game that we started way back in January, which feels good because for a while in June, I was too mad to play (during an argument over Matt's friend Zoe's birthday party that ended with Matt renaming all of the contacts in my phone to TATTLETALE). But because he loses, Matt has to be the one to clean our bathroom for the next three months (you think we play with no stakes?), and that leaves me in better spirits.

Another highlight of the summer is Mom's "work retreat"—a yearly trip she takes with her two sisters. The idea is they talk and plan for their recipe blog. I'm not sure how much work they actually do, but Matt and I are all for it because when Mom's gone, Dad relaxes all the rules (except video games and switching places). But school, bedtimes, naps, diets, exercise—he lets it all go, and Matt and I can do whatever we want. We usually watch a lot of TV, eat a lot of junk food, waste a lot of time online, and stay up late (and then complain to each other when we're tired or overdosed on sugar).

The Monday after Mom gets back, once Matt and I are adjusting to our normal bedtime again, I'm playing through his messages. In one he's so excited, I'm surprised.

"Hey! Jim! Guess what?" He's in the parking lot at church. "I'm going to play in a band!"

I'm curious how he worked that out, but I can't help smiling at his enthusiasm.

"Well, OK, it's not a band, and I'm just subbing." In the background of the video, I can see Mom and Dad walking with Matt to the car. "But it's for the group that performs at church on Sundays, you know? The drummer will be gone in a month, and *he asked me*! And it's my day!" Matt pumps a fist in the air. "I am so excited!"

I send a Vimer back. "No way! Congrats, Matt! That'll be sweet! Definitely get Mom and Dad to video it. I wish I could be there!"

Saturday, July 16
Matt

One of the most touristy things to do in Austin is see the bats. Meaning, the little flying mammals. Hundreds of thousands of them swarming out from underneath a bridge on Lady Bird Lake every sunset during the summer.

Because it's so touristy, I think it's kind of lame, but go figure, Mom likes to go, and she drags us every summer. At least she bribes me with an incentive. She gets donuts in the morning and saves them for when we're spreading out our picnic blanket on the grass overlooking the lake.

Dad opens the donut box. "Maple bacon—I believe this one's for you, Matt." These donuts are gourmet, with combinations and flavors you can't find anywhere else. We don't get them very often.

"Mmm." I eagerly take the donut from Dad and lick the maple icing, hungrily eyeing the syrup-covered crispy bacon on top.

"Bacon on a donut." Mom gives me a look as she picks up her own donut (plain glazed! How boring!). "That's just wrong."

"You're missing out," I say with a full mouth. "Come on, Dad, back me up."

"I agree with your mom." Dad stretches out the blanket and looks up at the darkening sky.

I roll my eyes at their lameness and enjoy myself. All around us are the sounds of voices talking, of other people spread out on their own blankets or standing around waiting. I can smell grass and someone's bug spray.

"So how's practice going, Matt?" Dad asks. He stretches out his legs in front of him and leans back on his arms.

"Great!" I say around another full bite. "Everyone's been really flexible and nice. It hasn't been hard to find times to meet together." Even though I'm only awake every other day. Even though I started schoolwork last week. Even though I haven't told anyone at church about my condition, and they think I'm Jett. "And I think they like me. Playing in church next weekend is going to be awesome."

"So, are you becoming more of a fan of the gospel music?" Mom asks. She takes a small lick of donut glaze on her fingers.

I send her a look that says, *Don't push it, Mom.* "Hey," I say. "I'm not being picky." Then I start to get excited again at the thought of next Sunday. "I'm getting to play with other people! In front of *other* other people! It's too great."

Mom and Dad smile.

"Next weekend's a big weekend for Jim, too." Mom pulls her legs up underneath her and leans against Dad. There's a slight breeze in the summer air that flips the ends of her hair up. Dad puts an arm around her.

"Yeah, soccer tryouts, right?" I lick my own fingers. "And he missed tryouts the last two seasons. So he's excited." I smile, remembering his Vimer I watched that morning. "He pretended to act all nervous and told me to wish him luck."

"Did you?"

"Nah." I pull my knees up and hug them loosely, turning in the direction of the bridge the bats will be emerging from soon. "I told him he doesn't need it. He'll do great."

Jim—Tue, Jul 19, 7:13 AM

are you ready to play in church this weekend???

Matt—Wed, Jul 20, 7:01 AM

so ready! are you ready for tryouts???

Jim—Thu, Jul 21, 7:30 AM

haha jk
yeah i'm ready
it's gonna be awesome

Matt—Fri, Jul 22, 7:01 AM

you'll do great
good luck!

Jim—Sat, Jul 23, 7:32 AM

i'll let you know how it goes

chapter
eighteen

Saturday, July 23
Jim

The day of soccer tryouts, as much as I've joked about it with Matt, I really am a little nervous. It's been over a year since I've tried out.

The season will last from August through November. Since I've played for Capital Soccer the past few years, I know a lot of the guys and coaches. I say hi to several of them as I walk with Mom and Dad onto the field. Then I send my parents a look that says *leave before you embarrass me* (I'm embarrassed enough that they both came in the first place), so with some good luck wishes, they go sit at the small section of spectator bleachers. I take my gym bag to the other side and sit next to the other players to change into my cleats. Then I slip on the numbered practice jersey they have waiting for me and join the players on the field.

We're arranged into teams for scrimmages. The pressure is on.

I play, trying to focus on the game and not the fact that I'm being watched. After a few minutes it's easy. I feel at home playing soccer.

After tryouts have been going on for a while, a guy on my team passes me the ball. Someone on the opposing team is in front of me. I glance to my right—Kahlil is upfield, open. I have to get around my defender to get the ball to him. I'm heading left and need to make a quick direction change. The defender steps closer to me than I expect. I plant my right foot and pivot—

And then I'm down. Something feels like it pops on my outer right ankle. It hurts like crazy. I fall to the grass, grabbing my leg. The guy who's defending me trips over me.

Certain details—like the patch of dirt I can see through the blades of grass, and the way the ridges of my sock feel under my fingers—stand out clear. Other details—like who comes over to me and what they say—don't register at all. I grimace and hold my right knee into my chest, afraid to touch my foot.

Here are the thoughts I have in order:

1) Ow-ow-ow-ow-ow-ow!

2) Did I just blow tryouts?

3) Oh *crap*. Matt.

No one's examined my ankle yet, and I'm not sure what happened, but I have a feeling it's bad. It *hurts*. And Matt needs this foot, like, tomorrow. For playing in church. His first performance on a stage. The one he's looking forward to so much.

He's going to hate me.

***

I sit in the waiting room of the urgent care, Mom on one side of me and Dad on the other. Neither of them have said anything since we walked in, other than giving the receptionist our insurance. We wait in silence, listening to the faint instrumental music playing over the speakers and the receptionist talking quietly on the phone.

Mom's face looks pained. Dad's handling it better. He looks at me with calm reassurance a few times.

An hour earlier at tryouts, after a coach helped me limp off the field, a physical therapist examined me and suggested I head to an urgent care.

I grimace. My foot's been wrapped in ice packs since the soccer field, but they're only slightly cool now. So am I. The AC in the room blows on my sweaty clothes, chilling my skin.

The room smells like disinfectant that I'm sure is supposed to smell clean but just makes me think of chemicals. Across the room, a kid holding a teddy bear sits next to his mom, staring at me. I stare back.

There's no way this isn't bad. From the way the physical trainer looked at it on the field to the way my ankle throbs now—yeah, it's bad.

Matt and I do this thing where, as much as we can, we pretend like our body is each of ours, individually. Meaning, when I'm in our body, it's *mine*, not ours. When it's Matt's turn, then it will be his body. He can play the drums with his body. But not on my day. I can play soccer with mine. We don't use phrases like "our body" or "our smile" or "our hair" unless we're talking about the fact that we share. No, all the other times I talk about the body Matt and I take turns in, it's *my* body, *my* smile, *my* hair. My foot. Things like this injury are painful reminders (this time literally) that that isn't the case. No matter what Matt and I pretend, we don't have our own bodies. We share one. We can't get away from the effects of each other's actions. And this time, I've done something awful. Something Matt is sure to hate me for.

***

A distal fibular fracture.

That's what I've done.

It means a break in my fibula, the bone on the outside of my right ankle. I feel sick when I hear the treatment: six to eight weeks in a medical boot.

Know what else it means? No exercising. No running. For the first two weeks, no walking at all unless I have crutches. For sure no soccer. No season.

Those are the implications for me. But just as quickly, I'm flooded with realizations of what it means for Matt. No driving to work. No dog walking. No ankle-bending. No bass drum. Oh *man*, he's going to want to kill me.

The only vaguely bright side I can see to this whole thing is that I won't be there tomorrow when Matt wakes up. But as I think of my parents, I only feel guiltier. They're the ones who are going to have to face him. And I know already that it's going to get ugly.

Sunday, July 24
Matt

The first thing I notice when I wake up in Jim's room is pain. The pain might be what wakes me up. I moan and roll in bed, then realize my right foot feels heavy. Actually, it feels like it's in a boot.

I sit up. It *is* in a boot. My right foot is in a medical boot. I gape at it for a moment in shock. What the heck! What happened!?

"MOM!" I yell as loud as I can. "DAD!"

They walk into my room together, like they've been preparing for this.

"What is this?!" I swing my feet over the edge of the bed. The boot on my right foot drags it to the ground. Pain shoots through my ankle and makes me grit my teeth.

"Matt." Mom kneels down in front of me. The light switch in the room is off, and the dim sunlight coming in from around the closed window blinds outlines her head. She puts a hand on my knee. Dad comes and stands next to her, a hand on her shoulder. "It was an accident. Jim was so, so sorry."

"What happened!?" I'm yelling.

"It's called a distal fibular fracture." Dad's voice is quiet. "An ankle fracture. It happened during Jim's soccer tryouts yesterday."

"What—why—agh!" I sputter for a moment. I shove aside the sheets tangled around my lap and grab my hair in my hands and stare ahead, wild-eyed.

"It was an accident," Mom repeats. "Jim is really sorry..."

"What about church?" I shout. "I have to play today!"

Even in the dim room, I can tell from the expressions on Mom's and Dad's faces that I'm not playing anywhere.

I swear and throw myself back on the bed. I close my eyes and pull at my hair again. I'm gritting my teeth. I'm *mad*. Boy, am I mad. Before I think through anything else, I sit up, reach over, and grab Jim's phone. I open Vimer.

"Matt." Mom puts a gentle hand on my arm. "Why don't you cool down for a minute, listen to us explain, before you say anything to Jim—"

I don't listen. I start talking into the phone camera. "Jim." I take in a slow breath. I'm having trouble knowing what to say. What *can* I say in a situation like this? "Jim, you *moron*," I settle for. "What the heck, man!" My voice gets louder. "Oh, I wish *so* bad I had my own body right now—not only so I wouldn't have to live with your stupid injury, but also so I could punch you in the face."

I wind back to chuck the phone across the room, but Mom takes it from me before I can.

I let her take it and flop back down on the bed violently enough that it shakes. I close my eyes and moan. Why? *Why?* I've been looking forward to playing in church more than anything else in my life. This sucks! It *sucks*! Is this going to be my whole life?

I roll onto my side, facing the wall.

"Matt." Mom puts a hand on my shoulder. "Matt, I know, this is so hard, and we can talk about it..."

I jerk away from her. That probably hurts her feelings. I don't care. My eyes are squinted shut and my jaw is tight. "I'm going to sleep."

"Matt..."

"Jane," Dad says softly. Then I hear footsteps and the door slowly creak shut.

I keep my eyes closed and I curl up, the boot on my right foot crushing my left foot. I do want to go to sleep. I don't want to be here right now. Let Jim deal with it, deal with the pain in our foot and the guilt Mom and Dad are feeling. Let him deal with all of it.

Sunday, July 24
Jim

I wake up in my own bed, which is confusing at first. My phone is on my nightstand. I check the day.

Sunday morning. The injury happened yesterday. This is supposed to be Matt's day. He's supposed to be in church in a few hours. Supposed to be... but won't be. Because of me.

I get my crutches and walk downstairs. Mom and Dad are in the kitchen. When they see me, they walk over to join me in the living room, where I sink onto the white fabric couch.

"Jim?" Mom sits next to me, picking up a gray throw pillow and hugging it to her.

I nod.

"How's your ankle feel?"

"It hurts." No one responds. The clock on the wall ticks the seconds by. "How's Matt?"

Mom and Dad are still both quiet, staring. Termite comes over and puts his head in my lap, but I ignore him.

"He hates me, doesn't he?"

This seems to wake Mom up from a trance. She sits straighter. "No, of course not. His message to you this morning might have been harsh, but he had just woken up and he wasn't—"

"He left a message for me?"

"Well." Mom lays the pillow flat on her lap and plays with the decorative stitching. "From your phone. You don't have to watch it yet—"

I pull out my phone and tap the most recent message to Matt.

"Jim." Matt breathes in slowly. I wince. "Jim, you *moron*." Then he starts to shout. "What the heck, man! Oh, I wish *so* bad I had my own body right now—not only so I wouldn't have to live with your stupid injury, but also so I could punch you in the face."

I set down the phone. No one in the room speaks for a few minutes, except Termite, who whines.

"He'll come around." Dad pets the dog. "It's understandable he would be upset. But he can't blame you. It wasn't your fault."

"Not the way he sees it," I mumble. "What happened this morning? Did he just go back to sleep?"

Dad nods. "We thought we would let him. He..." Dad searches for words, rubbing his temple with one hand.

"He seemed like he needed it," Mom finishes.

I nod. Still, I feel bad, taking Matt's day. "This should be his day. Should *I* go back to sleep?"

Mom and Dad look at each other before Mom turns to me. "You know, why don't you stay awake today. He'll take tomorrow and we'll get back on track with blue and orange days soon enough. But I think it's fair not to make Matt live through this day and have to miss church..."

I droop into the couch.

"Don't feel bad." Dad grips my shoulder. "It wasn't your fault."

"Not the way he sees it," I repeat in a mumble.

Monday, July 25
Jim

The next time I wake up, I'm in my bed again, and the time of day feels wrong. I look at my phone on my nightstand. It's Monday, after 10:30 in the morning.

I sigh and hobble downstairs on crutches. Mom isn't in the kitchen, so I sit down alone at the table. In the quiet room, Termite comes up to me, and I scratch behind his ears. "Hey, buddy," I murmur.

Mom hears my voice. She comes walking in from the homeschool room.

"Hi, Matt." Her voice is gentle. "How's your foot feeling? Jim took some extra pain medication last night. I thought you might sleep late this morning. Can I get you some breakfast?"

I stop petting Termite and look up. "I'm Jim. Matt must have gone back to sleep again this morning."

Mom looks sad as she sits down at the table with me.

"I'm worried about him, Mom. He hardly got any time yesterday. And no time the day before that. This should be his day."

Mom rests her forehead in her fingers. "I know. It looks like he doesn't want to be awake. I think every teenager feels like that sometimes." She crosses her arms on the table and sits up. "The problem with you two is... well, since Matt has you, he can let you take care of your body, eating and showering. Maybe he feels like he's free to check out as long as he wants."

I stare at the wall in front of me. There are framed photographs hanging there—not an official family portrait (because how can our family do a true family portrait?) but a collection of a bunch of candid photos of all of us. I make a face. "I don't want that."

"I know you don't." Mom rubs my shoulder. "Maybe you can nap later today. We can try to give him his day back."

"You might have to make him stay up."

Mom nods.

Tuesday, July 26
Jim

It's weird waking up for the third day in a row—no, wait, the fourth day in a row—in my own bed. I check Vimer. There's nothing from Matt. Nothing since the angry message he sent me after waking up in the boot.

"How's Matt?" is the first thing I ask my parents that day, before even reaching the bottom of the stairs. Mom and Dad are both in the living room. It looks like they've been talking.

Mom looks at me sadly. "He wouldn't get up, Jim. I tried, but he just wasn't responding..."

I stop right there, hovering on the steps. I feel terrible.

Dad looks thoughtful. "I have an idea."

Tuesday, July 26
Matt

Someone shaking my shoulder wakes me up. But Mom is rougher this time. I grunt and try to pull away.

"Sorry, bruh, I've got orders."

I roll over and squint. The light's been turned on, and it's shining in my eyes too bright. "Leo?" My voice is groggy.

"Your parents are worried about you." He takes a step back. "Jim's worried, too."

"Yeah, well, Jim can shove it." I roll over and close my eyes again.

"Nope." Leo starts shaking me again. "Sorry, pal." Then he yanks the blanket off me. In my groggy state, having the warmth ripped away is tormenting. I mutter and stick my head under my pillow.

"You're not allowed to go back to sleep." Leo takes the pillow too.

I glare at him. "Get out of my room."

He looks around. "Well, technically, this is Jim's room."

I'm unamused. I try again to turn away and face the wall, determined. Then Leo flicks my boot. Pain shoots through my ankle. That has me sitting straight up in bed fast.

"Ow! What the heck, dude!"

"Come *on*." Leo grabs my arm and tries to drag me out of bed. "Let's go play *Neutron 2*. Quick, before your dad comes home."

I groan and look up at Leo's face. I'm not getting rid of him any time soon. Wearily, I reach for the crutches.

***

I halfheartedly play video games with Leo in his game room. We aren't doing well in our two-player combat game because I don't contribute much. Leo tries to act as if everything is normal.

After the first game ends, I sit staring into space. The controller is slack in my hand, its weight pulling it down, the worn-smooth plastic threatening to slip from my fingers.

Leo looks over from the other couch. "You...want to play again?"

I don't respond.

"We can try a new game." Leo pushes some buttons and navigates the game menu on the TV screen. "I got this new one. I know it sounds bizarre, but it involves a hamburger joint in outer space—trust me, it's hilarious—"

"This is going to be my whole life, Leo." I let the controller fall out of my hand. It lands on the rug.

"Jim fracturing your ankle? I wouldn't be surprised if that only happens once."

"No." My voice is flat and dull. "Missing out on stuff. It's going to keep happening. Even if it's not Jim's fault. Even if he doesn't mean it. It's still going to keep happening."

Leo looks like he doesn't know what to say.

I don't know what else to say, either. I want to get up and hobble home. Instead, Leo convinces me to try his new silly outer space game, which doesn't make me laugh. It doesn't even make me smile. But it comes closer than anything else has today.

***

Later that night, after spending a strained evening with my parents and going up to bed, I check my messages. There are some Vimers and messages from Jim, but I don't watch or read them. I do listen to a voicemail from Zoe as I lay stretched out on my bed, flat on my back.

"Hey, Matt." Her voice is bright and makes me close my eyes and grimace. "I thought we were going to work today, and I didn't hear from you. How did playing in church go? Want to work Thursday instead?"

I know I have to talk to her, though I don't want to. Part of me still wants to go to sleep for six weeks until the boot is off. But I'm not insensitive enough to leave Zoe hanging.

"Hey, Matt," she answers after a couple of rings when I call. "How was playing in church?"

I close my eyes again and grit my teeth. I wish I could fade away and not have to deal with any of this. "I didn't go," I force out. One of my hands is gripped around my phone, and the other is gripped around a wad of my bedspread. If I could see my knuckles, I know they'd be white. "I couldn't go."

"Oh." Zoe's confused. "I'm sorry—is everything OK?"

"Jim hurt our foot." Before I can stop myself, I rush on in a messy deluge of an explanation. "He was playing soccer on Saturday and fractured something in his right ankle. On Sunday, I woke up with my foot in a boot and a lot of pain. There was no hope of playing the drums that day—or any time in the next six to eight weeks." I know I sound bitter.

It's silent on the line for a few seconds before Zoe speaks. "Oh, Matt, I'm so sorry." She does sound sorry. And her voice makes my shoulders relax, my jaw unclench, makes me exhale a breath I didn't realize I was holding.

Zoe goes on. "That's so...wow, that's got to be the worst thing in the world. I'm so sorry, Matt. Are you OK? Is your foot alright?"

"Yeah." I loosen my grip on my bedspread and rub my eyelids. "Yeah, it'll be fine."

It's silent a few seconds more. "That really, really sucks, Matt. I'm sorry."

"It's OK." My voice sounds flat and dull again. "But I can't come work with you this week. Sorry I didn't call you this morning. But I can't drive with this boot on, and I can't walk dogs because I'm on crutches."

There's a long pause. "OK," she finally says. "I'm so sorry, Matt. I'll... check in with you tomorr—I mean, the day after tomorrow."

"Bye, Zoe," I mumble. I end the call, take our medication, and roll over to go to sleep.

Thursday, July 28
Matt

The next time I wake up, it's again because someone is shaking my shoulder. But Leo? Again? Unlikely. Probably Mom. I decide to ignore her and roll away.

"Matt?"

I about jump out of bed in surprise. That's Zoe's voice.

"Zoe!" I jerk up in bed and scoot closer to the wall. "What are you doing here?"

"Jim asked if I would come over." Zoe pulls Jim's desk chair over and sits down. For the first time I've seen her since Camp Waller, she's wearing something other than the orange Pals T-shirt. She's in shorts and a shirt with a neckline that shows her silver hummingbird necklace resting on her skin. "So, how are things?"

I rub the heel of one hand into an eye socket, self-conscious to be in bed in my pajamas in front of her.

"Sorry I surprised you." She's opened the blinds—hasn't just slid the slats open but pulled them up all the way. Jim's room faces west and the sunlight that comes in isn't direct. But it's bright enough to shine a window-shaped square on the carpet behind Zoe's chair. "Your mom let me up. Apparently, you've had trouble getting out of bed."

I swallow, at a loss for words.

Zoe can tell and keeps talking. "So, I came to bring you to work."

"To work?"

"There's a collie with a litter of puppies. The owner needs someone to check on them and play with them. It's a team task. It's a little far, but I'll drive us there."

I don't know what to say. At my silence, Zoe looks down at her clothes. "I know I'm not in uniform. But I figure since we're not out walking, it's fine."

I sit still, slumped forward, messy hair, speechless like a dork.

Zoe's look softens. "Matt. Does anything sound better than cuddling a cute litter of puppies? Come on. Get up and get dressed. I'll wait for you downstairs."

I open and close my mouth once as she walks out of the room.

Well, I can't roll over and go back to sleep now. Not with Zoe downstairs in my kitchen. I get up and get dressed (grateful that Jim has been taking care of our body. Any other teenager who's spent days feeling sorry for himself in bed would be waking up smelly with patchy stubble. Thanks to Jim, I'm clean-cut and showered).

When I hobble downstairs, on crutches and wearing my baseball cap, Mom and Zoe are sitting in the kitchen talking.

Zoe stands up when she sees me. "Ready?"

Mom hands her a toasted bagel with cream cheese in a napkin and a bottle of orange juice. Zoe's hand around the orange juice bottle also grips her car keys.

I follow Zoe out to her car. Mom opens the passenger's side door for me and helps me get myself and my crutches inside.

"Thanks for coming down for him, Zoe." Mom smiles like everything is normal. She kisses the side of my head. "Bye, Matt."

I feel too numb to be embarrassed.

Zoe climbs in the driver's seat, setting the food between us.

I stare at it. "Did my mom give you breakfast?"

"No, silly." Zoe turns on the car and looks over her shoulder. "That's your breakfast. You've got a great mom."

I stare at the food as Zoe backs out of the driveway and heads out of the neighborhood.

"So..." Zoe says after five silent minutes. "Do you want to talk about it?"

"Talk about what?" I pick up the napkin and slowly tear off a bite of bagel, but I don't eat it.

Zoe is taken off-guard. "Anything. How much your foot hurts or how you've been feeling or why you're checking out..."

I don't answer right away. "I don't really want to talk about any of it."

"OK." Zoe nods. "I understand."

It's silent for a few moments as Zoe drives. Her car smells nice—something essential-oily, I think.

I finally speak. "It really sucks."

"Yeah. I know."

Then Zoe turns on some music she knows I like, and I start to eat. She sings along. I can't bring myself to sing along with her, but, like playing video games with Leo the day before, being with Zoe does help. So do the puppies. Working with her, I come the closest I have to smiling since before the accident.

***

I forget that Bradley is coming over tonight until he rings the doorbell. (He's started coming on Thursdays instead of Tuesdays recently, but even if

that weren't the case, I'm sure with the injury I would have spaced it.) I'm
upstairs in my room, lying on my bed flat on my back, lights off and blinds
shut, no music. My room smells like the stack of clean laundry my mom's put
on my dresser.

After the front door opens, Dad knocks on my bedroom door. "Matt?
Bradley is here."

I look at Dad sullenly. "Why? I can't play like this."

"Matt, Jim fractured your foot. Not your arms. Those work fine."

"But I can't play the bass drum without my right foot! There's no point!"
It's the most emotion that's been in my voice since I yelled at Jim when
I woke up and saw the boot. The bed shifts and squeaks as my body jerks
ramrod straight.

"No point at all?" Dad leans on the door frame. "Bradley drove all this
way. At least give it a shot."

I don't want to. I won't, except Dad comes and pulls me off the bed. He
guides me down to the basement on my crutches.

Bradley's sitting there, acoustic guitar on his lap, next to my drum set.
I glance at him, then look away as I sit down at the drums and dump the
crutches on the floor. The basement floor is concrete, and the crutches just
miss the rug under my drum set and hit the ground with a noisy clatter.

"Matt, that really sucks." Bradley must have been filled in on the injury
by Mom or Dad. "I'm sorry."

I don't reply.

"So..." Bradley plucks a few strings. "What do you want to play tonight?"

"Without the kick?" I mutter. Light reflects off the brass-colored
cymbals in front of me.

"You can't go six weeks without practicing at all," he reasons. "Let's try
something. Just leave the bass drum out."

I close my eyes, sigh, and pick up my drumsticks. Bradley names a song
with a light bass drum line and we start to play. I don't get far in, though. My
right foot, sitting uselessly under me, keeps trying to tap out of habit, and
that hurts, and the song doesn't sound good without the low, steady sounds
of the kick. When the missing bass drum throws me off enough to make me
miss a beat on the snare, I lose my temper. I exhale in frustration and crash
both sticks on the cymbals as hard as I can.

Bradley stops playing, and it's silent except for the AC humming and my
heavy breathing. Then he speaks. "You know what you need? A double bass
pedal. Then you can play the kick with your left foot."

I stare straight down, trying to control my breathing.

"It'll take a lot of practice, but if you commit, you'll get it."

I'm fuming mad. I can't look up. I'm afraid to say something because I'm worried I'll explode at Bradley, and he doesn't deserve that. I shake my head quickly, my neck tense.

"Well..." Bradley's chair twists under him as he rotates. "Do...you want to try something else tonight?"

I shake my head again, staring straight down at the snare drum. My hands are clenched around the drumsticks, shaking.

"Then...I'll see you next week, OK, Matt?"

When I don't reply, Bradley stands up, moves over, and bends down to where he's in my field of vision. "Hang in there, bro."

I jerk my head away.

I hear Bradley pack up and leave. I sit there at the drums, giving him time to go upstairs and out the door before I head back up to my room. But when I start up the stairs, I hear voices and realize he hasn't left yet.

"Yeah, I feel really sorry for him," Bradley's voice says from the kitchen. I pause halfway up the stairs and listen.

"He's had a hard time with it," Dad says.

"How big of a deal is it, really?" Mom's voice says. "Him not being able to use his right foot. Can't he manage without the bass drum for a few weeks?"

I can picture the look Bradley is giving my mom. "It's a big deal, Mrs. Mickelsen. For the type of music he likes to play? It's a big deal."

There's a loaded pause. I lean against the wall, trying to balance my right foot in a less painful position.

"But there's a solution," Bradley goes on. "There's something called a double bass pedal. It would let Matt play the bass drum with his left foot."

"So he could still play?" Dad sounds excited.

"Yes. It'll be hard at first." Bradley's voice echoes in the stairwell. "And it'll take time to learn. But if he wanted to, and if he really worked at it, he would be able to play the bass drum just as well as he used to."

"What's this double bass pedal?" Mom asks. "Another piece of equipment?"

"Yes."

"How much?" Dad asks.

"For a good one? Anywhere from three to seven hundred dollars."

There's a heavy silence.

"Well, thanks for coming, Bradley," Dad says.

"Do you think he'll want me back next week?" Bradley's voice is drawing further away. "I'm happy to come." They're walking toward the front door.

"We'll talk to him," Mom says. "I'll let you know..." She draws out of earshot.

I sink down onto the steps and lean my head against the wall, letting the crutches slip to the stairs, where they slide down a few feet, leaving me stranded.

Bradley's right.

I should learn to play the kick with my left foot.

It's something I've intended to learn how to do sometime anyway, play the double bass. Just not under the current circumstances. I'm very bitter about the current circumstances. I should be more cooperative, more excited, more willing. But I'm not. Not yet.

After I'm positive Bradley leaves and my parents are out of the kitchen, I slide down the stairs until I can pick up the crutches and make my way back to my bedroom. It's before dinner, but I want to lie down and go to sleep. I can't even bring myself to listen to music. I sit on my bed, but I don't lie down. I want to, but I know I shouldn't.

I'm sitting there, looking down, trying to make myself either lie down or get up but feeling stuck in the middle. Then the mattress creaks as someone sits on the bed next to me. It's Dad. He puts an arm around me. He doesn't say anything as I stare at the boot. We just sit there.

Jim—Sun, Jul 24, 10:03 AM

listen matt i'm so sorry
i know how much playing in church meant to you
i know you hate me

Mon, Jul 25, 10:56 AM

it was an accident
i never meant for it to happen

Tue, Jul 26, 11:14 AM

if i had known it was going to happen i would have
skipped tryouts and let you play in church instead

Wed, Jul 27, 8:24 AM

come on matt
talk to me bro
you can call me a jerk if you want

Fri, Jul 29, 9:32 AM

chapter
nineteen

Tuesday, August 2
Jim

The next Tuesday, Bradley comes over with the new drum pedal he's picked out. I'm in the homeschool room reading.

Mom lets him in. "Bradley. Thanks so much for coming."

"No problem, Mrs. Mickelsen." He walks in carrying a big cardboard box. He looks over and nods at me. "Hey, Jim, what's up?"

I'm surprised that he acts friendly. I don't know if I've ever had a real conversation with him, though I have seen him a few times (like when Mom and Dad took me to his high school graduation a couple years ago since it was on my day, and they couldn't take Matt).

I try to hide my surprise and act casual and cool in return. "Hey, Bradley."

Mom leads him downstairs. I grab my crutches and follow.

In the basement, Bradley is kneeling on the rug in front of the TV, opening the box and setting aside pieces of Styrofoam and plastic wrapping as he pulls out pieces of metal.

I hobble into the room. "Do...you need any help?"

He's surprised. "Sure. Thanks." He looks back down at the box, and I sit on the couch in front of him.

"Sorry about your foot, bro." Bradley hands me some pieces of metal to unwrap.

"Thanks." I feel uncomfortable as I slip off the plastic packaging. It feels like since he's Matt's friend he should take Matt's side and hate me for ruining Matt's life.

"Your mom told me about what you did, helping to pay for this." Bradley pulls another squeaky Styrofoam piece out of the box. "That was cool of you."

"Well." I drop the trash back in the box. "It's the least I can do after I ruined his life."

Bradley smiles down at the metal piece he's unwrapping. "Matt won't want to look at it like this yet, but learning to play the kick with his left foot will be a good thing."

I unwrap the next piece Bradley gives me. "Yeah, I have a feeling that if I try to point that out to him, I'll wake up with my fingers superglued together."

He laughs. Soon he has me putting metal pieces together while he's on the floor at Matt's drum kit, taking things apart with a screwdriver.

"What about the instrument you play?" He nods to the guitars on the wall. "You any good?"

I shrug. "Oh, I don't know. Not as good as Matt is on the drums. I haven't been taking lessons for a while." Then I add, "But I'm starting again this week."

"Nice." Bradley cranes his neck down to reach a piece to screw in. "I'm not that good on the guitar, either."

"That's not what Matt says."

He smiles. For a while I'm silent as I watch him work. He gets up to tap the pedals a few times and makes some adjustments. Finally, he stands up. "Well, let's see if we assembled this pedal correctly." He sits down at the kit and starts to play while I lean back on the couch and watch.

Bradley's good. He plays a few different beats and fills. Then he makes one more adjustment to the new pedal and sits down again. Before he starts playing, he looks at me. "Want to play along?"

I must look confused or surprised because Bradley laughs and nods to the guitars on the wall. I push off the throw blanket I've pulled onto my lap and stand up, hopping on one foot over to my guitar.

We find songs we both know and play. It's fun. I'm almost jealous that Matt gets to have a lesson with Bradley every week.

We play through a few songs before Bradley gets up and positions Matt's drumsticks across his snare.

"That was fun." He starts picking up the trash from the new pedal. It crumples and squeaks as he stuffs it back in the box. "A role reversal. Usually, it's the other way around."

I help him clean up. Soon we're standing, the empty box under Bradley's arm and my crutches under mine.

"You know what you and Matt need now?" Bradley surveys the basement.

"What?" I'm expecting another piece of equipment (hopefully one I won't have to pay for).

"A time machine."

I'm confused. "Huh?"

"So you could travel back a day and see Matt in person. You guys would love playing together."

Wednesday, August 3
Matt

That night before dinner, I'm heading upstairs to my room when the doorbell rings.

"That's probably Bradley." Mom walks to the door. "Are you ready for your lesson, Matt?"

"Bradley?" I freeze on the hardwood and speak over my shoulder. "You had him come back? I can't play like this, Mom!"

But Mom's at the door, opening it, letting Bradley in. She smiles at him like everything's normal. Bradley greets my mom, nods at me, and heads downstairs.

"No," I say under my breath to my mom.

"Yes." She points to the basement.

I shake my head and lower my chin.

Mom points again.

I give her my most stubborn glare.

She gives me the *you will right now or else* look.

I grunt and shuffle downstairs.

Bradley's sitting on a stool with his guitar on his lap. "Ready, Matt?"

I don't head to the drums. Instead, I sit on the couch.

"Aw, come on, man." Bradley swivels on his stool to face me. "Give it a shot. At least go look at your kit."

That sounds suspicious, so I do the crutches swing-and-step over to the drums, trying not to trip on the rugs.

I see it right away. Someone's installed a new double bass pedal. Bradley, judging by his smile.

"Jim and your parents paid for it. But I picked it out. Jim helped me set it up yesterday."

I don't say anything.

"Come on, Matt." Bradley's voice is quiet. "Just try it."

So I sit down and begin.

***

The drum lesson is...OK. Using my left foot is way hard. I feel bitter. But I don't lose my temper.

After Bradley leaves, I climb the stairs (which in my current state is basically equivalent to scaling a mountain) and plop on the living room couch. Mom and Dad sit with me.

Termite comes up to me, and I run a hand under his chin, feeling his loose folds of skin. "What's for dinner?" Usually after my lesson, Mom's in the kitchen, finishing cooking or setting the table.

"Dad ordered pizza." Mom's voice is cautious. "How was the new pedal?"

I don't respond right away. Instead, I look over my shoulder, out the window into the backyard. The sun is getting lower in the sky, peeking from behind trees. It's weird to think that just a few weeks ago we were watching the sunset and the bats downtown. It feels like another life.

"Matt." Dad's voice is stern. "Your mom and I, and Jim, spent a lot of money—"

"It was fine." I cut him off. I make myself look at my parents, realizing I haven't said thank you. "And I'm really grateful, OK? That was really nice of you, and Bradley, and Jim."

They look back at me. Mom's face says *You're suffering and I'm sad for you.* Dad's says *I know you're suffering, but that's no excuse to act like a jerk.*

"Will the pedal make drumming possible?" Mom tucks her hair behind her ear.

I lean my head back into the couch, sinking it into the padding as far as it will go. Termite puts his head right in my lap and licks my hand. "Yeah." My voice comes out quiet. "Yeah, it will. Thank you."

"You should tell Jim that."

I grunt, which maybe they take to mean OK.

***

Half an hour later, we're eating pizza around the table, and it's awkwardly quiet. I'm not talking. My head is bowed as I eat and try to ignore my right foot, both the pain and the uncomfortable boot.

"So..." Mom's finished eating. She twists a paper napkin in her hands. "Dad and I were looking at the calendar, and Camp Waller is coming up next month."

I don't look up. I don't say anything.

"I know you and Jim had fun last year," Mom says.

"Will our foot still be in the boot?"

"Most likely." Dad's finished eating too, and he leans back from the table.

"Then I don't want to go," I say without hesitating.

"But you and Jim had so much fun." Mom's voice is worried. "And I'm sure there's—"

"I don't want to go." I'm more forceful this time.

"What if Jim does?"

I look up sharply, and Mom can tell that wasn't the most sensitive thing to say.

"Then let him go." There's an edge to my voice. I reach for my crutches. "Let him go by himself. He can set an alarm for me every night and I'll go back to sleep." I stand and head for the stairs. "Not like I'd be missing out on anything anyway, right?"

"Matt, come back." Dad stands up and takes my crutches away. I wobble on one foot, scowling at him, before he guides me to sit back down at the table. "Are you sure?" He's making extra effort to make eye contact with me.

"Sure about letting Jim go to Camp Waller?"

Dad sighs. "We're not going to send Jim to Camp Waller alone."

Mom nods in agreement as she closes the empty pizza box.

"Why not? I don't care." It's hard to bring myself to care about anything in the next six to eight weeks.

"Are you sure that *you* don't want to go to Camp Waller?" Dad's still giving me that probing stare.

"*Yes.*" I sink deeper into my chair. "And seriously, if Jim throws a fit about it, tell him he can go by himself." I stand up again, determined to make it to my room this time. "He would love that, wouldn't he? He could go as Jim and not as Jett. No awkward one-week girlfriends to make him feel uncomfortable. No more Matt messing everything up." My words might be joking, except my voice is hard and bitter.

"Matt." Mom looks up at me, heartbroken. I pull my crutches away from Dad and head up the stairs.

Thursday, August 4
Jim

In Dad's car, I sit in the back seat, running my knuckles along the smooth window, staring out at buildings and cars passing by in the evening light. We're going to get my ankle checked out and hopefully hear that Matt and I can get off the crutches soon.

From the driver's seat, Dad speaks up. "Jim, I don't know if you realized, but Camp Waller's getting close."

I sit up straighter. "You mean you would let us go again? After what happened last year?"

Mom turns her head so I can see her profile and smiles. "Yes, we'd let you go again. As long as you learned your lesson."

"Oh, trust me, we did." I'm trying to sound funny and think Mom or Dad might laugh, but they don't.

"Would you want to go again?" Dad glances at me in the rearview mirror as we roll to a stop at a light.

"When is it?" I ask.

"Second week in September."

I look out the window again as we start moving. "So...we'll still be in the boot."

"Most likely."

I pull back at a seam of rubber on the top of the crutches sitting next to me and watch it spring back in place. "What did Matt say?"

"We're asking you, Jim."

I rub one eye. "I don't know. Wouldn't things be hard in a boot? The dance and the ropes course for sure." But I think about other parts. It could still be fun. Last year *was* really fun. "What about Matt? What does he want?"

Mom twists in her seat, pulling on the edge of it to turn around and look at me. "Why don't you talk to him about it?"

I sigh. "Because he won't talk to me about anything. Please, Mom? What did Matt say?"

"I don't think Matt's watching his messages, Jane," Dad murmurs. We're there, and he pulls into the parking lot.

I sink into the seat. I know Matt's not responding to my messages. I didn't know he isn't even watching them.

"OK." Mom picks up her wallet/phone case. "Jim, Matt said he doesn't want to go. He was adamant about it."

I sit up. "Well...OK, then." I feel the tiniest bit conflicted, the tiniest bit dejected. But I try to keep it out of my voice. "That's fine. I agree. So we don't have to go."

"Try to tell him anyway." Mom unbuckles her seatbelt with a click. "That might make him feel better."

"Yes, he was...bitter." Dad unbuckles, too. "He said—"

Mom interrupts in a low voice. "We don't have to tell him—"

"Tell me what?"

Mom sighs, her hand on the door handle, and Dad goes on. "He said if you threw a fit about it and wanted to go, you could go alone."

"And...how would we do that? We're kind of stuck with each other, if he hasn't noticed."

"Matt said you could set an alarm every night and he would wake up and go back to sleep."

"Oh." I lean back and look out the window, though in the parking lot there isn't much to stare at other than the sky, which is a desaturated gray. One of those deceiving summer skies that could almost be a winter sky, until you open the door and get blasted by a wave of heat. "Wow, he must really be depressed."

Mom and Dad open their car doors and get out, but I don't move. Dad opens my door. "He'll come out of it, Jim." His voice is gentle. "It's understandable. This is a big deal to him."

Mom stands next to my dad. "Not that it's your fault."

I sigh and close my eyes. They can keep saying that. I don't know if it makes it true.

Friday, August 5
Matt

Jim's getting creative. He must have realized I'm not reading his texts or watching his Vimers. He's started trying to communicate with me in different ways.

Monday morning, I wake up with an *I'm sorry* note taped around the medical boot. I throw it in the trash. On Wednesday, I pick up my phone to see that he's changed my wallpaper to a photo of Termite with a drawn-in speech bubble that says, "WOOF! That's dog for Jim says he's sorry!" Today there's a candy bar on my bed taped to a note in Jim's handwriting.

You know I helped pay for your new drum pedal right?

The note about the drum pedal makes me feel guilty enough to finally look at all the Vimers and text messages Jim's left for me. The first Vimer is of him sitting in the back seat of Mom's SUV, which is moving. Jim's in his soccer clothes with sweaty hair. He looks miserable.

"Matt, I'm so sorry." His face is screwed up in pain, and I'm guessing not just physical pain. "You're probably so ticked at me right now. It was an accident. I think you're going to have to miss church tomorrow, and I feel really, really bad. I'm sorry, Matt."

The rest of the Vimers follow, all apologetic:

"Matt, you didn't get up today. Come on, man, this should be your day. I'll try to take a nap later on and give it back to you."

"Matt, come on, don't do this! I'm sorry, alright? But don't check out. You've got to get up."

"Did Leo help? Zoe is coming tomorrow. If you keep staying in bed, I'm going to, too. Then we'll get smellier and smellier, and our body will need food and one of us will have to get up. I have lots of will power. It will probably be you."

When I had started to get up and engage again but continued to ignore his messages, Jim had changed tactics.

"OK," he says in one Vimer. "I admit my injury is a difficult thing you have to live through. And I am sorry. But it's not like you're the ideal body-sharing partner, either. Remember this incident?" Jim flips the phone camera around to show a video that's playing on his laptop screen.

In the video, fifteen-year-old me is kneeling on the kitchen floor, excitedly showing Jim a new trick Termite learned (licking me all over my mouth when I tell him "give kisses!").

Sitting on my bed watching, I can't help smiling. That had been a good one. I had known it would gross Jim out.

In the Vimer, Jim flips the camera around so it's pointing at his unamused face. "Seriously, Matt? Dis. Gus. Ting."

After I watch every Vimer and read every text, I send something back.

Saturday, August 6
Jim

I'm surprised to see a Vimer from Matt this morning. I've grabbed my phone and propped it up on my desk while I turn to get dressed, expecting to open Vimer and hear nothing, but at the sound of Matt's voice I rotate on my crutches (hopefully the last day I'll need them) to stop and watch it play.

"Hey, Jim." Matt's sitting on his bed staring down at his bedspread. There's a long pause when he doesn't say anything or move, just stares down. I slide into my desk chair.

In the video, Matt goes on. "I just watched all of your messages. The one with Termite made me smile." He smiles in the video, too, just barely. But then his face falls. "Part of me still wants to punch you in the face." His voice isn't angry; if anything, it's sad. "But it was an accident. I get it. And thanks for the drum pedal. I just..." He closes his eyes and looks pained. When he goes on, his voice is small. "Sometimes I wish so bad we could be normal."

The message ends. It's good to have him back, have him talking again, but what he says at the end makes me sad.

Matt—Fri, Aug 5, 7:43 AM

thanks for the pedal

Jim—Sat, Aug 6, 7:03 AM

don't mention it
and i'm really really really really sorry about our foot
did you talk to the drummer at church?
any chance he'll let you sub again?

Matt—Sun, Aug 7, 11:32 AM

no

Jim—Mon, Aug 8, 7:02 AM

no you didn't talk to him?
no you can't sub again?

Matt—Tue, Aug 9, 8:54 AM

haven't talked to him

didn't go to church

mom let me stay home

Jim—Wed, Aug 10, 7:25 AM

aw man matt
i'm sorry

chapter
twenty

Monday, August 8
Jim

Today marks the end of summer vacation for Leo and the start of his senior year. Mom has me and Matt start school, too. She's been lenient since the accident and hasn't made us do any schoolwork. But Monday morning, she makes sure I'm on time, and she sits with me while I do my history and economics.

During my lunch break, she drives me to the music studio where Matt takes drum lessons, and where I used to take guitar lessons. Now that I have more time on my hands (no soccer season for me), I've decided to take lessons again and brush up on my guitar skills.

Mom waits for me at the studio. (It feels humiliating not to drive.) In the car on the way home, she starts a conversation.

"Your soccer coach called just now." Mom slips on her sunglasses. A little rhinestone on the side sparkles in the sun. "He was wondering if he could come over tonight."

I look up from my phone. "My soccer coach?"

"Coach Turner. From last season."

I'm surprised. "Come over? What for?"

"He wants to talk to you, evidently." Mom sees my expression and smiles. "Don't worry, Jim, you're not in trouble. I think it will be a good thing."

***

After dinner, I'm sitting on the couch in the living room playing my acoustic guitar, feeling less and less like a poser as I practice. The doorbell rings. I put the guitar down and reach for my crutches.

"Stay there." Mom shoos me back down as she walks by. "I'll get it."

I stay on the couch listening as the front door opens. I hear Coach Turner's voice, and my mom's, and my dad's.

"Come in." Mom leads him into the living room.

"Hey, Coach." I half-stand, avoiding putting weight on my right foot, to give him a handshake. He shakes my hand and then motions for me to sit back down.

"How's your ankle, Jim?" Coach Turner sits on the couch perpendicular to mine. He was a good coach last spring season, particularly understanding of my condition. I've always liked him.

Dad sits next to him. Mom moves a throw pillow aside and sits next to me.

"The pain's gone down," I tell my coach. "And finally walking without crutches will be a big relief."

Coach smiles. "That's great. That will make everything possible."

I'm confused. "Make what possible?"

Coach leans forward, his elbows on his knees. "I have a proposition for you, Jim. I know how disappointed you must be, having to miss out on soccer season."

I look down and nod. It's quiet enough to hear the sound of the dishwasher running in the kitchen.

"I'm also wondering if there's a chance you might find yourself with some extra time on your hands?" Coach asks.

"Well," Mom starts right away. "It's been a good opportunity for the boys to refocus on their school—"

"*Yes*," I interrupt.

Coach smiles. "That seems funny to say, you having extra time on your hands. That wasn't insensitive, was it?"

"No," I assure him. "I miss soccer. It's nice," I look at Mom, "having something to do that isn't academic."

Mom taps her fingers on my guitar and pretends not to see my pointed look.

"Well, if your parents are OK with it," Coach glances at them, "I have an idea."

I sit up and move to the edge of the couch.

"There's a team on the kids' soccer league that could use an assistant coach."

I perk up. "Yeah?"

"The head coach is a volunteer, a parent of one of the boys on the team. And the league would be OK paying for an assistant for him."

"Pay?" My eyebrows raise. "You mean this is like a job?"

"Well, the pay isn't great," Coach warns.

"That's OK!" Then my smile falls. "But...I'm in a boot. How could I be an assistant coach?"

"These are six-year-olds. What their coach needs is someone else to stand on the field and help herd them. If you can do that, help call out to the kids, maybe walk around a little, that would be helpful enough."

I brighten again. "Really?"

Coach smiles and nods.

And then my parents jump in.

Mom uncrosses her legs and leans forward. "Are you sure this wouldn't tempt him to use his foot too much? He is still healing, after all."

"And what about days?" Dad asks. "You know Jim is only available every other day, and different days each week."

Coach nods like he's been expecting my dad's question. "There are two practices a week—Tuesday and Wednesday. And one game a week on Saturday. Jim will be able to go to one practice a week and every other game. On the days he's not there, the coach said he can bring his college-age son to help if needed."

"And Jim's foot?" Mom isn't going to give up.

"Again, all he'll need to do is stand on the field, maybe walk around a little."

Mom doesn't look convinced, sitting there biting her lip. Sigh. Mom. Why does she have to be such a worrier all the time?

"I'm in." I look at Coach Turner. "I'd love to. When do I start?"

Coach smiles again. "Next week."

"Just remember," Mom cautions me, "that this isn't just your ankle. If you slow down your healing, Matt is affected, too."

I exhale heavily and nod.

Mom and Dad copy Coach Turner when they see him stand. "I'll get you in touch with the team's coach. You can expect a call from him soon."

"Awesome." I try to stand too, but everyone waves me back down. Mom and Dad walk my coach out.

When they walk back in, they find me with a smile on my face.

"Come on, Mom," I say when she looks at me. "Be happy for me! This is great!"

"He will need something to fill his time," Dad says to her as she drags the curtains closed. "This way he gets to stay involved with soccer, and he'll be helping out a kids' team, too." Dad turns to me. "Six-year-olds, huh?" He smiles. "You'll have a blast."

I can't tell if he's being sarcastic or not.

Saturday, August 13
Matt

I'm getting stir-crazy at home. On Saturday after the sun goes down, I beg Mom and Dad to let me go for a walk. It's my first day of being allowed to walk without crutches. It's hot, but I don't care. I've hardly been out of the house lately. Mom and Dad go with me. We take Termite, and we do a slow circle around the neighborhood.

Mom's holding Termite's leash. "Matt, we wanted to check... The Camp Waller registration deadline is coming up. Are you sure you—"

"*Yes*." How many times am I going to have to go over this with them? "Yes, I'm sure. I don't want to go. And Jim doesn't, either. We agree."

Dad pats Termite on the head when he comes to walk next to him. "Agreeing with Jim does seem to make life easier."

"Yeah," I mutter so they can't hear. The hot weather outside is making the boot sweaty and uncomfortable. "So does not severely injuring our body."

***

Now that I've gotten past the knee-jerk reaction phase of not wanting to go to Camp Waller, deep inside I am sadder about it. Zoe and I talk about it on the phone at night.

"You're sure you're not going?" she asks.

I'm in my room, unwrapping the plastic from my boot after the boot-baths I hate taking. I miss showers. "Can you see me having any fun there with a boot on?"

"I'd hang back with you," she says. "I'd stand by you at the dance and during the ropes course, and the music workshop would still be fun."

That's so nice of her, I don't know what to say for a second. But I bring up my arguments, and we talk through them. What if we go and Jim insists on not going as Jett? What if we have to admit to everyone that we lied last year? What if we run into Andie and it's super awkward? What if there's no accessible tub for my boot-baths and I start to stink?

Zoe still works hard to convince me.

"I'd only be there half the time," I remind her as I towel my hair dry. "It would be Jim the other half."

"Well, I would have more fun half the time, then."

That comment makes me smile—the kind of dorky smile I'm grateful she can't see.

"Really, though." I sit down on my bed. "I seriously doubt Jim would be down with going as Jett. What would everyone think if me and Jim told them the truth and that we had lied to them last year?"

There was half a second of hesitation. "They would understand."

"Not all of them." I stretch out on my back. "Some kids would be hurt or weirded out. I know it."

"Well, they're dumb."

"And you're amazing."

Zoe doesn't talk for a second. I think (and hope) her face might have her own dorky smile.

so you got a job

yeah! 😛

i don't know how it will go but it'll keep me involved in soccer and i'll get paid

i'm not being picky

so a part-part time job as an assistant coach to a bunch of kids? how much can you possibly be making?

probably about as much as a part-part time dog walker

yeah whatever

chapter
twenty-one

Tuesday, August 16
Jim

    I'm nervous for my first time helping coach the little kids' soccer team. I haven't had a whole lot of experience with young kids. But kids or no, this is something that involves soccer, that will fill my free time, and that I'll get paid for. Triple bonus.

    The coach of the co-ed team, a dad who tells me to call him Coach Garrett, has me meet him on the field for the first practice I'll be attending. I've talked to Coach Garrett on the phone but never met him in person. I check the note I have written in my phone as I walk up to the field. The field farthest from the park... I walk over and see a man with black hair motioning to a group of young kids who are standing in a line, taking turns shooting a soccer ball into the goal.

    "Coach Garrett?" As I walk up, I wish I weren't in a boot. My approach feels painstakingly slow.

    "Jim?" Coach Garrett comes over to me. "Nice to meet you." He shakes my hand. "Is it OK if I put you to work right away? Peter!" He calls to a boy who looks up from his place in the line. "Come with me to the goal! Kids!" The rest of the kids look at him. "This is Coach Jim. He's going to be my helper. So listen to him like you would listen to me!"

    Coach Garrett leans closer to me. "Monitor the line, tell them when to kick, and send them to the back of the line. I'm going to work with Peter." Coach Garrett jogs over to the goal, and I walk to the front of the line of kids. I tell myself to act confident—these kids can probably sense fear.

    "Hey, guys." The late afternoon sun beats down on my neck. "I'm Coach Jim."

    "Why's your foot in that black boot?" a little voice asks.

    "I hurt it." I wave a bug away from my face. "The boot is helping it heal."

    "How'd you hurt it?" another kid says.

"Playing soccer," I admit. The kids stare at me with wide eyes. I have their attention. That's unexpected. "Which is why practice is important! So, who's next?"

Friday, August 26
Jim

It takes me a couple practices, but I start to feel at ease with Coach Garrett and the kids (our team is called the Sharks).

And then I start to enjoy it—even the hot summer air and the smell of bug spray and sunscreen that seems to follow the kids around like a cloud when they cluster together. I wish over and over that my foot was healed so I could help teach dribbling and passing, but I have to be content with standing, giving pointers, and helping herd the kids while Coach Garrett works with them one on one.

I get to enjoy the kids, too. Sometimes they're frustrating because they get distracted or won't listen, but once I get to know them, get to know their names and different personalities, they're a fun bunch. Coach Garrett tells me they ask for me when I'm not there. That makes me feel good.

My favorite kid is a little girl named Charlie (she hates it when the coach calls her Charlotte). She works hard. She listens well. She cares about the game. The only thing she doesn't seem to have a lot of is natural talent. Once after practicing shooting goals, Charlie misses the goal for the third time in a row. Frustrated, she kicks the grass and runs to the back of the line.

"Kids, keep taking your turn!" I catch the ball Coach Garrett tosses me and drop it on the grass at the front of the line. "Bo, you're next!" Then I walk to the back of the line.

"You'll get it, Charlie." I wait until she looks up at me. "You keep working hard like you do, and you'll get it."

She looks hopeful. Since then, she smiles when I compliment her or tell her she's doing well. It feels like a nice thing to do.

Tuesday, August 30
Jim

Coach Garrett is wrapping up the end of practice on Tuesday night. The kids' first game is coming up on Saturday, and they're all excited, nervous, or both.

Charlie is one of the nervous ones. After Coach Garrett leads a team cheer at the end of practice, she walks to the sidelines with a straight face.

"Hey! Charlie!" I walk up to her. "Did you know I was nervous for my first soccer game?"

"You were?"

For some reason, the kids think I'm a good soccer player, which is ridiculous because they've never seen me play, and all they know about me is that I was dumb enough to hurt my foot. I think Coach Garrett has planted the idea in their minds. Still, it's unexpected to see Charlie surprised that I, the mighty Coach Jim, was once nervous.

"Sure." I put my hands in my pockets. "It can be scary facing another team. But you know what?"

"What?"

"It's good that you're nervous."

She gulps from her pink and orange water bottle and looks at me like I'm crazy.

"It means you care. And that's a great quality in a soccer player." I get Charlie to smile at that. Then she looks past me and waves.

"Hi, Rachel!"

I turn around to see a girl walking up, about my age. She's wearing a T-shirt and gym shorts, but that doesn't hide the fact that she's pretty.

"Hey, Charlie." Rachel, I presume, walks up and gives Charlie a side hug. "How was practice?"

Charlie dangles her water bottle from one hand. "This is my sister, Rachel." They do look like sisters. They have the same straight, reddish hair. Charlie takes her sister's hand. "This is Coach Jim."

"Ah, *you're* Coach Jim." Rachel smiles. "We hear about you at home."

"Good stuff, I hope?"

Rachel puts a hand on Charlie's head and wiggles it. She smiles down at her. "What do you think?"

"Rachel's a *real* soccer player." Charlie hugs Rachel around the legs.

"Oh, yeah?" I fold my arms. "You play in the pros?"

Rachel laughs. "My high school team." She shoves Charlie away. "Not as big of a deal as she thinks. Well, come on, Charlie. Time to go home."

They walk toward the gravel parking lot, passing out from under the bright field lights into the shadows of the approaching evening.

"See you on Saturday, Charlie!" I call after them. "You're gonna do great!"

I'm grateful that Mom isn't there to pick me up yet. I would be humiliated if Rachel saw me getting picked up like one of the six-year-olds. Stupid boot.

Wednesday, August 31
Matt

"I love you very much and I know you love me." Leo paces the floor of his bedroom. "You know I'd do anything in the world for you and…" He closes his eyes in concentration. "And…"

I whisper-read from the script in my hands. "And I want you to do just this—"

"Just this little thing for me," Leo goes on as he remembers his line.

I put on my best old-lady voice and read, "What do you want us to do?"

"Don't *do* anything." Leo's pacing flips up the corner of the rug in his room, revealing the rubber backing. "I mean don't do *anything*. Don't let anyone in this house—and leave Mr. Hoskins right where he is."

"Why?" My old-lady voice creaks.

Leo stops pacing and turns to me with his normal voice. "Could you make Martha and Abby sound different? That would make it easier."

I'm unamused. "How many old-lady voices do you think I have?"

"Oh, just make one sound higher pitched, like this." Leo puts on an impressive old-lady voice I wouldn't be able to pull off and then repeats the line. I laugh.

Leo smiles, too, and sits down on his desk chair, which rolls a few feet across the hardwood floor. "I think I'm probably done for the night, anyway. I've got a ton of homework to do. Thanks for the help, Matt." He has a lead role in his school's upcoming play, *Arsenic and Old Lace*. I'm helping him practice his lines.

"No problem." I put down the script. I'm lying on my stomach on his bed, and I rest my chin on my hands. "And I'll work on that old-lady voice for next time." For a second it's quiet, and the smile I have from when Leo made me laugh fades. When I'm doing things like practicing lines with Leo, I'm able to forget that my foot is in a boot. It's always depressing to remember, to become aware of the weight of it as my foot hangs off the bed.

Leo notices. "How do you feel about doing my calculus proofs, too?"

"If you want to fail."

Leo rolls over to his beat-up orange backpack and pulls out his laptop. "What about writing a short English paper?"

"Probably not a good idea."

"Spanish homework?"

"*No hablo español*, Leo." (Mom hasn't made me and Jim learn a second language. Yet.)

"Typing up a government presentation?"

I pause. "Sure." I raise my upper body and hold out a hand. "I'll do that."

"Really?" Leo's surprised, but he happily hands over his laptop and a notebook with his handwriting and shows me what text to copy and where to put it. I prop myself up on my elbows and start typing.

"I can't believe school only started a few weeks ago." Leo pulls another notebook out of his bag and opens it. "I hope you like doing my homework and helping me practice lines, Matt. Between school and theater, it may be the only way we get to hang out this year."

"I sure hope not." Also, I'm not fooled. Leo's thrilled to have a lead role in *Arsenic and Old Lace*. I know he's going to do great, and I'm excited to watch the performance.

I create a new slide and keep typing. "I'm not good for much else until this stupid boot comes off anyway."

"That's not true." Leo leans over his desk, flipping pages.

"It's totally true. I can't work, I'm a crappy drummer all of a sudden, I can't go to the gym—" I have to stop myself. I've made Leo sit through enough of my complaining sessions.

"You *are* getting better at video games." Leo turns away from his notebook and picks up the giant plastic tub of candy on his shelf (right now it's licorice). He pulls out a stick and tears off a bite, then tosses another licorice stick next to me. "You can't deny that," he says with the candy hanging out of his mouth.

He's right about that one. Since the injury, I've started playing a lot more video games than I used to.

I pick up the candy. "No chance we'll play tonight, right?"

Leo's silent, and when I look up, I can tell that the answer is no.

"Sorry." He gestures to his notebook with his licorice stick. "Too much homework."

"That's cool. Don't worry about it." I tear off a bite of my own licorice and go back to typing.

Even though it isn't video games, even though it's practicing lines and helping with homework, I'm glad I'm able to hang out with Leo. It beats sitting at home wishing I could be at work with Zoe, or at drum lessons, or in yoga class.

Stupid boot.

***

The stupid boot has caused a lot of changes to my life. No working or exercising leaves me with a lot more time than I used to have. Dad tries to encourage me to find something different to fill my time, another hobby or skill. Mom tells me to focus on academics. Bradley says I should really throw myself into learning the double bass pedal, practice for hours every day. But trying to use my left foot is *hard*. Instead, I've started playing more video games at Leo's. I feel apathetic about everything, even the drums. I don't practice on my own as much as I used to, and I stop going into the studio for lessons. It doesn't seem worth it, especially when Mom has to drive me there.

But the worst part about not being able to drive is not being able to work. And the worst part about that is less time with Zoe.

I've forgiven Jim for breaking our foot. I don't hate him. It was an accident. I've accepted that. But I can't move past the sulky mood that all the disruptions to my half-life have caused.

Saturday, September 3
Jim

It's time for my little Sharks' first game. As nervous as some of them are, they were all thrilled when they got their bright blue uniforms, and they proudly wear them now.

Since it's a Saturday morning, my parents come out to see the team play. I guess I've started talking about the kids at home, entertaining my parents with their funny stories. So they make the drive to the Soccer Pros outdoor field to watch. (And, OK, because it isn't too big of a deal for them to stay after they have to give me a ride here. I can't wait to drive again.)

And we win! I couldn't be happier if I were a player on my own team. After the two teams high-five each other at the end of the game, and our

Sharks come running off the field, Coach Garrett gives them a post-game congratulatory speech, and they head off to meet their parents.

I congratulate them, too. "Way to go, Peter! Great save! You did great, too, Bo, awesome goal!" I give all the kids fist bumps as they walk by me. "Charlie!" I act super excited for her. "I can't believe that pass you made!" I give her a high five. She's all smiles.

I turn to see someone walk up, a woman I assume is Charlie's mom. She and Charlie start talking a few feet away from me, their voices drowned out by the parent chatter and little kid shrieks all around us. But Charlie's mom isn't the only one who walks up. Her sister soon follows.

"Hey, Rachel." I turn to face her.

"Congrats on the win." She's wearing athletic clothes again and a smile.

"Hey, the credit all goes to them." I gesture to the little six-year-olds stampeding to take juice boxes and granola bars from this week's snack mom.

Rachel nods at my boot. "What happened to your foot, by the way?"

I grimace and tap my left tennis shoe on the boot. "Distal fibular fracture."

She winces. "Ouch. Were you playing soccer?"

"Trying out." I fold my arms over my shirt, covering up the word COACH. "Big surprise, I didn't make a team. I ended up here instead. It's been fun, though."

"What team were you trying out for?" Rachel swishes a long ponytail off her shoulder. "The high school team? Do you go to Elliston?"

"No." I shake my head. "I'm homeschooled. I've been playing for Capital Soccer Club for the past few years."

"Oh." Rachel gets a sly smile. "Are you any good?"

I stammer for a few seconds before saying, "I don't know. I mean, I hope so."

She laughs. "Well, you *are* a good coach. Seriously, Charlie loves you. Thanks for encouraging her at practice. I know she can get discouraged sometimes."

I try not to smile too big at the compliment. "She tries hard. She probably wants to grow up to be like you and knows that the pressure's on."

Rachel smiles and rolls her eyes.

"Well, are you any good?" I ask. "How long have you played on your school's team?"

"I'm a sophomore. But…I am a starter on varsity." She sees my blank face and gives a small shy shrug. "Varsity's usually for juniors and seniors."

"Oh!" I nod. "Oh. Right. And—cool!" I feel like a dork. I hate when it shows that I'm homeschooled. "Yeah—see?" I try to recover. "The pressure for Charlie *is* on."

"Whatever, Jim." She lightly shoves me with her arm. Her skin is warm in the morning sunlight. I get excited to hear her say my name—not Coach Jim. Just Jim. Me. Maybe it shows on my face because she laughs.

"Well, I'll see you later!" Rachel walks away with Charlie and her mom toward the parking lot. I stand and wave.

Jim—Mon, Sep 5, 7:23 AM

so? did mom and dad show you the video? did
you see how awesome my team did?

Matt—Tue, Sep 6, 7:22 AM

i saw the video

brought back some memories

remember when we played when we
were like six and dad was our coach?

Jim—Wed, Sep 7, 7:06 AM

haha yeah
based on the videos of your games i'm pretty
sure you just played for the treats at the end

Matt—Thu, Sep 8, 7:31 AM

so? it was like the only time we got to drink capri suns

Jim—Fri, Sep 9, 7:29 AM

#howmattseesthegame

chapter
twenty-two

Thursday, September 8
Matt

It's the beginning of September, and Jim and I are supposed to start a break from school. But the thought of spending my break sitting at home with a broken foot instead of working with Zoe is so depressing, I beg Mom to switch the schedule around, to keep us in school longer and postpone our break until we're fully healed. She and Jim agree. So, two more weeks of school.

Hooray.

You know, it really isn't fair.

It's Jim's fault our foot is in a boot, but he seems to be doing fine with it on. Thriving, even. I can tell he likes his assistant coach job. And he's started taking guitar lessons again.

Then there's me. No work, no driving, less Zoe, super hard drum sessions, no yoga, no runs with Termite. Even hearing that Jim's getting the boot off tomorrow doesn't make me feel much better because we have weeks of physical therapy ahead of us before I can use my foot normally again. I even have to go to some of the physical therapy appointments, which I think is unfair.

I'd rather exercise like I used to than have to take baby steps practicing to bend a stupid hurt ankle. Over the past few weeks, we've been cleared to do some light strength training at the gym with our arms, but, other than the occasional walk, that's all the exercising I get to do.

Even though I'm glad when I can go back to the gym, another crappy consequence of the boot is not being able to go as myself. Jim and I have always scanned our own key cards when we enter. We have people there greet us by our own names. They assume we're normal twins. But what are we going to do now? Say that both Matt and Jim happen to be in medical boots at the same time? So I start going to the gym as Jim. He offers to go as me, but I want Jim to be the one people see in the boot, not me.

A few times people, like the yoga instructor, talk to me at the gym, thinking they're talking to me, Matt. But I have to correct them and tell them I'm Jim, that Matt is my twin brother. Where has Matt been? I don't know. I guess he got busy with life. When is he coming back to the gym? I'm not sure. Don't we talk? Sure, we're just not nosy. Why don't we ever do anything together? We like our space, like being treated as individuals instead of twins. The same conversations, the same explanations, the same lies.

Saturday, September 10
Matt

Saturday morning, I wake up and the boot is off.

Jim acts excited in his last message of the day, like getting the boot off is an early Christmas and is going to make me the happiest kid on earth. But I'm not elated. Don't get me wrong, it's nice to have the boot off, but it's bittersweet. Putting weight on my ankle comes with random pangs of pain. I have to take it easy, I have to go to physical therapy today, and I can't use my ankle to drum yet.

The rest of Jim's last message makes me grumbly like his others have lately. He likes his job, the kids are fun, he's getting better at the guitar...blah blah blah. I slouch on my bed in my still-dark bedroom as I listen. I know he isn't trying to make me feel bad. And I do try not to let it bother me. But I can't help reacting to the last thing he says.

"Yeah, coaching has been fun," he says. "But I'm looking forward to next season." His voice is casual as he sits at his desk, fiddling with his bendy lamp that squeaks as he moves it. "One of my old coaches checked in with me and said they miss me—isn't that cool? And there will be tryouts again in February, too, so I'll get another chance."

I prop myself up on one elbow and send something back right away. "What?!" My face is dimly lit in the dark bedroom, but Jim will have no problem reading my emotions. "You think you're playing soccer after this?" I gesture down to my foot. "Doesn't this prove that it's too dangerous? It's not fair for you to use our body to do things that have a good chance of injuring it again." My voice gets hard. "Yeah, Jim, I know, it sucks. But so does not getting to be a drummer in a band."

Sunday, September 11
Jim

Matt's first Vimer to me makes my mouth drop open. He wants me to quit soccer? Seriously? I forget about the shirt I'm about to put on, dropping it in a crumpled pile on the desk as I pull out my desk chair. I have to say something to him right away.

"That's ridiculous, Matt!" I hold the phone with one hand and twist in the office chair until I can lean forward against the desk. "Soccer's not that dangerous. We could get hurt doing any exercise—do you expect us to stop going to the gym? Not run anymore? Not ride a bike?" I frown and gesture down toward my foot. "This was an accident. Accidents could happen anywhere. I've played for years without any other big injuries. So you can't tell me I suddenly have to quit." I'm about to end it there, but I can't stop bringing the camera close to my face and adding something. "Yeah, you've always been jealous that I'm on a team and you don't get to play in a band." My voice is coming out louder and faster. "But that's not my fault. And you know what?" I pull the phone back from my face and tip it up so my bare right foot is visible. "Neither is this."

I end the message, realizing that Matt didn't even say anything about the boot being off. Of course, that only makes me madder.

Tuesday, September 13
Jim

A couple days later at breakfast, I speak up.

"Matt says I should quit soccer."

Predictably, both my parents look surprised.

"Why?" Mom asks, sincerely confused. Inside I rejoice. This is going to be easy.

"He says it's too dangerous." I try to keep my voice sounding honestly confused instead of pouty. "That I could get hurt again, so it's not fair for me to play a sport like that, since it's his body, too."

"He said that?" Dad asks.

"Yeah."

"Can we see what he said?" Dad sounds honest too, not like he doesn't trust me, but like he wants to help. But inside, I groan. I don't want to show my parents my conversation with Matt because I haven't been the nicest to him, either. But I pull out my phone and show it to Mom and Dad as I replay my and Matt's Vimers over the past few days.

There's the first one from me, casual and friendly, celebrating the boot being off and mentioning I want to play soccer again. There's the one from Matt where he gets mad. There's the one from me where I tell him he's jealous and the injury isn't my fault.

"The gym and running isn't the same as soccer," Matt says angrily in his next Vimer. "And, yeah, OK, I get it, you love it. So play casually. Keep coaching your little kid team and stay involved with soccer that way. But it's obvious that Capital Soccer now has too much pressure and is too intense. It's not fair for you to play a sport that'll result in injuries. Maybe not injuries all the time," he concedes. "But for sure more injuries than, I don't know, playing the drums." Then he scoffs. "And you really think the injury isn't your fault? That's crap, Jim."

Before I can stop it, my response to Matt starts playing, and I cringe as my parents watch it.

"You're just bitter that your life's been lame and you think it's my fault. You just want to make me miserable like you. Well, being miserable is your choice. Quit blaming me, grow up, and get over it."

Mom and Dad are quiet after the videos end. We all sit back in our chairs. I'm the one who speaks first.

"He can't ask me to do that, right? Quit soccer?"

"No," Mom says, looking distracted. "No, he can't ask you to do that. We'll talk to him about it." She looks at me. "But try to be more understanding. This has been a really hard thing for—"

"Yeah, I get it, poor, poor Matt," I interrupt. Dad looks at me disapprovingly. I sigh. I know they're right. But I don't like it. Not wanting to talk about it anymore, I grab half an untoasted bagel and head up to my room, careful to not put too much weight on my right foot.

Wednesday, September 14
Matt

Watching Jim's message after I wake up makes me grumpy all morning. Get over it? Really? He's been so nice and apologetic since the injury. Why's he now being such a jerk about it?

That evening, Mom, Dad, and I eat out. In a booth at our favorite Chinese place, Mom brings something up.

"Matt?" Her voice is gentle and calm, but I have a feeling I'm not going to like what she says next. "Can we talk to you about something?"

I sigh and nod.

"You can't ask Jim not to play soccer," Mom says gently.

I grunt. I should have known he'd tell them.

"That isn't fair to him," Dad goes on.

"I'm not asking him to never play soccer," I say. "Just not for Capital Soccer. Now that he's up a league, it's extra competitive. Isn't there a greater chance for injuries now?"

"Maybe," Dad says slowly. "But—"

I interrupt. "It's not fair to *me* for him to use our body in a dangerous way like that—"

"Soccer's not dangerous." Dad interrupts me now, sounding impatient. "If he wanted to get into extreme skateboarding or motocross stunt riding, that would be different, but—"

"But injuries could still happen," I say.

"Injuries could happen doing anything," Mom says. "You can't force Jim to avoid all hobbies because there's a chance he could get hurt. *You* could get hurt. Even from drumming." Mom glances at Dad and mutters, "Right?"

"Right," Dad says, smiling slightly. But he looks serious as he turns back to me. "The point is, Matt, yes, you and Jim share a body. But you can't dictate each other's lives."

"Half-lives," I mutter grumpily.

Dad ignores it. "As long as you're both being reasonable about any hobbies or sports you want to do, you should be free to do them. You may *rather* Jim not play soccer, but ultimately, it's his choice."

I grunt.

"And I think," Mom says gently, "after you calm down, you'll realize that you do want to let him play soccer because he loves it so much. You want him to be happy. Right?"

"Depends on the day," I mutter. Mom looks sad at that, but Dad smiles. He thinks I'm joking.

I don't think I am.

Thursday, September 15
Jim

"*Fine*, Jim," Matt says in his message this morning. "Mom and Dad said I can't keep you from playing soccer. So do what you want." His frown flattens out; he looks less frustrated and more pleading. "But please try not to get hurt. This has sucked. For you, too, I know."

I send something back.

"Of course I'll try not to get hurt," I say, exasperated. "I've always done that. You think I've liked this? And I know how awful it's been for you." I sigh. "Matt, believe it or not, I actually remember that you're in here, too. Well..." I tilt my head and look up at the ceiling, feigning thoughtfulness. "Most of the time."

Friday, September 16
Matt

Jim's message in the morning makes me feel better, even though I failed in keeping him from soccer. I think deep down I knew it wouldn't happen. But it was worth a shot.

Still, it isn't like I'm in a good mood during the day. And, like I've been doing lately any time Mom doesn't stop me, instead of doing my schoolwork downstairs in the homeschool room like I'm supposed to, I do it upstairs on my bed.

In the afternoon, after Mom goes over English with me, I sneak back upstairs to my room and do my science sitting on my bed with my back against the wall and my feet hanging over the edge. I'm being more or less a good student, maybe only half half-heartedly (so...three-quarters-heartedly?) going through my lesson. Things are fine, until I'm reading about a study that mentions a scientist named Dr. Gregory Burke. Burke... how common of a last name is that? *No way*, I tell myself. But...maybe way? I know it's a bad idea, I know I shouldn't do it, but I search my emails to find the one I forwarded to myself from my mom's account, the one originally from Dr. Anand, the one with the paper on the Burke-Dalton procedure attached. I find it, open it, skim it...

And yes way. Dr. Gregory Burke, apparently with his colleague named Dalton, is indeed the author of the same paper. Crazy.

But once I open the paper, I can't stop myself from reading bits of it. Just like I know I shouldn't.

Why do I know I shouldn't do it? Why is it a bad idea?

Because I've spent the last two months trying as hard as I can to not think about the Burke-Dalton procedure. Trying to forget it exists. Jim's soccer injury is depressing enough to make me want to spend eight weeks in bed. Knowing that life doesn't *have* to be like this, that there's a way out, but that we aren't going to take it—that's even worse. I realized early on that I can't do that to myself. There's enough to get depressed about without getting depressed about not doing the procedure, too. So I haven't let myself think about it.

Of course, it's hard to forget something exists when you're reading a scientific paper on it.

With effort, I close the window. I need to distract myself. I pull out my phone instead and start mindlessly scrolling, liking, and sharing. Funny animals. Dances. Stupid human tricks. News from family and friends. Ah. That's better.

I come across a post from my cousin Lacey. She's on my mom's side, our next oldest cousin, though she's nine years older than me and Jim. She's the best, the type of older cousin who loves and spoils and babysits all the younger cousins, and we all look up to and adore her for it. The post is a picture of her and her boyfriend announcing their engagement (no surprise there; we've all been predicting it for months). They look happy, and I'm happy for her, but as I start to like the post and comment with my congratulations, I find that I can't.

I'm feeling something else. A wash of hopelessness that comes with the realization that that will never be me. Announcing my engagement online. That will never be me. No, me is sitting on my bed crippled with someone else's injury. Even if it's not his fault. Even if he feels really bad about it and buys me drum pedals and candy bars as apology gifts. I'm still here, my foot recovering, nothing I can do about it. And even if the exact same thing doesn't happen again, stuff like it will. Again and again. *That's* me.

I drop the phone on the bedspread and push the computer off my lap.

Sometimes this thing happens to me, and I hate it so much that I've never told anyone about it, not even Jim. But sometimes I start thinking about life, about the way I live and my body and sharing it with Jim and all the implications it has, and I just start feeling trapped. Like, really trapped, like I'm actually trapped somewhere and I can't get out. Trapped in my body, I guess, with Jim, because I guess I am. And I start breathing fast, and I curl up and sweat, and I just lie there feeling scared until in a few minutes the feeling passes.

It hasn't happened in over a year, but now, sitting on the bed after seeing Lacey's post, so soon after rereading the paper on the Burke-Dalton procedure, I know it's going to happen again.

My mind starts racing as I think about all the other things, all the other hundreds of ways I will never be normal. And, without being able to help it, I'm soon on my side on the bed, my arms curled around my legs, breathing fast and getting warm.

Of course, that's when Mom comes into the room.

"Matt?" She comes over to the bed. "Matt! Are you OK?"

I don't answer—I can't—I stay there, curled up and breathing fast, shallow breaths.

Mom calls for my dad, and soon he's there, and Mom's sitting on my bed with a hand on my back and Dad's standing over me, and before they can say anything the feeling of terror passes and, shaking, I uncurl and lie on the bed.

"Matt, are you OK?" Mom says quietly.

I shut my eyes tight and nod, as embarrassed as anything else.

"What happened?"

I shrug.

"Has this happened before?" Dad asks carefully.

My eyes are closed, but I nod.

"Very often?"

I shake my head.

"Since when?"

I shrug again. But then, "Since we were thirteen," I mumble.

Mom hugs me, and I feel Dad put a hand on my back, too.

"It's called an anxiety attack," Mom says softly. "It happens to lots of people."

"Why didn't you tell us?" Dad asks. He doesn't sound stern or disappointed. He sounds concerned.

I shrug again.

"You can always tell us," Mom says, and she succeeds in getting me to sit up.

My eyes are finally open, and I look at the floor, nodding.

"Is this about the injury?" Dad asks as he pulls over my desk chair.

"About everything," I mumble. "Sometimes I just feel really...trapped. Like, in this body. In this life. Like this is how it's going to be forever and there's no way out."

Mom and Dad don't respond. Instead, Mom hugs me and brings me a bowl of mint chocolate chip ice cream. Dad pulls my laptop back over and sits with me on the bed. He opens YouTube and together we watch videos of a bunch of things exploding in slow motion.

Saturday, September 17
Jim

During Matt's last Vimer yesterday, he's sitting in bed, still dressed. Only his desk light is on, so his face is half illuminated. It looks like late at night.

"Hey, Jim." He's looking down and his voice is low. "I was thinking about the Burke-Dalton procedure today."

I admit I'm surprised.

"I know no one's talked about it in a while. I know Mom and Dad gave a pretty adamant no. But..." He breathes in deep. "I couldn't help it, even though I knew I shouldn't." His face stays pointing down, but his eyes glance up at the camera. "Um...have you? Ever thought about it again?"

I pause before sending something back.

"Sure, I've thought about it," I say honestly. "I would still do it. I don't know if Mom and Dad would feel any differently, though."

That Vimer has me a little worried about Matt. Later at breakfast, I find a reason to worry more.

"Jim," Mom says carefully at the table. "Do you ever get anxiety attacks?"

I look up, a little surprised. "I don't think so." I pause. "Do I?"

"I think you would know if you did," Dad says. "You might feel so scared or anxious that you have physical symptoms, like breathing quickly or sweating or your heart racing or not being able to stop shaking."

"Oh." I nod my head slowly, then shake it. "No, I don't think so. I mean, maybe when I was seven and scared to go off the high dive..." I pause and look at Mom's and Dad's faces, wondering why they're asking, when it hits me. "Does Matt?"

Mom and Dad both look at their plates.

"Sometimes," Mom says. "He had one yesterday."

"How often?" I say uncertainly.

"Not very often," Dad says.

I go on, still hesitantly. "What does he get anxious about?"

Mom and Dad don't answer right away.

"Oh," I say, looking down. "Right." Now him asking about the procedure makes sense. I look up. "Is he OK?"

"Yes." Mom forces a smile. "Yes, he's OK. If it ever happens to you, will you let us know?"

"Oh, yeah, sure," I say, a little distracted because I'm already wondering why Matt has never told me.

***

That night, I sit in the hall on the floor in the dark. Mom and Dad's room is open a crack and they're talking loud enough that I can hear almost everything they're saying. Matt and I have discovered that eavesdropping on our parents is surprisingly easy. As long as Mom and Dad see me take our sleep medication, they have no doubt that I'll be in bed snoozing because I can't stay awake for long after I take it. All I have to do is fake it, and they don't suspect a thing.

After hearing about Matt's anxiety attack, I admit I want to know more, but I don't know how to ask my parents without seeming nosy or Matt without making him uncomfortable. But I'm in luck; that's exactly what Mom and Dad are talking about.

"That was so scary to see," Mom's saying.

I'm worried and curious at the same time—how was it scary? What happened?

"I'm surprised it's been going on for years and we've never found out about it," Dad says.

Years?

"I thought he'd feel so much better now that the boot is off," Mom says. "But it hasn't picked him up like I thought it would."

"Yeah," Dad sighs. There's a pause, then he goes on. "But he'll be OK. You're right; it happens to lots of people. And now that we know, we can help him manage them more."

"Maybe we should get him in counseling." Mom's voice is quieter and harder to hear.

"I've thought about that, too," Dad says. "Honestly, I've thought before that counseling wouldn't be a bad thing for both of them."

I'm surprised, not expecting them to mention me.

"I hope he will tell us if it happens again." Mom sighs. "He probably won't want to."

"You know what was just as scary to me?" Dad says, and his voice is quieter. I strain to hear. "Sure, it was scary to see him curled up and having trouble breathing, but I thought it was worse to hear the way he talked about their life."

"Trapped? Is that the word he used?"

"Trapped forever and there's no way out," Dad says with a flat voice.

"I think that's just how the anxiety attack made him feel," Mom says. "That's normal, right?"

"I don't think those attacks are the only time he feels trapped," Dad says, and his voice sounds like his thoughts are far away. There's a pause. "It's probably worse now that he thinks there really is a way out."

"Are you talking about the procedure?" Mom asks.

Dad must nod because Mom moans. "Oh, I wish he had never found that email."

"It's so hard," Dad says. "I can see how to them, this procedure sounds amazing. But I think they're just too young to be capable of truly taking the risk into account."

I'm a little offended at that. Who says we're too young?

"They are," Mom agrees. "They're so young. I can't even imagine, Dave." She does sound tortured. "Sending them into an operating room and knowing there's a fifty/fifty chance we would lose one of them?"

"It would be awful," Dad agrees. He sighs. "But I wish Matt didn't have to feel trapped forever with no way out. I wish he didn't have thoughts like that."

"Let's get him in counseling."

"Maybe..." Dad still sounds distracted. "Maybe Jim, too."

I don't like that. I don't like the thought of doing counseling, and I don't like being lumped in with Matt.

"But we'll figure it out, Jane. They'll both be OK."

That seems to be the end of the conversation, so I sneak back to my room to talk to Matt.

Sunday, September 18
Matt

On Sunday, I open my phone almost apprehensively. What does Jim have to say about the Burke-Dalton procedure? Has he changed his mind?

His first message calms me down. He hasn't changed his mind. Unfortunately, he doesn't think Mom and Dad have, either.

But a few messages later there's another, late at night, in Jim's dark room where I can barely see his face.

"Hey, Matt." He's almost whispering. "I eavesdropped on Mom and Dad tonight. They were talking about you." He looks a little ashamed. "I hope that's OK that I listened. They, um, were talking about your anxiety attack."

Hearing Jim mention the anxiety attack makes my cheeks flush in embarrassment. I mean, it's only Jim. The person closer to me than anyone else. The person I share a body with, for crying out loud. I shouldn't be embarrassed that he knows. But I am.

"Sorry you have those."

Hearing Jim say that doesn't make me feel any better. I admit that I've been wondering if Jim gets anxiety attacks too, maybe even hoping he does. Hoping it isn't just me. But somehow, deep down, I think I've always known he never has.

Jim seems to get that I won't want to talk about the attacks, because he moves on. "Mom and Dad are worried about you. They want to get you into counseling. Me, too." He makes a face. "They talked about the procedure, too. It scares them and they don't want to do it. But..." He pauses. "If we're careful, this might be the best time to change their minds. They're worried about you, and after the injury and that disagreement about me playing soccer—" He takes a breath. "Anyway, things have been difficult. Maybe now is the time they'll listen."

***

After church I'm sitting on the couch in the living room, not doing much but staring into the backyard and thinking about if, when, and how I can talk to my parents about the procedure. Mom comes and sits next to me.

She looks at me quietly for a moment before speaking. "Will you promise to tell us if you ever have an anxiety attack again?"

I nod.

She rubs my back. "I'm so sorry, Matt. That looked awful."

I just shrug, not planning on saying anything. But then, "I just feel really trapped," I say, apparently taking a stab at expressing how I feel. "Sometimes life is really, really hard." I gesture to my right foot in a sock resting on the rug. "This, and other stuff, too. A lot of the stuff that's happened this past year." I take a deep breath. "Sometimes I feel like this year has been the hardest year with our condition yet. And I don't think it's going to get any easier."

Dad walks into the room then. He quietly sits down on the couch next to Mom.

Mom goes on. "I know the injury's been hard, Matt."

"And all the stuff that's happened this year," I remind her. "Lots of new stuff." Like jobs and summer camps and Andie and Zoe and concerts and haircuts that I'm starting to care more about than I did when I was younger. And, of course, the injury. "Isn't that new stuff going to keep happening?"

Neither of them replies right away. "I know it's hard," Mom ends up repeating.

I sigh. Is that all she can say? "Sometimes I just don't feel like I can do it," I say. "Like I can't live like this. That's when I get those attacks."

"But you *are* living like this," Mom says. "You have for seventeen years."

I exhale, frustrated. "But it doesn't make the feeling go away."

There's a pause.

"We're sorry it's been rough, Matt," Dad says in a gentle voice.

I close my eyes and take a deep breath. "The Burke-Dalton procedure…" I open my eyes and see Mom and Dad both looking at me like I've wounded them. I take another breath and forge ahead. "It's our way out. I could have a normal life. And it might even be years until there's a donor body and it could happen, but even just knowing that we're going to do it someday, to have that to look forward to…" I look at them pleadingly.

"We talked about this, Matt," Mom says, sounding sadly disappointed.

"Please?" My voice is quiet. "Please, Mom and Dad? I know it's risky. But it would completely change my and Jim's life. Let us do it? Please?"

Mom and Dad just look at each other, looking a little lost, until something in the kitchen beeps and Mom gets up to check on it. Dad grips my shoulder lovingly before standing up and leaving, too. I sink deeper into the cushions and exhale, feeling defeated.

Monday, September 19
Jim

I'm again in the hall outside my parents' room, but this time it's before bedtime. I take a breath before walking in.

Mom and Dad both sit on their bed. Mom has her laptop out and Dad has a tablet.

"Hey, Mom and Dad."

They look up at me. I walk over to their bed and sit down. "This injury has been really hard," I start.

"Well, yeah." Dad slides his tablet onto his bedside table. "Being in a boot for six weeks would be hard for anyone, and with you missing soccer and Matt not being able to work—"

"That's not what I mean," I interrupt. "What I mean is, the fact that Matt and I share a body has made the soccer injury especially hard." I take a breath. "For Matt, obviously, because it wasn't his fault and he's had to live with it and it really has messed up his life pretty bad." I pause again. "And—I don't want to sound insensitive or like I'm saying I've had it as bad—but it's been hard for me, too. I've felt really, really guilty."

Mom closes her laptop, and she and Dad sit up straighter, watching me.

"Matt has tried to guilt-trip me," I say, "which I don't blame him for, but even if he hadn't, I would have felt bad." I sigh. "And it's hard to have to feel that bad, that guilty, about things like injuries that aren't my fault, just because Matt and I are..." I falter, then start again. "And then with him wanting me to quit soccer. I don't want to. I won't. But I wonder, *am* I being fair? I *could* get hurt again. Or Matt could get hurt doing something. And then this whole thing would happen again, with one of us getting mad and the other feeling guilty."

There's a pause.

"I think part of what made this so bad for Matt was the day the injury happened," Dad says slowly. "The fact that Matt had to miss church the day he was going to play."

"And stuff like that could happen again, too," I say. "Even without an injury. Don't you see? Matt and I—we're—our lives are too—" I exhale a little frustratedly. "We're not normal," I settle with. "And I know I haven't ever had an anxiety attack, but I get why Matt has."

Neither of them says anything.

"Life is really hard," I repeat. "Matt..." I start slowly. "Matt brought up the Burke-Dalton procedure with me again."

Mom takes a breath and holds it, and Dad stiffens. I forge ahead. "What if we could do it? Or even just get on a list for a donor body? I know it's a huge risk and it's scary for you. But...but it could do so much for us." I look up at them. "Matt and I get that it's risky. We fully understand what's at stake. But the chance for us to have normal lives..." I look at Mom and Dad in turn. They're both quiet. "We wouldn't have to feel guilty for messing up each other's lives. We wouldn't fight over haircuts or going to concerts.

We'd get twice as much time. Matt could join a band. We could go to public school. College wouldn't be a logistical nightmare. We could date girls. We could get married someday." I pause, knowing this last one will mean a lot to Mom. "We could actually hang out together like normal brothers."

Mom doesn't say anything, but Dad sighs and shakes his head. "We've been through this, Jim. There's no way. The risk is too high."

I watch Mom closely.

"But…" I start. Then I sigh. "Dad, it's really hard living like this. And life's going to keep happening, and more new stuff is going to happen."

"Can't you keep living this way?" Mom speaks, almost pleading. "You've made it seventeen years."

"How much did your life change from seventeen on?"

Dad smiles a little wryly. Mom just sighs.

"We'll talk about it," Dad tells me quietly, which I take as my cue to leave.

Tuesday, September 20
Matt

On Tuesday after school, I'm lying on my side in bed. I've been doing a lot of that lately, usually with headphones on and listening to music. Melancholy music this time because I feel bored and lonely. I didn't get to see Zoe last weekend. And Leo's getting busier. His lead role in his high school's play has started taking up more of his time. Physical therapy appointments are lame, and it seems like it'll be forever until I'll get cleared to use my ankle again.

If we were normal, Jim and I could actually hang out together. What would that be like?

A knock at my door makes me lift my head. Mom and Dad walk in.

"Matt?" Dad asks. "Could we talk to you?"

I turn off the music and pull off my headphones, but I don't sit up.

Mom sits on the edge of my bed and Dad sits in my desk chair.

"Matt, we know this is hard for you," Dad starts.

I look at the floor and don't deny it.

"Your mom and I were talking and…we're OK with you and Jim getting on the list for a donor body for the Burke-Dalton procedure."

I look up, shocked. Dad looks pained. Mom's eyes are closed.

"Really?" I sit up.

"It could be years until a body becomes available." Mom opens her eyes. "You can't expect this to happen this year."

I move to the edge of the bed. "But we can get on the list?"

Dad nods. "It's hard for you two. We get it. Agreeing to this procedure isn't easy for us..." Dad looks at Mom, who looks down. "But we'll do it."

I hug Mom. She hugs me back, then Dad comes over and hugs both of us.

"Thank you," I say quietly. "Thank you."

Jim—Wed, Sep 21, 7:28 AM

are you sure you want to be the one transferred
to a new body? we could flip a coin online

Matt—Thu, Sep 22, 7:23 AM

positive. if we're gonna do it it's gonna be me

also WE'RE CLEARED FOR ALL ACTIVITY!!!

Jim—Fri, Sep 23, 7:44 AM

OK
if you say so

4:32 PM

mom talked to dr anand today and put us on the
waiting list. first i talked with him on the phone
a while and he went over all the risks again

there's some new stuff I learned. he said there's a chance
that your personality will change once you're in a new body

Matt—Sat, Sep 24, 7:23 AM

yeah i knew about that

Jim—Sun, Sep 25, 10:12 AM

why didn't you tell me? i kind of like
your personality the way it is

Matt—Mon, Sep 26, 7:44 AM

yeah i know

but it's just a chance

dr anand says the same thing can happen with patients who experience a head injury. what if it doesn't happen at all? and who knows maybe i'll become more caring or something

Jim—Tue, Sep 27, 7:50 AM

wait
you're admitting your personality could be improved upon?
is that humility i detect?
wow you must be experiencing some symptoms early
your personality clearly HAS changed

Matt—Wed, Sep 28, 7:23 AM

shut up

Jim—Thu, Sep 29, 7:38 AM

really though
that doesn't worry you?

Matt—Fri, Sep 30, 4:38 PM

hey so now that i have that new double bass pedal for the drums it sounds AWESOME

i never got super good at my left foot but i'm gonna practice way more now

it'll be even better than before

8:02 PM

i took some videos today. you should go downstairs and check it out

chapter
twenty-three

Thursday, September 22
Matt

"Matt!" Zoe hops out of her car, runs up, and hugs me. Surprised and happy, I hug her back. "Oh wow, seriously, I've missed you so much."

I can't help smiling. "Me, too. You have no idea." Even though the boot's been off for a couple of weeks, I haven't worked with her yet. We both look down, and I rotate my right ankle. "You have no idea how good *this* feels, either."

Zoe laughs. There's a pause when I think that maybe I should get out my phone to start looking for a Pals team task, but I realize I don't want to.

Zoe looks at me. "I don't feel like working yet. Want to go on a walk?"

I smile. "I was going to say the same thing."

We walk to Zilker Park, where we've walked many times before. Austin is having a mini cold front, and it feels really nice to be outside. It feels really nice to be with *her*.

We both talk animatedly, getting caught up and just enjoying being together. She does most of the catching up on things like Camp Waller. I feel like I don't have much exciting news to share about the last six weeks.

Except for one very exciting piece of news.

I lead the way to a bench. We sit down, and then I finally bring it up.

"So..." I don't really know how to ease into it, so I just blurt it out. "I'm going to get my own body."

Zoe looks at me without saying anything.

"There's a new procedure. To fix siblings with *duocordis unuscorporosis* like me and Jim. A cure. To take one of us and put us in a new body."

Zoe still stares at me. I'm starting to feel uncomfortable.

"It's...true. It's never been done before. Jim and I will be the first. We had to talk our parents into it, but they finally agreed."

Zoe finally speaks. "Are you serious?"

I can't help smiling. "Yeah!"

I think Zoe might smile, too, but she hasn't yet. "When?"

"As soon as a donor body is available."

"A donor body?" Zoe's voice is filled with disbelief. "Someone's going to donate their body to you?"

"There's a type of brain tumor," I explain. "It kills—well, not a person, but a person's consciousness. Their body would be fine, they just wouldn't be able to use it anymore. If they and their family gave permission, my and Jim's condition is the only thing doctors think that could make this transfer possible."

"How long until a donor like that comes around?"

I'm starting to falter a bit under Zoe's incredulity. "I'm not sure. Our doctor's not sure. Honestly, it could be years. But we're first in line."

Zoe turns away from me, faces forward, and shakes her head. "This is crazy."

"I know! But cool, right?"

"Who would get, um...transferred to a new body? You or Jim?"

"Me. We already worked that out." When I go on, my voice is quieter. "I'm the one who wants it more."

Zoe looks ahead and nods slowly. "And...this has never been done before?"

"No."

"But...how do you know it will work?"

"Ah." I look down. "Well, there's a chance...well, a chance it won't. It's a new procedure, and—"

"What's the chance?" Her voice is quiet.

"There's a...forty percent chance. A forty percent chance the transfer doesn't work and I—I—"

"You would just die?" Zoe is horrified.

"But look." I turn toward her. I try to laugh. "That's not what's going to happen! This is going to be a life-changing event! I'm going to get my own body! A whole life instead of half of one! And...and..." I look down at Zoe's hand by her side. Impulsively, I grab it. "I don't know if I've told you about all my parents' rules that I have to live by. There are some...about girls..."

Zoe is blushing. I don't know if it's what I said or the fact that I'm holding her hand.

"Anyway..." I look down but I don't let go of her hand. "If I...if I don't have to share a body with Jim anymore...the rules don't apply."

Zoe is looking straight ahead with a hard-to-read expression on her face. I start to worry that I've just made a mistake. I think maybe I should let go of her hand. But at the same time, I don't want to.

"Would you still want to be my friend?" I ask timidly. "If I were in a different body?"

Zoe looks at me, and *there's* the smile I've been waiting for. "Of course, Matt."

I smile back. "Even if I'm super ugly?"

Zoe's hand is still in mine. "If a new body could make *this* possible…" She squeezes my hand. Then she looks at me kind of shyly and smiles. "It doesn't matter what the body looks like as long as you're inside it."

Tuesday, September 27
Jim

Even when I got to officially take the boot off, Mom and Dad made me wear it to my coaching job so I wouldn't be tempted to use my foot before it completely healed. Now that I'm cleared for activity again, I get to leave the boot at home when I drive myself (*finally!*) to the field for practice. The kids notice right away.

"Coach Jim! Coach Jim! Where's your boot?"

"My foot's all better, guys!" I stand on my left foot and rotate my right ankle for them. "See?"

"Can you run with us now? Can you play?"

"Yeah!"

So that practice we have a blast. I run with the kids, pass to them, show them how to dribble, play goalie while they try to score. Coach Garrett is a good sport and lets me take up some extra time.

At the end of practice, Rachel comes to pick up Charlie. Rachel picks up Charlie all the time now, so I get to see her every week. Sometimes we just wave at each other. Sometimes, if I happen to be standing where she is when practice ends, we talk. I try to be standing there as often as I can. Especially today, the first practice without my boot on.

I'm wondering if she'll notice, or if it would be too kiddy if I said something like, "Rachel! Rachel! I got my boot off!" Luckily, she notices.

"Hey!" She walks up to me in her soccer practice clothes. "Your boot is off! Are you all healed?"

"Cleared for normal activity!" I hop up and down a couple of times. Man, it feels good to hop.

"Congrats."

Charlie comes running up to us then. "Rachel, Coach Jim's boot is off!"

Rachel smiles. "I saw."

"He can play soccer now!"

"Well, good for him."

Then, as if on cue, a soccer ball rolls toward us. It feels like a scene from a movie. It's coming right to me. I stop it and kick it back and forth a little bit, trying to convince myself that I'm not showing off...

Rachel smiles, reaches out a foot, and steals the ball from me. She dribbles onto the field and then turns back toward me, smiling, juggling the ball, daring me to come and take it back.

I smile and jog toward her.

We play, one on one, with the little Sharks watching and cheering. Rachel is good. Better than me, at least in my current state, out of the sport for two months. Still, I'm not terrible, and I laugh, and Rachel laughs, as we try to get the ball from each other. At one point, she's gotten the ball back from me, and we've worked our way closer to the goal. The net is behind me, and she kicks the ball into it. All the kids cheer.

I catch my breath as she jogs back to me. "Well, you're on varsity for a reason."

Rachel smiles. "No, you just got your boot off. I should have gone easier on you."

"Easier?"

She laughs as we make our way off the field, leaving the ball to the clump of six-year-olds. "I bet it does feel good to get your boot off." Rachel sits on the metal bench off to the side.

"You have no idea." I sit down next to her. "I can finally drive again, I can go running again, I can *play* again..." I rotate my right ankle carefully, checking to make sure it feels fine. If I hurt our foot again, Matt will *really* never forgive me...

"Are you going to play in your private league?" Rachel asks.

"Well, the season's half over." I sigh. "I'll have to wait until next spring." It's silent for a few moments.

"I get together with some friends from church and play sometimes." Rachel's voice is casual. She looks up at me. "We're playing Saturday evening if you want to come."

I'm tongue-tied for a moment. I try not to let her see that. She's asking me to do something with her? *Rachel?* A girl? A really attractive girl is asking me, Jim, to hang out with her? I almost stammer in disbelief before I get it together.

"Oh—Saturday—uh—yeah..." I clear my throat. "Yeah, for sure, I'd love to." I'm beyond grateful that this Saturday is mine and not Matt's.

Rachel smiles, and we get each other's numbers. As we're putting up our phones, Charlie comes over. She runs up to Rachel and hugs her legs. "Did you see me? I scored a goal!"

Rachel glances down at her and gives her a hug. They start to move to Rachel's car.

Rachel looks back at me. "See you Saturday, Coach Jim."

I stammer some more. "See—see you then."

After they drive off, I feel like it's safe to exhale, run my hands through my hair, and sink onto the bleachers. And smile. A lot. Rachel invited me to play soccer with her. I can't believe it.

I'm not sure how much Coach Garrett picks up on the interactions of nearby teenagers, but he winks at me as he leaves the field.

Jim—Sat, Oct 1, 4:37 PM

i played soccer for the first time today since the injury!
with rachel and her friends
don't worry
i was really careful
my ankle felt totally fine too

Matt—Sun, Oct 2, 11:21 AM

glad we're healing well

i feel fine drumming with my right foot too

so was it playing soccer that was fun?
or was it who you were playing with? 😌

Jim—Mon, Oct 3, 7:32 AM

both
but also definitely who i was playing with
i hope she invites me again

Matt—Tue, Oct 4, 7:33 AM

as long as you didn't do anything dumb
clumsy or stupid i bet your chances are high

Jim—Wed, Oct 5

chapter
twenty-four

Friday, October 21
Jim

    This is one of those mornings when, checking Vimer, it's easier to rewatch all of my and Matt's messages over the past week or so before responding. Matt and I have a long and heated conversation going, and I need to remember all of it. This one started with me over a week ago.

    Me, looking uncertain: "Hey, Matt. Listen…I was wondering if you'd swap days with me. Without Mom and Dad knowing, of course. Rachel, the girl I met at work—she invited me to play soccer with her again next Saturday. And…I really want to go."

    Matt, acting surprised: "Wait, what, Jim? A day swap? But—isn't that against the rules? Golly, Jim, I don't think we should. I don't think we could."

    Me, looking frustrated: "Knock it off, Matt. Look, I'll go to bed next Friday night, set an alarm in the middle of the night, you wake up, go back to sleep, and I'll wake up and take Saturday. Then I'll give you Sunday, and on Sunday night we'll do the reverse and you take Monday. We'll each get two days in a row. And we'll pretend to be each other over the weekend, and Mom and Dad never have to know. If you're OK with it. But lay off the theatrics. If you want to do it, fine. If not, just drop it."

    Matt, acting annoyed: "OK, I really am surprised to hear this coming from you. I don't know if you've forgotten that incident a few months ago when *I* had an event with a girl on one of *your* days and you were completely uncooperative about it."

    Me: "You didn't ask to swap with me—you asked me to go and pretend to be you."

    Matt: "I didn't think you'd go for a swap! I didn't think it was worth it to even ask! Why didn't you offer to switch days instead?"

    Me: "Because you made me mad when you asked me to be you."

    Matt: "Argh! You're the worst."

    That was yesterday.

I sigh. Today is Friday. Tomorrow is Saturday, the day I'm supposed to play soccer with Rachel. I haven't committed that I'll come...but I haven't told her I won't, either.

The problem is, Matt hasn't told me yes or no. I guess I can gather that it's a no. But maybe there's a chance?

I send a response to Matt, and later that night, before I go to sleep, I put Matt's phone on my nightstand and set an alarm.

Saturday, October 22
Matt

Music wakes me up.

I roll onto my stomach and groggily pull out the earbuds Jim's gone to sleep in. They're playing the song "Help!" by the Beatles.

I reach for the phone on the nightstand. It's mine, and the label of the alarm I turn off is "Please watch my Vimer." It's 1:00 AM.

I pull myself up onto my elbows and hang my head down between my arms. I know what day it is. It's Saturday, the one that's mine that Jim wants. I lift my head and open Vimer to see what Jim has to say.

"Listen, I'm sorry, OK? Sorry you had to miss Zoe's party. Sorry I didn't offer to swap with you. And if you don't want to swap with me—fine. Then don't. But..." Jim sighs. "...if you're feeling generous, I do want to go. And, yeah, it's tomorrow. So I'm going to set an alarm tonight. I'm putting your phone by my bed so you can watch this as soon as you wake up. If you don't want to swap, set another alarm for me, I'll wake up, go back to sleep, and I'll let you have your Saturday. But if you do want to swap..." Jim looks hopeful. "Then just go back to sleep? And you'll hear from me on Sunday."

I roll over onto my back. Truthfully, I don't want to argue with him. (Also, speaking selfishly, if we swap days I'll get Sunday two weeks in a row.)

So, without setting another alarm for Jim, I go back to sleep.

Saturday, October 22
Jim

When I wake up and it's light outside, I'm excited. A quick look at my phone confirms it: It's Saturday! Matt let us swap days! I check for a Vimer from him and find one short one. It's so dark I can't see his face, only hear his voice.

"OK," he says, sounding tired. "You win. Enjoy your Saturday. Have fun playing soccer. Don't hurt our foot again. And *don't* get caught."

My face falls at his last comment. He's right. We can*not* get caught.

So I'll have to be Matt for a day. I'll have to fool our parents. And instead of telling Mom I'm off to play soccer, I'll tell her I'm off to work with Zoe.

Soccer isn't until later that evening. I know there's a Sharks game I could go to, but it would be too risky to try. So I have a morning of schoolwork to get through first. But I start to get worried as I think about the day. Why haven't I thought this through more? How am I going to be Matt all day? For schoolwork? When Mom sits down with me for English, will she be able to tell? What if she figures it out?

So, apprehensively, I get up to start the day.

"Hey, Mom and Dad." I walk downstairs into the kitchen.

"Morning, Matt." Dad is at the table with a laptop. Termite comes up to me, and, like normal, I pat him on the head and move on. But then I stop.

Termite loves Matt more than me. He can tell the difference between us. What if I don't fool him and he gives me away?

So how does Matt treat Termite? I've only seen them together in videos. Matt's always excited, eager, exaggerated when he talks to our dog. Is that for the videos? Or is he like that all the time?

"Hey, Termite!" I get down on his level and hold his doggy face in my hands. I put my face right up in front of his nose and make my voice sappy, like Matt does. "Hey, who's a good boy? Who's a good boy? That's right, good dog!"

Termite wiggles and licks my face (I try not to flinch).

Mom and Dad are looking at me. Am I too exaggerated? Not happy enough? I let go of Termite and stand up.

"Good morning, Matt." Mom is sitting next to Dad with a bowl of granola.

"Any Saturday plans?" Dad types something on his laptop.

I go to the sink to wash my hands. "I'm gonna work with Zoe this evening. After I finish schoolwork and stuff."

"Are you going to hit the gym today?" Dad's been eager to encourage me and Matt to get back to our workout routines now that the boot is off.

"Sure." I turn around to see Mom looking at me.

She tilts her head. "Why are you washing your hands?"

Oops. Matt must not wash his hands every time he touches Termite, like I do. (Gross.)

I shrug and try to brush it off. "I don't know."

Mom thankfully brushes it off, too.

Making it through breakfast is exhausting. I'm constantly stressed about giving myself away. When I go upstairs to get dressed, I'm glad for the break.

When I go to the gym, I take Matt's wallet and driver's license and scan his key card instead of mine, in case anyone sends word back to my dad. I work out, head home, and try as hard as I can to be Matt all day. English is stressful. I try not to show Mom that I've finished *The Autobiography of Benjamin Franklin* (when Matt hasn't).

And then, happy for the first time all day, I put on Matt's Pals shirt, grab one of my shirts to change into, hop in our truck, and head out to play soccer. And to see Rachel.

***

Rachel plays soccer with her friends from church, fittingly enough, at their church. Well, it's a park across the street. But I drive to the same parking lot I went to last time, park my car, get out, and walk across the street to the group of kids on the field.

Rachel is there. She steps away from everyone when she sees me. "Hi, Jim."

I smile. "Hey."

"I'm glad you made it."

"Me, too." I don't mention how (or why) it's such a miracle that I'm there. The day before, I told her I had a family thing going on that I'd try to get out of.

No, I haven't told Rachel anything about Matt. It's not like I'm keeping a secret from her. It just...hasn't come up yet.

Rachel smiles at me, and two kids pick teams. I end up on Rachel's.

We play like last time. All the other kids there, teenagers of varying high school ages, are nice and fun. Rachel is the best player.

The game is casual and fun, not like the games and scrimmages I have at Capital Soccer. There's a lot of laughing involved. It reminds me of Camp Waller when I was Jett.

My and Rachel's team wins the first game. She smiles and we high-five, then they change the teams around and Rachel and I are on different ones.

That's more fun. Somehow, it works out that every time I have the ball, she's the one guarding me, laughing.

I'm in uncharted waters. I've never hung out with a girl like this before. But I'm pretty sure she's flirting with me. And, as unsure and awkward as I feel sometimes, I think I flirt back.

Sunday, October 23
Matt

I wake up on Sunday in my own bed and then remember that Jim and I swapped days. I'm supposed to be him all day.

I'm curious to see what he says in his Vimers from yesterday. Did he have fun playing soccer? Did he get to talk to Rachel? I hope for his sake it was worth it.

I walk into Jim's room (reminding myself that I have to be him) and pick up his phone. I make sure the door is shut before watching his messages.

"Hey, Matt." Jim looks happy. "So soccer this evening was a blast. Thanks for swapping with me." He's sincere, and I smile. He gives me some more details on playing (and on Rachel) before wrapping up his message. "So, listen..." His smile fades. "Mom and Dad might be a little suspicious. I tried as hard as I could to be you. But be careful. Remember you've got to fool Termite as well as Mom and Dad."

Jim at the end of his message does look nervous. I smile. This little act of rebellion has to be freaking him out. Lucky for him, I can keep my cool and no doubt won't get caught.

***

"Good morning," Mom says as I walk downstairs, conspicuously leaving off my name.

"Hey, Mom, hey, Dad." I sit down at the table.

I can tell immediately that Mom and Dad are suspicious. Jim must have done a lousy job of being me yesterday. I groan inwardly.

"I made your favorite." Dad puts a plate of waffles on the table. "Waffles."

"You mean *Matt's* favorite," I correct. "Come on, Dad." I shoot him a frustrated look.

Mom and Dad look at each other in a calculating way. And I take a bite of waffles.

***

After church, wanting to be extra convincing, I pull out the Spider-Man costume Jim's started. (It's his year for Halloween.) He's replicating Peter Parker's homemade suit from *Spider-Man: Homecoming*. I think I'll work on the costume, but as I look at the blue sweats and red hoodie, I'm not sure what to do with them. I don't want to mess something up and make Jim mad. So I head to the basement to watch the movie, for research, I tell Mom and Dad.

After a while I hear Mom. "Hi, Jim." She walks down into the basement.

"Hey." I stay lying down on the couch, eyes on the TV. Termite is stretched out on the floor next to me, and I'm idly petting him. I stop, wondering if that's something Jim would do.

"Can I ask you something?" Mom sits down on the other couch.

"Uh-huh." My eyes don't leave the TV screen.

"I'm going to give you the opportunity to tell the truth."

For the first time I glance at her. "OK..."

"Are you Matt or Jim?"

"Mom!" I sit up. "Are you serious? You're asking me that? You know that's, like, the most offensive thing ever, right?"

She doesn't smile, just looks at me earnestly. "Answer the question, please."

I roll my eyes. "I'm *Jim*, Mom! Come on." Then I lie down again and pretend to concentrate on the movie. Termite gives a soft whine, but I don't touch him.

Mom isn't done. She gets up and stands in front of me.

"I'm Jim, Mom, I swear."

Mom picks up the remote and turns off the TV.

"Mom!"

She looks more serious now. "Then play something on the guitar for me."

"Mom!" I sit up and laugh in disbelief. "Come on, where is the trust?"

Mom isn't smiling. She steps to the side as Termite, dog tags rattling, gets up and walks past her upstairs. "If you are Jim, then why so reluctant to prove it?"

"Mom!" I try to laugh again. "Because I'm trying to make a point! I shouldn't have to *prove* it. You know how much that hurts. When you mix up me and Matt?" I pantomime stabbing a dagger through my chest.

Mom stares at me, eyes narrowing. I try to look innocently hurt. Seconds tick by.

"You're Matt," Mom finally announces.

"Mom! No, I'm not!"

"No." She's firm. "You *are* Matt, and you are in a heap of trouble, unless you want to correct me by proving to me you're Jim." She gestures to his guitar.

"Alright!" I grab the guitar from off the wall and sit down on the couch. "Alright, fine! Though I'm deeply offended."

I swallow as I pull the guitar on my lap. I have this crazy hope that muscle memory will take over and my fingers and hands will start playing of their own accord.

When that doesn't happen, I stall. "So...what song do you want to hear?"

"Oh, any of the ones you've been practicing recently. Surprise me."

"OK. OK, fine." I pluck out a few single notes before glancing up at Mom's face and realizing I don't have a prayer.

"Argh!" I toss the guitar onto the couch. "This is totally why I told Jim we should learn the same instrument!"

Mom, though mad, gives a small triumphant smile.

"It's his fault, though, right?" I stand up. "He was me yesterday, and he made you suspicious, didn't he? He did a lousy job. If it weren't for him, we could have gotten away with it."

By Mom's look, I can tell that wasn't the wisest thing to say.

"You're not supposed to get away with it!" Mom pushes past me up the stairs to the kitchen. "Dave!"

"Yes?" Dad appears at the top of the stairs.

"He's Matt."

Dad frowns at me as I follow Mom up the stairs.

"What?" I shrug. "It was his idea, OK? I was doing him a favor. He's the one you should be mad at." Do I feel bad for immediately throwing Jim under the bus? No, not even a little.

"Dream on, bud." Dad is stern. "You know that's not allowed." He points to the table. I sigh and sit down.

Mom sits next to me. "What was so important it was worth breaking the rules and swapping days?"

I open my mouth, but then pause. "You know, I'm going to let Jim tell you."

Sunday, October 23
Jim

Someone is shaking my shoulder to wake me up. I roll over.

"Mom?" I squint up at her. The room is dark, but the door is open and the light in the hall is on. There's a dark shape standing behind her. "Dad? What time is it?"

"Night. Just after your brother went to sleep." Dad's hands are in his pockets, and he steps closer to the bed. "Any idea why we're waking you up?"

I sit up, rubbing my eyes, trying to get my bearings. Mom is sitting on the edge of my bed frowning at me, and Dad is watching me. I have a bad feeling about this.

"Um...no?"

"You're already in trouble," Mom sighs. "You can make it worse by lying to us. Now do you want to tell us what your name is?"

I groan and put my head in my hand. "You caught Matt?"

"We caught both of you." Mom is frustrated. "Jim, what were you thinking? You know switching days is against the rules."

I moan. Dad flips on the light and I squint. He sits down next to Mom, and I can tell I'm in for one big lecture.

Monday, October 24
Matt

On Monday morning, I wake up in my own bed. I don't have anything from Jim from last night, but I know he must have been up because otherwise I wouldn't be the one awake.

I cautiously go downstairs. Maybe-just-maybe Mom and Dad talked to Jim, realized the whole swap thing was his idea, and will decide to take it easy on me.

The kitchen is empty. I get myself some cereal and sit down at the table. In a few minutes, the back door opens, and Mom walks in, just getting home from the gym.

"Hey, Mom." I take a bite of cereal, deciding not to bring up Jim or the swap and maybe she won't—

"Matt. Your dad and I talked." Mom frowns at me as she puts her water bottle down on the counter. "We decided on a punishment for you and Jim for your little deception."

"OK…"

"It starts today."

"…And?"

Mom smiles then, barely, I swear it. "You want to pretend to be Jim? Fine. For your next three awake days, you're not allowed to do anything Jim wouldn't be able to do."

I try to sort through that for a second, then give up and scrunch up my face. "Huh?"

"If you were trying to fool me right now," Mom said with the air of explaining something to someone dim-witted, "and pretend to be Jim, you wouldn't do any 'Matt' things. So that's what you'll get for the rest of the week."

"But—"

"That means no playing the drums."

"Wha—!?"

"No working."

"But—"

"And you'll go to sleep in his bed, wear his clothes, and study in his room."

"OK, *that's* just cruel and unusual."

"Matt." Mom frowns at me. "What you and Jim did is serious. You broke one of our most important rules, *and* you lied about it. No, not a lie—an elaborate scheme you planned out in advance. When you break rules, there are consequences."

"But what about drum lessons?"

"You'll skip them this week." Mom turns toward the fridge to get her own breakfast.

I sputter for a second.

"Oh." Mom turns around again. "And today you will have a double load of schoolwork since you missed your Saturday."

I groan.

The clothes thing isn't a big deal. We wear each other's clothes all the time. Falling asleep in his room feels a little different, but other than colors, our beds (mattresses, pillows, sheets) are the same, so it doesn't make a big difference. I wake up in his bed every morning, anyway. Even hanging out in Jim's room all day instead of mine isn't too big of a deal.

It's the no drums, no work, no Zoe thing that's killer.

***

We've been planning on working this afternoon, so in the morning I call her.

"Matt?" she answers.

"Hey, Zoe."

"Hey." Then immediately, "What's wrong?"

I sigh. "I can't come work today."

"Are you sick?" She sounds concerned.

I slump back in the chair in the homeschool room I'm sitting in. "No. I'm in trouble."

There's a pause, and I have the impression that Zoe is smiling. "What happened?"

I sigh again. "It's Jim's fault. He's been hanging out with this girl Rachel, and she invited him to play soccer on Saturday, and he wanted to go so he talked me into switching days with him."

"But I thought...I thought you weren't allowed to do that."

I wince. This is why I didn't tell Zoe on Sunday that I switched days with Jim. Back on her birthday, she had basically asked me to, and I told her no because it was against the rules. And here I am, breaking the rules for Jim's benefit.

"Yeah. That's why I'm in such big trouble. Jim, too."

"So are you, like, grounded?"

"Not exactly." I tap a pencil on the table. "In theory, I could go anywhere Jim would go. Just not anywhere *I* would go."

"Like to work with me?"

"Yep. Or drum lessons. Bradley can't even come over this week."

"That's lame. I'm sorry."

"Yeah." I sigh. "Jim's really gonna owe me one. Anyway...I won't be able to see you until next week."

"OK." She's as dejected as I am. "I'll miss you."

"Me, too. Bye, Zoe."

"Bye, Matt."

Tuesday, October 25
Jim

"But what about soccer?" I'm downstairs in the kitchen, where Mom's just told me my punishment for the next three days. I'm basically going to be forced to be Matt. A cruel punishment if I ever heard one. "I started private lessons last week! I can't skip my second one! And this week is the last Sharks' game I'll be able to make!"

Mom turns back to her computer like it's not a big deal. "You're welcome to send Matt in your place."

"Aargh!" I turn and stomp out the door.

***

After a grumpy day of schoolwork, I think working on my Halloween costume might make me feel better. But when I go to pull it out of my closet, it isn't there.

"Mom, where's my Spider-Man costume?" I'm still angry from hearing my punishment, and I stomp downstairs.

Mom's cooking dinner. "I put it up." She doesn't look up at me.

"Put it up...where?"

"Just up." Mom stirs a pot on the stove. "Matt wouldn't work on your Halloween costume. So this week, you can't either."

"What!?" I explode.

Mom looks calmly stubborn.

"But—but I need to finish it!"

"And starting Monday, you can."

"But the party is on Monday!" I can't believe this.

"I guess you'll have to work fast."

"I can't finish that costume in a day!" I pace around the kitchen.

"Maybe Matt will finish it for you."

I snort. Yeah, right.

Mom is pleased, I swear. "Then you'll need to figure something else out."

I grunt again and stomp away.

Matt—Mon, Oct 24, 11:22 AM

way to go on getting caught

Jim—Tue, Oct 25, 7:17 AM

i got caught? are you serious? i believe
you're the one who couldn't pull it off

Matt—Wed, Oct 26, 7:22 AM

yeah well i would have been able to if you hadn't been
so conspicuous the day before. mom and dad knew
right away that something was up. there was no way i
was going to fool them after your lousy performance

plus i hope you remember that the whole thing was YOUR
idea. it's unfair of mom and dad to punish me at all and if
you were a caring brother you'd try to talk them out of it

and NO

i will NOT finish your costume for you you rat

Jim—Thu, Oct 27, 7:02 AM

fine thanks for nothing. hope you're happy that now i have
to go to the party dressed as unoriginal harry potter

if mom and dad knew i was faking it they
would have said something on saturday and
they didn't. you're the one who blew it

and you were breaking the rules along with me.
you should be punished as much as i am

Matt—Fri, Oct 28, 7:06 AM

that's such a jerk attitude to have. don't know why i
would have expected anything different from you

Jim—Sat, Oct 29, 7:02 AM

shut up matt

Matt—Sun, Oct 30, 7:01 AM

go kiss a dementor jim

chapter
twenty-five

Wednesday, November 2
Jim

The day-swapping punishment is lame enough that Matt and I stay mad at each other the rest of the week. (Also, when it ends, both of our rooms are trashed because we had no motivation to keep each other's clean.) But on Saturday, Rachel texts and says how much fun it was having me at soccer. I realize how great it was, playing with her, and how it was worth the punishment, even worth missing the Sharks' second-to-last game. (Though my Halloween costume is a shame. The party is still fun, even in the Harry Potter costume, but that Spider-Man one would have looked so cool.)

***

Next Saturday is the Sharks' last game of the season, and I'm bummed that I'm going to have to miss it (it's Matt's day). It's been a good season. They're a fun group of kids. I'm going to miss it when the season ends.

Today is their last practice, and at least I get to be there for that. Then Coach Garrett has planned a little end-of-season get-together with all the kids and their families, and he's nice enough to schedule it on Sunday when I can come.

***

At the Sharks' practice in the evening, I have fun. I laugh and play and chase and *am* chased and enjoy goofing around with the kids. As practice is ending, I'm being chased by four or five kids when I see Rachel coming to pick up Charlie. I shake off the kids.

"Hey, Rachel." I jog over to her, smiling.

She looks up like she hasn't seen me coming. "Oh. Jim. Hey." She looks down again and is quiet, even cold, as she stares at her car keys in her hands, fingering an Eiffel Tower keychain.

"Uh...is something wrong?"

"No." Rachel is still looking at her keys. "No, nothing's wrong." Then she looks up at me, and I can tell that absolutely something is wrong. She sighs frustratedly. "Just because you see me when you're with your girlfriend—who you never mentioned, by the way—doesn't mean you have to ignore me."

"What?!" I take a step back. "I don't have a girlfriend. What makes you say—" Wait. I know *exactly* what would make her say that.

Rachel glares at me. "I saw you downtown holding hands with her yesterday."

"Holding—!" I stop myself. Matt and Zoe are *holding hands*?

"And when I started to say hi, you looked away from me like you didn't know me."

"Rachel, that wasn't me," I say immediately. She looks at me, unamused. "It was my twin brother."

She looks suspicious. "You never mentioned you had a twin brother before."

I shrug. "It never came up before. But believe me, that wasn't me yesterday."

"He looked just like you."

"We're super identical."

When she still looks skeptical, I pull out my phone. "Look. I'll show you. His name's Matt."

"Bye, Coach Jim!" one of the kids shouts as he walks by. I nod at him without looking up.

I open my text messages. "See him there?" I hold my phone in front of Rachel. "These are our texts." I scroll through the conversation too quickly for her to read anything.

"OK..."

"You want more proof? Look me up on Instagram."

Rachel pulls out her phone and opens the app, pulling up my profile.

"Look at that." I point. "See in my followers? Matt Mickelsen? That's him."

Rachel taps Matt's picture, and we go to his profile.

"See?" I ask as she scrolls.

Rachel wrinkles her nose. "Still fishy. Why aren't you in any photos together? What if you invented this Matt personality so you can date two girls at once?"

I look down, close my eyes, and put a hand to the bridge of my nose. *Why?*

"Well?" Rachel presses. "Why aren't you in any pictures together?"

"Because we share a body!" I blurt out.

She stares at me, eyes wide.

I hold out my hands. "See this body? We take turns with it. I'm awake right now, and he's dormant. Tomorrow it will be his turn. Yesterday, he was the one you saw downtown."

Rachel lowers her chin. "Dormant."

"Yeah." Now that I realize what I've done—blurted out the complete truth about me and Matt—I take a breath and go on more slowly. "Always one of us is awake, and the other is dormant. Not conscious. When Matt wakes up tomorrow, he'll have no idea what I did on my day. I had no idea he was holding hands with Zoe on his day yesterday." I make a face as I remember that fact and remind myself to send some carefully chosen words to Matt later.

Rachel stands looking at me like she doesn't know what to make of me. Behind me in the field some kids laugh. I'm grateful Charlie hasn't run over to us yet.

"It's true," I offer weakly. "The condition is called *duocordis unuscorporosis*. It's super rare. Matt and I are just lucky, I guess." My lame attempt at humor through sarcasm doesn't land well.

It's silent for a moment, and then Rachel laughs in disbelief. "Wow." She takes a step back. "Just—wow. This is incredible, Jim. If you made up such an elaborate lie so you can, I don't know, live a double life—" She starts to back away from me. "Charlie!" she shouts. "Let's go!"

"It's not a lie!" I hurry after her. She starts walking toward the parking lot. "I promise, Rachel! What else would convince you? Do you want to read a scientific article about us? Do you want to ask my parents?" I'm getting desperate. "Do you want to meet him?"

Rachel stops walking.

"I'm sorry." I look down and run a hand over the back of my head. "I...I didn't know when to tell you. It's just that it didn't come up and..." I keep my head lowered but glance up at her with my eyes.

She studies me. "I can meet him?"

"Y—yeah."

"So then I'll be able to prove that he's you pretending to be him?"

"If you want to look at it like that, sure."

She studies me some more. "Either way, Jim. Whether you're some sick pathological liar or whether you have..." She pauses, searching for words. "...some...really, really weird..."

I wait. Before she can finish, Charlie comes running up, hugs Rachel around the legs, calls, "Bye, Coach Jim!" and heads toward Rachel's car.

"I'll text you," I say lamely as Rachel walks away.

Thursday, November 3
Matt

"Matt." Jim starts his message to me today with a straight face. He looks angry. He goes on, his voice the dangerous sort of quiet. "Why in the world didn't you tell me you and Zoe have been *holding hands*?"

I wince.

No, I haven't told Jim that I've been holding Zoe's hand. And no, I haven't stopped. Zoe and I hold hands all the time now. On some dog walks it's harder than others, but if we're walking some less excitable dogs and we're able to, we hold hands—and when we move between tasks, when we're not riding scooters.

I don't know why I haven't told Jim. Maybe I'm worried he'll tattle on me. I know what I'm doing is against the rules.

I think the main reason is the Burke-Dalton procedure. In my mind, I've gotten used to the idea that the way Jim and I live has become temporary. One day, it won't matter that I've been holding Zoe's hand when it's against the rules. One day, I'll be allowed to. I know that it could be years until I'm normal. But that hasn't sunk deep into my head. I'm going to be normal someday. Should I wait until that day to start living?

Jim doesn't seem to see it the same way. "What were you thinking, Matt!" he yells. "You know that's against the rules. I could get you in so much trouble if I told Mom and Dad."

I wince again. It'll be a miracle if he hasn't.

"And," Jim goes on, "did you stop to think about me, that other guy who occupies your body half the time? Know who saw you with Zoe on Tuesday? Rachel. Yeah. That Rachel."

I'm paying close attention.

"Know who's now mad at me because she thinks I have a secret girlfriend? Rachel."

Wait a second...

"Thanks a lot, Matt." Jim huffs. "I'm mad that you did it, but I'm madder that you didn't tell me about it."

I tap my phone screen and open my and Jim's text messages.

One fact about my relationship with Jim—for better or worse—is that literally everything we have ever said or written to each other is recorded. I scroll back through our messages until I find the ones I want. Jim was telling me about Rachel. I was happy for him, sending him thumbs-up GIFs and asking for details. And then I sent: "And what about the whole duocordis thing? She doesn't think you're weird?" And Jim replied: "She doesn't think I'm weird."

I start a Vimer to Jim right away. "Wait a second, Jim..." I start. "Rachel saw me and thought it was you...does this mean you didn't tell her about me?" I shake my head. "Ha! You hypocrite! You told me over and over when I started hanging out with Zoe that I should tell her about you. And you never told Rachel—and, on top of that—" I make air quotes with one hand. "'She doesn't think I'm weird'? That's lying to me about it. I don't know what you're mad at me for. Seems like it's your own fault."

Friday, November 4
Jim

I watch Matt's video to me this morning and wince. He has a point. I didn't tell Rachel about him, and I was misleading about it. I just...didn't want to tell her, and I didn't want to hear Matt tell me I should.

I make a face as I lean back in bed. This whole thing sucks. But I know that I need Matt's help, so I know what I have to say.

I hold the camera up to my face and tap the red record circle.

"OK, Matt," I say. "About me not telling Rachel about you...can we agree I've been punished enough without you getting on me again? And about you and Zoe..." I sigh. "I won't tell Mom and Dad. Promise. So, if we can move past all that...I need your help again."

Saturday, November 5
Matt

"Hey, Mom?" I ask when I go down for breakfast. "Is it OK if Jim's friend Rachel comes over today?"

Mom is in the living room folding laundry. She looks up at me. "The one he had you switch places for?"

"Yeah."

"Why would she come over?" Mom stands up and walks into the kitchen.

"Well." I get out cereal and milk. "This is his fault more than mine, but on Tuesday Rachel saw me downtown working with Zoe, and she tried to say hi and I ignored her—because, hello, I don't know her, and I didn't even notice her—"

Mom is looking at me suspiciously.

I pour cereal in my bowl. "And Jim had never told her about me, or about his condition, so when she saw me ignoring her downtown, she thought it was Jim, and she confronted Jim about it, mad, and I guess the truth came out." I add milk.

"The truth about you and Jim." Mom joins me at the table.

"Right," I say around a mouthful of cereal. "So, the thing is, Rachel didn't believe him because, you know," I swallow. "Our condition is weird and hard to believe, right? So then she got mad at him and thought he was a liar, and he said, 'Well, why don't you meet my brother so you can see for yourself he's real?' And I guess she was like, 'OK,' and so now Jim asked if I would have Rachel over and show her that I do exist so she can stop being mad at him if that's OK?" I look at Mom with raised eyebrows.

She's suspicious. "Why didn't Jim tell us this?"

I shrug. "He asked me yesterday if I'd meet her. I think he didn't want to tell you until he knew for sure I'd say yes."

"Why wouldn't you say yes?"

I sigh. "Because I got mad at him for not telling Rachel the truth about us." I stir my cereal. "After I first met Zoe, Jim told me to tell her the truth, and now he's had this friend for a while, and he even had us switch places so he could hang out with her, and he hasn't told her?" I look at Mom like, *Can you believe that?*

Mom looks back.

"So anyway." I take a bite. "I told Jim I'd meet Rachel and try to convince her that he's not a pathological liar."

"OK..." Mom stands up from the table. "Sure. That's fine. When?"

"She can come over during my lunch break."

"OK. Until then it's gym, then school?"

"Yep." I take another bite. "Gym then school."

***

Around lunchtime, I sit on the living room couch, petting Termite. Mom and Dad are both in the kitchen. We're all quiet.

I break the silence. "Based on what Jim said, in Rachel's mind, she's hoping today to prove to herself that she's right. So it sounds like…"

"Like she's not coming over with an open mind?" Mom says from the kitchen. She's cutting vegetables for a salad.

"Sounds like you've got your work cut out for you?" Dad's eyes are on the cucumber he's chopping.

I look toward the front door. Dad is right. From what Jim says about Rachel, she's out to prove he's some sort of sick liar. I have a job to do—convince Rachel, a girl I've never met, that my brother is telling her the truth.

The doorbell rings and I go to get it. I open the door to see Rachel. She's taller than Zoe, and athletic. Her reddish hair is long and straight, and she wears it tied back in a ponytail. She has on shorts and a T-shirt. Her legs, I try not to notice but do anyway, look great.

Maybe she's untrusting and accusatory, but I'll give Jim this much. She is pretty.

"Hey, Rachel." I stick out a hand. "I'm Matt."

She shakes it. "OK, 'Matt.' But I'm pretty sure you're Jim, so I'm going to call you that."

I roll my eyes. "Not like I haven't been called that before." I step to the side. "Come in."

"Thanks, Jim."

I make a face behind her back. She's trying to annoy me/Jim, I know it. Trying to get me/him to "slip up."

In the kitchen, Rachel meets my mom and dad, where they all work out that they've seen each other before at Jim's little soccer team's games. Mom and Dad talk about Rachel's little sister and how highly Jim thinks of her. Rachel fills them in on the team's game this morning (they won). I stay bored off to the side.

"Don't you want to speak up, Jim?" Rachel asks me. "You're not going to say something nice about Charlie?"

"I don't know Charlie," I say deliberately, "because *I'm not Jim*."

Mom shoots me a look that tells me I better be nice to Jim's friend.

I send her one back that says, come on, she's being super rude, cut me some slack.

Dad comes to my rescue. "This is Matt, Rachel." He gestures to me. "He and Jim really are different people."

Rachel looks at me, more unsure, and I give her a sarcastic smile and a wave.

"What's more likely?" Dad goes on. "That Jim and his parents are lying, or that all four of us are telling the truth?"

Rachel looks like she doesn't know what to say.

"Come on." I tap her on the arm. "I'll show you our rooms."

Upstairs, I show her Jim's room first. "As you can see, he's pretty neat."

Rachel peeks in as I turn on the light. Jim's bed is made and his room is neat, as usual. All the pictures and posters on his wall are framed. His books, pens, and notebooks are tucked into the wooden organizer hanging above his desk. The guitar and soccer jerseys on the wall hang straight. His floating white box bookshelves are full of books, trophies, and knickknacks, but not cluttered. The only thing not put away is the Mastermind game on the small table against the wall.

"What's with the game?" Rachel points.

"It's called Mastermind. Have you played?"

Rachel shakes her head. "No. Why? Do you want to play n—"

"Stop!" I pull her back before she touches the game. Rachel looks at me like I'm crazy.

"That's my and Jim's game," I explain. "It's been going on for…" I glance at the board. "…about eight weeks now. And I'm pretty sure I'm going to win. So please don't mess up the board."

She still looks at me like I'm crazy. "But…how do you play with each other?"

"We each take one turn a day. That's why it takes so long." I lead the way out of Jim's room, across the hall, and into mine.

Rachel looks in. "Not so neat."

That's a little unfair of her to say. Just because I have more stuff than Jim doesn't mean I'm messier. So my concert posters aren't framed (it *is* an impressive collection though, a giant collage taking up a whole wall). So the bulletin board above my bed is close to overflowing, just like the glass jar of ticket stubs. So I made the clay pencil cup on my desk nine years ago and it's a little crooked. So what? It's not like I have clothes on the floor or food wrappers left all over.

I smile. "I like to think of myself as more artistic than Jim."

"Sure."

I roll my eyes.

Rachel points to my bed. "Your bed's nicely made, though. I'll give you that."

"Yeah. Jim does that."

Rachel looks at me, confused. "Jim comes in and makes your bed?"

"Jim sleeps in my bed."

Now she's extra confused.

I go on. "Well, you could say we both sleep in both of our beds. We switch places at night, right? So every night we go to sleep in our own beds and wake up in each other's."

Rachel nods a slow, confused nod.

"We're good about making each other's beds, though." I leave my room and head down the hall. "That's an unspoken rule. If either of us got sloppy and started skipping days, the other would, too, and then we would never have made beds. And Jim would hate that." I turn around with a shrug.

***

"OK." I've given her a tour of the house, introduced her to Termite, and played the drums for her. Rachel and I are walking back into the living room. "There's one more thing Jim wanted me to show you. He asked me..." I sigh, thinking about how much I must love Jim for doing this. "...to play soccer with you, because apparently I'm horrible enough that if nothing else convinces you that Jim's telling the truth, that will."

Rachel smiles at that. "You have a ball?"

"*Jim* has a ball," I clarify. "Let me grab it."

***

At the bottom of our sloped backyard, I hold the soccer ball. Rachel stands across the yard and squints in the sun.

"Kick it!" she calls.

I drop-kick the ball to her. I think about missing it on purpose, but I don't want to be too obvious.

The ball lands in front of Rachel. She passes it back and forth between her feet (showing off, if you ask me) and kicks it back to me. I do a not-too-terrible job accepting her pass and send it back.

"You're not so bad." She stops the ball with her foot.

"Yeah, well you haven't sent me anything hard y—"

BAM! I can't finish my sentence because the soccer ball hits me full in the face.

"Oww!" My head snaps back. I grab my nose. "What the heck, Rachel!"

She purses her lips like she's trying not to smile. "You're right, Jim would have been able to head that back."

"Argh." I glare at her and finger the bridge of my nose.

"It's not broken, is it?" She comes close and looks at my face.

"I don't think so," I say sullenly. "But thanks a lot."

She shrugs innocently. "I was just trying to find out if you're really not Jim."

"You couldn't have found a less painful way to do it?" I turn toward the house, stomping up the yard to the door.

"Wait, are we done with soccer?"

"YES!" I walk inside, holding my face.

***

I say goodbye to Rachel at the front door, after my parents say goodbye and try to press on her one last time that Jim is telling the truth and that I, Matt, do indeed exist.

"Sorry about your face, Matt." Rachel reaches for the door handle.

"Hey." I smile. "You called me by my name. Does this mean you believe us?"

She sighs and folds her arms. "Yeah, I guess so."

"Jim will be relieved to hear that." I pause. Jim will kill me if he finds out I say this, but I say it anyway. "He likes you, you know."

Rachel stammers and blushes. I enjoy making her feel thrown off for once.

"Well, nice to meet you." Rachel recovers and turns away. "You can tell Jim I'll text him."

"Will do."

She starts to walk down the sidewalk.

"If Jim wakes up with a bruised face, I'm telling him it's your fault!" I call.

She glances back with a half-smile as she gets into her car.

A few minutes later, I'm sitting at the table with Mom and Dad for lunch.

"So?" Mom takes another bite. "What did you think?"

"She was kind of rude." I poke at my salad with my fork. "And the whole soccer-ball-in-the-face thing."

Dad looks at his plate and smiles.

"Dad," I complain.

"I think she was rude because she thought you were a lying Jim," Mom says. "She seemed very polite otherwise."

Dad swallows a bite of salad. "But now she knows Jim's telling the truth?"

"Seems that way."

"Well, Jim will be glad to hear that," Mom says with a smile. "So you didn't get hit in the face for nothing."

I sigh and lean my head back. "I am such a good brother."

Sunday, November 6
Jim

Before checking Vimer in the morning, I check for something from Rachel. I have a string of text messages from her.

> *hey jim*
> *i went to your house*
> *i met your parents*
> *and matt*
> *your parents are really nice*
> *matt was def not you*
> *im sorry i didnt believe you*

I text her back and move on to Matt's messages. I watch the ones from earlier in the day until I get to the one I want, Matt's last message of the day.

Matt is frowning. "So your friend Rachel kicked me in the face with a soccer ball today."

I open my eyes wide in surprise.

Matt feels his nose. "If your nose is black and blue tomorrow, that's why." (I touch my nose. It does feel a little bruised.)

"I was nice to her, too," Matt goes on. "Promise. Maybe I was annoyed at the beginning, but that's because she was calling me 'Jim' on purpose, trying to get to you. I'm assuming she wasn't nice because she was mad at you and taking it out on me. You're welcome."

I smile.

"Either that or she was freaked out that this weird stranger who played the drums and was kind of snarky had taken over her friend's body. Also a possibility. Too bad we're so weird, huh, Jim? Well, the good news is that I'm ninety percent sure she believes you now. She realizes *duocordis* is a real condition and you're not a pathological liar. Again, you're welcome. And because of the soccer ball in the face thing, I think either you or she owes me one. Just saying."

I laugh to myself as I get up. From what Matt and Rachel both said, her coming over was a success. Now Rachel knows I wasn't lying to her. But... does that make it any more likely that she'll want to be my friend?

Later today the Sharks are having their end-of-season party at Coach Garrett's house. Families are invited. I hope Rachel will be there.

Going downstairs in the morning, I ask Mom and Dad right away.

"So?" I'm cautious. "What did you think of Rachel?"

"She was nice." Mom stands up from the living room couch to walk into the kitchen.

I look at Mom pointedly.

"Well," she amends, "she was nice to *us.*"

"We talked about the game yesterday morning," Dad adds as Mom and I join him in the kitchen. "Good news—the Sharks won."

"Great!" Then I look back at Mom. "But back to Rachel...?"

"She wasn't the nicest to Matt," Mom admits. She looks at my face. "But I'm guessing you heard about that."

I smile. "Yeah. Does my face look bruised?"

Mom comes close and examines my nose. "No, I don't think you can tell."

"Matt said he thought Rachel was mad at me and taking it out on him, since she thought he was me."

Dad laughs. "That sounds about right." He flips a pancake on the griddle. "The good news is she knows you're telling the truth now."

"Yeah." I sit down at the table. "So now she knows I don't have a secret—" I stop. I'm about to say *girlfriend*, which would be disastrous for Matt. He told Mom that Rachel had seen him working with Zoe and that Matt ignored her and that's why she was mad. He didn't mention anything about them holding hands, or Rachel thinking that I had a girlfriend. "A secret," I finish awkwardly.

Mom looks at me funny, and I pretend not to notice as I pull a pancake onto my plate.

"I don't think I heard the whole story." Dad sits down at the table with us. "What exactly happened?"

I take a breath. "Rachel saw Matt downtown with Zoe on Tuesday while they were working, and she thought he was me, so she got mad at me. At first, I tried to pass Matt off as my normal identical twin brother, but then she kept thinking my story was fishy, so I blurted out the whole truth about Matt on accident. And then because it sounded so weird she didn't believe me, so she thought I was a pathological liar trying to pull off two identities or something. So I told her she could meet Matt and see for herself."

"She got mad just because she saw 'you' working with Zoe?" Mom pours syrup on her pancake.

Inside I squirm, hoping I won't give anything away. "Well, she said she tried to say hi to 'me,' but said I looked away like I didn't know her. I bet Matt didn't even notice."

Dad laughs. Mom nods. I take a bite and hope we can talk about something else.

★★★

Later after church, I go to my room to change. If I *am* going to see Rachel at Coach Garrett's house, I want to look good. I have my shirt picked out in my head. But I frown as I start leafing through the shirts on hangers in my closet and don't see the one I want.

I walk down the hall into Mom and Dad's room. "Mom, have you seen my gray collared shirt?"

"Um..." Mom looks up, distracted, from her laptop. "Did you check Matt's dirty clothes?"

"He wore it this week? Argh..." I rub my face.

Dad's also been changing out of church clothes. He walks out of their bathroom in a T-shirt. "I thought you guys have an open closet policy."

"Yeah," I mutter. A policy that's a real pain sometimes.

"And it's not like he can ask your permission when he's here."

I send Dad a glare that makes him smile.

"I'll wash it for you." Mom stands up. "Do you have time?"

I look at the clock on the wall and sigh. "No, I'm supposed to be there in an hour."

"Sorry, Jim." Mom does look sorry. "If it helps, you look nice in that blue striped polo."

I grumble as I turn to go back to my room.

"Are you sure you don't want us to come with you to your party?" Mom calls after me. "Didn't you say families are invited?"

I whip around. "*No!* I mean, um...no. Please. Families of the *kids* are invited. If you came that would be, um..." I make a face. "Different." Meaning totally uncool.

Mom looks disappointed, like she did the first time I told her they couldn't come. Dad chuckles.

***

An hour later, I stand on Coach Garrett's doorstep (in the blue striped polo). He opens the door before I have a chance to knock.

"Jim, hey!" He holds out a hand, and I shake it. I've never seen him in slacks and a polo before.

"Hey, Coach."

He leads me into the house. "I'll tell you, I've had a lot of six-year-olds ask where you are." Coach Garrett switches a can of soda back to his right hand. "I'm glad you made it."

"Sure, I wouldn't miss it." I glance up the hall. Coach Garrett and I are alone. I lower my voice. "So, um, I was wondering...do the parents know about my condition? I don't care either way, it's just nice sometimes to be prepared..."

He smiles gently. "I haven't talked about it with anyone."

I breathe out, relieved. Meeting a bunch of parents will be easier if I don't have to spend the whole time explaining a weird condition and watching people look at me in fascination and pity.

A few of the team members bombard me when they see me, but they're all distracted soon enough, running into the yard and chasing each other around a play set and a trampoline. I grab a bottled water and wander out to the backyard, watching them. There are a lot of kids there, siblings in addition to the team members. Speaking of siblings...

"Hey." Rachel has been sitting outside on the porch. She stands up and walks over to me.

"Hey." It's quiet for a moment. I've never seen Rachel in anything but soccer clothes before. Today, she's wearing hoop earrings, jeans, and a decidedly non-athletic shirt. I've always thought she was pretty. This is a whole new level.

"So, um..." Rachel starts, but she's interrupted by her dad walking up.

"Oh, hey, Coach Jim, right? I haven't had a chance to meet you yet." He has a big, enthusiastic voice. He holds out his hand and I shake it. "You've been a big help to Charlie this year."

"Yeah—I mean, sure, no problem. It's been fun." We talk more, and then Rachel's mom comes up and talks with us, and then a few more parents come up and introduce themselves. Everyone is nice. They make me feel welcome and appreciated. It's easy to smile, to make small talk, to feel at ease and share my favorite stories of the season about their kids.

At some point, Rachel slips away. When I can, I excuse myself from the other parents and go wandering around, hopefully not too obviously looking for her.

I find her inside an office, sitting in a chair and looking at her phone.

I take a breath and walk up to her. "So, who's better looking, me or Matt?" I lean on the desk next to her.

She glances up at me. "Is that supposed to be a joke?"

I feel uncomfortable, but I try to smile and shake it off. "Yeah."

Rachel sits up straighter and puts her phone away. "So...sorry I didn't believe you when you first told me about...you know."

I droop inside, wishing she weren't so uncomfortable with all this. On the outside, I try to act reassuring. "Oh, no problem. It's OK, I'm used to it."

Rachel laughs nervously and leans forward in her seat.

Looking at her, my smile falls. "I'm sorry I'm weird, Rachel. And I should have told you sooner." I pause, but she doesn't say anything. "Um, now that the season is over, I'll miss seeing you after Charlie's practices. And I've loved playing soccer with you and your friends. But I understand if..." I trail off pathetically.

Rachel twists back and forth in the office chair, her hair falling forward over her shoulder. The pause feels too long. "We're playing next Saturday." She looks up at me. "If you want to come."

I try not to jump for joy. "Oh, yeah, sure! I'd love to!"

"It's not Matt's day?"

"Nope. It's mine." I've never been happier to say those words.

She smiles cautiously. "OK," she says. "Cool."

Jim—Sun, Nov 6, 3:49 PM

rachel told me to tell you she's sorry about your face
thanks for convincing her you exist
but it was probably easy
all you had to do was be your normal disagreeable
self and that would have done it

Matt—Mon, Nov 7, 7:30 AM

pretty sure you're mixing the mickelsen brothers up
there. matt's the fun one and jim's the disagreeable one

don't worry it happens all the time

Jim—Tue, Nov 8, 7:11 AM

seriously though thanks
i'm playing soccer with her again this weekend

Matt—Wed, Nov 9, 7:14 AM

oh yeah?

way to go bro

8:54 PM

also

if i happen to hold a girl's hand again while we're
in the same body i'll try not to keep it a secret

Jim—Thu, Nov 10, 8:00 AM

yeah since when do we keep secrets from each other?

Matt—Fri, Nov 11, 7:43 AM

since we turned 17 and started hanging out with girls

chapter
twenty-six

Saturday, November 12
Jim

On Saturday, after I play soccer with Rachel and her friends, we're all walking across the street to the church parking lot so we can hop in our cars and leave.

I walk with Rachel toward my truck.

"Thanks for inviting me again," I say to Rachel.

One of the guys walking by hears. "Hey, Jim, you're invited any time!"

"Yeah!" a couple of other kids agree.

I look at Rachel with an apologetic shrug and she laughs.

We keep walking until she stops before the front doors of the building.

"I came with my mom," she says. "She's inside at a Bible study group. I'm going to wait until she's done."

"Want me to, uh, wait with you?" Someday, I'm going to get the hang of talking with her and will be at least a little smoother.

"OK," she says. "Sure."

***

A few minutes later, we're sitting on the curb in the parking lot. Everyone else has left.

Rachel holds a soccer ball under one foot, rolling it back and forth across the asphalt. Every now and then she rolls it to me, and I roll it back.

"So...what's it like?"

I know what she's talking about, but I pretend not to. "To drive a really crappy truck?" I nod at my car a few spots away in the parking lot.

She rolls her eyes. "No. You know—what's it like to live with—your condition—what do you call it?"

"Duo-COR-dis you-nus-cor-por-OH-sis," I supply. "Yeah, it's a mouthful."

She nods. "So...?"

I sigh. I never know how to answer a question like this. Answer it honestly? Tell her it sucks? "What do you mean?" I go with. "That's a broad question."

She smiles and kicks the ball toward me. "OK, fine. Here's a specific one. At your house, I saw your room and Matt's room. Matt tried to explain it, but I didn't get it. If you switch places at night, why do you have two beds?"

I lean back on my arms and tap the sidewalk with my fingers. "We *would* need only one bed, but what we like is having two rooms."

"They were different," Rachel observes.

I get embarrassed again at the thought of her looking into my bedroom when I wasn't there. "Yeah," I say. "Right. We're different. And we have our own tastes. And, like lots of brothers, we want our own rooms."

"And you sleep in your own beds...?"

"But wake up in each other's," I say. "Yeah, I know, it's weird and complicated."

"Right..."

"OK, specific question number one down. Any others?" I know she has to have more. Maybe being casual and open about Matt will be the easiest way.

"Did I bruise your nose when I kicked Matt in the face with a soccer ball?"

I laugh out loud at that. "Yeah, a little. But it didn't really hurt me. Matt was mad, though."

She smiles and winces. "Yeah...oops." Her smile falls. "OK, though, but my real question was...like, I didn't realize, but if Matt got hurt on his day, it would affect you, huh? And vice versa? Would you be mad at him if you woke up with a bruised nose?"

"Only if it wasn't your fault." I nudge her leg with my knee, and she smiles shyly. Then I get more serious. "But yeah, that happens. Like, we can't make it through a summer without one really bad sunburn, which will make one of us mad, but we've both done it. Then we've had little gashes or cuts or bruises here and there that we'll get mad at each other about, but nothing serious." My face falls. "Up until the Jones fracture."

Rachel's eyes widen. "Oh," she says softly. "I didn't realize... What did Matt think?"

"When he woke up with his foot in a boot and a lot of pain? He didn't talk to me for weeks."

"Huh." Rachel looks down.

It's quiet for a few seconds.

"So, I have another question," Rachel says, and I'm glad she's moving on. She's been rolling the ball, and she kicks it back to me. "How come it never came up before? Your condition, I mean? I saw you at Charlie's practices and games, and you came and played with us a couple times. All those events just happened to be on your days?"

"Well, not quite." I smile a little. "Back during soccer season, I made it to every other practice and game. Didn't you notice?"

"Well, there was the coach's son. I thought you took turns with him."

"Yeah. Because of the condition."

She shrugs, embarrassed.

"Then the first time you asked me to play soccer," I say, "yeah, it happened to be my day." *And I was elated*, I don't add.

"And the next?"

I shrug. "Yeah...well, that time it was Matt's day."

"Then how did you...?"

"We switched days," I say with a casual smile.

"You can do that?"

"Oh, sure, we can. Are we supposed to? No."

"What do you mean?"

"It's our parents' rule. We're not allowed to switch days for *anything*."

"How come?"

I roll my eyes. "Go ask them." I pause. "But I guess I can see why. If Matt and I were able to swap days with each other whenever we wanted, we'd have a lot more arguments than we already do."

"So, what did you do when it was Matt's day and you wanted to come play soccer?" Rachel looks at me curiously.

I smile. "We did it behind our parents' backs. First, it took some persuading to get Matt to swap with me, but he finally agreed."

"Not a natural rule-breaker?"

I laugh. "No, Matt's fine with breaking rules." I clear my throat. "He was just being kind of a jerk about it."

"Uh-huh." Rachel looks at me. "How do you do it behind your parents' backs?"

"If we set alarms in the middle of the night, we can switch places without them knowing. Then we pretend to be each other for a couple of days until we get the days switched back how they're supposed to be."

"So, the day you came and played soccer at the park...?"

"I was pretending to be Matt all day around my parents, until I came to hang out with you."

Rachel eyes me critically. "You could have told me then."

I look down, ashamed. "Yeah. I know. If Matt hadn't agreed to swap with me and I hadn't made it, I would have. But when I realized I'd be able to come..." I look up at her and shrug apologetically.

She considers me for a moment, then nods.

It's quiet for a few seconds as we both resettle in our sitting positions on the curb. "We got caught, though," I say after a pause.

"You did?"

"Yeah. Our parents realized what we were doing. They realized that I wasn't Matt." I start talking more quickly. "Actually, Matt was the one who got caught the next day, but he claims Mom wouldn't have been so suspicious if I had done a better job pretending to be him the day before..." I trail off, realizing how whiny I sound.

Rachel smiles. "So did you get punished?"

"Oh, yeah." I nod emphatically. "And Mom and Dad's punishment was borderline cruel and unusual. Since Matt and I had pretended to be each other when we weren't supposed to, they kind of forced us to be each other for the rest of the week."

Rachel scrunches up her nose. "Did they call you by the wrong name or something?"

"No, they just wouldn't let me do anything that Matt wouldn't be able to do. Like play soccer or the guitar. Same for him. He has a job, and they wouldn't let him work." I stop to remember. "We also had to wear each other's clothes and sleep in each other's rooms, but that wasn't as big of a deal."

"Wow. Sounds rough."

"It was super lame."

"Was it worth it?"

Her question catches me by surprise. I glance over to see Rachel looking at me out of the corners of her eyes with a sly smile.

"Uh—" I stammer for a second. "Um, yeah. Totally. Definitely worth it."

She smiles.

Tuesday, November 29
Matt

It's late November, and life is going well. Jim is happier now that Rachel knows about (and is OK with) his condition. I tell Zoe the whole story, and we laugh about it together. I keep holding her hand. It does feel better that I'm not keeping it secret from Jim anymore. (Though I do continue to keep it secret from my parents. Jim keeps his word and doesn't tell on me.)

Earlier this month, we went to visit Mom's sisters on the East Coast. We went the week before Thanksgiving—since Mom homeschools us, we can travel whenever, and we've found that doing actual holidays with extended family gets complicated. If we do it by ourselves at home, no one else feels like they have to do Thanksgiving dinner twice. But it's always great to be with our closest cousins and family, so we enjoyed a few days up there before actual Thanksgiving. We get to meet Lacey's fiancé, who seems like a decently cool guy. I tell her I approve. It's fun hanging out with our cousins, and it's nice having Thanksgiving at home, too.

Zoe and I continue to work for Pals, walking dogs or checking up on them and feeding them when their owners are out of town. We complete two more training sessions and start taking tasks with cats and the occasional rodent. Being inside homes checking on animals is a plus because it's getting cold enough to require jackets, gloves, and hats. But even walking outside between assignments, there's something fun about experiencing the cold, like it was fun experiencing the heat in the summer. No matter what, it's always fun with Zoe.

Saturday, December 10
Jim

Saturday is my first opportunity to see Rachel outside of soccer. Her high school team is having a blood drive, and she invites me to come. It isn't that special, but it does make me feel good to be invited. I run the idea of donating some of our blood by Matt and he's fine with it, so I'm all set to go.

All morning long, I'm looking forward to seeing her. I go to the gym in the morning and hurry through my schoolwork. When my math tutor leaves at 11:00, I drive to Rachel's school. I figure I can see Rachel, give blood, and then eat lunch. Because if she's eating lunch around the same time, and we can eat together...

At the high school, which I've been to a few times for Leo's plays, I park in the back parking lot and walk into the gym. There are rows of dark-blue chairs and adults in scrubs helping kids give blood. When I walk in, I'm smiling, looking forward to seeing Rachel, scanning the room for her. As

I get close to the first blue chair, I pause and stare wide-eyed as a nurse holds up a needle, studying it before inserting it into a girl's arm. Wow. That needle sure looks—

"Jim!"

I look up and see Rachel walking over to me.

"Hey, Rachel." I smile. She looks pretty in jeans and a blue sweater.

She smiles at me. "Thanks for coming."

"Sure." I walk over to her. "I'm glad I can help."

"I'll show you where you can sign in." Rachel leads the way to a folding table against one wall. I follow.

I sit down in a row of chairs with a clipboard of paperwork, trying with effort to concentrate on filling it out. I'm still unnerved by the sight of that needle. And Rachel sitting next to me, smiling at me, doesn't calm me down as much as make my insides flutter.

As I'm finishing the paperwork, a few girls walk up. Rachel and I stand.

"Hey, this is my friend Jim," Rachel says. Then to me, "Jim, these are girls from my soccer team."

Rachel tells me the names of the small group of girls. They're all nice.

"Hi, Jim!"

"Thanks for coming!"

"Rachel told us you play soccer, too."

I smile and try to be nice and social. I tell them that I'm homeschooled but that I play for Capital Soccer Club, and I'm bummed that it's the off-season. I try to ignore the nearest nurse inserting another needle.

"How's the blood drive going?" I ask.

"Oh, it's great!"

"Tons of people have come."

"It's been perfect."

Throughout it all, while I'm trying to be nice and social and smile and ignore the needles, Rachel stands there, smiling at me.

"There's an open chair." She points to one of the dark-blue chairs. "Want to go now, Jim?" Then she pulls me by the hand over to the empty chair.

It isn't like she's holding my hand (which would be against the rules anyway). But the feeling of her hand holding mine has my insides keyed up and my mind frozen.

A lady in scrubs is by the chair, and she has me sit down. I do so distractedly. Part of me is still fixated on the feeling of Rachel's hand. And the rest of me is getting more nervous as I see the needle the nurse is about to stick in my arm.

Rachel talks to the lady in scrubs. I sit there, feeling more and more nervous about the whole giving blood part of this thing. When it comes time for the lady to prick my arm, I shut my eyes and look away.

"Are you nervous, Jim?"

I open my eyes to see Rachel smiling at me.

I try to smile back. "I've never done this before," I admit.

She smiles and puts a hand on my free arm (the keyed-up insides again).

I didn't know I would feel squeamish around needles. It didn't cross my mind. Blood in movies and shows, and even in injuries, has never bothered me. And I get yearly vaccines without a problem...mostly... Well, OK, it's not like I look forward to them. And if I'm honest with myself, any time I can swing it so Matt gets the shots, that's fine with me. And if I *do* get shots, I guess I always look away when they stick it in my arm. Still, I can handle it. But there's something about these larger-than-average needles...

My eyes are closed, and I hear Rachel talking, asking about how I'm doing. I say things like, "I'm OK" and "fine" without registering much. Finally, the lady pulls the needle out and I open my eyes.

She's wrapping a green bandage around a wad of cotton over the crease in my arm. My number one thought and desire is to get out of that chair and as far away from the other needles as fast as I can. As soon as she's done, I stand up. But I'm surprised at how weak I feel.

"Are you OK, Jim?" Rachel says, sounding worried.

I turn my head to look at her, but before my eyes find her, they close as my body goes limp.

Saturday, December 10
Matt

"Jim."

My eyes are closed.

"Jim!" Someone pats my face, and I flinch. "Jim, come on, wake up!" The voice is gentle but has a slight note of panic.

"He should come to in a few seconds," another voice says. "This happens sometimes."

I'm on something hard, somewhere with lights above my head. I scrunch up my face and groggily think. Where am I? Why am I being called Jim? What's going on?

Someone pats my face again, and I open my eyes and squint up. There are several people leaning over me. One looks like a nurse. There are some teenage girls I don't recognize. But there's one I think I do.

"Rachel?" My voice is weak.

"Jim!" She leans back in relief. "Wow, you had us worried—"

"No, I'm not—" I start to say. I stop when I see Rachel's face. Her mouth pops open and she covers it with her hand.

Then Rachel speaks to the girls and nurse. "I think he's confused. Let me talk to him for a second." Before I can do anything else, she leans down so she can talk in my ear. I stiffen.

"Matt?" she says quietly. "Is that you?"

I nod.

"OK, listen. We're at my school at a blood drive. Jim just gave blood and fainted."

"He what!"

"Shh! The thing is, no one here knows about you. So you can either sit up and pretend to be Jim, or you can help me explain your condition to everyone right now."

I glance up at the girls and nurse kneeling around me. I don't hesitate much before I whisper back. "I'll be Jim."

Rachel nods. I think she's happy with my decision. Then she leans back and speaks to the nurse. "He says he feels OK. I think he'll be alright."

I lift my head off the ground. "Was I out long?"

"Just a little bit." The nurse starts touching my legs and arms. "Do you feel any pain? Did you hurt yourself as you fell?"

"Um, I don't think so..." I start to sit up.

"Wait, wait." The nurse pushes me down. "You need to lie down longer." She looks up and raises her voice. "Does anyone have a backpack or something we can prop his feet up with?"

Someone must bring a backpack or something they can prop my feet up with because they lift my legs and slide something underneath them before setting them down.

"Can't I get up?" I try to push myself up to sitting. "I think I'm OK..."

"Jim." Rachel looks at me. "You should do what the nurse says."

I close my eyes and shake my head. I'm pretending to be my brother around his...well, the closest thing to a girlfriend he's going to have. This feels too weird.

In a humiliating moment, many hands drag me across the floor of the high school gym, moving me out of the way of the chair so other people can continue donating blood. I decide to give Jim the benefit of the doubt and assume it wasn't his fault he fainted.

The nurse, Rachel, and a few other girls stay by me while I lie down.

"You looked like you were getting a little woozy while you were giving blood." The nurse looks at me with concern. "Have you given blood before?"

"No."

"Do you usually get queasy at the sight of blood?"

"No!" I say automatically. But is Jim the same? "I mean, I don't think so."

"What about food and fluids today? Did you eat lunch and drink plenty of water before you came?"

"Um…" I look up at everyone's faces. Rachel gives me the tiniest shrug. I try to pay attention to my stomach, which does feel empty. I settle with, "I probably could have eaten more."

A few girls from Rachel's soccer team, I assume, start asking questions, first about how I'm feeling ("Yeah, I'm OK, I'll be fine, thanks") and then about more Jim specifics.

"Has Capital Soccer ever done a blood drive?" one of them asks.

"Nope." I hope it's the right answer.

"What position do you play on your team?"

"Um…defense." I know Jim plays defense. I know there are multiple positions on defense. I know Jim has played several of them. But I can't remember what all the names are. Fullback? But right or left? (That's a thing, right?) Or is there a center fullback? And isn't there, like, a…scrubber? Or is it a sweeper? To be safe, I go with, "Just…all-around defense."

Rachel is looking at me funny.

"I think he's feeling weak," she says to the rest of the girls. "We should let him rest."

I close my eyes and nod, and thankfully they give me some space.

After a few minutes, they help me to a chair. Someone brings me a water bottle, someone else brings me a granola bar, and I'm told to put my head between my knees if I start to feel faint again. I'm starting to feel uncomfortable with all the attention, so I'm relieved when the nurse feels like she can leave me.

Before she does, she looks at Rachel. "Will you sit with him and keep an eye on him? He should rest a little more. Make sure he eats and drinks." The nurse walks away before Rachel, who looks as hesitant about it as I do, can say anything.

So she takes a seat next to me. After an awkward silence, we both pull out our phones (well, mine is Jim's). Rachel scrolls through a feed, and I text Leo, telling him what happened and laughing about it with him. Then I put my phone down and start sipping the water.

"So," I say after a pause. "What happened?"

Rachel looks up from her phone. "Jim gave blood, and I think it made him more squeamish than he thought it would. I think he was eager to be done and stood up too quickly, and he just...collapsed." Rachel doesn't look happy to be reliving the memory.

I shake my head. "Idiot."

Rachel looks at me, surprised. "It wasn't his fault!"

"I know, I know." I roll my eyes. "I'm kidding. He told me he wanted to donate blood and asked if it was OK, and I said sure. We both assumed that because we're healthy he'd be fine." I shake my head. "Apparently not. Now I feel like a loser. Does this happen often?"

"The nurse said sometimes. There was someone else who fainted today."

"Phew." Still, though. Jim and I are healthy and fit. What gives?

"So what made you and him switch places?" Rachel asks in a quieter voice. "I thought you switch places when you fall asleep. You were only unconscious for, what, a minute or less."

"That's all it takes." I shrug. "The second our body goes to sleep, Jim's gone and I'm here."

"So for him to come back...?"

"I either have to lose consciousness or sleep again."

"There's not any other way for you to switch?" Rachel asks. "Like, some sedative you can take or something that will make you briefly go to sleep?"

I shake my head.

"What about hypnosis? Like when magicians make people fall asleep for a second and then wake them up again?"

"That's not a thing."

"What do you mean that's not a thing—"

"It's not a thing. Go look it up."

She makes a face. "OK, what about anesthesia?"

"Oh, yeah, since Jim and I are certified anesthesiologists."

She rolls her eyes. "What about stuff like they do in the movies? Like breathing into a rag soaked in that chemical?"

"Chloroform? Too dangerous."

"What about when they hit people over the head to knock them out for a little bit?"

"Also not a thing."

"What! What do you mean? In all the movies—"

"Wait, Hollywood's unrealistic?" I pretend to be shocked. She's unamused. I roll my eyes. "It doesn't work like in the movies. Getting hit in the head is dangerous and unreliable and more likely to cause lasting head trauma than knock you out. Also, I would imagine it hurts."

"Hmm..." Rachel looks at me critically, out of ideas.

We sit in silence a few seconds more while I start on the granola bar.

"So," I say around a mouthful. "You haven't told your friends the truth about Jim."

Rachel looks annoyed. "I've told my close friends. The ones Jim hangs out with, the ones from my church that we play soccer with." She looks uncomfortable. "With my team it hasn't come up."

"Like it could have just now?"

Rachel just scowls at me.

I laugh a little. "Hey, I get it," I say. "Our condition doesn't exactly make things easy." I take a drink of water. "You must really like Jim if you hang out with him despite that."

This makes her blush, and I smile triumphantly.

After a few seconds, Rachel regains her cool. "Well, what about you? The first time I saw you, you were holding hands with a girl. Who is *she*?"

I look straight ahead and, at the mention of Zoe, have to try not to smile. "None of your business."

"Things going well, I presume?" She's teasing me.

"None of your business." I'm really fighting a smile now.

"Guess I'm going to have to get the details from Jim."

I laugh and shake my head.

"Hmm, maybe your mom, then." Rachel smiles wickedly. "She was friendly... I could visit Jim one day and casually bring up—"

"No!" I sit up straight, and my loud voice shocks Rachel into silence. She looks at me in surprise. "I mean..." I try to think of the right thing to say. "My parents, um, don't really know. And I want to keep it that way."

"Matt, are you telling me you have a secret girlfriend?" Now she looks impish, sounding like what I would imagine a little sister sounds like.

"No," I say quickly.

"Aw, are you embarrassed, Matt? That's kind of cute."

"No." I'm frustrated now. "I'd get in mega trouble, and my parents wouldn't want me to see her again."

Rachel is surprised.

I take a careful breath. "Jim and I have to live by a lot of rules. Some are about...girls." It's hard to get the last word out without sounding awkward.

"Oh." Rachel looks away from me, staring straight ahead.

I watch her sitting there, quiet, and realize that she didn't know. She didn't know that Jim and I aren't allowed to have girlfriends. But that isn't surprising. With Jim and Rachel just friends, I can see how discussing I'm-not-allowed-to-date-you rules would be awkward. If I put myself in Jim's shoes (like I'm literally doing in his canvas lace-ups at the moment), I would have done the same thing.

It's silent for a moment as Rachel looks away, and I try to relax again. "So..." I try to change the subject. "Have you kicked soccer balls in any other guys' faces lately?"

Rachel rolls her eyes. "Are you still bitter about that?"

"Oh, no, not bitter at all..."

We spend the next few minutes arguing over whether or not I'm bitter and whether or not she's mean. Then the conversation ends, and we sit in silence.

"This feels weird," Rachel says.

"You're telling me."

"I mean," she says, "last time I saw you, you were dressed in your own clothes. This time you look just like Jim...I mean, obviously you do, but you know what I—I mean, you *were* Jim less than an hour ago..."

I smile, amused. "But now I'm not?"

She shakes her head and gives me an unamused look. "Nope. Now you're not."

Finally, the nurse comes over, sees my empty water bottle and granola bar wrapper, and tells me I can leave. I reach in Jim's pocket for the keys and stand up. When I unknowingly head to the wrong door, Rachel impatiently leads me out the right door, walks me a few feet into the parking lot, and points out my truck.

"Need me to walk you farther?"

I roll my eyes. "Sorry you were stuck with me instead of Jim."

She smiles wryly. "Tell him I hope he feels better."

I looked at Rachel, amused. "Rachel, *I* feel better. So obviously—"

"OK, OK, you know what I mean." She's peeved. "Tell him I'll talk to him tomorrow."

"Yeah...about that..."

Rachel raises her eyebrows.

"Well," I explain. "Tomorrow's my day. I think my mom will want to keep it that way."

"Are you going to give Jim the rest of his day back?"

I shrug. "Depends on whether my mom wants me to nap or not."

Rachel looks at me critically. "That seems unfair to Jim."

"Unfair?" I walk backward away from her toward my truck. "No, that's crazy talk. Nothing about me and Jim is unfair at all." Then I turn around and leave.

***

"Jim." Mom comes into the kitchen from the office when I walk in the door. "That took longer than I thought. We were supposed to start English already."

"Sorry it took so long, Mom, and, oh, by the way, I'm not Jim." I open the fridge.

Mom looks at me, confused. "Matt? Why are you here?"

"Good to see you too, Mom." I move aside a dish of leftover lasagna.

She rolls her eyes. "You know what I mean. Have you two been trying to switch days again?" She's stern, so I shut the fridge, turn around, and speak quickly.

"No! It was an accident. Get this—Jim fainted!" I bend down to check the freezer instead.

Mom's eyebrows raise. "After giving blood? Are you OK?"

"Yeah, Mom, we're fine." I pull out a frozen breakfast sandwich, open it, and put it in the microwave. "They made me sit for a while and drink and eat some, but then I got to come home." I punch the microwave buttons and wait for my sandwich to heat up.

Mom stands next to me and feels my forehead.

"Mom." I'm unamused. "What are you doing?"

She looks at me, worried. "Well, I'm glad you're OK. I'm sure that was scary."

I shrug. "Mostly confusing. I woke up on the gym floor with a bunch of strangers leaning over me. And then I had to pretend to be him because no one knew about his condition."

Mom smiles. "I'm sure he'll be grateful." Her smile falls a little. "Do you know why he fainted?"

"I don't think he ate enough beforehand. And from the sound of it..." I can't help grinning wickedly. "I don't think he handles needles very well."

Mom smiles. "Try not to tease him too much."

The microwave beeps, and I reach inside to pull out my sandwich. "No promises."

After my late lunch, Mom does try to make me nap, but when I go to lie down in bed, I know right away that it isn't going to work. I'm too awake. My brain is too active. I make a mental list of things to tell Jim while I lie down, humoring my mom until she gives me permission to get up.

Things to tell Jim:

1. You fainted because you gave blood?! Ha! You wimp.
2. Bad news: I accidentally told Rachel about the we're-not-allowed-to-date-girls rule.
3. Good news: She was sad about it and is clearly into you.

Saturday, December 10
Jim

"Jim."

Someone is shaking my shoulder.

"Jim."

I roll over and blink. I'm in Matt's room, and it's dark. I sit up so quickly I almost hit Mom's head. She backs out of the way.

"What happened?" My voice is groggy.

Mom sighs. "You fainted after you gave blood today. Matt was awake the rest of the afternoon and evening. He tried to nap, but it wasn't working. He went to sleep an hour ago, and..." She makes a face that tells me she's about to break bad news. "I'm sorry, but tomorrow is an orange day and we've got to stay on track."

I give an exasperated sigh and flop back on my bed. So Mom's waking me up just to send me back to sleep so Matt can have his day tomorrow.

"That's so unfair," I mutter with my eyes closed.

"It's not his fault," Mom says.

I open my eyes. "Can I check Vimer?"

Mom hands me my phone.

First, I check my text messages, which are almost entirely fainting GIFs courtesy of Matt and Leo.

There's one Vimer sent *from* my phone. Matt is sitting in the truck, parked outside the school.

"You *passed out?*" he laughs. "Ha! You wimp!"

I groan. He's never going to let me live that down.

The other update was sent in the evening, a few hours ago before Matt went to sleep.

"Hey, Jim," he says. "Sorry I took your Saturday afternoon. But it wasn't my fault. I guess not your fault either that you're a big baby. Unless —" He looks stern. "Did you really skip lunch? Because that would have been really dumb."

I wince.

Matt goes on to tell the whole story of him waking up, seeing Rachel, and pretending to be me, which makes me feel partly grateful to him but partly resentful.

"And one last thing…" Matt adds. He looks hesitant. "I didn't mean to, but I stumbled into telling Rachel about Mom and Dad's rule that we're not allowed to date girls." He looks at the camera, wincing. "She didn't know. Heads up, now she might ask you about it."

My heart sinks. I can't imagine that not being awkward.

"But," Matt says, starting to smile, "if it makes you feel better, she was disappointed."

I swallow, feeling anxious and nervous and unsure and excited all at once.

Jim—Mon, Dec 12, 7:02 AM

OK OK enough
it's not like i'm the only one who's fainted giving blood

Matt—Tue, Dec 13, 7:31 AM

just you and all the other morons who
give blood on an empty stomach

or is it because you keel over when you see a needle?

i honestly can't decide which one i'd rather mock you for

Jim—Wed, Dec 14

chapter
twenty-seven

Monday, December 12
Jim

    After Matt tells me he accidentally told Rachel about the no-girlfriend rule, I decide I'm not going to say anything about it. Rachel doesn't bring it up, either, which I'm glad for. There's no way I can imagine that conversation not being awkward. It's probably best that she found out about the rule from someone other than me.

    Mom and Dad explained the rule to each of us a few years ago. They spelled out that Matt and I will never be able to get married. Or have kids. Or have girlfriends. Ever.

    Matt and I are not normal teenage guys, but we're still teenage guys, so we've liked girls throughout the years, girls at the gym or church or a homeschool group. One summer, there was a lifeguard at the neighborhood pool who Matt and I both had a crush on (but since she was older than us it wasn't a huge deal).

    Still, aside from Andie last year (which we all know doesn't count), neither Matt nor I have broken the rule. But thinking of Matt telling Rachel does make me think about him and Zoe. This is the first time one of us is breaking the rule. What's going to happen? What will Mom and Dad do if they find out? I know that if they do, it won't be from me. I have no desire to get Matt in major trouble.

    But still, it doesn't seem quite...fair. That Matt has what you might call a girlfriend (it feels so weird to say). All I have is a friend-that's-a-girl. I've told myself that's all I need, but the more time I spend around Rachel, the harder it is to convince myself that it's true.

Monday, December 19
Matt

Monday is the start of a three-week break from school, and I'm in good spirits. I'll have more time to hang out with Leo, who has finished (and killed) his performance of *Arsenic and Old Lace*. And he only has a few days of finals before he's out of school for Christmas break, too.

Although Leo is great, the biggest reason I'm happy about the break is spending more time working with Zoe. The income is nice, and Zoe and I have fun walking dogs and doing our other tasks. But those times aren't as nice as the times we have between tasks, going on walks, bundled up, holding hands even though it's cold, warming up by buying hot chocolate or fresh-baked cookies at the end.

***

In the afternoon, we work together. Even after I get home and walk into the house, I'm smiling. I hang up the keys to the truck and, when Termite walks over to me, bend down to hold his head in both of my hands.

"Hey, hey, bud!" I smile as he wiggles and whines, acting a little funny like he always does after I work because he can smell so many other dogs on me. I try to give him extra attention. "Hey, didja miss me? How much do you love me? How much?"

Termite lunges for my face to lick me, forgiving me for my strange smell, and I laugh and stand, scratching him behind the ears. That's when I see Mom and Dad sitting at the kitchen table.

"Hi," I say uncertainly. The way they're both sitting, looking at me... something has to be up.

I sit down next to them. "What, did somebody die?"

Mom looks at me seriously. "Matt, we need to talk about something."

"About what?" And, though on the outside I'm confused, somewhere deep down inside, part of me is aware of what they're going to say next. A part so deep down, I pretend like it doesn't exist.

"About Zoe." Dad is serious.

The part of me that isn't supposed to exist rears up, claiming control of all my internal organs. It isn't a pleasant sensation. I slump in my seat and stare into space.

"Matt." Dad tries to move so I'm looking at him. "You know the rules. And you've been breaking them."

"We just work together," I protest.

"Holdings hands is not 'just working together.'"

Crap. I'm torn between dejection and anger. I scowl. "Did Jim tell you?"

"Jim *knew*?" Mom says.

Oops. I shrug. There goes the anger.

Dad frowns. "You were spotted downtown by one of my employees, who will remain nameless."

Dang it. Stupid employee.

Dad softens. His next words are more disappointed than stern. "Matt, you know better."

Mom sighs. "This can't keep going on."

"I'll stop holding her hand, OK?" My voice is sullen.

Mom shakes her head. "No. Even becoming emotionally attached to a girl is something that isn't wise for you to do."

Those words sting. My body tenses up when Mom says them. I stare down at the table, clenching my teeth. I have to exercise a lot of control to stay sitting at the table. There's a pause when I don't move, and neither of my parents says anything.

"Matt." Mom's voice is gentle now. "I know that it's unfair."

Unfair is right. That's the phrase that's screaming through my head, over and over. *IT'S NOT FAIR!*

"Certain people are born with certain conditions that limit their lives in different ways." Mom is still gentle. I tense up more, knowing exactly what she's going to say and hating it. It's an oft-repeated explanation. "It's not fair for someone to be born with Down syndrome, or with spina bifida, or—"

"With a congenital heart defect, I know, I get it," I snap. I keep my eyes down on the table. I'm sick of that approach.

Dad tenses up. I'm sure there's a "don't talk to your mother that way" waiting behind his lips.

Mom sighs. "We're sorry, Matt."

Dad speaks. "This is nothing new. We've talked about this before. You know girlfriends are off-limits. If you've been telling yourself that what you've been doing with Zoe is OK, we're here to tell you that it's gone too far."

"So what am I supposed to do?" There's more of an edge to my voice. "What do you want me to do? Stop talking to her? Quit my job? Never see her again?"

Mom and Dad are silent.

"It's a difficult situation," Mom admits. "But there's a line you and Jim can't cross. Now that you have, adjustments will need to be made."

There's something she says that I pick up on. "Has Jim crossed a line, too?"

Mom and Dad look at each other. "We're planning on talking to him about Rachel," she admits.

I gape. *That* is crazy. He hasn't broken any rules. Are we not allowed to have girls as *friends*?

"Why don't you lock us up so we never get to know any girls, then?" I say angrily.

"Matt, it's not that. Of course we want you to have friends—"

"It sure doesn't seem like it!" I yell and jump up from the table at the same time.

"Matthew." Dad stands up too and looks at me sternly.

I glare back at him. I'm shaking. Without saying anything else, I stomp away from the table, away from my parents, and upstairs.

"Matt—"

I ignore her and, when I get to my room, slam the door shut.

***

The first thing I do is put on my headphones and play the loudest, angriest music I can. Then I pace before grabbing my phone and slamming myself down on my bed. I turn off the music and open Vimer to talk to Jim.

"Jim. Get ready for a super unfair conversation with Mom and Dad." I force myself to take a breath. "They told me I'm too serious with Zoe." I pause. "Yeah, they found out about the hand-holding. But I said I'd stop. And they still said no! They made it sound like because I like her, I can't be her friend! Here's the kicker." I stand up to pace. "They said *you've* been too serious with Rachel!" I look at the camera in disbelief. "OK, I admit, I shouldn't have held Zoe's hand. I was dumb. But you and Rachel? Unless they know something about you that I don't, you haven't broken any rules." I shake my head. "But Mom and Dad said you've crossed a line! Word-for-word quote!" I'm yelling. "Super unfair, right? If we're not allowed to get to know girls as *friends*?" I collapse on my bed again. "This *sucks*!"

Tuesday, December 20
Jim

When I wake up in the morning and check Vimer, I notice that Matt didn't leave me a message at the end of his day. I don't think much of it, though. It's happened before. Our break from school just started. He probably stayed up late watching movies and went to bed half asleep.

During the day, I go to the gym for some weight training, and I have soccer lessons, and guitar lessons, and after Leo gets home from school, I go over to help him study for his last day of finals. Then his mom invites me over for dinner. It isn't until about eight o'clock that I'm home.

I walk in the front door and call, "Hey, Mom and Dad! I'm home!" I'm on the way to my bedroom when I hear my name and turn around to see Mom and Dad both sitting at the kitchen table.

I slow in my tracks. They're both looking at me seriously.

"What's wrong?" I say, unnerved.

Dad gestures for me to sit, so I do, on the edge of my chair, no idea what's coming but with a feeling it isn't going to be good.

"Mom and I want to talk to you," Dad says, "about Rachel."

I'm silent.

"We think you've been spending too much time with her," Mom says carefully.

"What?" My voice is small.

"Too much time," Mom repeats. "You know our rule about girls."

"But I haven't broken any rules," I say. "Right? I mean, I haven't, like..." I feel myself getting warm. "Like, held her hand or anything. We're just friends." I look at Mom and Dad pleadingly.

"You have to be careful," Dad says. "You and Matt both. We've talked about this. You know we have. Certain things for you and Matt are off-limits—like girlfriends."

I feel like I have the wind knocked out of me, like someone just hit me in the chest. "But Rachel's not—I mean—she's not my—"

"Maybe not yet." Mom says gently. "But, from what Dad and I see, you might be heading that way."

"But..."

"Jim, look what's happened these last few months. Because of her, you convinced Matt to break the rules."

"You've been seeing her frequently," Dad adds.

"We can tell how you feel about her."

I feel myself getting warm again. "So I'm not allowed to like a girl?"

Mom and Dad look at each other. "It's complicated, Jim."

I'm speechless for a second, until I know exactly what to say. "Wait, what about Matt and Zoe?" If Matt is going to get away with what he's been doing with Zoe while I get punished, I'll be seriously tempted to go back on my word and tell Mom and Dad about the handholding.

"We've talked to him, too," Mom says.

"When?"

"Yesterday."

And he didn't tell me about it? Thanks for the heads up, Matt. "He didn't tell me about that."

"Well..." Mom looks down, uncomfortable. "He, um —" She glances at my dad, who looks back. I watch suspiciously.

"He'll either find out from us or find out from him," Dad says to her in an undertone.

Mom nods. "Matt did leave you a message about it. We removed it from your video thread, but —"

"WHAT?" I jump up from the table. "*You deleted one of Matt's messages to me?!*"

"Jim!" Dad stands up too. "Don't shout. You'll see the message. We saved it. He was angry, and we wanted a chance to talk to you first —"

"You watched it, too!?"

"No, we didn't watch it." Dad sounds impatient. "He was shouting so loud we could overhear the whole thing. And we didn't like what he was saying —"

"And that makes it OK?!"

"He was angry, Jim." Mom sits and looks up at me. "He was telling you things we wanted to get a chance to talk to you about first. We didn't want that message to be the first thing you saw this morning."

"That's not fair!" For some reason I'm way more upset that they've kept Matt's message from me than the fact that they're telling me I need to stay away from Rachel. "You can't do that. You can't keep us from talking to each other."

"He was very angry," Mom repeats.

"So?" *I'm* very angry. "I still have a right to hear about it. If we were normal brothers, you would never do something like that. It's like locking one of us up so we couldn't talk to each other."

"If you were normal brothers, we could have a conversation with both of you at the same time instead of giving you time to vent to each other about it behind our backs." Dad is getting angry, too.

"Vent to each other?" I turn to face him. "Since when? We can't talk in real time. That's unfair enough. Now you're trying to censor his messages to me?" I exhale loudly in frustration.

"Plenty of parents monitor their kids' cell phone usage." Mom tries a different angle.

"This is different, and you know it!"

"Jim!" Dad says. But I ignore him. I turned toward the stairs.

"Jim, wait—"

But I'm not looking back.

I slam the door to my room and start pacing, stomping every step. It's so unfair. *So* unfair.

I can think of one thing I want to do. The more I think about it, the more elaborate the idea becomes.

Matt and I will go down to our truck. We'll sneak around our parents so they don't see us leaving. We'll argue over who gets to drive and who has to sit in the passenger's seat. We'll drive to Sonic. I'll get my usual favorite—a cherry limeade—and Matt will get his favorite, which is—shoot, I don't know. We've never been to Sonic together. Anyway, he'll get it, whatever it is, and we'll get our drinks and talk about how unfair our parents are being and how mad we are at them. Then we'll get in the car and drive home, blasting loud, angry music and singing along.

Of course, it can never happen. Not until the procedure, and there's no telling when that will be.

I sit slowly on the edge of my bed.

My whole life, I've had to deal with this feeling of being cut off from Matt, who—despite all the arguments, despite how much I have to share with him, despite how annoying and manipulative and cocky he can be—is my brother. That's one of the hardest things about our condition that a lot of people don't understand. Mom and Dad have always done so much to help me and Matt get along, to be best friends, even. And now they're interfering with us talking to each other? It's like everything is flipped upside-down.

Since Matt and I can't go to Sonic, I have to settle for what we always settle for—Vimer. I pull out my phone and have it pointed at my face when my door opens.

It's Dad. I look at him disgustedly. "Can I have some privacy, please?"

Dad instead comes in and sits on the bed next to me. "No. We'll do what we should have done yesterday—talk to Matt together."

Mom joins us in the room.

I glare at them. "That's still not fair."

Dad sighs. "Jim, nothing about this is fair. For you, for Matt, for us." That makes me clench my teeth. It isn't fair for *them*? "Can we throw out the 'it's not fair' phrase please?"

I grunt.

"Come on." Dad pulls me off the bed. "Let's go to the basement."

I roll my eyes, knowing I shouldn't let myself go along with this but doing it anyway.

We go downstairs. Mom, Dad, and I sit on the couch. Mom turns on the camera on the TV and starts talking.

"Matt," Mom says evenly to the camera. "We think we made a mistake yesterday. We took one of your messages away from Jim—"

"Which isn't fair." My arms are folded, and my body is sunk into the couch.

"It was the message you sent last night," Dad says to the camera. "The one where you told him about our talk with you about Zoe. We didn't think it was fair for Jim to see that message first thing in the morning, before we had a chance to talk to him about Rachel."

My body tenses so tight, thinking about the injustice of it all, that I start shaking. I look away from the camera and keep my arms folded.

"Now, can we please talk about girls?" Mom says. She turns toward me. "Jim." She looks back at the TV. "Matt. You know this. You know you can't have girlfriends. I know it's tough, and a hard distinction to make, but we think—"

"No!" I jump up from the couch, unable to take it anymore. "I want to talk to Matt myself! This isn't fair!" I start to walk away. Dad stands up and makes a move to grab my arm. I jerk away. "Stop it!"

"Jim!" Dad's starting to look angry. "That's uncalled for."

"So is what you're doing!"

Mom sighs. "Please, Jim. Calm down."

"I'm not going to calm down!" I can't stop yelling.

"Jim, do not shout at your mother."

"Who should I shout at?" I turn and yell in my dad's face. "You?"

That's too far, and I know it. For a second, looking at my dad stare at me with his eyes open wide, I'm afraid. But Dad doesn't lose his temper. Instead, he holds out his hand.

"Give me your phone." His voice is steady, quiet, and dangerous.

My mouth drops open. Mom and Dad have never taken our phones away before, no matter how bad we've been.

"Give it," he repeats.

I exhale frustratedly, take my phone out of my pocket, and slam it into his hand. Then, before they can stop me, I stomp to my room again.

Later, I hear a knock on my door.

"Jim?" Mom says. I don't respond. "Jim, we're not trying to keep you from talking to Matt." She sounds sad. "Of course we want you to talk to each other. You can use the basement webcam, or his phone, or your laptop. And you can have your phone back as soon as you promise to talk with us calmly."

I don't respond and she leaves.

At night, after I pull out a notebook and write a note to Matt asking him what his favorite Sonic drink is, I write a letter and put it under my pillow. I just need to make sure Matt finds it.

Wednesday, December 21
Matt

In the morning when I wake up, I don't see the message written on my hand until I grab my phone and flop down on my own bed. As I hold up my phone in front of my face I get a glimpse of my left palm. LOOK UNDER MY PILLOW, the words say in ballpoint pen in Jim's handwriting. So before I check Vimer or my other messages, I head back to Jim's room.

There are several folded pieces of paper under his pillow. I sit on the edge of the bed I just made, unfold them, and read.

> YOU WILL NOT BELIEVE WHAT MOM AND DAD DID TODAY!!! They TOOK AWAY MY PHONE! Why? Because I was super angry and shouting at them. And why was I angry? Because last night they TOOK AWAY YOUR MESSAGE TO ME! Without even telling me about it!

My mouth drops open. The rest of Jim's letter, where he tells the whole story, just makes it drop farther. The letter ends like this:

> Seriously, what are we going to do if there's a risk of Mom and Dad taking away what we leave for each other? How are we

supposed to trust them now? We've got to think of something, Matt. We can't let this stand. Right?

Wish you were here.

I lower the papers and sit in shock. Then, at first slowly but moving more quickly, I stand up and go downstairs.

By the time I reach the bottom of the stairs I'm running.

"MOM!" I shout before I reach the living room. "What is this!?" I hold up the papers. "*You tried to censor me to Jim?!*"

"Matt!" Mom jumps, surprised, and turns around. Dad rushes in from the office.

"Is this true?" I yell.

"Matt, calm down!" Dad says. "Is what true?"

I hold up the papers again. "Jim says you took one of my messages away from him—*without telling him about it!*"

Mom and Dad look pained.

I hold up the papers a third time. "Under my pillow. Guess you didn't check there, did you? What about this?" I hold up my palm. "Guess you didn't think to sneak in at night and wash it off? You're going to have to work harder than that if you want to keep me and Jim from talking to each other."

"Matt." Mom reaches toward me. "Of course we don't want to keep you and Jim from talking to each other. Come here. Let us explain." She tries to lead me to the living room couch. I stiffen.

"And you took away his phone?!" I say. "You can't do that! That's like—it's not—" I sputter, searching for words. "That's like taking away *me*!"

"Taking away the phone was a symbol." Dad looks at me sternly. "He was showing some seriously unacceptable behavior. He can have his phone back tomorrow once he recognizes that. And we never said he couldn't talk to you." Dad nods at the papers in my hand. "Looks like he found a way."

"Argh!" That makes me *super* mad. No matter what they say, they're trying to make it difficult for me and Jim to talk to each other. "You can't do that! That's so unfair!"

"Please calm down," Mom begs.

"No!"

Dad isn't as calm as Mom is. "Matthew, stop shouting, or you will lose your phone, too!"

"Is that what you want? Fine!" I take out my phone, toss it onto the couch, and stomp up to my room.

Later when I try to leave the house, Mom catches me and tells me I'm not allowed to. Without a phone, she explains, I can't drive around. And until I apologize, I'm not getting my phone back. I can't even walk down to Leo's house because he's at school. So I spend a very angry day at my drums, in the yard with Termite, and up in my bedroom on my computer.

Thursday, December 22
Jim

Something wakes me up around midnight. It's an alarm clock, the little battery-operated kind, the one Matt and I took to Camp Waller last year. I turn it off and automatically reach for Matt's phone to see what time it is. The nightstand is empty.

I sit up, rubbing my face, and look around. The chair to Matt's desk has been dragged into the center of the room. On it sits our laptop, open, with a sticky note on the screen that says, "Log in as me and play the video."

I swing my legs out of bed and pull the chair over. In Matt's video, he's wearing pajamas and dressed for bed. He doesn't look happy.

"So guess who else lost a phone today? Wow, I was so mad at Mom and Dad after I read your letter. They didn't like it when I yelled at them any more than when you did." Then Matt fills me in on everything—everything Mom and Dad said to him on Monday night, everything he said to me in the deleted message, everything they said to him after he found my note.

"Anyway," Matt says after the updates. "You're right. There's no way we can let Mom and Dad treat us like this and we've got to do something. And I have an idea."

He outlines his plan to me, and I start to get excited.

"I started today," Matt goes on. "But I need your help. Also, I think we should get this done as fast as we can—I *really* want my phone back—so we won't get much sleep tonight. If you think this idea is enough—" Matt stops. "Actually, I'm not sure you will. I know you were really mad at Mom and Dad. Because—" He smirks. "Bruh. Do you know what got recorded on the basement webcam yesterday? I was surprised Dad didn't hit you, Jim!"

I groan but smile.

Matt goes on. "Anyway, if you're on board, you can work on it tonight as long as you need to. When you're ready, go to sleep and set a short alarm, and I'll wake up and take over. To help us survive the night, I did bring up this..." Matt shows me a handful of snacks and water bottles. "And... this." Matt holds up a small 5-hour Energy bottle and looks at the camera unsurely. "Leo gave it to me. I know we've never tried one before. I'll let you decide."

I sit up fully, rubbing my face to wake myself up. I move to Matt's desk, putting the laptop on it. Next to me on the desk is the 5-hour Energy. Hesitantly I pick it up. After reading the bottle and thinking for a second, I chug the whole thing.

Thursday, December 22
Matt

I open my eyes and blink a few times while I listen to the sound of the alarm going off. Rubbing my eyes heavily, I sit up in bed. I'm in my room. It's still dark outside. Looking at the clock tells me that it's 6:00 AM.

I grab the computer, eager to see what Jim has said and what he's been up to the past five hours. Did he like my plan?

His video tells me that he did. "Great idea, Matt," he says. "I did what you said. I found some clips and made some suggestions to the script. Also, I took this..." He holds up the energy shot. "And wow, it really worked! I've felt so awake! Though..." He makes a face. "I hope you don't have to deal with a crash. I'm giving you a solid hour of sleep. Hopefully you feel alright when you wake up."

I do feel alright. Maybe not great or rested, but what can I expect? Our body has been up all night. I feel well enough to do what I need to.

The first thing I do is quietly open my door and tape a note on the outside.

WE DON'T WANT TO TALK
LEAVE US ALONE

Then I unwrap a pack of cookies, sit down at the computer, and get to work.

Thursday, December 22
Jim

The next time I wake up, I'm not feeling nearly so alert as I did when I went to bed twelve hours earlier, and I have a killer headache. I drag myself up, rub my eyes, and stumble over to Matt's desk.

I watch his video message to me first.

"I'm done." Matt yawns and rubs his face. "I finished. But you can change anything you want to. When you're happy with it, send it to Mom and Dad. And then..." Matt yawns again. "You might want to go back to sleep. I'm exhausted. I know it's your day and it's almost over anyway, but I'll give you tomorrow if you want."

I gulp a bottle of water as I pull up the other video, the one Matt has spent the day creating. I pay close attention as I watch it.

It starts with a really old clip of me. I'm wearing a blue sweatshirt, and Mom is standing behind me, holding me in front of the camera and cheerfully encouraging me to say hi to Matt. Then comes Matt's response from the next day, same thing (except he's in an orange shirt). As far as we can tell, it's the first time we ever talked to each other. We were four.

The screen goes black and text appears.

Everything we've ever said to each other is recorded

Then comes a montage of clips, all of me and Matt talking to each other, from when we were little up until this past year. In some, we're happy and joking, in some we're down and commiserating, and in some we're ticked and yelling at each other. There's music playing in the background, which is a nice touch. The clips play faster and faster, eventually flashing on the screen one after the other. So many clips. So many conversations. Then the screen goes black, and more text appears, explaining how difficult our condition is and how much our phones mean to us.

It isn't mean. It isn't angry. But it's powerful. Shoot, it almost makes *me* want to cry. I know it's going to get to Mom, and hopefully to Dad, too.

I export the video and send it to them. I leave a message for Matt telling him I think the video is great. I set another alarm and, very gratefully because my head is killing me, I let my head hit the pillow and fall almost immediately asleep.

Thursday, December 22
Matt

I creep down the stairs. There are sounds coming from the kitchen, low voices and water running in the sink and a pot being put on the stove. When I reach the bottom of the steps, Termite rushes over to me, wagging his tail. I pat him quietly, but Mom and Dad still notice.

"Jim," Mom says, coming over and hugging me like she hasn't seen him in a week.

"Actually, it's Matt." I pull away. "Sorry to disappoint."

"Matt." She smiles. "Of course I'm not disappointed."

Dad walks over too, and I'm surprised to look down and see him holding my phone and Jim's. He offers them to me. "Ready to talk?"

I take the phones almost hesitantly. "OK." My voice is low and I'm looking at the floor, but I mean it.

Mom and Dad have been making a late dinner. The smell of spaghetti sauce and garlic bread soon fills the kitchen. Dad sets the table, and we all sit down.

"Want some real food?" Dad asks, dishing me up a plate. "What have you and Jim been living off of all day?"

"Crackers, cookies, and granola bars." I pick up my fork and start playing with my food. "And a 5-hour Energy shot."

Both Mom's and Dad's eyebrows shoot up and they stare at me.

"*What?*" Dad seems like he would be mad if he weren't so shocked.

"It's alright," I say. "We're fine. It helped, but..." I rub my left temple. "I have a huge headache. I don't think we'll be tempted to drink another any time soon."

Mom sympathetically rubs my back, and Dad thankfully shakes his head and lets it drop. For a few minutes we all eat in silence.

"So." I break it. "You watched the video." It's a statement, not a question.

"We watched it." Mom says. "It communicated your message very well."

"We were wrong to take your phones," Dad says with effort. "And to take away your message. We won't interfere with you and Jim talking to each other again."

I nod, look down at my plate, and don't say anything. Mom and Dad eat in silence some more, but I mostly sit and twirl spaghetti on my fork without taking a bite. For some reason, I don't have much of an appetite.

"That was a well-done video," Dad says. "Did you make it?"

"Me and Jim together. He helped me find clips and figure out what to say. I put the videos together." My voice sounds dull, or maybe I'm just tired.

"Maybe you guys should go into advertising." Dad is smiling when I glance at him.

I'm surprised. No one in our family talks a lot about what Jim and I will do when we grow up. We know it will happen. But it won't be easy to figure out. Will we each get our own part-time job? Will we share a full-time one? If so, how on earth are we going to agree on what to study and what to do? Will we get the procedure done before it becomes an issue? Our family has reached an unspoken agreement that we'll put off talking about it until it gets closer.

"Maybe." I shrug and look down again.

"How's Jim feeling?" Mom asks. "Is he still angry?"

"He'll be alright now that he has his phone back." For the first time I smile, though slightly. "Though he was pretty mad." I address my dad. "I saw what happened in the basement before you took his phone away."

"Whew." Dad exhales and opens his eyes wide in disbelief.

"I'm surprised you didn't hit him," I say, smiling wider.

"I about did." Dad smiles, too. "Maybe we should go down and delete that clip."

"No," I say. "Don't. It'll be the type of thing that will be really funny to watch in a few years."

And then Mom and Dad laugh, and, as long as I can avoid thinking too much about the Zoe conversation we'll have to have, things between me and Jim and our parents feel normal again.

Friday, December 23
Jim

A sound wakes me up, music playing in my ears through headphones. I sit up and groggily take them off, then look around.

I'm in Matt's bed and my phone is on his nightstand. I jump to pick it up and see that it's just after midnight.

I sit up in bed and open Vimer.

"Hey, Jim." Matt is sitting in bed. "I think everything's OK now. Mom and Dad watched the video. It worked. They gave us our phones back and said they were sorry."

In the video, Matt goes on. "We're still in for lectures about girls, which I promised to be more mature about." Matt sighs dramatically. "Man, life is hard sometimes. But I'm glad we made that video. Dad said it was so good we should go into advertising." Matt gets a funny expression on his face, like he can't believe he just said that. Then he brushes it aside and moves on. "You're sure about giving me tomorrow? You can set another alarm and have some of it if you want. I don't mind. Oh, and I did take care of your chores for you, so either way you're covered there." Matt gives a big yawn. "My head still hurts. I drank a lot of water, which is supposed to help. Hope you feel better next time you wake up. All for staying away from energy shots from now on say 'aye.'" He smiles briefly. "Talk to you later, Jim."

My response is one word: "Aye." Then I yawn and put the phone away, relieved to have my phone back and feeling better than I thought I would about the whole thing with our parents. And for all the times Matt can be a jerk, he can be nice, too.

Hey Matt what's your favorite drink to get at Sonic?

Eh I always get something different. If I'm not in the mood to try something new I get a cherry limeade. Why? What's yours?

Cherry limeade??? NO WAY ME TOO I GET EXACTLY THE SAME THING! What a coincidence. Seriously what are the odds?

Haha. kinda weird that we share a body and we don't know each other's favorite Sonic drink huh!

I was thinking the same thing. I guess not surprising since we've never been together

That's what I wish mom and dad would understand

Yeah me too

chapter
twenty-eight

Friday, December 23
Matt

When I come downstairs the next morning, Dad is alone in the kitchen.

"Where's Mom?" I head to a barstool.

"Christmas shopping." Dad is in warm athletic clothes unloading the dishwasher.

"Are you going in to work today?"

"I took it off." Dad puts a bowl and a box of cereal in front of me on the bar.

I pour myself some cereal. "You're not going to try to talk me into running with you, right? Because I'm fine going to the gym." I take a bite. "Unless I can skip my whole workout?"

Dad comes to stand in front of me. "I was actually wondering if we could go for a walk."

I glance at his face and know this isn't an ordinary walk. I'm tempted to groan, but I hold it in.

***

After I have breakfast and change into sweats, a hoodie, and a beanie, Dad and I head out the back door with Termite on a leash. We walk down the sidewalk that slopes down the hill behind our house until we reach the gravel trail at the bottom. Dad turns right and I follow.

"So," Dad starts.

"This is going to be about Zoe, isn't it?"

Dad looks at me. "Are you going to blow up again?"

I sigh. "No."

"Good."

I wait for him to go on.

"Matt," he starts, "this is nothing new. When you started holding her hand, you knew you were breaking the rules."

"But..." I start. "Jim and I are going to be normal. We're going to get the Burke-Dalton procedure done. I swear I didn't hold her hand until I knew about that."

"And finding out that you and Jim could get on the waiting list for a donor body changed everything?"

"Right." I nod. "Exactly. Because...well, one day, those rules won't apply anymore." I look at him. "Right, Dad?"

Dad sighs like this pains him. "Matt, I know this is tough. And I can see how you want to look at it like that. But you have to understand that it could be years until—"

"I know," I interrupt bitterly.

"I wish I could change this for you, Matt. But until the day you and Jim do have your own bodies, these rules still stand."

I grumble under my breath.

Dad sighs. "There might not be harm in you holding Zoe's hand right now. The rule is about what would happen later on. You know we've talked about why you and Jim can never get married."

I look at the ground. "Yeah."

"Well, girlfriends and dating are the start of the road that ends in marriage."

"That's dumb," I protest. "You're saying I can't hold Zoe's hand now because there's a chance I might marry her someday? We're just teenagers!"

"But it's a road," Dad says. "A road that, once you start down, isn't always easy to get off. So, the easiest thing to do is never start."

"So what do I do?" I say it this time without getting angry and yelling. "Go back to being her friend?"

"Well, for starters," Dad says, "you stop breaking the rules you've already broken."

I look down at my feet and don't reply.

"That means no holding Zoe's hand," Dad clarifies.

"OK," I mumble.

"And your mom and I talked, and we have two new rules we're going to ask you and Jim to follow from now on, with any girl."

"OK...?" I look up nervously.

"One," Dad says matter-of-factly. "You're not allowed to spend more than two days a week with her—or any girl."

"More than two days a week!?"

Dad cringes. "We don't want you spending most of your time with her—or, again, any girl. Matt, some weeks, you get as little as three days. Twice a week is the limit Mom and I decided on."

My mouth hangs open. "So I can only work two days a week?"

"Well." Dad clears his throat. "I haven't gotten to the second rule. That is you're not allowed to be alone with Zoe, or any girl."

"Alone...?"

"Yes." Dad nods. "And walking dogs around the city with her counts as being alone."

"So, you're saying...I can't work with her?" I sputter. "But that's not—"

Dad looks at me, and I swallow the "fair" I'm about to say.

"This is how we keep relationships from happening," Dad says. "Mom and I want you and Jim to have friends. We want you to have normal interactions with other teenagers. And if you follow these two new rules, it should keep those interactions as friendships. Not as relationships."

"So what am I supposed to do about Pals?" I can't help sounding angry this time. "Quit?"

Dad shrugs. "You don't have to work with her. You can go back to working on your own, right?"

"But we have the perfect system," I argue. "We take all the team tasks." Not to mention working alone won't be near as much fun. For either of us.

"I know it's tough, Matt," Dad says.

I grunt. "You're basically making it so I can't see Zoe again. That's not fair, Dad."

"Who said you can't see her again? You can do things with her. As long as someone else is around—Leo, or me and Mom, or her parents or friends. Invite her over to our house for dinner. That's fine with us."

I moan. Can't Dad see that that's *so* not the same thing?

"Well, look at it this way," Dad says. "You want to be with her when you're 'normal,' right? When you have your own body? That's why you think it's safe to hold her hand now?"

I nod.

"Well, the more of that you do with her now, the stranger it will be for her when she sees you in a new body."

"No, it won't," I say immediately and stubbornly. "Zoe's not like that. She said she'll want to be with me no matter how I look."

"I know," Dad says placatingly. "I know. But the more time you spend holding her hand, and if you were rebellious enough to try more than that..." Dad looks at me pointedly and I look away. "Well," he goes on. "When the day comes that you and Jim get your own bodies, and you and Jim can spend time together, and you'll naturally want Zoe to spend time with our family... well, every time Zoe looks at Jim..."

"OK!" I say, feeling my cheeks get warm. "I get it." I don't want to admit it, but I can see my dad's logic in that one. It will be one thing for Zoe to get used to me in a new body. It will be another for her to get used to my *old* body with someone else inside it, especially when that someone is my decently cool brother with a fair amount in common with me.

It's silent for a few minutes. Our shoes crunch along the path, and Termite pants along beside us.

"So what am I supposed to do in the future?" I ask. "Only be friends with plain girls I'm not attracted to?"

Dad smiles. "It's tough, Matt. I'm not going to deny it. It will be something you and Jim will have to learn how to do."

I sigh.

"Hey." Dad looks at me and waits until I look back. "I'm proud of you."

"Thanks," I say sarcastically. "That makes it all better."

Dad smiles and puts an arm around me. "Thanks for talking."

"Yeah," I sigh. "Whatever."

Then Dad's phone rings.

"Sorry." He reaches in his pocket. "I thought I had this on silent." Dad looks at the screen. "It's your mom. She called twice. Hang on." Dad answers the phone. "Hey, Jane." Pause. "Yes, we're on a walk." Dad glances at me. "Is everything OK?" Pause. "OK, we'll see you soon." Dad hangs up.

"What was that about?"

"She's on her way home from shopping. Are you ready to head back?"

"OK."

***

When Dad and I get home and say hi to Mom, I check my phone and see a message from Zoe. She wants to work this evening. Before I text her back, I go up to my room and shut the door. Then I start to pace.

I need to digest these two new rules my dad gave. Only two days a week and never alone with her? Can't Dad see that those would change everything? I shake my head. No, no way I'm keeping both of those rules.

But Dad is right. Things do have to change. Because of the fact that my body will one day be all Jim's, I'll stop holding her hand. But I don't have to quit Pals. I can tell my parents I've started working on my own—I even can, some of the time—but still secretly work with Zoe.

I take a breath, feeling better in deciding that I'll still get to be with her, even if it's less frequently. But there's so much I have to tell her. I'm not looking forward to that conversation.

I think I should check with my parents before I work out a time with Zoe, especially because it's my Christmas Eve and I don't know if Mom and Dad have plans for us. I go all the way down the staircase before I realize that neither of them are in the kitchen.

"Mom?" I walk back upstairs. "Dad?" I make it to their bedroom door, which is cracked, before knocking and pushing it open. "Mom and Dad?" I stop.

My parents are sitting on the edge of their bed. I'm shocked to see my mom...crying. I stand there not knowing what to do.

"Yeah, just a second, Matt." Dad has an arm around my mom. Mom is looking down and doesn't look up. "I'll be out in a second."

I awkwardly leave the room, starting to worry, and in a moment, Dad joins me in the hall.

"What's wrong?" I ask. "Why's Mom sad? No one died this time, did they?"

Dad shakes his head before veering into my bedroom. Surprised, I follow and sit on my bed. Dad sits on my desk chair.

"Matt," he starts, "Mom heard from Dr. Anand. There's...a teenage male donor body available for the Burke-Dalton procedure."

I jerk up straighter and my eyes widen. "Really?"

"Dr. Anand says the body is in perfect condition. If you and Jim still want to, the surgery could happen next week."

"*What?!*" I jump up. "Are you serious!?"

Dad looks up at me. He isn't smiling, but he nods.

I laugh. "No way!" I start to pace around the room. "This is incredible!" Still smiling, I turn to look at my dad.

No smile from him yet. "So I take it you want to."

"Um, yeah!" As if it weren't obvious.

"We'll have to check with Jim."

"Yeah, yeah, of course." A tiny thought creeps in, a fear that Jim will change his mind, but I push it away.

Dad nods as he stands up. I do, too, and he hugs me.

"Can I tell Jim?" I ask as Dad pulls back.

He nods.

"Dad?" I add hesitantly. At the doorway he pauses and turns around. "I was going to work with Zoe tonight...does this mean I don't have to quit? Since in a week the rules won't apply?"

Dad exhales, closes his eyes, and rubs them with one hand. "Let's say... you follow the rules for this last week. But no, you don't have to quit." He opens his eyes. "And instead of working with her, why don't you invite her to eat dinner with us?"

"You and Mom and me?"

"Yes." Dad looks amused.

"OK..." I say a little hesitantly.

"Matt," Dad says. "This could be your last—" He stops. "This is Christmas. Your Christmas Eve. Today is a day for family."

I nod. "OK."

Dad gives a sad-looking smile and leaves.

I sit down on my bed.

I know what he was about to say. This could be my last week alive. But I'm not going to think about that. Why think about that? In a week, life is going to be amazing. I pull out my phone and start a Vimer for Jim.

***

Dinner that night with Zoe and my parents is OK. She's cool around them, and it doesn't feel that awkward. Mom seems normal again, no sign she was crying earlier. The biggest emotion I feel all dinner long is anticipation. I can't wait to tell her that the procedure is going to happen.

When we're walking out of the restaurant, I give my dad a look.

He nods. "We'll see you at the car, Matt."

I turn to Zoe. It's the first time we've been alone all evening. She smiles wryly at me. "So. Dinner with your parents."

I laugh. "Yeah. Sorry about that. But...it's because something's changed."

Zoe looks concerned, so I smile so she'll know it's good news. "Remember that procedure I told you about?"

***

In the car on the way home I'm quiet. Zoe's reaction to the news wasn't as positive as I hoped it would be. She mostly looked shocked.

She just needs some time to get used to the idea, I tell myself. It's crazy, I have to admit. Me in a new body. But she'll get used to it. She'll get excited. She has to.

Saturday, December 24
Jim

"Jim." Matt is sitting on his bed looking excited. That's weird, considering everything that's gone on in our house over the last few days. I watch the phone screen curiously. "Jim. This is crazy. Remember the Burke-Dalton procedure? *They have a donor body ready!* I can get transferred to my own body next week! Isn't that nuts!"

My mouth drops.

Matt takes a big, happy breath. "You know the best thing? The timing is perfect! All this mess with girls and Zoe and Rachel—none of it will matter next week! We were going to have to follow two *new* rules—Dad told me today. No being alone with a girl, and no seeing a girl more than *twice a week*." Matt makes a disgusted face, then smiles. "Not anymore! And we won't have to worry about not trusting Mom and Dad to stay out of our Vimers—*because we won't need Vimer anymore!*" Matt pantomimes his mind being blown. But then he becomes serious. "But, hey. I know it's been a while since we talked about this. I mean what I said. We shouldn't go through with this unless you really want to." Matt makes deliberate eye contact with the camera. "Jim, do you still want to do it?"

In a daze, I lower the phone.

Next week? Next *week*? That's so soon! But is Matt right that the timing is perfect? All the drama over the past week—gone! Mom and Dad won't need to sit me down and tell me I've been spending too much time with Rachel.

Rachel! Not only can I keep spending time with her, but I can also spend even *more* time... I inhale and lean back into my pillow.

Without thinking much, I send Matt a response.

"Matt, are you serious!? Yes, I'm sure, let's do it. Let me ask you—" I look at the camera like Matt had. "Are you sure you want to be the one to be transferred? We could flip a coin or pick one of us randomly. That seems more fair." Then I exhale and shake my head. "This is nuts though! Next *week*?" I pantomime my own mind being blown, like he had. Then I smile. "This is gonna be awesome."

"Jim?"

I hear a knock at my door and look up.

"Good morning." Mom enters my room slowly, followed by Dad.

"So, you heard the news?" Dad asks.

"Yeah!" I stand up and can't do anything else before Mom hugs me.

"We haven't seen you since Tuesday," she says gently. "Good to have you back."

"Sorry for getting mad," I mumble as I hug my mom back. But the donor body pushes all thoughts of the fight with my parents out of my mind. "It's true?" I look at her and then my dad. "There's a donor body? We can get the procedure done next week?"

Dad looks at me seriously. "If you want to."

"Of course I do! We've been looking forward to this for months and—" I glance at Mom's face and falter. She looks close to tears.

Dad puts his arm around her. "OK." Then he guides her out the door.

***

When I go downstairs later, there's a pot of homemade hot chocolate on the stove and Christmas music playing. Mom is wearing a red and white sweater and is sitting at the bar with her laptop.

"What book review are you working on?" I come up to look at her screen.

"Charles Dickens' *A Christmas Carol*. Doesn't Aunt Theresa's Christmas turkey look good?" Mom shows me her screen.

"Looks awesome." I smile. "Is that what we're having for dinner tonight?"

Mom laughs. "I wish." She turns around and smiles at me, and for a second everything feels normal.

I head over to the stove for a mug of hot chocolate.

Mom comes and stands in front of me after I turn around holding the mug, blowing on it. For a second we look at each other.

"Are you OK, Mom?" I say quietly.

She takes a deep breath. "If you and Matt have made up your minds, I've accepted that it's going to happen." Then she smiles, though it looks forced. "Let's spend Christmas break together and enjoy it as much as we can."

***

The majority of the morning is spent on the phone with Dr. Anand. He has a lot to go over with us. He details all the risks and gives us a complete rundown of how the surgery will work. It will start next Friday, on my awake day, when we'll drive to Houston in the morning. I'll be the one put under on the operating table. If everything goes well, within twelve hours I'll be waking up in one hospital bed, and Matt will be waking up in the bed next to me.

Dr. Anand also sends lots of paperwork to fill out and pictures of the body that's being donated. I'm surprised to learn from Matt that he hasn't seen it.

"I feel weird about it," he confesses to me in another Vimer from this morning. "Maybe it's weird, but...I don't want to see it beforehand. Will you look at it for me? I trust you. If you tell me the body looks OK—like, obviously not as good-looking as us, but not super ugly—then I'll be OK with it."

So I look at the pictures Dr. Anand sends. The body belongs to an eighteen-year-old white guy named Joseph Nelson. He's taller than me and Matt—5' 10". His hair is dark, almost black, and his skin is a little darker, too. He wears glasses/contacts. He played the piano. (Matt will be glad to learn he was a fellow musician.) Dr. Anand says the body's deceased consciousness and the brain tumor have both been taken out. Joseph Nelson's—for all intents and purposes—empty body is in a medically induced coma, waiting for us in Houston.

I tell Matt the body is great (not as good-looking as us, but what can we expect?). But I still feel nervous about it. What if Matt wakes up in Joseph Nelson's body in a week and hates it? And Dr. Anand makes it clear that this is an irreversible process. Once Matt leaves our body, he's never coming back.

When Dr. Anand says goodbye, Mom taps her phone to end the call and collapses onto the couch. I do the same thing. Dad sits next to Mom, putting his arm around her.

"Kind of an exhausting morning, huh?" he says.

No one says anything. I pet Termite when he comes over.

"What do you want to do today, Jim?" Dad asks.

My brain feels foggy, and I'm not sure what to say. Luckily, the doorbell interrupts us. Dad gets up to get it.

"Merry Christmas, Mr. Mickelsen!" an enthusiastic voice says from the doorway. I raise my head to see Leo walking in.

"Hey, Jim! Hey, Mrs. Mickelsen!" Leo says. Then he takes in me and my mom lying back on the sofa, looking wiped out. "Sheesh, what did you guys do today, run a marathon?" He pushes my feet off the end of my couch and sits down while Mom and I both sit up.

Leo doesn't know. I found that out from another one of Matt's messages. Matt said I can be the one to tell Leo about the procedure.

"Jim, we're going upstairs." Dad helps my mom stand. "But don't go anywhere, OK? You're welcome to stay, of course, Leo."

"Cool." Leo relaxes into the couch cushions. "My mom went shopping." He smiles.

I force a smile back as Mom and Dad leave the room. Leo glances around, watching them go, and realizes something is up. "Dude, what's been going on around here?"

"A lot," I admit.

***

"No way." Leo sits, staring straight ahead. "No freaking way."

"Yes way. It's happening. Next Friday."

Leo shakes his head. "I can't believe it." He looks at me. "So you and Matt—you'll really be—"

"Yeah."

"Whoa." Leo looks straight ahead again. "But you're the first ones?"

"To have the procedure done? Yeah."

"How do they know it will work?"

I don't answer.

Leo's voice gets quieter. "They don't know it will work, do they?"

I look down and shake my head.

"How risky is it?" Leo says quietly, like he doesn't really want to know the answer.

"Our doctor says there's a forty percent chance that Matt won't—"

"Forty percent?"

"Yeah."

"*Forty?*"

"Stop repeating it!" I take a breath. "And a twenty percent chance I won't make it."

"There's even a risk to you?" Leo asks incredulously.

"It's brain surgery. They have to get to the part of our brain that holds Matt's consciousness. Mine is right next to it, and it's all super small, so..."

It's silent, so I glance up to see Leo's shocked face.

"How in the world did your parents agree to this?" he asks.

"It was after I broke our foot. Matt was struggling—"

"I remember."

"Mom and Dad told us then we could do it. We first heard about the procedure almost a year ago and asked to do it then, but they said no."

It's silent again. I have to try something to lighten the mood. "Know what this means?"

Leo looks at me blankly.

"When you spend the night from now on, you'll be on the floor. But it'll probably be worth it since we'll all three get to hang out together."

Leo laughs in disbelief, then he gets serious again. "What's the donor body look like?"

"Want to see it?" I stand up and walk to my laptop at the bar.

Leo watches as I scroll through the photos. There are some of the body as it is now, empty on an operating table, but there are some of Joseph Nelson when he was alive, too, with family and friends. It feels weird to look at the pictures. Though I didn't know Joseph Nelson or his family, thinking about someone as young as us dying is sad. But it's also weird to think about this body, Matt's future body, belonging to someone else. In less than a week, Matt is going to look like Joseph Nelson's dad instead of ours. Weird, right?

Leo watches in silence, processing similar things. "So that's what Matt will look like next week?"

"Yep."

He's focused on the screen. "Does Matt like it?"

"He hasn't seen it," I confess.

"Really?" Leo looks at me. "Is he going to?"

I shake my head. "Matt says he doesn't want to see it beforehand. Isn't that weird? He told me he trusts me, and if I give him the go-ahead, that's all he needs."

Leo turns back to face the computer, but his eyes are staring into space. "It's because he's scared."

"Matt? Scared? Yeah, right. He's been looking forward to this for months."

"No," Leo disagrees. "He's got to be at least a little scared. He's scared that if he sees the donor body, he'll change his mind."

Sunday, December 25
Matt

On Sunday, Mom, Dad, and I do presents in the morning, recording the event for Jim. I can't help getting excited at the idea that this is the last holiday we'll ever have to record.

Mom and Dad get me and Jim a new board game to play together. It's a two-player turn-based game that we can play now, taking one turn a day, but how much more fun will it be to play in real life next week? From my parents, I get some colored LED strip lights that will increase the coolness of my already awesome room. And, somehow, Jim and I get each other the same gag gift: a men's leave-in conditioner (but the gag part is it works overnight). I don't know if it was coincidental or if Jim did some detective work, but either way, I crack up.

Mom, Dad, and I are eating breakfast later when someone rings the doorbell. I go to the door and open it to see Leo standing there. For a second we stare at each other.

"No way," Leo finally says.

I smile. "Yes way."

***

It isn't until later that evening, after Leo helps me hang my new lights up in my room, that Mom and Dad sit me down and go over all the details of the procedure, everything they heard from Dr. Anand the day before. Everything that's going to happen—and everything that could go wrong.

Here are all the risks.

For one, they're not even sure that Jim and I can survive without each other. The act of cutting my consciousness out of our brain might kill both of us.

And then, even if that doesn't happen, the surgery could damage either of our consciousnesses independently of each other.

And then, even if that doesn't happen and we both survive me being taken out, my consciousness might not survive long enough to make it to a new body.

And then, even if my consciousness does survive that long, they might not be able to correctly attach it to the new body, and then I'll cease to exist.

And then, even if that doesn't happen, even if I make it to the new body and am alive and well, my personality might change. Maybe a lot. No one knows for sure.

All those risks get rolled together and weighed and calculated and somehow mathematically come out to Jim's 20 percent and my 40 percent.

I listen to all the risks. I talk through them with Mom and Dad. I tell them that I understand them. We sign all the paperwork. And I try to focus on the rewards.

Monday, December 26
Jim

Monday is my Christmas morning. I get Dad some new compression socks for running and Mom a children's novel that takes place in China. I hope it will provide some good recipe opportunities for her blog. In a surprising coincidence, Matt and I get each other the same gag gift: a men's overnight leave-in conditioner. It *is* pretty great watching the video of Matt opening the gift yesterday because he cracks up so hard.

After presents, after watching Matt's Christmas from the day before, we all sit on the couch in the basement. Mom has turned on Christmas music. I'm going through the rules for the new game Matt and I got. Mom is leafing through her new book. Dad is reading something on his phone. Things feel calm and normal. I almost forget that at the end of the week things will change so drastically.

***

Later Leo comes over. We sit at the bar and eat stocking candy while he tells me about his Christmas presents.

"And I got this new video game— Hey!" His eyes open wide. "Now that you and Matt are going to be awake all the time, do you think your dad will let you play video games?" He's so excited I laugh.

"I don't know," I admit. "Sometimes I think he just doesn't like video games."

"Worth a try though, right? If your parents let you, would you play?"

"Sure."

"Even if they didn't let you? You'll try it? All three of us together?"

I laugh again. "Sure."

"You'll have twice as much time," Leo reasons. "Seems like you could spare some on video games." He smiles and stares ahead. "Matt's favorite is *Neutron 2*...you'd like it, too. And *Go Dash* would be a perfect three-player game. Even if you just watch Matt play this space hamburger game, it would be entertaining. He always gets a kick out of it."

"Hopefully he still will next week," I say without thinking.

Leo is confused. "What do you mean?"

I look down and pause. "Matt's personality might change," I confess to Leo. "Once he's in a new body."

"What?" The news takes Leo by surprise.

"Yeah," I say, not smiling anymore. "Our doctor doesn't know for sure how much, but there's a chance."

"Like...Matt will start to...become this other guy?" Leo looks scared.

"No..." I say slowly. "Matt and I are in the same body, and we have different personalities. It's just, when he has a new brain, there might be changes. Our doctor made it sound like changes in his mood."

Leo looks like he's trying to process.

"Matt said his preferences won't change," I say. "Like his likes and dislikes. Just...I don't know, maybe the way he responds to certain things."

"Like...pranks?"

"Maybe taking risks."

"His sense of humor?"

"Maybe."

"And how would his preferences not change?" Leo asks. "Like, he'll have different taste buds, right? Wouldn't that change what foods he likes? And if his new body is used to doing different things, like..."

"Playing the piano," I supply.

Leo and I both sit in heavy silence.

I play with a foil chocolate wrapper in my hand and speak in a low voice. "He didn't tell me at first, either."

"Jim..." Leo says. When he goes on it sounds like he's afraid to say what he wants to next. "What if...what if this isn't as great as you and Matt think it will be?"

I open my mouth to say something, take a breath, find I don't know what to say, and shut it again.

***

Later that afternoon, Mom and Dad are in the kitchen, and I'm playing the acoustic guitar on the couch, so when the doorbell rings, I don't go to the door. Not until I hear a chorus of voices say, "Merry Christmas!" I think I detect a little kid's voice in the mix... I stand up and hurry to the entryway.

Standing on the doorstep is Rachel with her family, including Charlie and a younger brother I haven't met before. Charlie is holding a plate of cookies.

"Why, thank you!" Mom says.

Rachel's mom smiles. "We were deciding who to bring cookies to, and Charlie said she wanted to bring some to Coach Jim."

Charlie beams up at me and I take the cookies, stealing a glance at Rachel's face. She's smiling, too. I hope Charlie wasn't the only one excited to come over.

I'm elated when Dad joins us at the door and Mom says, "Come in!" So Rachel's family walks in the house.

The adults don't make it far. They stand in the entryway and start to chat. Termite comes running up, distracting Charlie and the brother, who bend to pet him. I slip into the kitchen to put the cookies away and hope Rachel will follow.

She does. I start to get nervous as I realize this is it—this is my chance to tell her about the procedure.

"Merry Christmas, Coach Jim," she says as we walk into the kitchen.

I laugh. "You, too." I put the cookies on the counter and turn to face her.

Termite has one of his toys and is now playing tug-of-war with Rachel's brother, and Charlie walks over to join them. Seeing their fascination with our dog, I pull out some dog treats they can give him and a ball they can play fetch with. They all head into the backyard.

Saying a silent thank-you to Termite, I turn back to Rachel.

"What did you get for Christmas?" she asks as we walk to the couch and sit down.

"Oh, um, a new game, and some clothes..." I'm distracted and nervous. "Actually, the biggest thing that happened at our house this past week wasn't Christmas."

"It wasn't?"

"Yeah..." Why does this feel like such a hard topic to bring up? "So, there's this procedure that Matt and I are going to try."

That gets her attention. "What procedure?"

"Well..." My guitar is still next to me on the couch, and I lightly pluck a few strings. "It's I guess what you'd call a cure."

"A *what?*"

"Yeah," I say, smiling at her expression. "A cure to our condition."

"Uh...*how?*"

"This is kind of weird," I preface, "but they'd take Matt's consciousness out of our body and put it in a new body."

Rachel's mouth is hanging open. "Which new body?"

"A donor body," I say. "Our parents told us we could get in on the list for the procedure a few months ago. We've been waiting for a donor body since, and we heard last Friday that there's one ready now."

Rachel tilts her head in disbelief. "What type of person would donate their body to you?"

"Someone very selfless with a very selfless family," I admit. Then I explain. "There's a type of brain tumor that kills a consciousness but leaves a body intact. It's happened to a guy one year older than us. And we're lined up to have the procedure done on Friday."

Rachel's mouth still hangs open. She sits for a second staring ahead. "So—wait. You're telling me that in a few days...?"

"I'll be normal," I say, and my voice comes out small. "Just me. No more taking turns with Matt."

Rachel sits for another second, then lets out a half gasp/half laugh. "Wow!" She turns to me. "That's fantastic!" And she leans over and hugs me. I sit there stiff; she's never hugged me before.

"Yeah," I say as she pulls back. "Yeah, I know, right?"

"Jim, that's—that's incredible! Are you so excited?"

"Oh, yeah." I debate for a second whether or not to bring up the risks. But I decide not to. She's so excited, which by itself is filling my stomach with butterflies. There's no reason to make her feel scared.

"That's really, really great, Jim," she says. "I'm so happy for you!"

"Rachel!" her mom calls. "Charlie! Preston! It's time to go."

We stand up from the couch.

"Uh, merry Christmas," I say, feeling awkward.

"Merry Christmas." Rachel's beaming at me. She starts to head out, but then turns half around. "I'm excited!"

I dare to hope what she's excited about, but I'm too nervous to ask her.

***

That night, I'm up in my room getting ready for bed, and I'm surprised when my phone rings. When I see that it's Rachel who's calling, I jump for the phone.

"Rachel?"

"Hi, Jim," she says, and her voice is a little higher pitched than normal. "So...remember when you told me how your life is going to change this weekend?"

Does she mean like seven hours ago? "Um, yes..."

"So, I was thinking, um, maybe your parents' rules will change, too? About girls?"

My stomach drops. We've still never talked about the rules.

Rachel doesn't pause too long before going on. "And, um, if they do, I was wondering if you would want to..." Rachel's voice gets higher. "...go to a dance with me?" She starts speaking quickly. "It's next month, and it's a winter lower-classmen dance at my school, which might be totally lame for you, I don't know, because you're, like, a junior, but if you want to come..."

My mouth is open, and I'm frozen. Talk, Jim, talk! But also play it cool... "Um..." I start. Never mind, forget about playing it cool. "Um, *yes*! Yes, I'd love to go with you!"

"Really?" She sounds relieved. "It won't be too lame for you? A bunch of freshmen and sophomores?"

"Are you kidding? Do you know how many dances I get to go to? I'm—" I clear my throat and try to play it a little more cool. "Yeah, I would love to."

"OK," Rachel says. "That's awesome."

Over the phone, I hear a noise in the background, something that sounds like a door opening.

"Charlie, get *out*!" Rachel's voice says, sounding like she's pulled the phone away from her face. There's a pause. "No, I won't! I'll tell Mom."

"Tell her Coach Jim says hi," I say, smiling.

She laughs. "I better go. Talk to you later?"

"Yeah," I say, wondering if she can hear the ginormous smile on my face. "Talk to you later, Rachel."

She hangs up, and I do a victory dance.

Tuesday, December 27
Matt

The weather is crisp but sunny as I walk across our yard, across the neighbors' yard, through Leo's yard, and knock on his front door.

His mom answers and lets me in. She says Leo is in his room, so I head upstairs and open the door.

Leo is lying on his bed on his back, listening to music.

"Hey, bro, what's up?"

Leo takes out his earbuds but stays lying down. He glances at me, then looks away.

My face falls. "What is it?"

"Why didn't you tell me your personality might change?"

I sigh. Jim must have told him. I sit down in Leo's stuffed chair and think for a minute before responding. "It's not a big deal."

"It kind of is, Matt."

I avoid looking at him. "OK. So it might. But whatever happens, it'll be worth it to have my own body, to be awake all the time."

It's quiet and I glance over to see Leo's face. He still isn't smiling. "I just don't know why you wouldn't tell me. You could come back on Saturday and hate playing video games. You weren't going to warn me?"

"That won't happen," I say, exasperated. "My likes and dislikes won't change."

"Well, you might be really bad at video games, then."

"I'm already bad at video games. If anything, I'll get better."

"Maybe you won't be rebellious enough to play them behind your parents' backs," Leo tries.

"Maybe their rules will change and that won't be an issue."

"You could get more insecure. Too insecure to do yoga. Especially in a new body."

"So?" I say, faltering only a little. "I'll trade in yoga if it means I get to date girls."

Leo looks at the ceiling. "You might be a bad drummer."

"No," I say forcefully. I sit up straight. "Don't you dare say that."

Leo sits up, slouching forward. "But it's true, Matt." He looks honest-to-goodness worried. "You *have* to admit to yourself that you're not going to be as good at the drums."

I hesitate. "OK, maybe not *as* good. But I'll still be me. I'll still know everything I know. So maybe I'll need extra practice at the beginning to train my new body and get caught up. So what?"

Leo gets more distressed. "But what if you don't think the same stuff is funny anymore? What if you're studious all of a sudden and think making videos is a waste of time? What if you get mad about pranks instead of laugh at them? What if you're not as—"

"Leo!" I interrupt. I lean back in the chair, and the Styrofoam balls inside creak. "I'll still be me."

"Will you?"

His statement and the hard expression on his face catch me off-guard, and I have to think a moment before I can respond. "Dude, this is going to be the best thing that's going to happen in my and Jim's life. And you're sad about it?"

"No, it's just..." Leo sighs. "I hope you've thought it through."

"Of course I've thought it through," I say, offended. "This has been on my mind for months."

"But have you thought about everything?" Leo looks at me. "Sometimes you get so excited about something good, you don't stop to think about the bad stuff that might happen."

"No, I don't." I'm still feeling offended.

"So, you've thought about the possibility of coming back on Saturday, walking down into the basement with Jim all excited to play music together for the first time ever, sitting down at your drums, and realizing that playing is way harder than it used to be?"

I scowl.

"Have you thought about coming back on Saturday as an only child?"

His question hits me like a blow. I can't think of anything to say, other than wanting to call Leo the least supportive friend ever.

"Or Jim coming back as an only child?" Leo goes on.

"But the odds are still—"

"No." Leo shakes his head. "Huh-uh." He stands up from his bed and grabs a deck of cards from his desk. He looks through them, pulling certain cards out, glancing darkly at me as he does. Finally, he holds out a fan of ten cards face down in front of me.

"A black card, you live. A red card, you die. Pick one."

I grunt but, to humor him, lean forward and draw a card.

It's the six of hearts.

"You see!" Leo shuffles the rest of the cards back into the deck.

"This doesn't prove anything!" I say. "I could have drawn a black card—"

"The point is, it's a big risk."

"But think about the reward!" I throw the card like a ninja star in the direction of Leo's desk. "Do you get what this procedure could do for us?" I glare at him. "No, you couldn't possibly. You don't know what it's really like, do you?"

Leo smiles bitterly. "I've been your and Jim's friend for like six years. I think I have a pretty good idea of what life is like for you."

"No, you don't." I sit up straighter in my stuffed chair. And now I'm more than irritated or offended. I'm mad. "You can't say that. You're like, 'Matt, it's not worth risking death over.' Easy for you to say. You're not the one stuck in a body with someone else." My voice comes out harsh, and Leo is quiet.

"Okaaaay," he says. Then he sighs. "Look, I just hope you realize what you're getting into. You're either going to die or change. Face it."

If my last statement came out as a blow, Leo's has to be worse. We both sit there looking away for a few seconds.

"Fine," I say.

"OK," Leo says.

"I'll talk to you later, then."

"Sure."

I get up and walk home.

Wednesday, December 28
Jim

On Wednesday, I wake up to a text from Rachel with a picture of the dress she's planning to wear to the dance (the *dance!*). That gets me excited enough to do a victory dance all over again. I told Matt she asked me, and in his first Vimer of the day, he's the perfect sort of excited brother you'd want, celebrating and congratulating me and talking about how great our new life is going to be.

Watching his message makes me smile, but almost as soon as it ends, my face falls.

Matt, the perfect sort of excited brother... What sort of brother is he going to be next week? How much will the personality changes really affect him? I'm so used to looking at his face. But it's going to change. His voice will change. Yeah, I'll be with him in real life. But will it even feel like him?

And then, like a spiral, my thoughts get darker. Next week, he might not be here at all.

But if you survive, a voice in my head says, *you could still go to the dance with Rachel.*

I let my head fall back and hit the headboard, disgusted with myself for thinking that. But I can't help turning the thought over in my head a few times. Even if Matt were gone, even if I could never talk to him again, even if I missed him, even without his sense of humor and personality in our family, even without him making videos with me and Leo, even though he's my brother...can I really say that life wouldn't be better if I had our body all to myself?

***

That night I'm on my stomach in my bed scrolling through my phone. There's a knock on my door and I look up.

"Jim?" Mom walks into my room and sits on my bed. "How are you?"

"I'm fi—I'm OK." I sit up and move cross-legged to the head of my bed.

"The surgery's on your next awake day."

"Yeah."

"Are you scared?" She looks at me, searching my face, looking earnest and worried. Dad knocks lightly on the door and walks in, too.

I shrug and look down.

"It's OK if you are," Mom says gently.

"Anyone in your position would be," Dad says. "I've never faced the possibility of death so head-on like you and Matt are."

"Yeah, and..." I take a breath. "What if Matt changes a lot? What if...what if he doesn't like the same stuff? What if he's not as funny?" *What if we're not friends anymore?* I look down. "I know I'm not supposed to think like that. As long as he's in the new body, that's what counts. I mean, that *should* be what counts. But..." I let my sentence trail.

"That's a normal thing to be scared about," Mom says softly.

"There's more," I say. "I'm afraid...of Matt...dying."

"We're all scared of that," Dad says softly.

"Yeah, but..." I close my eyes tight, not sure if I can say this next part. Then I go on more quickly. "Yeah, I'm afraid of Matt dying and getting sad. But I'm almost more afraid of him dying and me being...happy."

I peek my eyes open. Dad looks a little confused, but Mom looks like she gets it.

"Afraid of feeling guilty if Matt dies and you end up enjoying life more than ever?"

I close my eyes and nod again. "Man, I'm a horrible brother."

"Jim." Mom picks up one of my hands. "Jim, no."

"This is a complicated situation," Dad says. "There are no easy answers."

I just take a breath and look down.

"So are you ashamed to admit how much you want the procedure?" Mom asks carefully.

I shake my head. "No." I gulp. "Will you swear you won't tell any of this to Matt?"

They both nod.

"If it were up to me—" I stop. I can't do that. I can't tell my parents. What if they do tell Matt? And if Matt suspects that I want out of this... "I mean—" I start. "This is such a big deal to Matt. If he wants to do it, so do I."

Mom and Dad are silent.

"Sooo," Dad says slowly after a second. "You feel guilty for thinking that life might be better if you had your own body, even if it means Matt dying?"

I cringe but nod.

Dad goes on. "But the thought of the procedure and all its unknowns still scares you?"

I nod, closing my eyes, feeling worse.

"But you want to do the procedure anyway, even though you're scared, not for your sake, but for Matt's?"

I open my eyes. Is that true?

"You don't sound like a horrible brother to me," Dad says gently.

Thursday, December 29
Matt

I wake up with the surgery on my mind. This is it. The last day of my old life. The last day in this *body*. My feelings are...mixed.

Despite having to share it with Jim, I do love our body. I like how we look. I like that we're fit. I like our arms, I like our hands, I like the way they play the drums. I know Jim assures me that I'll like my new body...but it's weird to think about.

After I've had enough lying in Jim's bed and pondering difficult things like this, and after I tell myself to cheer up and be excited like I have been for days, I walk to my room, grab my phone, flop down on my bed, and watch Jim's messages. The first few are from his morning, one right after he woke up and one when he's walking onto the field to play soccer with Rachel and her friends (I cheer for him again inside when I remember Rachel asked him to a dance).

The last message of the day, Jim's sitting in his bed. It's obvious he's not feeling great. His face is long, and his voice is low.

"So...hey. I guess the next time you hear from me will be face-to-face from your new body. Weird, huh? It's hard to imagine what this is going to be like." Jim pauses. It's a long pause. When he goes on, I'm surprised to see that he's gotten emotional. "And I know you don't like to talk about the risks, but there's a big chance and...and if you don't see me again..." Jim rubs one eye. "I love you, Matt. And I know your mind is made up, but if you change it, I hope you know that you can stay. You can stay here, in this body, for the rest of our life. I don't mind."

I lie on my back and put the phone down. It's a few minutes before I sit up, make myself smile, and send a response.

"Man, moved to tears, huh? But Jim, don't worry about it! It'll all be fine! Great, even! Can you imagine what it's going to be like, having our own bodies? And you know what I'm most excited about? Meeting you in real life! How weird is that going to be? We'll get to hang out together! I can't wait! See you tomorrow from my new body—which I'm convinced will be ruggedly handsome and superior to yours in every way. No offense."

It's not too long after I send Jim that message that there's a knock at my door. I look up to see Mom and then, even more surprising, Dad walking in.

"Whoa." I sit up straighter. "Morning, guys. What's this?"

"Breakfast in bed." Mom's smiling as she brings a white box to me. She holds it out.

"Really?" I smile. "Sweet! Thanks!" I open the box to see a donut—but not just any donut. "Wait—is this a bacon maple donut?"

Dad sits on the edge of the foot of my bed. "The one you liked but we both thought was disgusting? Yes."

"We thought we'd make this a special day of Matt's favorite foods." Mom pulls over the chair from my desk.

"Not just your favorite foods," Dad says with a smile. "Your *weirdest* favorite foods. The ones you'll have the greatest chance of no longer liking once you're in a new body."

I laugh out loud. "No way. You guys are the best." I pull out the donut and pretend to offer some to them. Mom shakes her head and pulls out a bag with donuts for her and Dad. For a second we all eat in silence.

"So what's for lunch and dinner?" I can't help asking.

"Well," starts Dad, "we're open to suggestions for lunch, but we're thinking tacos for dinner, with the hottest taco you can stand, just in case it's the last time your taste buds will let you really enjoy it."

"I might get more spice tolerance," I say. "You never know."

Mom makes a sound, maybe like a gasp or a sigh. Dad reaches over and grabs her hand. Neither of them look at me for a moment, and no one says anything. I awkwardly look down and take another bite of my donut.

In a moment, Mom speaks up, and if anything was wrong before, I can't detect it in her voice now.

"Oh, Matt, did you see that text from Bradley?" She looks at her phone. "I guess he's back in town. You could have your first drum lesson in two weeks today, if you want...?" She looks at me searchingly.

"Oh...yeah," I say. "Yeah, sure." Playing the drums today would be cool...I mean, my last time in this body...I have to take advantage of it... right?

"And, uh, Mom and Dad?" I wait until they look up at me. "I was wondering, can I go work with Zoe this afternoon?" I look at Dad especially. He knows what I want and why.

He looks at me and nods. "OK, Matt. For an hour or two."

***

Sometime later that morning, I answer a knock at the front door. It's Leo.

He comes right up and hugs me.

I stand there, stiff, arms straight at my sides. "Um, OK..."

"Sorry, man." He draws back, looking at the ground. "So, I was thinking we need a code word."

"A what?"

"Well, when I see you in this new body I've never seen before, how will I know for *sure* it will be you inside? So, let's agree on a code word, and you've got to swear not to tell anyone, and when you give it to me, I know it'll be you in that stranger's body."

"OK... Um, any ideas?"

He has one right away. "Glockenspiel."

I smile. "OK. Glockenspiel it is."

***

I don't realize until almost lunch that I've been avoiding the basement. But for some reason, every time I walk through the kitchen by the basement door, I feel anxious and turn the other way. But once I realize I *am* avoiding it, I make myself go downstairs.

It's my drum kit. I stand looking at it, knowing that today will be the last time I'll play the drums in this body. But Bradley is coming over later. I can't be feeling jittery like this when he gets here.

Before I can sit down and play, Dad comes home with lunch. He and Mom come downstairs with paper Whataburger bags, and we eat on the couches. We start in silence, and after a few minutes, Dad goes to the TV and plays something.

"What are you doing?" Mom asks.

"Just scrolling back to a random date on the webcam," he says, sitting back down next to me on the couch with his chicken wrap. "To watch for fun. I have no idea what it'll be. Let's find out."

"How about you pull up that clip of Jim yelling at you before you took his phone away?" I take a bite of my sandwich.

Dad winces. "Too soon, Matt. Too soon."

What ends up playing is Christmas morning with a twelve-ish-looking Matt or Jim.

"Which one of us is that?" I ask around a mouthful of Texas toast, chicken strips, cheese, and honey barbecue sauce.

"This is why I dressed you in different colors when you were little," Mom says in a flat voice as she takes a bite of a French fry. "Do you know how many confusing home videos we would have otherwise?"

"It's Jim," Dad says, eyes on the TV. "It's the year we got Termite. Look."

We all watch the video of kid-Jim getting a box with puppy-Termite for Christmas. I can't help laughing at Jim's face. "Man, he really wasn't that excited, was he?"

"You definitely were the lucky one that Christmas," Mom says.

"Go back to the day before," I say. "I want to watch me getting Termite."

So we watch me opening the box with my brand-new puppy inside. I can't help smiling. I was so excited. Man, that was an awesome Christmas.

My parents watch me smiling at the TV.

"Poor Jim," Mom sighs. "I still feel bad that you liked that present so much more."

"Don't feel bad," I say. "Jim loves Termite. He loves the fact that we have a dog that can tell us apart." I smile at my mom. "Promise."

"It's true, Jane," Dad says. "Though telling you apart won't be a problem anymore," he adds to me.

I nod. True. Though that's kind of weird to think about. I look at Termite lying on the rug, and he lifts his head to look at me and thumps his tail. Termite will still love me just as much in a new body...right?

***

After lunch, Mom and Dad go upstairs, and I realize I don't have an excuse not to play the drums anymore. So, trying really hard not to think about what Leo said, about me being a worse drummer in my new body, I sit down and play my heart out.

Time passes, maybe hours. I don't stop. When a voice speaks during a pause, it startles me, and I jump.

"Wow, you're all in, Matt." It's Bradley.

I turn to look at him, breathing heavily. I haven't realized so much time has passed.

"You even need me, or are you in the zone?" Bradley puts his messenger bag on the couch.

I take a few more deep breaths. For some reason, I'm having a hard time finding words right away.

Bradley notices. "So...your parents told me you have some news?" He uncertainly sits down on the stool next to me, sensing something is different.

"They didn't tell you what?"

He shakes his head.

I take one last deep breath before explaining.

***

"Wow," Bradley breathes after I tell him about the procedure. He's moved to the couch, and I've followed. I'm worn out from so many hours of playing anyway.

"This is nuts, Matt."

"Yeah."

"Are you scared?"

It's not like he's trying to pry or change my mind; he's just asking. I feel like I can be honest.

I blow out a huge breath. "Yeah," I finally say. "I guess so." I pause again. "Don't tell my parents."

"Why not?"

"I want them to think I'm excited. Not scared. They're already reluctant for us to do this at all. If they think I'm scared, they might try to talk me out of it."

"Or they might think you're human."

I shrug as I consider. Maybe. But maybe he's wrong.

"Bradley..." I start carefully. He's a drummer. More experienced than me. Maybe he has an answer I can trust. "How much harder do you think playing the drums will be when I'm in a new body?"

I watch Bradley's face as he puffs out his cheeks and exhales. "Depends on the body, I guess. It didn't happen to belong to a drummer, did it?"

I shake my head. "A piano player. But...that's...kind of similar." My voice gets high and uncertain. "Right?"

Bradley exhales again. "I think you're going to have to expect it to be hard," he finally says. "There's no way it won't be. You just have to face the fact that you won't be as good. At least not at first."

My face falls, and I look down.

"Sorry, Matt. I know how much drumming means to you," Bradley says, his voice almost sad. Then he perks up a little. "But I'll still be here. I'll tutor you all over again."

I smile back. "Thanks." I stop to think. "And maybe I'll finally find a rock band to join. Eventually. After I get caught up."

"Sure," Bradley says, sounding excited. "Man, that's what you've always wanted, right?"

"Yeah!" But I don't say anything else, and my face falls again. Bradley can tell something is up. But he just looks at me until I go on. "I...I hope I still do," I confess in a quieter voice. "With the personality changes, I..." I sigh, frustrated. "I'm just not a hundred percent sure I'll want the same things."

Bradley nods. "This must have been a hard decision to make, huh?"

I don't reply. A hard decision to make? It hasn't felt like that. From the moment I heard about the procedure, choosing to do it has felt like the easiest no-brainer decision in the world. But...should it be?

"Well," Bradley says, interrupting me from my deep introspective thoughts. "Do you still want to play more today?" He checks his watch. "I've still got time." He looks at me searchingly. "It's your last chance..."

I breathe deep. "Yeah," I say. I stand up from the couch. "Yeah. Let's play."

So I sit down and he grabs a guitar, and I play my heart out. Again.

***

In my car on the way downtown, I don't listen to music like I usually do when I drive. I don't think about Zoe like I usually do when I'm headed to see her. I think a whole, whole lot about the procedure, and about everything that's happened this morning. About what Jim said in his Vimer. About how nice my parents are. About Termite, and Christmas, and my body. About Bradley and playing the drums. About his comment on the decision being hard when I feel like it's actually been really easy. About what Leo said the day before.

It's the most unpleasant, stressful, anxious car ride I've ever taken. But by the time I pull up by the park downtown, I feel like I've made up my mind.

I kind of lied to my parents. Zoe and I aren't planning on working today. We're just going to meet in the park. When we find each other, we walk next to each other quietly. It's cold out. Our hands stay in our jacket pockets.

When I see the stone wall overlooking the creek where I first told her about Jim, I lead the way, and soon we're sitting on it, staring down into the water.

"So, this is your last day."

"Yeah..." My voice must sound unsure enough that she looks at me. I look down and go on. "I don't know if I can do it, Zoe."

She watches me, her dark eyes opened wide.

I lean over and put my head in my hands. My voice is small and hesitant. "I'm scared. I don't want to die. And..." I swallow. "I don't want to give up my body. Or my personality." I take a breath and close my eyes. "And I don't want to be the reason Jim dies."

Zoe leans over to hug me.

I sit up straighter. "I'm sorry, Zoe," I mumble.

"It's OK," Zoe says. "You were basically taking a fifty-fifty chance with death. I was scared, too." Then she cuddles closer to me, scooting in under my arm. "I like you the way you are," she says quietly. "Whether you have your body to yourself or whether you share it with a brother—I don't care."

I sigh. This is the hard part.

"Yeah...only...there's more." I take a breath. "I can't work with you anymore."

Zoe pulls back and looks at me. I cringe when I see her face.

"You know my parents' rules," I say. "I'm not allowed to have a girlfriend."

Zoe looks shocked for a moment, and I let her think. "Weren't you..." Zoe starts. "Weren't you OK breaking the rules before?" And then, pretty boldly, I have to say, she reaches over and holds my hand.

I close my eyes. "Yeah. But it's not just the rules..." I look down at Zoe's hand around mine, our fingers intertwined. Why is this so hard? I take a deep breath. And then I pull my hand away.

"I'm sorry, Zoe. I can't. I like you. A lot. And you like me. And if we do that stuff...holding hands and all that... Well, maybe one day we'd break up like most teenagers do. But maybe we wouldn't. Maybe I'd start to love you—"

Zoe ducks her head, and I wonder if she's blushing.

"—and maybe you'd start to love me back," I go on. "And then you would want more—more that I couldn't give. I can never have a life like that. Jim and I can never have a life like that." It's hard to swallow. "So we can't start."

Zoe sits in silence for a while.

"I'm sorry," I say quietly. Feeling lame, I can't think of anything else to say. It takes me a few moments to notice she's crying.

"Oh, no," I moan. I pull her into a hug. And I hold her until we stand up from the bench, say goodbye, and walk away.

***

When I get home, I don't go in right away. I turn off the engine and sit in the driveway in my truck, staring at the steering wheel, not moving.

Mom and Dad will know I'm back. We're going to go out for tacos together. They'll be waiting for me inside. But I can't make myself go in yet.

Someone knocks on the driver's side window. I look up, startled. Mom and Dad are both standing out in the driveway, looking at me with concerned expressions.

Dad opens the truck door. "Everything OK, Matt?"

"Yeah." I sniff and wipe my nose with the back of my hand. "Yeah, sorry. I was just about to come in."

But before I can get out of the truck, Mom surprises both me and Dad by stepping around him and climbing up into the truck. Surprised, I hurry to flip the center console up so I can scoot over to the middle. Then Dad walks around and climbs in the other side, and soon they're sitting on either side of me. The open doors let in cold air, but with the doors closed, the cab starts to feel warm again.

At first, it's quiet. It's like Mom and Dad know they don't need to say anything.

"Mom and Dad..." My voice is small. "About tomorrow...would you be mad if I changed my mind?"

"Oh, Matt." Mom hugs me. "Of course not, honey."

Dad hugs me too. "Of course we wouldn't be mad."

Mom's voice is gentle. "It's a hard decision to make, isn't it?"

I nod. And I look down. And the muscles in my lip start to get all funny and my eyes start to sting and—*shoot*! I'm almost crying.

I take a deep breath and make my face more normal. "Jim told me I could stay." I'm able to keep my voice steady. Mom and Dad don't say anything, so I look over at Mom. "Do you think he means it?"

"Yes," she says.

"You're sure?" I look at Dad. "Because he's been thinking that tomorrow he's getting this—" I gesture to my body "—all to himself. That's a pretty big deal. And now I'm supposed to tell him, 'Psych! I'm staying!'"

Dad smiles gently. "He'll be OK."

I look at him, searching his face. "Really? You swear?"

Mom speaks up. "We're positive."

I inhale deeply and exhale, looking down at the floor. "OK."

Mom hugs me again, and I lean against her and breathe deeply.

After a few seconds, I pull out my phone. I open Vimer, point the camera at my face, tap record, and start talking.

"Hey, um, Jim." I don't look at the camera. "So these guys—" I move the phone to show Mom and Dad in the video. "—are saying to me that they're sure that it's OK with you if I change my mind about the procedure, so..." I close my eyes. "If that really is true, please don't go to Houston tomorrow and get me removed from our body." I open my eyes and look at the camera. There's one more thing I want to say to him, but I'm embarrassed to say it in front of our parents. So I say, "Thanks."

Mom and Dad are both hugging me as I end the message and put my phone down.

"I thought you were going to go with the 'Psych! I'm staying!' approach," Dad says.

That makes me and Mom laugh, even if it's a kind of gaspy/half-sob laugh. But it still feels right.

Friday, December 30
Jim

The morning of the surgery. I wake up in bed, staring out the window in Matt's room at the sunlight. And I stay that way for at least ten minutes.

As I check Vimer, I can't help thinking that this is the last time I'll see Matt's face—our face—talking to me from a phone screen. I try not to think about the fact that this might be the last time I hear from him at all.

In the first Vimer, Matt's sitting on his bed in pajamas. It's bright outside and he's smiling. He's happy and optimistic, making fun of me for crying, telling me not to worry and that everything will be great, saying how excited he is to see me in real life, joking and smiling.

As the message ends, I can't help it. My nose starts to sting and the muscles in my lip tense up. I'm going to cry again. I put down the phone and quickly rub my eyes, hoping Mom and Dad won't walk in.

It takes a few seconds before I feel OK enough to watch Matt's next Vimer. I expect more of the same from him—joking, optimism. But when I tap the video to play it, Matt's face is serious. He's in the truck, of all places, sitting between Mom and Dad, who are scooted in close around him.

I sit with my mouth open as I watch Matt tell me not to go to Houston and get him removed. He's changed his mind.

There's one last Vimer from Matt from yesterday. Matt's in pajamas in bed. The message is short.

"I love you, too, Jim."

I realize my mouth is still hanging open. I shut it. *What?* Really? He changed his mind? Wow! Without thinking about what I'm going to say, I send Matt a response.

After I send the Vimer, I hear a knock at my door. First Mom and then Dad poke their heads into the room.

"Jim?"

I look up at them and breathe deep and exhale, and they can tell that I know. Then none of us really seems to know what to say, but we have a group hug that seems to say it all.

***

Breakfast with Mom and Dad is happy. But I would be lying to myself if I don't admit that, as the morning goes on, I start to have mixed feelings. Having our body to myself would be amazing, and for a week I've been getting used to that idea. I'm glad Matt chose what he did. But...it's a mental adjustment. The hardest part is when I think of one person in particular.

I think about texting Rachel to tell her I want to talk to her, but I don't know how to word what I want to say. I know she's at breakfast at IHOP with some of her church friends, because she invited me, but I said I couldn't come because of the surgery.

So, feeling melancholy, I drive to the IHOP, park in the parking lot, and watch the front door. It isn't too long before Rachel comes out with three girls and two boys from her church group. I have to make myself do it because I'm getting more and more reluctant, but I open the door and step outside.

Rachel sees me before I say anything. "Jim! What are you doing here?"

We're walking toward each other. Rachel's friends say hi to me, and I nod and smile back.

"I need to talk to you," I say to Rachel. My hands are in my pockets. "Just for a second?"

Though she's surprised, she says OK, and her friends walk off to their cars while Rachel follows me to my truck.

"Are you getting ready for your procedure?" Rachel asks as we climb in and shut the doors. Since I had the engine running earlier, it's warm enough inside and I don't start it.

"Yeah..." I say. "About that...it's not going to happen."

Rachel's eyes get wide, and her face gets serious. "Why not?"

"Well..." I finger the bottom of the steering wheel. "I wasn't completely honest with you when I told you about it. It's actually really risky."

"Oh." Her voice is small. "Risky how?"

"Risky like Matt might not survive being transferred. Or the surgery to take him out of our brain might damage my consciousness and I might not survive."

It's silent for a few minutes, and I'm afraid to look at Rachel's face.

"What are the chances of that happening?" Rachel asks.

"There was a twenty percent chance I wouldn't make it," I say.

"What about Matt?"

"Forty percent."

"Wow." Rachel looks straight ahead. "I had no idea."

"Yeah," I say quietly. "Maybe I should have told you. But I wanted you to be excited, not scared." I pause. "There was also a risk of Matt's personality changing—they're not sure how much—once he was in a new body."

Rachel nods. "That's a lot of risks."

"Sorry I didn't tell you about them," I mumble.

"I'm glad you told me now." Rachel turns to look at me. "And it's not happening?"

"Right." I exhale. "This morning, I woke up to a message from Matt saying he changed his mind. And I'm glad. I was scared about the risks, too." I look at her uncertainly. "But...I wanted to say sorry. I know, um, that...well, I was excited to, um, spend more time with you..." I wish I could be smoother. I'm tripping and stumbling through this.

Rachel looks down at her lap. "I was, too."

"Um..." I clear my throat. "I...I don't think I can come to your school dance with you anymore."

She looks up at me, her eyes opened wide. I hate seeing that sad expression on her face and knowing it's my fault that she's making it.

"I'm sorry." I look down again. "It's my parents' rules. The procedure would have changed things, but now..." I sigh and don't know what else to say. I look up at her. "So...friends?"

Rachel surprises me by reaching over and hugging me. "Friends."

***

The conversation with Rachel is a downer. But later I have a happier one.

"Leo!" I say excitedly as he opens his front door.

"Jim!" Leo is surprised, then unsure. "I thought you guys were getting the procedure done today."

"Matt changed his mind!" I walk in. Leo's mouth falls open, then he smiles. And hugs me.

I laugh as I stand there uncomfortably (he's pinned my arms down by my sides).

Leo pulls back. "So just like that?"

"Well," I say, "I can't say for sure what changed his mind. Maybe it was my moved-to-tears goodbye I left for him."

"You *cried*?"

"Shut up." I punch Leo in the shoulder. We walk into the kitchen, where I sit on a barstool and Leo pulls two sodas from his fridge.

"Like, for real cried? You weren't faking it to try to convince him?"

I roll my eyes. "Can we get away from the subject of me crying? And no, I didn't fake it. Come on, give me a break. I'm not that much of a manipulator."

"Oh." Leo opens his soda. "I am. I was trying to get Matt to change his mind, or at least think about it more seriously, so I held out ten face cards to simulate a forty-sixty chance of survival. If he picked a red one, he died." He takes a drink. "Of course, they were all red."

I sputter on my soda.

"Do *not* tell him that," Leo says with a stern look at me.

I smile. "Alright. Fine. Your secret's safe with me."

Leo smiles too. "Well, even though I was looking forward to the mind-blowing possibility of being with both Mickelsen brothers at the same time..." He holds out his soda can. "Here's to both of you not dying."

I tap mine against it and smile. "Yeah. Here's to both of us living."

Saturday, December 31
Matt

It's weird, waking up to a morning that, for a while, you weren't sure you'd wake up to. But Saturday morning, there I am, in Jim's bed, in our same body. So Jim hadn't done it. No procedure.

In Jim's Vimer he's sitting in our pajamas on his bed. From the light coming in the window, it looks like morning. He's probably just seen the Vimer I sent the night before. The one where I told him I changed my mind.

"Wow..." Jim says. He looks shocked. And he actually looks like he's been crying again. I'm amazed that we share the same tear ducts.

In the video, Jim hesitates like he doesn't know what to say. "Wow, I—*man*, you took me by surprise." Jim raises his eyebrows and lets out a deep breath before he goes on. "But of course, I'm serious, you can stay." Then he actually smiles. "So I guess we're still stuck with each other. Or without each other, however you want to look at it. But I'm glad you chose this. Yeah, I know, it's a crappy, weird, frustrating half-life that we have to share. But... it's still a good one, isn't it? At least most of the time? I think so." He smiles. "Talk to you later, Matt."

I take a big breath and flop down on my bed on my back. Crappy, weird, frustrating—he's right about that. But...maybe he's right about the last one, too.

you swear you're OK with me staying?

geez matt
not if you won't drop it

alright alright
so we'll stay like this
for now

for now?

well for now
or forever
who knows?

maybe science will get better and the risk will go
down and the procedure will happen someday

maybe they'll find a way to clone our
body so we each get a copy

that would be amazing

no kidding!

maybe they'll invent time travel and i can go
back a day so we can meet each other and
have two copies of our body that way

haha
i guess you never know
probably not worth holding our breath over

but you never know

Jim—Wed, Jan 11, 7:20 AM

even if we're like this forever it'll be OK

right?

Matt—Thu, Jan 12, 7:24 AM

well we'll probably always fight over things

Jim—Fri, Jan 13, 7:19 AM

and have prank wars

Matt—Sat, Jan 14, 7:22 AM

and i'm still bummed i'm not in a rock band

Jim—Sun, Jan 15, 10:02 AM

don't forget public school
and i don't even want to think about college

Matt—Mon, Jan 16, 7:34 AM

yeah and life after
and if you ever break our foot again i'm
not talking to you for a month

Jim—Tue, Jan 17, 7:19 AM

is it too soon to mention girls?

Matt—Wed, Jan 18, 8:33 AM

YES

but if we can survive with all that

then yeah

I guess life's OK

about the author

Paige Ellsworth Lyman has loved writing and creating stories for as long as she can remember. She attended Brigham Young University and resides outside of Houston, Texas with her husband and three children. She's written about games and escape rooms online as the Game Gal and in *The Do-It-Yourself Escape Room Book*. This is her first novel.

Follow her at www.paigelyman.com.